LABYRINTH OF SHADOWS

THE WITCH'S REBIRTH

Part 1

By

Michaela Riley

Michaela Riley

Copyright © 2025 by Michaela Riley.

East Roman Empire 553-600
Seats of patriarchates
Scale 1:36,000,000
Miles
Northmen
NORTH SEA
Austrasia
KINGDOM OF THE
FRANKS
Aquitaine
KINGDOM
OF THE WEST GOTHS
MEDITERRANEAN
EAST ROMAN EMPIRE
Mauretanians
PATRIARCHATE OF CONSTANTINOPLE
PATRIARCHATE OF ANTIOCH
PATRIARCHATE OF JERUSALEM
PATRIARCHATE OF ALEXANDRIA
Corsica
Sardinia

Michaela Riley

"The feaefull aboundinge at this time in this countrie, of these detestable slaves of the Devil, the Witches or enchanters, hath moved me (beloved reader) to dispatch in post, this following treatise of mine (...) to resolve the doubting (...) both that such assaults of Satan are most certainly practised, and that the instrument thereof merits most severely to be punished."

Daemonologie, by King James

Prologue

In the early fifth century, the tribal landscape of Europe was forever changed by the invasion of the Huns. This forced the Sicambrian Franks, led by Merovech, to cross the Rhine and establish themselves in Gaul. This migration was not only a quest for safety but also the beginning of a new era for the Merovingians, whose lineage was steeped in mystery and fascination.

Rumors spread about the origins of their mystical powers, with many believing their bloodlines were entwined with ancient magic, an enigma that captured the imagination of all who heard it. Some whispered that their ancestors were fey, hiding deep within the dense forests of Europe, while others traced their lineage back to the legendary Minotaur of Crete, a creature that embodied both fear and grandeur.

Even more unsettling were the chilling stories of the Deep Ones, otherworldly sea creatures whose essence was believed to flow through the veins of the Merovingian kings. This connection granted them supernatural powers that defied the understanding of ordinary mortals. These rulers were far more than mere monarchs. They embodied an ancient wisdom and an unmatched mastery of arcane forces, capable of telepathic communication with creatures from both the earthly and ethereal realms. Their long, flowing hair was not only a symbol of their regal stature but also thought to serve as a conduit for their mystical abilities. To their people, the bees that swarmed around them represented a promise of immortality. As the Western Roman Empire disintegrated, the Merovingians capitalized on the ensuing chaos, expanding their power through brutal and relentless conquests, etching their name into the history of Europe.

However, The Merovingians' chaotic ambitions were matched by the unraveling of the natural world. A massive earthquake struck the Mediterranean, causing destruction in far-off lands, and civilization seemed to be on the verge of collapse. Unusual events, like unexplained eclipses that plunged entire regions into darkness for years, and disastrous volcanic eruptions, mirrored the turmoil of human fate. Comets, bright and fiery, streaked across the sky, their presence both awe-inspiring and terrifying to those who looked up in fear. Each natural disaster added to the sense of dread hanging over the world, as it seemed that nature itself was turning against humanity, signaling a time of great uncertainty and peril.

In the middle of the turbulent time of despair and change, a witch appeared, her arrival whispered about in prophecies spread across Gaul. She was said to possess mysterious powers predicted by ancient seers, making her a figure surrounded by myth and legend. Many believed she was the chosen savior, destined to lead her people through the dangerous times ahead. However, her arrival did not bring peace. Instead, it unleashed a storm of war and chaos, as her influence began to shift the very course of destiny. As her powers grew, the balance of fate itself seemed to waver, hinting that the era of the Merovingians was not only defined by their conquests but also by the rise of a new force. One powerful enough to challenge even the mightiest of magical bloodlines.

ACT I

THE PROPHESY OF REBIRTH

"There can be no rebirth without a dark night of the soul, a total annihilation of all that you believed in and thought that you were."

Pir Vilayat Inayat Khan

Chapter 1

Copenhagen, Denmark, 1590

The cobblestones cut into Anna's bare, bleeding feet as rough hands dragged her through the bustling streets of Copenhagen. Each painful step sent sharp jolts through her legs, the wounds reopening with every stumble. The thick hood over her head left her in complete darkness, only amplifying the sound of jeering voices that echoed around her.

"I'm innocent," Anna whispered, her voice barely audible and hoarse from screaming. The words were lost, swallowed by the coarse fabric covering her face, unheard by the angry crowd and her tormentors. She stumbled again, nearly falling, but the ropes around her wrists yanked her upright, jerking her forward.

The guard's grip on the rope tightened. "Keep moving, witch," he snarled, his voice cold and filled with contempt.

Anna's heart pounded in her chest, her thoughts a jumbled mess of fear and desperation. How had it come to this? Just days ago, she had been a respected midwife, trusted by the community. Now, she was labeled a servant of evil, condemned to die for crimes she hadn't committed.

"Please," she begged, her voice trembling, "I've done nothing wrong. I've only ever helped people."

A sharp blow to her back cut off Anna's plea, and she gasped for air, her body jolting forward. "Save your lies for the devil," the guard spat, his voice dripping with disdain.

Anna's feet slipped and slid on the slick cobblestones, her blood leaving a dark stain with each agonizing step. The ropes around her wrists dug deep into her raw, bruised skin, a constant reminder of her helplessness. She tried to steady her breathing, fighting to maintain some semblance of composure amidst the chaos around her. But the seething hatred from the crowd pressed in on her, overwhelming her with its palpable cruelty. Every jeering voice felt like a sharp blow to her already battered spirit.

"I don't understand," Anna thought, her heart heavy with confusion and sorrow. "How can they believe such lies? How can they forget all the good I've done for them?"

Suddenly, the procession came to a halt, and the air seemed to shift. The raucous noise of the crowd faded into an eerie silence, broken only by the shuffling of feet and hushed whispers. Anna felt a cold chill run down her spine as a deep, unsettling realization crept over her. She knew exactly what was coming. Her heart raced in fear and anticipation, her breaths coming in shallow gasps. The atmosphere was thick with a tense mix of excitement and dread, like the oppressive stillness before a storm, waiting to break.

The guard barked with grim satisfaction, pointing toward the towering pyre ahead. "Your time has come, witch," he sneered, his voice dripping with malice as he reveled in his power over her. The flames crackled and roared; their fiery tongues eager to consume their next victim accused of witchcraft.

Despite the fear gnawing at her insides, Anna stood tall and defiant, facing her fate with unwavering determination. Her legs trembled beneath her, threatening to give way. This was it, the end of her life. She gathered every ounce of strength she had left, lifting her chin even though the heavy hood still covered her face.

"I may die today," Anna said, her voice steady and clear, though fear churned within her. "But my conscience is clear. Can you say the same?"

The guard's retort was drowned out by the deafening roar of the crowd. Anna was roughly shoved forward, closer to the blazing pyre. The acrid smell of smoke filled her nostrils as she was pushed even closer to her fate. Her heart hammered in her chest; each beat a silent cry for mercy. Suddenly, a sharp voice cut through the crowd, filled with venom and hatred.

"Die, witch!" someone screamed from the throng, the word a bitter curse aimed directly at her soul.

Anna flinched as the words struck her, deeper than any physical wound could. She longed to cry out, to defend herself, but her voice was trapped in her throat. The harsh accusation hung in the air, a bitter reminder of the fear and ignorance that had led her to this moment.

Then, another voice rang out, dripping with self-righteous fervor, "May the flames cleanse your soul!"

A bitter laugh escaped Anna's lips, surprising even herself. "Cleanse my soul?" she thought, a flicker of defiance sparking within her. "My soul is far purer than those who condemn me."

She lifted her chin, wishing she could see the faces of the people who had sentenced her to this fate. Instead, she turned toward the crowd, her voice steady despite the storm of fear inside her. "You speak of cleansing, yet it is your own hearts that are stained with hatred and fear."

The guard standing beside her growled, "Silence, witch! Your words hold no power here."

Anna faced the voice, a sad smile forming on her lips as she turned to him. "Perhaps not," she replied softly, "but neither do your flames have power over the truth."

Anna's long, wavy red hair hung in wild disarray, matted with sweat and dirt, falling loosely around her shoulders and down to her waist. The once-soft linen chemise clung uncomfortably to her skin beneath the coarse wool robe, offering little comfort against the harsh, biting chill of the morning air. She could feel the eyes of the commoners fixed on her, their gazes burning with a mix of fear and twisted fascination.

"Look at her hair!" a woman's shrill voice sliced through the crowd. "Red as hellfire itself! Proof of her wickedness!"

Anna's face, streaked with tears, burned with shame. The weight of the crowd's malice pressed down on her like a physical force, suffocating her. She wanted to scream, to defend herself against their ignorant accusations, but her throat felt raw and tight, as if the words could not escape.

Instead, she closed her eyes tighter, trying to block out the world around her. In the darkness behind her eyelids, flashes of her life before this moment danced before her; a peaceful herb garden she had lovingly tended, the grateful smiles of those she had healed with her knowledge. How quickly they had all turned on her.

"Please," Anna whispered hoarsely, her voice barely audible over the roar of the crowd. "Please, Gods... save me."

As the words left her lips, a sudden gust of wind swept through the square, causing the flames of the nearby torches to flicker and dance wildly. For a brief, fleeting moment, Anna dared to believe it was a sign; an answer to her desperate plea.

But the wind died as quickly as it had come, leaving only the harsh, mocking jeers of the crowd in its wake. Anna's heart sank as the last remnants of hope within her began to flicker and fade, threatening to extinguish entirely.

"The Gods won't save you, witch," a gruff voice sneered from beside her. "They've abandoned you to your fate."

Anna turned her head toward the voice, her green eyes flashing with a mixture of defiance and despair. "And what do you know of the Gods' will?" she challenged, surprised by the strength in her own voice. "They see beyond your petty fears and superstitions."

The man spat at her feet; his face twisted with disgust. "Your words mean nothing now," he hissed. "Soon, the flames will silence you forever."

As the crowd's bloodlust grew, Anna retreated into herself once more. "If this is to be my end," she thought, her resolve hardening with each step, "let it be on my terms. I may die today, but I will not give them the satisfaction of breaking me."

The burly guard's meaty hand clasped Anna's shoulder, his fingers digging into her flesh as he shoved her forward. The rough cobblestones beneath her bare feet felt like jagged stones, each step cutting deeper into her, a constant reminder of the pain that awaited her.

"Here we are, witch," the guard growled, his hot breath searing her ear as he pushed her roughly towards the execution site. "Your pyre awaits." He removed the hood from her head. "I want you to see what's coming next."

Anna stumbled, nearly collapsing under the weight of her own despair, and found herself face to face with the towering wooden stake at the center of the execution ground. The acrid scent of pitch and oil filled her nostrils, making her stomach churn in dread. She could see the remains of others accused of witchcraft that were burned at the stake…flames still smoldering. The stench of burnt flesh filled the air.

"This can't be happening," she thought, her mind spinning as she stared at the carefully arranged kindling. "How can they not see the truth?" The thought swirled in her head, a mix of disbelief and sorrow, as she faced the cruel finality of her fate.

Anna was dragged up the stairs to the pyre by the guard. He began securing Anna to the post, the rough ropes biting into her already bruised wrists and ankles, each knot pulling tighter. As he worked, Anna's gaze swept over the sea of faces before her; neighbors, friends, people she had known her entire life. Now, their expressions were twisted with hatred and fear, unrecognizable from the faces she had once trusted.

"You're making a terrible mistake," Anna called out, her voice cracking with emotion. "I'm innocent of these charges. Please, listen to reason!"

But instead of a response, a deafening roar consumed her senses, drowning out her desperate pleas for mercy. The chants of the crowd, demanding her death, reverberated through her body, each word feeling like a physical blow. With trembling hands, she squeezed her eyes shut in a futile attempt to block out the cruel reality that was crashing down upon her. Tears streamed down her cheeks as she braced herself for the inevitable.

The executioner, a towering figure draped in black, stepped forward. His voice, deep and commanding, boomed across the square, silencing the crowd for a brief moment. "This witch and mother of the devil has been cursed and brought evil to our village!" he declared, his words echoing through the air with authority.

Anna's heart skipped a beat, and her mind reeled. "Mother of the devil? Cursed? How can they believe such lies?" The weight of their false accusations crashed over her like a tidal wave, overwhelming her reason. How had everything spiraled so far out of control?

The executioner continued, his words growing more frantic and unhinged with each breath. "She caused the storm that sank the princess' ship on her way to Scotland. We must burn her now!"

A fresh wave of terror surged through Anna, flooding her veins with ice-cold dread. "The princess' ship. I've never even seen the sea!" she wanted to scream.

"Can't you see I'm innocent?" Anna pleaded, her voice quivering with fear and desperation. The words tumbled out; each one soaked with the terror coursing through her veins. "I've done nothing wrong! Please, don't do this!"

She searched the guard's face for any sign of compassion, any flicker of doubt. But his expression remained as cold and unyielding as stone. He used a torch and lit the pyre, laughing and sneering at Anna.

"Why won't they listen?" Anna thought, her heart pounding so fiercely that she feared it might burst from her chest. "How can they condemn me without proof?"

Anna closed her eyes, shutting out the hateful glares and jeering faces. In the darkness behind her eyelids, she found a fleeting moment of stillness. It was the only peace she could find in that unbearable moment of chaos.

"Gods, if you're out there," Anna prayed silently, her thoughts a desperate whisper in the void. "Hear me now. I don't deserve this fate. Let justice be served."

The smell of smoke filled her nostrils, sharp and suffocating, pulling her from her thoughts. Anna's eyes snapped open, and she saw the flames growing larger, their hungry dance reaching toward her. The crowd's cheers grew louder, a twisted celebration of her impending doom.

"No," she whispered, her voice barely audible over the roar of the crowd. "Please, no."

But as the first lick of flame caressed the hem of her tattered robe, Anna felt a sickening certainty settle in her stomach. Divine intervention would not come. The pain, the heat, and the injustice of it all hit her like a wave, drowning out every ounce of hope she had left.

The painful reality wrapped around her like a shroud, suffocating any remaining hope and leaving only bitter despair. She could no longer deny it. This was her end.

"How did it come to this?" she thought, her mind reeling with disbelief. "Yesterday, I was Anna Koldings, a respected midwife and healer. Today, I'm to die in agony, branded a witch and a monster by the very people I once called neighbors and friends." The weight of it all felt unbearable, and yet, she could do nothing to change it.

The heat intensified, and Anna's breath came in short, panicked gasps. "I don't want to die," she thought, terror clawing at her insides. "Not like this. Not for nothing." The flames reached higher, their blistering warmth wrapping around her, making every breath feel like it might be her last.

As the fire roared, Anna's gaze swept across the crowd one last time, searching desperately for a single sympathetic face, someone who might see the truth behind the lies. But all she saw was a sea of hatred and fear, their faces contorted and twisted by the shimmering heat.

"Remember me," she wanted to scream, but the words stuck in her throat, swallowed by the chaos. "Remember the truth. I am innocent!" The words never left her lips, drowned by the gut-wrenching screams of agony as the flames began to lick at her lower body.

Her world was consumed by an inferno of blistering pain, searing every nerve and fiber of her being. The pain was all-encompassing, a fire that spread through her flesh, until all that remained was the suffocating heat and the unbearable ache.

The crowd's chants grew louder, their voices like the pounding of a drum, relentless and unforgiving. "Burn, witch, burn!" they cried, their words driving deep into Anna's soul, amplifying the suffering.

Her heart pounded like a hammer against her chest, each beat a brutal reminder that time was running out, that her life was slipping away with every passing second. The smoke clawed at her eyes, the sting making them water as she fought to stay conscious, to keep a grip on the reality that was slipping away in the smoke and flames surrounding her.

"I am not a witch," Anna thought desperately, clinging to the last remnants of her identity, her mind frantically repeating the words in the hope they would somehow make sense of the nightmare she was trapped in. "I am Anna. I heal. I help. I am innocent." The mantra was the only thing that kept her tethered to the woman she once was, but it felt fragile, as if it might slip away at any moment.

Her silent protestations were drowned out by the deafening jeers and taunts that came from all directions. She recognized the voices of people she once knew well; like the baker's wife who had always smiled at her as they passed in the market, the blacksmith's son who had once been a playful child; now their voices filled with anger. Their words consumed by something dark and hateful that seemed to burn hotter than the flames themselves.

As the heat intensified, Anna's thoughts spiraled, racing through the memories of her life. She thought of the people she had helped; the countless babies she had delivered, the sick she had soothed, the lives she had touched. "This can't be how it ends," she pleaded silently to any god who might listen, her heart aching with the weight of her fate. "There must be a purpose to this suffering. Please, let there be meaning in my death." But the words felt hollow, swallowed by the rising flames and the crowd's unrelenting chants.

A thick cloud of smoke rose around her, and the flames began to engulf her, suffocating her in their fiery embrace. Every breath became a struggle; each inhale a burning reminder of her body's slow destruction. It felt as though her very lungs were alight, each gasp a desperate plea for relief. She tightly squeezed her eyes shut; tears unable to form before they were evaporated by the scorching heat.

"Gods, take me now," she prayed silently, her thoughts a tangle of terror and regret. "Let this end quickly." But even as she begged for release, death did not come swiftly. Instead, memories began to flash before her eyes. She saw the herbs she had gathered in the wild, the ones that healed so many. She remembered the comforting words she'd whispered to the dying, the soft touch of her hands as she had tried to ease their suffering. Now all of it; her care, her service; felt twisted and condemned by the very people she had sought to help.

Through the thick smoke and pain, Anna struggled to keep her eyes open, focusing on the crowd one last time. And then, in the distance, she saw a face she knew. Old Willem, the carpenter, the husband of the woman she had helped deliver their child. His eyes met hers, and for a fleeting moment, she saw something shift in them; a flicker of doubt, perhaps a memory of her kindness.

"Willem," she croaked, her voice barely rising above the roar of the flames. "You know me. You know I'm no witch." The words were weak, but in them, she hoped to find the thread of humanity that still existed in the crowd.

But Willem turned away, his eyes filled with an unbearable guilt, unable to meet her gaze any longer. And in that moment, as his back was turned, Anna realized the full weight of her fate; not just to die, but to be forgotten, erased, her existence rewritten as a lesson to the fearful. In the eyes of those she had known, she was no longer the healer, the friend, the woman who had once helped them. She was a monster, a symbol of everything they feared.

As the flames climbed higher, something strange happened. An unexpected calm washed over Anna, a stillness that seemed to separate her from the world around her. The chaotic jeers of the crowd faded into the background, as if muffled by an invisible hand.

The air thickened, humming with an unseen energy. It was a brief moment, but in it, Anna's heart found a flicker of something she hadn't felt in what seemed like an eternity…hope.

"Could it be?" she thought, her pulse quickening. "Have the Gods heard my pleas?" The thought was absurd, yet the sensation of power gathering in the air around her felt undeniable. The flames continued to lick at her, but the sensation of them no longer felt all-encompassing. The sky above Copenhagen seemed to shimmer with a strange energy.

Then, the night sky above her exploded in a magnificent, blinding display of light. It was unlike anything Anna had ever seen; brilliant and overwhelming, a breathtaking eruption of color that illuminated the entire square. The crowd gasped in fear, some dropping to their knees, others crying out in confusion and terror.

"What sorcery is this?" one villager shouted, his voice trembling, eyes wide with disbelief.

Anna, stunned and gasping for air, could hardly comprehend what was happening. She had no words; only wide eyes filled with awe and fear as the radiant light descended upon her. "I don't understand," she whispered to no one in particular, her voice shaky, caught between wonder and confusion.

But unknown to the onlookers, a powerful spell was at work. The Magi's magic, ancient and deep, was taking hold. As the arcane light from the heavens poured down, Anna could feel something extraordinary surge within her. It was as if the very earth beneath her feet and the skies above her had reached out to touch her, filling her with an energy she had never known. The air crackled, charged with an unstoppable force, and Anna felt, for the first time in what seemed like forever, that something beyond her suffering was happening; something powerful, something that could change her fate.

"By all that's holy," the executioner stammered, stepping back, his voice shaking with disbelief. "The witch...she's... changing!"

Anna's body shimmered, her skin glowing with an ethereal light. The flames, once ravenous and eager to consume her, now seemed to bend away, recoiling from her like a hesitant animal. She felt an overwhelming surge of power, a flood of energy coursing through her veins, as if the very air around her was alive and charged with something ancient. In that moment, she knew. She was no longer the woman who had been condemned. She was something different, something greater.

"This can't be happening," Anna thought, her heart pounding as the transformation swept through her. "Am I truly becoming... a witch? I shall return from the ashes."

A surge of fear and awe gripped her heart, but amidst it all, there was a sense of clarity. Her body was no longer bound to the earth, no longer shackled by the mortal limits that had once defined her. The power was flowing through her, transforming her into something that was both terrifying and liberating.

From the shadows of a nearby alleyway, Murdach watched the scene unfold. His long silver hair, now loose and flowing in the night air, fluttered around his face, caught in the gentle breeze. His sea-green eyes, filled with both sorrow and wonder, reflected the radiant light surrounding Anna. Tears streamed down his weathered face; his heart heavy with the realization of what was happening.

"My beloved, it begins," Murdach whispered, his voice thick with emotion, his breath catching in his chest. The weight of centuries-old prophecies pressed down on him as he watched Anna's transformation.

His hands balled into fists at his sides, every inch of him yearning to rush forward, to hold her, to protect her. But he knew this was her journey, one that had been foretold long before either of them had been born. He was not meant to intervene, only to guide her through the trials that lay ahead.

"I will be there for you," he vowed silently, his heart torn. "Always."

As the villagers stood frozen in shock, Anna's form began to fade from view. The ropes that had bound her unraveled, disintegrating into wisps of smoke that vanished into the night. The stake, once solid and unyielding, seemed to blur and flicker like a mirage. The very air around her shifted, as if reality itself was warping to accommodate her new, otherworldly presence. The fire that had threatened to end her life was now a distant memory, unable to touch her as she ascended beyond the reach of those who had once condemned her.

"She's disappearing!" a woman cried, clutching her child tightly against her chest. "The witch is escaping!"

His eyes never left Anna…no, *The Witch* now, as her form shimmered, fading in and out of existence. He felt the raw cosmic energy swirling around her, a force so powerful it seemed to bend the fabric of reality itself. She was being pulled through time and space, her body dissolving into something beyond the reach of the mortals who had condemned her.

"Remember, my love," he thought fiercely, his mind reaching out to her, desperate for her to hold on to the truth. "Remember who you truly are."

With one final, blinding burst of light, Anna vanished completely, leaving only the lingering echo of her presence in the air. The villagers erupted into chaos, their bloodlust quickly turning to confusion, then fear.

"What does this mean?" an old man cried out, his voice shaking. "Has the end of days come upon us?"

Murdach stepped back, retreating into the deeper shadows. His heart raced as he felt the weight of what had just transpired. He knew the wait would be long. This was not the end, but the beginning. The Witch would return, reborn in a time of even greater danger and possibility, and he would be there to guide her when the time came.

"Until we meet again," he whispered to the winds, his voice soft but resolute. "May the Gods watch over you."

In the crowd, a woman with trembling hands pulled her shawl tighter around her shoulders, her wide eyes filled with dread. "Is she gone?" she whispered to no one in particular, her voice barely audible above the whispers of the onlookers. "Or has she become something... else?"

Chapter 2

In the year 478 AD, the ancient and once-mighty land of Gaul found itself shrouded in the haunting shadows of an ominous legacy, a legacy mired in the remnants of the splintered Western Roman Empire. These remnants lay scattered across the countryside like autumn leaves caught in an unrelenting gust, each leaf a whisper, a ghostly echo of power now faded, carried by winds that howled through the crumbling ruins that once echoed with the sounds of prosperity. Amid this backdrop of decay and suffering, a young boy named Clovis walked the forested paths with an air of innocence, blissfully unaware that his destiny was intimately intertwined with the very fabric of the tumultuous world around him.

As the time for Samhain; a night rich in old traditions and mysterious spirits drew near, Clovis' father, Childeric, led the fierce Franks in relentless battles. They hunted the last fighters of the Western Roman Empire, warriors clinging to a fading past as history moved on without them. Driven by ambition, bloodlust, and dreams of domination, the Franks pressed forward, blind to the growing storm on the horizon. This storm, a reckoning with fate, hovered just out of sight, waiting for the right moment to descend.

As the clash of steel rang through the air and dark storm clouds gathered overhead, the whispered prophecies grew louder, almost as if they had taken form; the Witch. Each gust of wind shaking the ancient trees carried an unsettling sense of dread as if the world itself was holding its breath, waiting for the boundary between the living and the dead to fade. Lightning streaked across the sky, lighting up the shadowy forest for a brief moment, each flash revealing glimpses of a dark future shrouded in secrets yet to come. The air was thick with an unearthly energy, amplifying the fear and tension that cloaked the land like an unwelcome shadow.

Hidden among the tall trees, Clovis watched the raw power of both nature and war. His father, Childeric, a fierce and relentless warrior, had pulled him into a world where the clash of swords and the cries of the dying blended into the background of everyday life. These sounds were as familiar to him as the rustling leaves above, as the tribe carved out their place through raids and pillaging. Their lives were woven into a relentless cycle of conquering and revenge, each victory securing their hold on newly claimed lands while fueling the fires of future battles.

As a Sicambrian Frank, Clovis came from a tribe surrounded by mystery and bound by the weight of history. Their ancestry linked them to Merovech, a legendary figure whose life was shrouded in tales of war and strange secrets that left listeners uneasy.

These stories spoke not only of Merovech's skill in battle but of a bloodline touched by something beyond the natural world. A heritage whispered to be connected to dark and mystical powers.

Young Clovis was drawn to these tales, mesmerized as he stood by the fire, watching its flickering light play across the faces of the elders. They spoke in soft voices, their old-fashioned Dutch flowing like a song in the still night. Some said Merovech had been cursed by a mystical being from the forest, while others claimed he had been blessed by the Minotaur, the mythical creature said to roam the labyrinths of far-off Crete.

At just 12 years old, Clovis carried himself with a confidence that went far beyond his years. Dressed in the attire of Frankish nobility, his tall and strong frame stood out, while his long dark hair, flowing past his shoulders, and piercing eyes hinted at a wisdom and depth that seemed far older than his age. He wore a narrow red tunic with vivid blue borders that stopped just above his knees, paired with a sleeveless fur jacket that marked his high status. His low-cut leather shoes, intricately laced at the instep and folded at the ankles, left his legs bare from the thighs down, reflecting the hardy life he had been raised to endure.

At his side hung a small sword, a mark of maturity that stood out like a rare jewel against the innocence of his youth.

In a time, heavy with despair, whispers began spreading through the villages about a mysterious figure: the Witch. Tales of her, described as a living prophecy destined to emerge during the chaos, drifted like smoke, wrapping around the thoughts of the people. Clovis wasn't alone in his curiosity; he and his friend Alix, a boy whose playful mischief often brought light to dark moments, found themselves drawn into the growing buzz.

"She will come on the wings of a storm," an old man proclaimed one evening, his gnarled staff supporting his frail body as he addressed a crowd. His voice, thick with foreboding, captured the attention of all who dared to listen. "Her fingertips will reach the heavens, and she will call down lightning to cleanse the earth of the unworthy!"

Another voice rose above the murmurs, harsh and foreboding. "She will bring the dark magic of the Deep Ones," a shadowy figure growled, spitting into the earth as if to ward off the very thought. "She will unleash horrors upon our enemies and claim the rightful throne of the Merovingians for herself!" The crowd shifted uneasily, the tension thickening like the storm clouds overhead.

"Do you believe it, Clovis?" Alix's voice broke through Clovis' thoughts, pulling him back to the moment. His friend's eyes glimmered with a mix of mischief and curiosity. "Do you think we descend from beasts or from magic?"

Clovis thought for a moment, his mind churning like the dark clouds on the horizon. "I think we descend from both," he said, his voice quiet but sure, a sly grin playing at his lips. "The world itself is a tapestry woven from threads of the unknown."

With laughter echoing between them, they ventured further into the woods. The ancient oaks, their roots tangled in a thousand forgotten yesterdays, seemed to whisper secrets older than the fading light of twilight. Yet, even in their playful wandering, an unsettling shadow hung over Gaul, as dark and heavy as the stories shared by the campfires where they had once found solace.

Nature, once their faithful ally, seemed to turn against them. Relentless storms lashed the land, shaking it with endless fury. The ground trembled as eruptions tore through its surface while an invisible dread crept ever closer, wrapping tighter and tighter around them like a closing noose.

Clovis felt the creeping chill slide down his spine, a shiver that tugged at the edges of his thoughts. Yet, instead of giving in to fear, he found himself drawn to the idea that the Witch: this mysterious figure of change might bring a transformation for him and his people. Though he was only a boy caught in the chaos of unrest, he felt deep within that he was meant to be part of this change. Whether it would make him an enemy or a bringer of a new dawn, he did not yet know.

Even with the peaceful beauty of the forest around him, Clovis couldn't shake the feeling that unseen eyes were upon him. The trees stood tall and still, their branches barely swaying, while their shadows stretched long under the moonlight, wrapping the woods in an air of quiet unease.

As Clovis drifted into an uneasy sleep that night, his dreams became a maze of shadow and sensation, filled with a presence he could not name. Rest eluded him as the forest around him seemed alive, humming with a strange, pulsing energy. Each rustle of leaves and every whisper of the wind sent shivers through him. Despite the mounting dread, he felt an irresistible pull, a magnetic lure that led him toward the soft glow of bioluminescent flowers lighting the path deeper into the unknown.

In the enveloping darkness, he found her. She was both a stranger and someone achingly familiar, stirring emotions that clashed within him. Before him stood a figure cloaked in midnight blue, her raven-black hair cascading like a gleaming waterfall down her back. Her piercing blue eyes, ageless and commanding, seemed to hold the secrets of centuries, their gaze both unsettling and mesmerizing.

It was her…the Witch. Feared and revered, her name was carried in whispered tales shared around campfires. Now, she stood before him, her presence no longer a rumor but a powerful reality.

Clovis stood frozen, unable to move, his wide eyes fixed on the Witch. He wanted to run or cry out, but his body refused to listen. Then, as if she could sense his fear, her voice broke the silence.

"Rise, child of blood and magic," she said softly, her tone like the rustling of leaves. "You are a harbinger of change."

"Who are you?" Clovis finally managed to ask, his voice barely more than a whisper.

The Witch tilted her head, her hair cascading over her shoulder like a shimmering veil. "I am called many names," she replied, her words as cryptic as the mystery surrounding her. "But for now, you may call me The Witch."

The name struck something deep within Clovis, stirring a sense of importance he couldn't quite place. Though he didn't understand why, he felt an undeniable pull toward her as if the powerful energy she radiated was drawing him in, captivating him completely.

"You've been searching for something," the Witch continued, taking a slow step closer to Clovis. "A purpose beyond this village."

Clovis nodded slowly, his voice still trapped in his throat, unable to speak.

"And I believe that purpose is tied to me." Her words flowed like a spell, settling deep in Clovis' mind, filling him with an urgent feeling he couldn't shake.

"What do you want from me?" Clovis finally managed to ask, his voice shaking with uncertainty.

The Witch's eyes glowed with intense determination as she spoke, her voice steady but urgent. "I need your help," she said firmly. "The land is in chaos, and my powers alone are not enough to save it. But together, we can bring balance and restore peace."

A heavy sense of foreboding filled the air as she went on, "But be warned, there will be great challenges ahead. Battles that will test your strength and choices that will echo through generations."

Clovis could feel the weight of her words pressing on him. This was no ordinary woman before him; she was something powerful and otherworldly.

The Witch's lips curved into a knowing smile. "You are the chosen one, Clovis," she said cryptically. "You have been marked by the gods since birth, destined for greatness or destruction."

He took a deep breath, trying to steady himself. "What do you need me to do?" he asked, his voice quiet but firm.

The Witch smiled again, as if she knew something he didn't. "You will know what needs to be done when the time comes."

Clovis stood still for a moment, trying to shake off the confusion.

"Why me?" he whispered, still trying to understand what had just happened.

"It is in your blood," the Witch answered mysteriously. "Your ancestors carry a powerful legacy that has been passed down to you."

Clovis thought back to the stories his grandmother used to tell him stories of brave warriors and wise leaders who once ruled over their people with strength and honor. Could it be true that he was descended from such legendary figures?

But then a sense of determination filled him. If he really had such power and responsibility inside him, he wouldn't let it go to waste. He would use it to bring change to the people of Gaul.

"How can I be of significance?" Clovis asked, his voice a little shaky. To him, those words carried the weight of ages, and in them, he felt destiny calling him.

The Witch's voice was filled with malice as she replied, "Only you can decide the path you take, but beware each choice has its own consequences. Will you fight for the good of all people and protect the land of Gaul, or will you give in to your fate and let darkness rule?" Her cold eyes locked onto him, daring him to make the wrong choice. The weight of the world seemed to rest on his shoulders as he struggled to decide his future.

"I wish to fight," Clovis said firmly, a fierce determination burning in his chest. "I want to change the fate that has fallen on my people."

The Witch stared at him with eyes that seemed to see beyond the world around them. "Know this, Clovis of the Merovingians," she said, her voice steady but full of power. "Your fate is tied to the flames of ambition and chaos. May the sleeping powers of your ancestors and the ancient knowledge within you rise in a storm, forever changing the course of your destiny."

Clovis hesitated, feeling the heavy presence of his ancestors' spirits pressing down on him. The call from the forest was strong, tempting him with promises of ancient power and knowledge. But he also knew that with the Witch's Rebirth, a great change was coming; one that could bring both destruction and salvation. Should he embrace this power or resist it? His mind and heart were in conflict, torn between duty and desire.

With that final warning, the Witch vanished into the air, leaving Clovis alone in the dark once again.

When he awoke, he could still feel the cold of the forest, the wind's breath carrying secrets too old to understand. The image of the Witch stayed with him; her midnight blue cloak and raven hair etched into his memory. It was more than just an encounter; it felt as if the threads of fate had woven their lives together.

As the sweat dripped down his body, Clovis couldn't help but wonder if what had just happened was real or just a trick of his mind. His heart raced as he sat up, trying to make sense of it all. Was it just a dream? Or was it something darker? He couldn't shake the feeling of unease that weighed on him like a heavy burden.

Yet, deep inside, Clovis felt the stirrings of change, a power rising within him, waiting to be unleashed. The witch had awakened not just the ancient wisdom of his bloodline but also the strange allure of the fey and the mystery of the Deep Ones. As he stood on the edge of his destiny, he wondered if he could find the strength to change the course of fate.

The weight of his family's legacy pressed down on him, and he felt the shadow of doom drawing closer. The earth seemed to tremble and roar, as if responding to an unknown force, and all he could do was prepare for what was coming. Standing at the edge of the forest, the winds of autumn whispered with voices that both intrigued and terrified him. He knew that after the end of the Merovingians' rule, a new age would rise, but at what cost?

Chapter 3

October 31, 478 AD

In the distant land of Gaul, there was a village called Septimania, nestled between the Garonne and Rhône rivers. These rivers flowed through valleys shaped by the towering Pyrenees and Cévennes mountains. As Samhain drew near, shadows stretched across the land. This part of Gaul was home to the Celts, who spoke their own language and held pagan practices and beliefs.

The village was alive with activity, filled with the energy of preparation and the smell of freshly harvested crops. The people were busy getting ready for Samhain. They wore rustic garments in shades of earthy orange, moving quickly to finish their tasks. The crops were gathered at the end of summer, and bonfires were lit to confuse the spirits. During this time, the veil between worlds thinned, allowing the living to communicate with those from other realms for three days. The season of life was about to meet the season of death.

Dark clouds moved quickly across the sky, pushed by an unseen force, while the moon struggled to shine through the growing darkness. Deep shadows covered the land, leaving only the sparkling stars and the occasional flicker of bonfire flames to break through the gloom. It felt as though the heavens themselves were holding their breath, waiting for the night to arrive.

The fires crackled and popped, casting lively shadows on the cobblestone streets. Villagers gathered around the bonfires, their faces glowing with the light in their eyes. Both old and young listened closely as the elders began to tell stories of past Samhain's; tales of spirits crossing the thinning veil between worlds, of life and death forever connected.

"Remember," one old woman whispered, her voice soft against the howling wind, "this is the time when the boundary between our world and the next is the weakest. Stay alert, for the unknown is near."

Mairead stood out sharply against the ancient stone altar, her fiery red hair glowing like a flame in the dark. Her hazel eyes sparkled with a hint of magic as she surveyed the busy square below. The intricate runic tattoos on her forearms pulsed with a soft, glowing light, casting faint, glowing lines on her skin.

Over her tunic, she wore a Gallic coat, draped elegantly over her shoulders. The coat, made from a heavy wool blend, dyed in deep shades of auburn and forest green, echoing the autumn leaves that crunched underfoot. The hemline was embroidered with motifs of twisting vines and leaves, invoking the natural world and the spirits she sought to commune with on this sacred night. The coat's wide lapels framed her face, adding an air of authority and mystery.

Standing tall next to a bonfire, Mairead's figure was framed by the darkening sky. Her sharp eyes took in every movement in the square below. The wind whipped her vivid auburn hair around, tangling the strands like a firestorm. The glowing marks on her forearms drew attention with their detailed patterns.

"Hurry now," she commanded, her voice rising above the noise. "The veil is growing thin, and we must be ready when darkness falls."

The villagers moved faster, carrying armfuls of firewood, and hanging garlands of autumn leaves across the square. Mairead's eyes landed on a young man struggling with a bundle of branches.

"Careful, Eoghan," she warned. "We can't afford to waste even a single twig."

Eoghan nodded, his face turning red with a mix of embarrassment and respect. "Yes, High Priestess. I'll be more careful."

Mairead's face softened just a little. She understood the weight of the responsibility on their shoulders this Samhain night. The signs had been clear change was coming, for better or for worse.

As she walked toward the villagers, they stepped to the sides for her, like water moving around a stone. Mairead could feel their eyes on her, a mix of awe and fear that she had grown used to over the years.

"Elder," an older woman approached, wringing her hands nervously. "Do you truly believe the prophecies? That this Samhain will be different?"

Mairead paused, carefully considering her words. "The stars do not lie, Brigid. We must be ready for whatever this night may bring."

She continued her walk around the square, checking the preparations with a keen eye. The bonfires were arranged in the sacred pattern, waiting to be lit when the moment came. Piles of herbs and offerings sat beside each pyre, their strong scents mixing with the crisp smell of fallen leaves.

"It is nearly time," Mairead announced, her voice firm. "Take your places and remember your parts in the ritual. The fate of Septimania and perhaps all of Gaul may rest on our actions tonight."

As the villagers quickly followed her commands, Mairead closed her eyes and stretched out her senses. The veil between worlds was already becoming thin, and she could feel the whispers from the otherworld brushing against her mind. Whatever was coming, she knew they would face it together.

A strange darkness settled over Septimania. Mairead shivered as the last light disappeared, leaving the village in an eerie twilight. The air felt heavy with expectation, filled with the scent of damp earth and burning herbs.

"It begins," she whispered, her words carried away by a sudden gust of wind that swept through the square.

The villagers huddled closer, their faces showing a mix of excitement and fear. Mairead could hear their quiet whispers and feel their eyes nervously watching the shadows that seemed to grow darker with every passing moment.

"Light the fires," Mairead commanded, her voice steady even though unease twisted inside her.

One by one, torches were touched to the carefully arranged pyres. Flames sprang to life, casting flickering shadows across the faces of the crowd. The crackle and pop of burning wood filled the air, offering a comforting sound against the heavy silence that had settled over Septimania.

As the warmth from the bonfires washed over her, Mairead let out a small sigh of relief. "The fires will protect us," she murmured, mostly to herself.

A young man stepped forward; his face partly lit by the dancing flames. "High Priestess," he said, his voice shaking a little, "I've never felt a night like this before. It's as if... as if the air itself is alive."

Mairead nodded, her expression serious. "You feel it too, Aedan. The veil grows thin, and with it comes both danger and opportunity." She paused, choosing her words carefully. "Stay alert. Keep your eyes on the fires and watch the shadows between them. This Samhain may bring more than we expect."

As Aedan hurried back to his post, Mairead looked up at the dark sky above. The fires gave the village a warm glow, but beyond their light, the darkness seemed to grow, waiting. She couldn't shake the feeling that something was coming. Something that would change everything.

A collective gasp moved through the crowd, pulling Mairead's attention to the sky. A brilliant cone of light pierced through the dark, its brightness shining brighter than the bonfires below. The villagers, who had moments ago looked serious and focused, now stared up in awe and wonder.

"By the gods," whispered an elderly woman, her wrinkled hands tightly clasped to her chest. "It's a sign!"

Mairead's sharp hazel eyes narrowed as she watched the strange light. Her voice, low and urgent, cut through the rising whispers. "Silence," she commanded, and the villagers immediately quieted.

The light pulsed, sending shimmering waves across the sky. Children pointed up, their eyes wide with excitement, while their parents exchanged worried glances.

"High Priestess," a man called out, his voice trembling. "What does it mean?"

Mairead's brow furrowed, the runic tattoos on her forearms glowing faintly in response to the strange light. She opened her mouth to answer, but the words vanished as a cold chill ran down her spine.

Something was wrong.

The light that had once seemed pure and hopeful now felt... tainted. Mairead's senses, sharpened by years of ritual and connection to the unseen, screamed a warning she couldn't ignore.

"Extinguish the fires," she commanded, her voice firm and unyielding. "Now!"

Confusion spread through the crowd, but none dared question her. As the villagers hurried to put out the bonfires,

Mairead's mind raced. What kind of force had entered their world? And more importantly, what did it want?

On a jagged ledge, Armaeus stood like a dark silhouette against the night sky. The wind howled around him, whipping his long black hair wildly, but he stayed still, his obsidian eyes locked onto the village below. The flickering candlelight from distant windows gave his sharp features an eerie glow, highlighting the powerful presence that seemed to surround him.

Silence weighed heavily in the air as he spoke, his voice a deep rumble that seemed to shake the very ground beneath him. His intense gaze swept across the land, taking in the sight of the extinguished bonfires and the frantic villagers rushing around. "A change has come," he growled, his words carrying a sense of dark warning. "Even the witch-priestess can feel it now."

A cold shiver ran down Armaeus' spine, an unfamiliar feeling that made him curl his lip in disgust. Uncertainty was a feeling he didn't know well. He was the Daemon, the most feared being in the entire realm. What could possibly make him feel unsettled?

"What is this?" Armaeus muttered, his brow furrowing as he searched for the source of his unease. "A tear in the very fabric of reality?"

He stood still, appearing calm, his powerful body set in a stance of deep thought. The moonlight cast a pale glow on his sharp features, highlighting the depth of his dark eyes and the proud curve of his jaw.

The darkness shifts into a vivid display of swirling colors and shapes. The air around him crackles with flashes of bright light, each one bursting in every color imaginable. The energy pulses and hums, a mix of electric blues and fiery reds that stretch far into the distance.

Armaeus' eyes snapped open, burning like fiery orbs, full of both rage and curiosity. His fingers dug into the hard stone beneath him, leaving deep marks as his grip tightened. "No force can escape me," he growled, his voice thick with anger. "I am the supreme ruler of this realm, and no one will challenge my power."

As he spoke, a plan began to take shape in his mind. He would have to investigate this strange force himself, understand what it was, and if needed, crush it completely. The thought of facing a new challenge stirred something deep within him, a thrill of excitement he hadn't felt in centuries.

"Perhaps," he thought aloud, "this is the challenge I've waited for centuries. A worthy opponent... or a powerful weapon."

Armaeus straightened, his towering figure outlined against the starlit sky. A cold wind whipped around him, carrying whispers of change and trouble. He breathed deeply, savoring the scent of fear and anticipation in the air.

Armaeus bared his teeth, the muscles in his jaw tightening with each word. His eyes burned with a fierce determination as he faced the unseen force before him. "No matter what you are," he snarled, "I, Armaeus, will conquer you. This realm is my right, and I will not stop until it bends to my will."

With a quick, smooth movement, he shed his daemon form and took on the appearance of a human, a striking figure with dark hair and a presence that hid the evil inside.

A sly grin curled at the corners of his mouth as he whispered, "I will harness this power by any means necessary." His dark ambitions surged like a storm within him, fueling a relentless pursuit to claim the power he knew was coming, a force that could reshape the very fabric of existence and plunge the world into chaos.

Chapter 4

43

The forest whispered secrets as Mairead led the villagers through its dark depths without fear. Each step sank into the thick carpet of fallen leaves, creating a silence that built an eerie tension in the air and sent shivers down her spine. Her sharp hazel eyes sparkled with determination in the dim light, scanning the twisted branches above for any signs of danger. Vines twisted around trees like serpents, adding to the spooky atmosphere of the dense forest. The faint smell of moss and decay filled the air, heightening their senses as they followed Mairead deeper into the unknown.

"Stay close," Mairead whispered, her voice soft yet full of authority. "The veil grows thin tonight."

The villagers huddled together, their faces showing a mix of curiosity and fear. Mairead felt their anxiety and wonder pressing against her like a living thing. She took a deep breath, drawing strength from the ancient power that pulsed through the earth beneath her feet.

As they neared the sacred grove, cloaked in dark garments, the flickering torchlight cast eerie shadows on the twisted tree trunks. The flames danced, creating strange shapes that seemed to move and stretch toward the huddled group. Mairead's eyes narrowed, and her tattoos began to glow softly, responding to the magical energy swirling around them.

"Gather around the altar," she ordered, pointing to the weathered stone at the center of the clearing. "But do not touch it. Its power is not to be taken lightly, especially tonight."

The villagers obeyed, forming a loose circle around the altar. Their eyes flicked nervously between Mairead and the dark shadows beyond, as if expecting something from the other world to appear at any moment. Mairead allowed herself a small, grim smile. They were right to be cautious. Samhain was a time when the line between worlds grew thin, when ancient powers awoke, and forgotten prophecies whispered in the wind.

"Elder Mairead," a trembling voice called out, "what... what are we searching for here tonight?"

Mairead turned and locked eyes with the speaker, her gaze sharp. "Answers, child. And maybe... a sign of what's to come."

As she spoke, a cold wind rushed through the grove, making the torches flicker and blaze. The villagers gasped and huddled closer together. Mairead felt it too, a strange tingling on her skin, a pressure in her chest. Something was approaching. Something that would change everything.

She closed her eyes, reaching out with her senses, trying to feel the thin boundary between worlds. "Be ready," she whispered, more to herself than to the uneasy villagers. "The Gods have heard our call. Now we must be ready for their answer."

Mairead stepped forward, her auburn hair shining in the torchlight, and her runic tattoos glowing with an eerie light. The whispers among the villagers faded as she raised her arms, drawing their full attention.

"Children of Septimania," her voice rang out with strength, breaking the silence of the night. "We gather here, on the edge of Samhain, to understand the omens that haunt our land."

Her sharp hazel eyes scanned the crowd, taking in the mix of fear and respect on their faces. "The Labyrinth ceremony is not just a ritual, but a journey into the core of our being. Tonight, we walk the twisted path between worlds, seeking guidance from Cernunnos and Danu themselves."

A shiver ran through the villagers as Mairead spoke again, her words carrying the weight of ancient power. "The signs are clear change is coming. We must be ready."

As she spoke, the villagers instinctively began to form a circle around the altar. Mairead nodded in approval, feeling the energy growing in the sacred space.

"Join hands," she commanded, extending her own arms. "Let your fears fall away. Tonight, we are one with the earth, one with the sky, one with each other."

As the circle formed, Mairead closed her eyes and reached out to the ancient forces that surrounded them. The air grew thick with expectation, and even the trees seemed to bend closer, eager to witness what was about to unfold.

"Great Cernunnos, Lord of the Wild," Mairead called, her voice rising with an unearthly strength. "Guide our steps through the Labyrinth of life. Great Danu, Mother of All, embrace us with your wisdom."

The wind began to pick up, swirling through the clearing, carrying the scent of autumn leaves and something more. Something ancient, something powerful. Mairead felt it pulse through her, a force both frightening and thrilling.

This is it, she thought, her heart pounding. The moment of truth. The fate of Septimania, perhaps even all of Gaul, is hanging by a thread.

As she opened her mouth to continue the chant, a sound like distant thunder rumbled across the sky, and the very air seemed to hum with energy.

A deep silence fell over the villagers. The clouds parted, and a full moon emerged, casting its pale light over the clearing. The moon's glow filtered through the trees, casting long shadows and illuminating the stone altar in the center of their circle. Mairead's breath caught in her chest as she looked at the sight before her…something that sent a chill down her spine.

There, on the cold stone altar, lay a small bundle wrapped in simple cloth. Its presence was both miraculous and unsettling. The baby's sudden appearance seemed to defy all reason, yet Mairead felt an undeniable pull toward the infant that she couldn't explain.

"By the Gods," she whispered, her voice barely a breath. The villagers shifted, murmuring in a mix of awe and fear.

Mairead took slow, deliberate steps toward the altar, her legs trembling slightly with each movement. As she got closer, she noticed the cloth was covered in faint, glowing runes that seemed to shimmer in the moonlight. Her heart raced in her chest as she reached out to touch the bundle.

The moment her fingers brushed against it; a shock of energy surged through her. Mairead gasped, her eyes widening as she recognized something beyond the reach of mortal understanding. Her hands shook, despite her strong will, as she carefully lifted the baby into her arms.

"What is it, Elder?" a villager called out, his voice laced with worry.

Mairead held the infant close, feeling waves of energy flowing from the tiny form. She turned to face the circle, her voice steady even though her heart raced with confusion and awe.

"This child," she began, pausing to find the right words, "is unlike any I have ever seen. The very fabric of our world seems to bend around her."

As if to confirm her words, the baby stirred, opening eyes that shone like the starry sky above them. Mairead felt a powerful connection, a bond that went beyond the physical world.

"But what does it mean?" another villager asked, her voice trembling with fear.

Mairead looked down at the infant, her mind racing with possibilities and signs of what was to come. "It means," she said slowly, "that everything is about to change. Whether for better or worse, the fate of Septimania and perhaps all of Gaul now rests in our hands."

As her words filled the air, a collective gasp passed through the gathered villagers. The High Priestess gently shifted the infant in her arms, revealing a birthmark on the baby's right forearm. The intricate pattern of swirls and lines formed a clear labyrinth.

"By the Gods," someone whispered, their voice almost drowned out by the sound of rustling leaves.

Murmurs of awe and fear spread through the crowd. Mairead scanned the faces around her, feeling the mixture of wonder and uncertainty in the air. She knew that she had to act quickly and with certainty.

"This mark," Mairead declared, her voice strong and clear, "is a sign from the Gods themselves. This child is destined for greatness."

A villager stepped forward; his face filled with worry. "But what does it mean for us, Elder? Are we in danger?"

"This child is a gift," she said firmly, her voice leaving no room for doubt. "I shall name her Merona, for she is our guiding light in these dark times."

"Merona," the villagers repeated, the name spreading through the grove like a chant.

Mairead raised her voice, letting it carry the strength and certainty of her words. "Merona is a child of the Gods, chosen to fulfill the prophecy that has been whispered in our sacred groves for generations. From this day forward, she will be like my own daughter."

The High Priestess felt a deep sense of protectiveness well up inside her. She had never imagined becoming a mother, but it seemed fate had other plans. "We will raise her together," Mairead continued, her eyes glowing with resolve. "We will guide her along the path the Gods have set for her."

As she spoke, Mairead's mind raced with the weight of this moment. What trials lay ahead for this child? What dangers would they face? But beneath the uncertainty, a strong determination grew in her heart. No matter what happened, she would prepare Merona for her fate.

A quiet fell over the gathered villagers, their faces lit by the soft glow of the torches, showing a mix of emotions. Elara, the village midwife, stepped forward, her old face showing respect. "Blessed be," she whispered, kneeling before Mairead and the infant Merona.

One by one, others followed, bowing their heads in respect to the child's divine importance. But not everyone was so quick to accept. Bran, the blacksmith, stood tall, his eyes filled with doubt.

"How can we be sure?" Bran's voice cut through the quiet night, filled with doubt. "What if this child brings doom upon us all?"

Mairead's hold on Merona tightened without thinking. She looked at Bran, her gaze sharp and filled with power. "The Gods have spoken, Bran. Would you dare question their will?"

Bran hesitated, but the doubt had already been planted. Whispers spread among the villagers, a mix of fear and awe.

Mairead looked down at Merona, safely cradled in her arms. The baby's bright blue eyes met hers, full of a wisdom that seemed far beyond her age. In that moment, a rush of love overwhelmed Mairead, nearly taking her breath away.

"Listen to me, all of you," she said, her voice strong and clear, reaching every ear in the grove. "I know you are afraid. These are uncertain times, and this child's arrival is like nothing we've seen before. But I swear to you, by everything sacred, Merona will bring good to this world."

She paused, letting her words settle into the air. "We will raise her as our own, teaching her our ways and our magic. And when the time comes, she will stand as a shield against the darkness that threatens to swallow us all."

Mairead's eyes glowed with resolve as she continued, "This is not a burden, but a blessing. Together, we will guide Merona on her path, and in doing so, we will secure a future for ourselves and for the generations that follow."

As she spoke, Mairead felt the mood of the villagers beginning to change. Fear turned to hope, suspicion shifted to curiosity. She knew the journey ahead would be difficult, but in that moment, holding the child of prophecy, Mairead felt a sense of purpose stronger than anything she had ever experienced.

A quiet fell over the grove as Mairead's words took root in the hearts of the villagers. The flickering torchlight threw shifting shadows on their faces, revealing a mix of emotions. Slowly, one by one, they began to step forward.

Aoife, the village midwife, was the first to speak. "I offer my knowledge and care to the child," she said, her weathered hands trembling slightly as she placed them over her heart. "May my herbs and wisdom help her grow."

One by one, others followed, their voices growing steadier with each promise.

"I give my strength to protect her," proclaimed Bran, the blacksmith, his strong frame outlined by the firelight.

"And I, my stories and songs to nurture her spirit," added Saoirse, the bard, her eyes shining with unspoken emotions.

Mairead watched, her heart swelling with pride and relief. She could feel Merona stirring in her arms, as if the infant sensed the importance of the moment unfolding around her. The High

Priestess glanced down at the child, a small smile forming on her lips.

"You feel it too, don't you, little one?" she whispered, her voice barely audible over the sound of the villagers' continued pledges. "The threads of fate weaving around us all."

As the last villager stepped back, a noticeable energy filled the sacred grove. Mairead took a deep breath, knowing it was time to begin the next phase of the ritual.

"My brothers and sisters," she said, her voice filled with strength, "you have shown great courage tonight. Now, let us call upon the Gods to bless our endeavor."

Mairead raised her free hand towards the star-filled sky, her eyes closing as she focused. "Great Cernunnos, Lord of the Wild, and Danu, Mother of All, we ask for your help. Guide our steps as we begin this sacred journey."

The air grew heavy with anticipation as Mairead began to chant, her words forming an ancient spell to start the Labyrinth ceremony. As she spoke, the villagers gathered in a circle around her and Merona, their hands joined in unity.

Mairead's eyes snapped open, glowing with a strange, powerful light. She stood from the altar, holding Merona in one arm while raising the other to the sky. The air seemed to vibrate with energy, making the villagers shiver in awe.

"North, South, East, West," Mairead said, her voice ringing through the grove. As she spoke, four villagers stepped forward, each standing tall to represent a cardinal direction. Their faces showed a mix of determination and reverence.

Mairead's gaze moved across the group, her hazel eyes sparkling with ancient knowledge. "The Labyrinth Ritual begins tonight," she announced, her words carrying the weight of centuries. "We have called upon Cernunnos and Danu."

The High Priestess paused, allowing the names of the deities to resonate through the sacred space. Merona stirred in her arms, letting out a soft coo that seemed to harmonize with the mystical atmosphere.

"Cernunnos," Mairead continued, her voice dropping to a reverent whisper, "god of the wilderness, protector of wild animals, wanderer of secret paths. We seek your guidance as we navigate our own paths." She raised her voice, commanding, "Cernunnos, guide us!"

The villagers echoed her call, their voices coming together in a strong and united chorus. Mairead felt a wave of pride at their unity, even as she continued with the ritual.

"Danu, Great Mother of the Celts, Mother Earth herself," she called out, her voice softening with warmth and care. "We ask for your love and guidance, that we might better understand your heart." She paused for a moment, then added, "Danu, embrace us!"

Once more, the villagers' voices rose together, their sound carrying through the ancient trees. Mairead closed her eyes for a brief moment, feeling the energy flowing around them, binding them all to something much larger than themselves.

"Tonight," she said, opening her eyes and meeting the gaze of each villager, "we walk the path of the Labyrinth. "With courage in our hearts and the strength of our ancestors guiding us, we shall confront the shadows that dwell within." As the moonlight cast an ethereal glow upon the ancient stones, a hushed anticipation swept through the crowd, uniting them in a shared resolve to face whatever trials awaited in the depths of the maze. The air crackled with energy as they stepped forward together, each footfall echoing the unspoken promises of bravery and unity that bound them as one.

Merona shifted again in her arms, as though the infant understood the weight of the moment. Mairead looked down at her, feeling a rush of love mixed with fear. What future awaited this mysterious child?

Pushing aside her doubts, Mairead raised her voice again. "Join me now in a chant to raise the energy, so we can connect with Cernunnos and Danu: Cernunnos guide us, Danu embrace us."

As the chant began, Mairead felt the power growing around them, a force that seemed to pulse stronger with each repetition of the sacred words. She closed her eyes, giving herself fully to the ritual, knowing that whatever came next, they would face it together the village, the gods, and this special child in her arms.

Mairead's eyes snapped open, her focus sharpening as she felt the ancient power rushing through her. The air crackled with unseen energy, and the villagers' chanting softened to an expectant silence. She pulled Merona closer, the warmth of the infant a sharp contrast to the cold of the night.

With a voice that seemed to come from the earth beneath them, Mairead began to whisper, "Elements of the Sun, Elements of the Day, please come this way." The words hung in the air, shimmering like heat waves.

As she spoke, Mairead's mind raced. Would this be enough to protect the child? To shield the village from the darkness that was creeping closer? She pushed aside her doubts, focusing on the task before her.

"Powers of the Night and Day, I summon you," she continued, her voice growing stronger. The runic tattoos on her forearms began to glow softly, pulsing with each word she spoke.

Mairead felt a presence stir in the shadows beyond the grove. Murdach. She knew he was there, watching, protecting. His dragon form, hidden from mortal eyes, added another layer of power to her incantation.

"I call upon you to protect this village and this baby," Mairead declared, her hazel eyes shining with determination. She raised Merona slightly, presenting the infant to the cosmic forces she was summoning.

The villagers gasped as a sudden gust of wind swept through the grove, carrying the scent of smoke and sea salt – the very essence of Murdach.

"So mote it be," Mairead finished, her voice falling to a whisper once more.

As the final words left her lips, she felt a surge of energy flow through her and into Merona. The baby cooed softly, her tiny hands reaching up toward the starry sky.

Mairead breathed out slowly, her shoulders relaxing. "It is done," she told the villagers, who stood in awe. "The pact is sealed.

We are now bound to protect this child, just as she will one day protect us all."

As the villagers began to disperse, speaking in hushed, respectful tones, Mairead held Merona close to her chest. The baby's eyes seemed to shine with an otherworldly wisdom, and Mairead felt a deep, unspoken bond with this small, powerful child.

"Rest now, little one," she whispered softly. "Your journey has only just begun."

Mairead felt a change in the air, a strange tingle at the back of her neck that told her he was close. She turned, her eyes scanning the trees until she saw him step out of the shadows. His human form was tall and commanding.

He walked toward her; his eyes locked on the bundle in her arms. "So, it's true," he said, his voice smooth and deep. "The Witch is reborn."

Mairead nodded, her grip on Merona tightening without thinking. "You felt it too?"

"I did," Murdach replied, his finger gently brushing Merona's cheek. "The very elements sing of her arrival."

Mairead frowned, her thoughts racing. "But why now? Why here?"

Murdach's gaze locked with hers, steady and unblinking. "Because the time has come, Mairead. The prophecy is unfolding, and I am here to make sure it is fulfilled."

Mairead's eyes widened as the truth hit her. "Who are you?" she asked, her voice tinged with disbelief.

Murdach's answer was simple yet heavy. "I am here to protect her."

Chapter 5

The morning sun cast long shadows across the cobblestones of Septimania's town square, its light weak and struggling to break through the mist that hung heavily over the village, creating an eerie quiet. The usual sounds of the bustling square were missing, replaced by a thick, uneasy silence. Villagers stopped in their tracks, sensing something was wrong.

Mairead stood tall in the midst of this strange stillness, her auburn hair glowing in the weak sunlight, forming a fiery halo around her face. She held baby Merona close, instinctively shielding the fragile child against her chest. The warmth of the baby's tiny body was a sharp contrast to the chill that seemed to seep through the air, creeping into Mairead's bones.

Her eyes swept over the crowd, alert for any sign of danger hidden in the shadows. The villagers, who had once been chatting and going about their morning tasks, now wore faces full of worry and uncertainty. Their eyes darted around, trying to make sense of the strange tension in the air. Mairead's gaze met Bran's, the village blacksmith. He was a tall, strong man, with hands hardened by years of work, but his sharp mind was what truly stood out. In that moment, a silent understanding passed between them, and Mairead felt a shiver run down her spine. The hairs on the back of her neck stood up, as a deep, instinctive feeling warned her that something dark and dangerous was coming.

"The air itself seems to hold its breath," Mairead whispered, her voice low and urgent, tinged with a touch of fear.

She glanced down at Merona, whose bright blue eyes seemed far too aware for a baby of her age. They sparkled with a depth of intelligence that both reassured and unsettled Mairead.

"What darkness comes, little one?" she murmured softly, her protective instincts rising, her thoughts clouded by an overwhelming need to shield her child from whatever was drawing near.

As though answering her unspoken question, the crowd began to part, like the waters of a stormy sea, revealing a figure stepping out from the thick mist. Cloaked in shadows that clung to him, the man moved slowly, each step deliberate, his presence heavy and suffocating. His face remained hidden beneath a dark hood, but Mairead could feel his eyes on her, cold and intense, as though they could see straight through her, piercing to her very soul.

The silence around them was broken suddenly by the man's voice, sharp and cold, cutting through the stillness like a knife. "Show me the child," he demanded, each word dripping with malice, filling the air with an oppressive, foul feeling.

Mairead's instincts kicked in, and she tightened her grip on Merona, even though a wave of fear twisted in her stomach. She could feel the raw power pulsing within her, ready to burst forth at any moment. But she held back, knowing that revealing too much in front of the villagers could put everyone she loved in danger.

"And who are you to make such a demand?" Mairead asked, her voice firm, a shield of defiance against the fear creeping into her heart. She took a small step back, raising her free hand in a protective motion, ready to use her magic if needed.

The man moved forward quickly, his cloak billowing around him like a dark cloud, the sound of the fabric swishing sending an unsettling whisper through the air, as if the cloak itself carried hidden secrets. His cold eyes glowed with an evil light, casting eerie shadows across his face as he came closer.

"I am the one who knows the truth about that cursed child you hold," he snarled, his voice full of hatred. "Give her to me, sorceress, or face the consequences."

Mairead's mind spun, filled with a storm of questions and fears. How did this stranger know about Merona? Who had sent him, and what did he mean by "cursed"? Her heart hammered in her chest as she glanced around the square, seeing the fear and confusion on the villagers' faces. The reality hit her hard; she couldn't risk a fight here, not with so many innocent lives at stake.

Holding baby Merona tightly against her, Mairead felt the tiny body trembling in her arms, a clear sign of the danger that was closing in. The air around them felt heavier, thick with tension. What had once been a peaceful square now felt dark, the energy almost suffocating. The leaves rustled like whispers in the wind, and the distant howls only made her nerves tighten. But through it all, she held on, her determination growing stronger as she prepared to protect this fragile life from whatever dark forces threatened them.

"You speak of things you do not understand," Mairead declared, her voice rising above the quiet fear that gripped the crowd, carrying through the square with a fierce determination. "This child is under my protection, and I will not give her to someone like you."

The man's laughter echoed through the air, cold and sharp, like the sound of broken glass. "Protection?" he mocked, his voice dripping with contempt. "You deceive yourself if you think you can protect her from her destiny or from those who will do anything to control it." His eyes flashed with a dark promise, daring anyone to step in his way, as if a storm was gathering behind them.

As he spoke, Mairead felt something stir deep inside her. A surge of energy pulsed from Merona, an unknown force full of life and power. The birthmark on the child's skin, like a twisting labyrinth, glowed softly for a moment, casting a gentle light that broke through the thick shadows surrounding them. A warm breeze swept through the square, clearing the fog and filling the air with the earthy scent of autumn leaves and the comforting warmth of wood smoke. A quiet promise of change, of hope, and the strength to stand firm against the dark forces closing in.

Mairead's voice trembled with barely contained anger as she faced the man. "You have no right to decide her fate," she spat, her eyes burning with defiance. "Leave now, or you'll regret crossing me." She stood tall, ready to fight for what was hers.

The man's cruel laugh echoed in Mairead's ears, a sharp reminder of his power and her supposed weakness. But Mairead squared her shoulders and glared back at him, refusing to be scared by his mocking and threats. She would protect Merona with everything she had, even if it meant giving her life.

At the edge of town, where the cobblestone streets gave way to thick grass and wildflowers, Murdach stood watching. His sharp gaze never wavered, and his eyes narrowed, filled with the wisdom of centuries. He felt the strange, dark energy coming from the cloaked figure in the distance. This man was no ordinary enemy; the darkness that clung to him seemed alive, whispering of evil and fear.

Murdach's silver hair shone in the soft light of the morning, giving him a halo-like glow. He stepped forward, his muscles tensing like a bow ready to fire, prepared for action at any moment.

Every part of him felt danger, a deep instinct sharpened by years of battles and shadows. His eyes stayed locked on Mairead and the baby, Merona, whose fate now rested on the fragile balance between light and darkness.

"I will not ask again," came the voice from the cloaked figure. It was smooth and captivating yet filled with dark intent. The words floated across the square, calm and controlled, but hiding a deep threat beneath the surface. "Give me the child or face the consequences."

Mairead's heart sank as the weight of his words hit her like a wave. She held Merona closer, instinctively trying to protect the child from the danger before them.

"Never," she said, her voice shaking but firm, like a strong flame fighting against the wind. "This child's fate is hers alone, not yours to decide."

A dark smile twisted the man's lips, a disturbing expression that showed no sign of humanity. As he lifted his hands, the air around them grew heavy, thick with a strange energy that seemed to promise destruction.

"Then you leave me no choice," he hissed, his voice full of hatred.

In that moment, as if pulled from a dark, ancient world, a powerful wave of energy surged through the air, sending a cold wave of fear through the town. Flames suddenly shot from the man's fingers, twisting and spinning in a deadly dance, growing larger and more dangerous with each passing second. The heat and the burning smell of smoke flooded the square, choking the townspeople as they were caught in the fire's grip. Screams filled the air as people ran in all directions, trying to escape the flames. The once peaceful town square had turned into a nightmare, as if the very fires of hell had been set loose on them.

Murdach's heart pounded in his chest like a war drum as he watched the fire rage, a bitter realization sinking in. "Armaeus," he growled, the name leaving a sour taste on his tongue.

Knowing that this was the work of the demon filled him with a deep, burning anger. His muscles tensed, ready to act against this evil force, but he paused, torn by doubt. Was now the right moment to step forward and face the darkness threatening to control Merona's fate?

Then, in a terrifying turn, the flames consumed Armaeus' human form. The fire tore away his disguise, revealing the twisted and powerful demon beneath. His eyes glowed like burning embers, a malicious light cutting through the chaos. Armaeus let out a roar of dark power, his voice booming through the square like a curse from the depths of hell.

"The child's power will be mine," Armaeus declared, his voice carrying a dark promise. "And this world will burn to ashes under my command!"

Mairead staggered backward, instinctively pulling little Merona closer to her chest, desperate to shield the child from the growing heat that threatened to consume them both. Her mind spun, a whirlwind of panic and urgency, searching for a way to protect the precious life in her arms.

"Murdach," she whispered, her voice barely audible over the roar of the flames. It was a prayer, a desperate plea for help. "Where are you?"

The question hung heavy in the air, laced with fear and the need for hope as the darkness closed in.

Then, in the midst of the chaos, Mairead's prayer was answered. A powerful chorus of voices rose above the crackling flames, defying the fiery destruction that threatened to overwhelm the town. From the frightened crowd, the coven appeared, a sisterhood bound by their ancient vows and a common purpose. Their faces, lit by the dancing firelight, were set in grim determination, each one reflecting the unwavering spirit of witchcraft. Mairead felt a rush of pride fill her chest at the sight of her sisters, united and ready to stand against the darkness.

"CIRCLE OF PROTECTION!" Mairead shouted, her voice cutting through the chaos. Each word carried its own power. "Channel the elements, sisters! Earth to ground us, air to lift us, water to flow through us, fire to ignite our will!"

The witches quickly formed a tight circle around Mairead and Merona, their hands joined together in unity. Their voices rose as one, singing an ancient chant filled with power. As they spoke the words, a glowing barrier began to take shape before them, a bright shield that pushed back against the fierce flames that threatened to devour everything in their way.

Armaeus, a creature of pure evil, snarled from the edge of the chaos, his demonic face twisted in fury. "Your weak magic won't stop me!" he growled, his voice filled with hatred and disdain.

Mairead, standing strong against his fierce presence, met his fiery gaze without hesitation. "We are the daughters of the earth, protectors of the old ways. Your fire may burn, but it will not destroy us." Her words sparked a new strength in her sisters, filling them with fierce determination that strengthened the protective barrier.

As the witches' chanting grew louder, Murdach felt a powerful, ancient force awakening inside him. His skin tingled, and a surge of adrenaline rushed through him, his muscles tightening as a long-forgotten power stirred. In that moment, everything became clear to him. He could no longer stay on the sidelines.

"Merona needs me. Mairead needs me," he thought, his heart pounding with purpose.

Mairead gasped in surprise as she watched Murdach transform right before her eyes. "A dragon," she whispered in awe, her heart filled with wonder and reverence. "The legends were true."

Mairead felt a powerful surge of hope, a belief that their combined strength might be enough to change the course of the battle. The coven's chanting faltered for a moment as they looked up in awe at Murdach in his sea dragon form. His shining scales, a dazzling blend of colors, glimmered in the fiery light of the burning town. With a mighty flap of his massive wings, he soared into the air, sending a gust of wind that scattered glowing embers into the night sky. High above, he became a shining beacon of strength amid the chaos below.

In response, Armaeus let out a terrifying roar that echoed through the crumbling streets. His fiery breath shot toward Murdach, a blazing arrow aimed with deadly intent. But Murdach was ready. With sharp instincts honed through countless battles, he dove toward the demon, his tail lashing out with precise force, a deadly weapon in this fight for survival.

The demon dodged and weaved with surprising speed, but Murdach's aim was true. His tail slammed into Armaeus, sending the demon crashing backward, his body slamming into a nearby building. The impact shook the ground, temporarily stunning him.

Seizing the moment while Armaeus remained disoriented, the coven poured their magic into the air with renewed strength. The circle they formed began to glow brighter, their voices rising together in a powerful song of resistance. Their energy flowed into Murdach and Mairead, binding them with an unbreakable shield of protection.

Murdach could feel the surge of power coursing through him, filling him with new life and strength for the battle that raged around him. With a mighty, deafening roar that shook the very air, he dove once more toward Armaeus, now empowered by the magic of the witches surrounding him.

But this time, Armaeus was ready. His claws shot out like lightning, slicing through the air with terrifying speed. They aimed for Murdach's vulnerable underbelly; a deadly strike intended to end the fight.

Murdach tried to dodge, but he was caught off guard. Armaeus's claws struck him, tearing through his shimmering scales and drawing blood. Sparks flew into the dark sky, like fiery stars being born from the chaos below.

Pain and fury surged through Murdach, and he reacted instinctively. With a mighty roar, he unleashed a powerful wave of water from his jaws toward Armaeus. The force of the blast knocked the demon back, sending him sprawling and temporarily putting out some of the flames that were tearing through the town. The water hissed as it met the burning remnants, a warning sound of steam rising in the air.

Murdach coiled gracefully in the air, his iridescent scales glowing in the fiery chaos below. He gathered his strength and released another torrent of water, this time a massive wave that crashed down to quench the flames. The air was filled with the deafening hiss of steam as the water met the fire, a sound that echoed through the square and shook the very ground beneath them.

"By the gods," Mairead whispered, her voice barely rising above the noise of the battle. She held Merona close, the infant strangely calm amidst the chaos that raged around them.

Murdach's voice echoed in her mind, deep and comforting like the rumble of thunder. "Hold fast, our combined strength will defeat this evil."

Mairead's heart lifted at his words, and with renewed strength, she focused on maintaining the protective barrier. She turned to her sisters, her voice strong and commanding, "Push harder! The tide is turning in our favor!"

The witches, fueled by Mairead's call, gave everything they had. Their chants grew louder, blending with the sounds of battle, as they pushed back the flames inch by inch. Sweat beaded on their foreheads, but their eyes burned with determination, their spirits unbroken and resolute.

"We will not yield," Mairead declared, her eyes burning with determination as she fixed her gaze on Armaeus. "This land, these people, Merona... they are under our protection. Your dark ambitions end here!"

Armaeus sneered, his form shifting like a shadow in the dying light of the flames. "This is just a temporary setback, witch. The child will be mine," he hissed, his voice filled with malice and unwavering confidence.

Murdach swooped low, his massive wings casting a dark shadow over the town square. "You will not touch her while I still breathe," he growled, his eyes glowing fiercely with restrained anger.

As the last of the flames died down, leaving behind only charred earth and lingering wisps of smoke, Mairead felt an overwhelming wave of exhaustion wash over her. But as she looked down at Merona, peacefully asleep in her arms, she knew their fight was far from over.

"What comes next?" she wondered quietly, her gaze meeting Murdach's in a moment of silent understanding. An unspoken promise passed between them: no matter what trials lay ahead, they would face them together, side by side, to protect Merona.

But Armaeus was not finished. His form shimmered as he began to fade into the growing darkness, his blackened skin blending with the shadows. His fiery red eyes remained locked on Merona, filled with both hatred and longing.

"Mark my words," he hissed, his voice a low growl that seemed to come from deep within the night. "I will return, and the child will be mine. No amount of water or witchcraft will stop me."

With those final, chilling words, Armaeus disappeared, leaving behind only the cold presence of evil that lingered in the air.

Mairead held Merona close to her chest, feeling the quick beat of her heart echo in her ears. The air still felt heavy with the chaos of their battle, the shadows of what had happened lingering like ghosts. She looked at Murdach, who had changed back into his human form. His silver hair shone softly, like stars caught in the moonlight.

"We've won this battle," she said, her voice heavy with both exhaustion and relief, "but at what cost?"

Murdach met her gaze, his eyes softening as he looked at her. He moved closer, his calm presence filled with determination. Reaching out, he gently placed a hand on top of Merona's small head. As he touched Merona, Mairead noticed that the labyrinth birthmark seemed to glow brighter.

"Any cost is worth her safety," he said, his voice warm and strong. "She is our future, our hope."

A tired smile began to pull at the corners of Mairead's lips, despite the weight of exhaustion that pressed on her. "You're right, of course," she said, glancing at the scorched earth littered with the remains of their magical battle. The smoldering embers crumbled into ash, a silent reminder of how fierce their struggle had been. "But Armaeus will come back. We have to be ready."

"And we will be," Murdach said firmly, his voice filled with unwavering determination. "Together, we're stronger than any demon from hell."

They stood side by side, their bodies aching and drained, but their spirits unbroken by the events they had just faced. As Mairead thought about the challenges that still lay ahead threatening prophecies, Merona's unique destiny, and Armaeus's constant hunger for power, everything seemed overwhelming. Yet, in that moment, looking at Murdach's steady face and feeling the warmth of Merona in her arms, Mairead discovered a strength within herself she hadn't known was there, waiting for the right moment to rise.

"We've defended our home today," Mairead said softly, her words drifting into the quiet, as much for herself as for Murdach. "And we'll do it again, as many times as we must."

Murdach nodded, his gaze sweeping over the town, which lay in ruin, its people peering out from the shadows in fear. "For Merona," he whispered, his voice filled with reverence, a promise made in the wake of the chaos. "For all of us."

The heavy silence that surrounded them was suddenly broken by the sound of doors creaking open and the cautious shuffle of villagers stepping out of hiding. Their eyes, wide with both awe and fear, watched the trio closely as they approached Mairead, Murdach, and the precious Merona. They moved carefully, as though afraid that any sudden movement might bring the horrors of the battle back to life.

Mairead instinctively tightened her grip on Merona, feeling the weight of the villagers' stares upon her. Their silent questions hung in the air, thick as the smoke that was only just beginning to clear. From the crowd, an elderly woman stepped forward, her face lined with years of wisdom, now softened by gratitude.

"You saved us," she said, her voice shaking with emotion. "You and your... your dragon," she added, her eyes briefly glancing at Murdach, who seemed to carry both the presence of man and magic.

Pride sparkled in Murdach's eyes as he spoke. "We did what was necessary." His voice was calm and steady, like the gentle rhythm of waves crashing on the shore, offering comfort after the storm.

More villagers gathered, forming a circle of grateful faces around Mairead and Murdach. They whispered their thanks, some reaching out hesitantly to touch Mairead's sleeve or lightly rest their fingers on Murdach's arm, as if trying to confirm that their saviors were real and not just a dream born from the chaos they had witnessed.

Mairead felt warmth spread through her chest, lifted by their gratitude. But that warmth was shaded by the uncertainty that still lingered, the weight of what lay ahead. She looked down at Merona, whose eyes sparkled with a strange wisdom, far beyond her age, as if the child carried a future already written a destiny waiting for its moment.

"This is just the beginning," Mairead thought, her mind racing with growing fears. "How many more battles must we face? How can we keep her safe in a world full of darkness?"

Sensing the weight of her thoughts, Murdach stepped closer and placed a firm hand on her shoulder, offering comfort. "We should rest," he said softly. "The town is safe for now."

Mairead nodded, letting herself take a deep breath as her eyes swept over the destruction. The scorched ground and the thin wisps of smoke rising into the night. "Yes," she agreed, though her voice still carried caution, "but we must stay alert. Armaeus won't give up so easily."

A young man, his cheeks smudged with soot and his eyes full of determination, stepped forward. "We'll stand with you," he said, his voice strong despite the slight shake in his hands. "We've seen what you can do, what you're willing to sacrifice for us."

Murmurs of agreement spread through the crowd, each voice a heartbeat that echoed unity. Mairead felt a lump rise in her throat, a wave of gratitude and admiration for their bravery sweeping over her, though it was quickly overshadowed by the sharp awareness of the danger their bravery could bring.

"Your courage is admirable," Mairead said, her voice heavy with the wisdom of experience. "But this is not your battle. We cannot ask you to risk your lives."

Murdach's gaze softened with both pride and concern as he shook his head thoughtfully. "Perhaps," he said slowly, his brow furrowing, "their support is exactly what we need. Unity in the face of darkness can be a powerful force."

"We cannot let our guard down," Mairead whispered softly, almost reverently. Her fingers gently traced the intricate runic tattoos spiraling across her forearms, symbols of her strength and vulnerabilities intertwined. "Armaeus will return, and he will be stronger."

Murdach nodded, his silver hair catching the last light of day, glowing faintly against the darkening sky. "But so will we," he replied, his voice filled with fierce resolve. "We will protect Merona and ensure she fulfills her destiny, no matter what it takes."

Turning her gaze back to the small bundle in her arms, Mairead felt the full weight of their duty settle upon her. "The road ahead will be perilous," she thought aloud, "but we cannot shy away from it. Our journey is for Merona's sake. For what lies at the end of this uncertain path."

Chapter 6

Merona's tiny fingers moved lightly over the old rune stones, their carved symbols glowing faintly as she touched them. The dim light of flickering candles sent long shadows dancing across the rough walls of Mairead's cottage, filling the room with a mysterious energy that matched the magic in the air.

"Now, little one," Mairead's voice broke the silence, firm and steady. "Focus on the flame in front of you. Feel its warmth, its life. Command it to grow."

Merona leaned forward, her dark curls falling over her face as she focused intently. Her eyes narrowed in concentration. The flame on the candle flickered, wavered, and then suddenly rose high, stretching toward the wooden rafters above.

"I did it!" Merona's voice rang with excitement and pride.

Mairead's lips curved into a rare smile, her hazel eyes sparkling with approval. "Yes, you did, child. You have a gift for the elements." She knelt beside Merona, her long raven hair flowing over her shoulders. "But remember," she said, her tone soft yet serious, "with great power comes great responsibility. We must always respect the balance."

Merona nodded solemnly, her young mind working to understand ideas far beyond her age. The magic in her veins hummed softly, a constant reminder of who she truly was.

"Mother," she asked quietly, her voice filled with curiosity, "why can I do these things when others can't?"

Mairead's face grew serious, and the runic tattoos on her forearms seemed to glow faintly. "You are special, Merona. Chosen by forces we cannot fully understand. In time, you will discover your true purpose."

As Mairead spoke, a chill ran down Merona's spine, like a warning of challenges yet to come. Even at just five years old, she felt the weight of her destiny. She knew she would need to face whatever the future held. The magic inside her stirred, answering her resolve, and she turned back to the candle, ready to keep learning.

Merona focused intently, her small hands reaching out toward the flickering flame. Taking a deep breath, she concentrated, picturing the fire responding to her will. Suddenly, the flame stretched and twisted, forming a dancing figure that spun gracefully above the wick.

"I did it!" Merona cried out, her face glowing with happiness. "Mother, look!"

The elder witch nodded with approval, her sharp hazel eyes reflecting the glow of the magical fire. "Well done, child. Your illusions grow stronger every day."

Encouraged by her success, Merona shifted her focus to a nearby quill. Her small brow furrowed in concentration as she willed the feather to rise. Slowly, it lifted from the table, hovering gently in the air before her.

"How am I doing this?" Merona asked, her voice filled with wonder and curiosity.

Mairead's voice was calm but firm. "That is the power of your mind. Remember, such abilities must always be used wisely."

Merona nodded, her dark curls bouncing slightly as she kept her focus on the floating quill. "Can you teach me more? I want to understand how magic works!"

A flicker of concern crossed Mairead's face, though her tone remained steady. "Patience, little one. Magic must not be rushed. Now tell me, why do you think we practice these arts?"

Merona paused, deep in thought, and the quill slowly settled back onto the table. "To help people? To... to protect people?"

"Both true," Mairead said, her voice serious. "But also to keep balance in the world. Our power comes with great responsibility."

As Merona listened, her chest tightened, a strange sensation prickling at the edge of her mind, as though unseen eyes were watching her. She shivered, the weight of her destiny pressing down on her even though she couldn't fully understand what it meant.

The torchlight flickered, casting eerie shadows on the cottage walls, reflecting the tension that seemed to seep in from the world outside. Merona's small hands shook as she held a worn parchment, her eyes filled with both fear and fascination.

"Mother," she whispered, her voice almost lost amid the faint sounds of conflict in the distance. "Who is Childeric?"

Mairead's face grew tight, her gaze unfocused as if lost in thought. "He is the ruler of the Franks, child. A man of immense ambition and even greater power. His choices will shape the future of this land... and your destiny."

"My destiny?" Merona asked, a small smile breaking the tension. "But I'm just a girl!"

Mairead chuckled softly at her innocence but said nothing more. Outside, the villagers spoke in hushed tones of the Franks and their victories in Gaul, how they had overtaken the Romans with relentless force.

Standing at the window of the cottage, Mairead peered out at the darkening world. Merona joined her, stretching onto her toes to catch a glimpse of what lay beyond, the shadows of her future hidden in the twilight.

"Why do they fight?" Merona asked, her young voice filled with confusion as she tried to understand the violence.

Mairead sighed, placing a comforting hand on Merona's shoulder. "Power, child. Control. And faith. The old ways are being replaced by a new god who promises unity and peace. We are living at a time of great change."

Merona's brow furrowed, her mind racing with questions. "But what about our magic? Will it survive?"

Mairead crouched slightly to meet Merona's gaze, her voice soft but firm. "That, little one, may depend on you. The road ahead is filled with challenges, but it holds great possibilities too. You must be ready for what's coming."

The world was shifting, and Merona found herself at its center, a small but vital figure who could shape its future. Mairead's heart swelled with love as she looked at her, feeling the weight of both hope and fear. Wanting to ease the tension, she suggested a walk to the edge of the forest to escape the heavy talk of war and destiny.

Merona's face lit up with joy at the idea. She was a curious and adventurous child who loved to explore. As they entered the forest, it felt alive, as though the trees were whispering ancient secrets. Sunlight filtered through the leaves, casting golden patterns on Merona's dark hair, giving her an almost otherworldly glow as she skipped happily ahead.

Suddenly, she stopped, her breath catching as a soft breeze brushed against her face. Her eyes widened with wonder, reflecting the magic she felt in that moment.

"Hello," Merona whispered to the wind, her voice so soft it barely stirred the air. The leaves rustled in reply, as though inviting her deeper into the woods.

She closed her eyes, feeling the steady pulse of the earth beneath her bare feet. With arms outstretched, her small fingers spread wide, she seemed to reach for the very essence of the world around her.

"I feel you," she murmured, a gentle smile curving her lips. "The trees, the rocks, the water... you're all alive."

As she stood there, immersed in the natural energy surrounding her, a shadowed figure lingered in silence. Armaeus, cloaked in his human form, watched her intently. The guise barely masked the dark malice that flickered within him.

"So small," he muttered under his breath, his voice a rough growl. "Yet so deeply tied to the elements. She is the one foretold."

Unaware of his presence, Merona wandered to a bubbling stream. She knelt by its edge and dipped her hand into the cool, clear water, laughing softly as it swirled around her fingers.

"Water," she said, her voice laced with awe. "You bring life. You shape the land." She paused, tilting her head as though hearing a secret only she could discern. "And you remember. You remember everything."

Armaeus's fists tightened, his nails digging into his palms. "She grows stronger with every breath," he hissed under his breath. "If she reaches her full potential..."

His dark thoughts were cut short as Merona suddenly stood, her gaze sweeping the forest with an unsettling awareness. For a brief, paralyzing moment, Armaeus feared she had detected him. But her eyes passed over his hiding spot without pausing.

"The forest is afraid," Merona said, her expression tightening with concern. "Something dark is here. Something that doesn't belong."

She placed her small hand on the rough trunk of a nearby tree, her fingers pressing gently against the bark. Closing her eyes, she whispered softly, "Don't worry. I'll protect you. All of you."

A faint glow began to radiate from her palm, spreading into the tree and down through its roots. The light pulsed gently, moving as though it carried life itself. Around her, the forest seemed to exhale in relief, the tension melting away as the energy flowed through the ground.

Hidden in the shadows, Armaeus's jaw tightened as he watched the scene unfold. His voice, low and filled with disbelief, broke the silence. "Impossible," he snarled. "She's just a child. How can she command such power?"

As he retreated deeper into the shadows, unseen and unheard, Merona's voice carried after him, steady and filled with quiet conviction:

"The earth remembers. The wind carries stories. The water shapes destiny. And the fire... the fire will cleanse."

Her words seemed to ripple through the forest; a quiet promise carried on the air. Nearby, a shimmer of light appeared, coalescing into a figure. Stepping from behind an ancient oak, Murdach emerged silently, his presence calm yet commanding. He watched the young girl with measured pride, and his silver hair gleamed in the dappled sunlight, giving him an almost otherworldly aura.

"Well done, little one," Murdach said softly, his voice carrying on the gentle breeze. "You're learning faster than any of us dared to hope."

Merona spun around, her eyes shining with joy. "Murdach!" she exclaimed, running toward him. "Did you see? I made the forest happy again!"

Murdach knelt to meet her gaze, his eyes warm with approval. "I saw, little one. Your bond with the elements grows stronger every day."

Merona's smile faded as her brow furrowed in thought. "Why was the forest scared?" she asked softly. "It felt like... like shadows were trying to eat the light."

Murdach's expression grew serious, the warmth in his eyes replaced by concern. "There are forces, Merona," he said carefully, "that seek to destroy what is good and pure. But that's why I'm here to protect you."

Merona tilted her head, her gaze unfocused as if listening to something only she could hear. Her expression brightened. "Mairead is coming," she said, her voice filled with excitement. Then her tone shifted, quieter now. "She feels... worried."

Murdach rose, his stance suddenly alert. "She's sensed something," he murmured, his voice low and cautious, more to himself than to her. "We must remain alert."

Moments later, Mairead stepped out from the treeline, her auburn hair flowing behind her like a streak of fire. Her piercing hazel eyes swept across the clearing until they landed on Merona.

"I felt a disturbance," Mairead said, her voice sharp with urgency. "Armaeus. He was here, wasn't he?"

Murdach nodded solemnly. "His presence still lingers," he confirmed. "But Merona... she cleansed it, Mairead. Without even realizing the depth of her power."

Mairead's eyes widened, pride and fear mingling on her face. "So soon?" she whispered, more to herself. "The prophecy... it's moving faster than we thought."

Murdach's jaw tightened as he spoke. "It is. And Armaeus grows bolder with each passing day. His determination to snuff out the light knows no bounds. We must be on guard at all times."

Merona stood quietly, watching their serious exchange. She didn't understand all of their words, but she could feel the weight of their emotions pressing down on the air around them. Her small brow furrowed as she tugged on Mairead's sleeve.

"What does it all mean?" she asked, her wide blue eyes searching Mairead's face for answers.

Mairead knelt beside Merona, her hand resting gently on the child's shoulder. Her voice was soft yet filled with meaning. "You are special, Merona," she said. "You have powers that others can only imagine. And with those powers comes a responsibility you must take seriously."

Merona glanced down at her small hands, her fingers curling slightly as she thought about what Mairead had said. A weight, heavy and unfamiliar, seemed to settle on her young shoulders. She had always felt different. The way the forest seemed to whisper secrets to her, the way she could sense the emotions of others as if they were her own.

"But why me?" she asked, her voice barely above a whisper as she looked back at Mairead.

Mairead's expression softened, though her tone remained steady. "Because the elements have chosen you," she said. "They see you as their protector, their guardian."

Merona's eyes grew wide with wonder, and a spark of determination flickered deep within them. She didn't fully understand what it all meant, but one thing was clear; she loved this forest and the life it held. If she had been chosen to protect it, she would do everything in her power to keep it safe.

With a small nod, Merona straightened her back. "I'll protect them," she said quietly but with growing confidence. "I promise."

"We will train you," Murdach said, his voice pulling Merona out of her thoughts. "To control your powers and get you ready for what's coming."

Merona nodded eagerly. She was ready to do anything needed to fulfill her purpose.

"But we must begin right away," Mairead added. "Armaeus is growing stronger, and it won't be long before he makes his next move."

Murdach and Mairead led Merona deeper into the forest, taking her to a quiet clearing where a small, hidden cottage stood. Merona could feel a gentle hum of magic coming from the cottage, though it was hidden from sight.

"This will be our training place," Murdach explained, pointing to the cottage.

Merona's eyes lit up with excitement as they entered the cottage. Inside, the room was filled with shelves of books, tables covered in scrolls and potions, and various magical tools scattered around.

"Wow..." she whispered, taking in the sight of everything.

Mairead smiled at Merona's excitement. "We have a lot to teach you," she said. "But first, we'll start with the basics."

For the next few years, Merona threw herself into her training. She learned how to control her powers. How to call fire without burning herself or anyone else, how to summon water without flooding everything around her.

She also learned more about the elements and the importance of attaining knowledge to master them. With each lesson, Merona felt a deeper connection to the elements as she practiced controlling them under Mairead's watchful eyes.

But even as she made progress, there was always a sense of urgency. Armaeus was never far from their minds, and they knew they had to move quickly before he grew stronger.

One day, as Merona practiced controlling the air element, she suddenly stopped.

"What's wrong?" Mairead asked, noticing Merona's change in focus.

"I... I can sense something," Merona said quietly. "A darkness... it's coming."

Mairead and Murdach exchanged a worried glance, then turned their attention back to Merona. The time was drawing near for her to fully awaken her powers and face the battle against the darkness that was closing in.

Chapter 7

The flickering candlelight cast eerie shadows across Merona's face as she stared into the cracked mirror. Ten years old today, she thought, tracing the curve of her cheek with a slender finger. Ten years since I appeared on that altar, wrapped in ancient runes and destined for... what?

A chill ran down her spine, and she shivered, pulling her woolen cloak tighter around her shoulders. The small cottage suddenly felt stifling, the weight of expectations pressing down on her from all sides.

"Merona?" Mairead's gentle voice called from the other room. "Are you ready, child?"

Merona took a deep breath, steadying herself. "Coming," she replied, her voice calm despite the tremor in her hands.

As she stepped into the main room, Murdach's wise eyes met hers. A flicker of concern crossed his weathered face. "How do you feel, little one?"

"I'm not sure," Merona admitted, furrowing her brow. "There's a... heaviness in the air. Can you feel it?"

Murdach nodded gravely. "The wheel of fate turns, Merona. Your journey truly begins today."

Deep beneath the earth, in a cavern untouched by the sun's warmth, Armaeus paced like a trapped beast. His claws scraped against the stone floor, leaving deep gouges in their wake. His eyes burned with crimson fury as he muttered to himself, his voice a low, menacing growl.

"Ten years," he snarled, spinning to face the ancient texts scattered across a rough-hewn table. "Ten years I've waited, watching her grow stronger with each passing day."

He slammed his fist down, shaking the cavern. Dust and small stones rained from the ceiling, but Armaeus barely noticed. His thoughts were consumed by the witch-child above, the one foretold to be his undoing.

"I will not be bested by a mere girl," he hissed, his form flickering with rage. For a moment, his demonic appearance wavered, showing the handsome face of his human guise before returning to its monstrous shape.

Armaeus closed his eyes, drawing in a deep breath to steady himself. When he spoke again, his voice was smooth, dripping with malevolent charm. "Soon, little witch. Soon, you'll learn the true meaning of power... and the price it demands."

Back in the cottage, Merona suddenly felt a chill, as if icy fingers had brushed the back of her neck. She spun around, half-expecting to see a shadowy figure lurking in the corner.

"What is it?" Mairead asked, her face lined with worry.

Merona shook her head, still unable to shake the uneasy feeling. "Nothing, I... I just felt something strange."

"The veil between worlds is thin today, Merona," Mairead said gently. "It's Samhain, and it's your birthday. You must stay alert. Your powers are awakening, and there are those who would try to use them... or destroy them."

Merona nodded, her expression firm with resolve. "I'm ready, mother. Whatever comes, I'll face it. I have to."

As soon as the words left her lips, a gust of wind howled outside, rattling the shutters. The candles flickered, and for a brief moment, the cottage was plunged into darkness. When the light returned, Merona stood tall, her eyes glowing with a fierce inner fire that seemed beyond her years.

The battle lines were drawn. Below in the depths and above in the world, two forces were preparing for a confrontation that would shake the very foundations of reality. And in the middle of it all stood a ten-year-old girl, bearing the weight of destiny on her slender shoulders.

In the depths of his cavernous lair, Armaeus raised his arms, his crimson eyes glowing with dark intent. The air around him crackled with sinister energy as he spoke, his voice a low growl that echoed off the damp stone walls.

"Come forth, my brethren of shadow and flame! Hear my call and gather for the battle ahead!"

The ground shook as cracks split the rock, and grotesque forms began to emerge. Demons of all shapes and sizes clawed their way into existence, their eyes burning with an unholy light.

Armaeus smiled cruelly, his gaze sweeping over the assembled forces. "At last," he whispered, savoring the sight. "The time has come to destroy that meddlesome witch and her protectors."

A massive demon with twisted horns stepped forward, bowing its misshapen head. "What is your command, master?"

Armaeus paced, his claws leaving scorched marks on the stone floor. "We will exploit their weaknesses," he said, thinking aloud. "The child, Merona, is still untrained, her powers raw and unpredictable. Mairead, for all her wisdom, is weakened by her love for the girl. And Murdach..."

He paused, a brief flicker of respect crossing his features before it was replaced by contempt. "Murdach's loyalty will be his downfall. He would sacrifice everything for them."

The demon nodded; its rough voice filled with eager anticipation. "How shall we proceed?"

Armaeus's eyes gleamed dangerously. "We'll strike when they least expect it. Divide and conquer. We'll isolate the child, overwhelm her protectors. And when the time is right..." He clenched his fist, dark energy swirling around it. "I'll snuff out her light myself."

As Armaeus continued to explain his plan, the demons listened intently, their forms twitching with barely contained bloodlust. In the shadows of the cavern, unnoticed by anyone, a small, ethereal wisp floated silently, carrying with it a warning of the danger to come. It vanished into the air, leaving only the faintest trace behind.

The cavern shook as Armaeus raised his arms, dark energy pulsing from his fingertips. "Go forth, my minions," he commanded, his voice rumbling like distant thunder. "Spread chaos across the land. Let no village know peace, and no heart find solace."

As his demons scattered, blending into the shadows, and slipping through cracks in the earth, Armaeus turned his focus inward. He could feel Merona's power growing, a distant light that threatened to overshadow his darkness.

"Not long now," he muttered, pacing the cold stone floor. "The witch-child's awakening is near."

His claws scraped against the rock as he clenched his fists. "I must be ready."

Armaeus closed his eyes, tapping into centuries of dark knowledge. The air around him thickened with twisted energy as he began to chant, his voice a harsh mockery of ancient Celtic incantations.

"Trí fhuil is cnámh, le sgáth 's le lasair, ceanglaím mo thoil leis an aidhm mhínaofa seo, By blood and bone, by shadow and flame, I bind my will to this unholy aim," he chanted, dark symbols flickering in the air around him. "Let the witch's power fade as mine grows. Let her allies fall, their strength turning to dust."

As he continued to weave his spell, Armaeus's thoughts fixated on Merona. How could such a small creature be such a threat? Yet, the prophecy was clear – she had the power to undo everything he had built.

"I will not be undone," he growled, putting more force into his words. The walls of the cave seemed to pulse with each chant, the very earth reacting to his dark intent.

In the depths of his black heart, a flicker of doubt stirred. What if the child was truly as powerful as the prophecy foretold? He crushed the thought instantly, feeding it to the growing storm of dark energy swirling around him.

"Doubt is weakness," Armaeus reminded himself. "And I am anything but weak."

As the incantation reached its crescendo, Armaeus felt his power surge, dark tendrils reaching out across the land, seeking his enemies. He would be ready when the time came. The witch-child would fall, and with her, any hope for a future free from his dominion.

As the sun began to dip below the horizon, Mairead and Murdach led Merona toward the labyrinth and the ancient grove. The towering standing stones loomed before them, their surfaces weathered and marked with symbols that seemed to pulse with a strange, otherworldly energy. Merona took a deep breath, grounding herself as Mairead's steady voice echoed behind her.

"Focus, child. Feel the earth beneath your feet, the air in your lungs. Let the elements flow through you."

Merona closed her eyes, reaching out with her senses. The cool grass brushed against her bare feet, and a soft breeze kissed her face. She could almost taste the raw power coming from the stones.

"I can feel it," she whispered in awe. "It's like... the whole world is singing to me."

Mairead's hand rested gently on Merona's shoulder, warm and comforting. "Good. Now, channel that energy. Shape it to your will."

Merona began to weave the elemental forces around her, but suddenly, a cold wind swept through the clearing. Her eyes snapped open; her focus broken.

"Something's wrong," she gasped, her eyes wide with fear. "I can feel... darkness. It's closing in."

Murdach's eyes sharpened as he scanned the treeline. "Armaeus," he muttered, his voice low and tense. "His demons are near."

Mairead's voice was tight with urgency. "We must hurry. Merona, we don't have much time. You need to finish the ritual before..."

A bone-chilling howl echoed through the air, followed by the sound of wood cracking. Merona's heart raced as grotesque figures began to emerge from the forest, their red eyes locked on her, filled with hunger.

"I can't," she whispered, panic creeping into her voice. "There are too many. I'm not ready."

Murdach's strong hand gripped Merona's arm firmly. "You're stronger than you think, Merona. Remember why we fight. Remember who you are."

Merona swallowed hard, gathering her courage. She thought of her village, of the innocent people depending on her. With a steady breath, she raised her hands, feeling the power of the elements stir within her.

With fierce determination in her eyes, Merona declared herself as the descendant of the ancient ways. Her voice rang out, growing louder and stronger with each word until it echoed through the air, filled with power.

As demons charged towards her, Merona tapped into her deep well of strength, unleashing a powerful wave of energy that surged through the darkening air. The ground beneath her feet trembled as her power expanded, creating a shimmering barrier between her and the advancing demons. But just as quickly as it formed, the shield flickered, its light dimming. Merona's face twisted in effort, sweat gathering on her brow.

A dark, mocking laugh broke the tense silence. The demons parted, revealing a tall, shadowed figure. Armaeus stepped forward, his eyes glowing with an eerie, unholy light.

"How touching," Armaeus sneered, his voice filled with contempt. "The little witch thinks she can stand against me."

Merona's heart raced in her chest, but she stood firm. "Why are you doing this?" she demanded, her voice trembling slightly. "What do you want from me?"

Armaeus's lips twisted into a cruel smile. "Your death, child. Nothing less will do."

Mairead stepped forward, her hazel eyes burning with fury. "You will not touch her, monster!"

"Ah, the Morrigan's puppet," Armaeus mocked. "Still holding on to false hope, I see."

Murdach's voice rumbled like distant thunder. "Enough talk. Face us, coward, if you dare!"

Armaeus raised his hands, dark energy swirling around him. "As you wish."

The air erupted into chaos as demons charged forward. Merona felt panic rising inside her. How could she possibly defeat such darkness?

"Focus, Merona!" Mairead shouted, her hands weaving protective magic in the air. "Remember your training!"

Merona closed her eyes, drawing deep from the power within her. She thought of the elements, of the ancient bloodline flowing through her veins. When she opened her eyes, they burned with determination. The labyrinth birthmark glowing brightly as she tapped into her powers.

"I won't let you win," she said, her voice steady and strong. "Not now, not ever."

With a fierce cry, she unleashed her power, light bursting from her hands to collide with Armaeus's darkness.

The clash of light and shadow sent shockwaves through the air, lighting up the battle-scarred landscape. Merona felt the raw power surge within her. She gritted her teeth, fighting back against Armaeus' onslaught.

"You cannot hope to match me, child," Armaeus sneered, his crimson eyes blazing with malevolence.

Merona's voice faltered for a moment, but her resolve remained unbroken. "I don't need to match you. I just need to stop you."

Beside her, Mairead's voice rose in an ancient chant, her runic tattoos glowing with an ethereal light. The high priestess's magic blended with Merona's, creating a shield of protective energy.

Murdach's dragon form towered above them, his shimmering scales reflecting the light as he unleashed powerful blasts of flame at the advancing demons. "Hold fast, Merona!" he roared. "We are with you!"

Merona's mind raced, recalling everything she had learned during her training. The elements, she thought. I need to call on them all.

Taking a deep breath, she focused, feeling the earth beneath her, the air around her, the fire within her spirit, and the water of her blood. As she drew on these ancient forces, she sensed Armaeus' attack starting to weaken.

"Impossible," the demon hissed, his smug sneer faltering for the first time.

Merona allowed herself a small, determined smile. "Nothing is impossible when the fate of the world is at stake."

With each demon they defeated, Merona's hope grew stronger. Could they really overcome this endless nightmare?

Suddenly, the demons vanished, but their dark presence still lingered in the air.

Armaeus paced back and forth in his cold, cavernous lair, his claws scraping against the stone floor. The sting of his recent defeat burned in him, feeding his anger and resolve. He stopped, his crimson eyes narrowing as he stared into the shadows of his dark sanctum.

His mind raced with dark thoughts. He had underestimated the witch and her allies, but he wouldn't make that mistake again. Armaeus clenched his fists, feeling the raw power surge through him.

"Twelve years," he muttered to himself, his voice a bitter hiss. "That's when her powers will reach their peak."

"The prophecy," he said aloud, his words echoing in the icy silence.

"The sky will darken for three days before she is revealed in her full glory." A sinister smile spread across his face. "But I will not let that happen."

He started pacing again, his steps quick and restless. "I must find a way to end her life before she grows too powerful. But how?"

Armaeus' eyes gleamed with a cruel thought. "Perhaps," he whispered, "I don't need to confront her directly. There are other ways to destroy a witch."

Armaeus' laughter echoed through the cavern, cold and cruel. "Oh, little Merona," he sneered. "You may have won a battle, but the war has only just begun. And I have eternity to see it through."

Chapter 8

The scent of damp earth and autumn leaves filled Merona's lungs as she stepped into the village square, her raven hair fluttering in the crisp breeze. At eleven years old, she moved with an ethereal grace, a presence both enchanting and unsettling to the villagers of Septimania. With each step, it felt as though she wove magic into the very air around her.

"Good morning, Merona," called Agnès, the baker's wife, her weathered face crinkling into a smile as warm as fresh bread from the oven. "What brings you out so early?"

Merona approached the makeshift stall, her eyes shining with excitement as she took in the vibrant colors of the market. The air was alive with the scent of fresh herbs and spices, a natural melody mixing with the laughter of villagers preparing for the day.

"Mother and I are crafting a special potion for the upcoming harvest festival," she exclaimed, her voice light like wind chimes in a gentle breeze. "I've come to gather the herbs we need."

Her gaze swept over the jars and bundles of dried plants, her mind racing with ideas for their mystical concoction.

At that moment, a robin landed gently on her shoulder, its tiny claws barely grazing her cloak. She turned her head, listening closely to its sweet chirping.

"What news does your feathered friend bring?" Agnès asked, her voice a mix of awe and unease.

Merona's brow furrowed slightly. "He speaks of storm clouds gathering on the horizon. We may need to hurry with our preparations for the festival."

Her gaze drifted to a patch of wild herbs near the village well. With a wave of her hand, the plants stretched toward her, their leaves unfurling eagerly. A nearby villager gasped, and whispers began to ripple through the square.

"By the gods," one muttered, his voice filled with both fascination and fear.

Merona felt a familiar pang of isolation tug at her heart. *They love me,* she thought, *but they will never truly understand me.* She pushed the sadness aside and refocused on her task.

"Mother says these herbs are strongest when gathered under the waxing moon," she explained, carefully plucking leaves and stems. "The potion will bring a bountiful harvest for everyone."

Agnès nodded, her eyes filled with gratitude. "We are blessed to have you and the elder watching over us, child. Take what you need, and please, have a sweet roll for your trouble."

As Merona accepted the warm pastry, a sudden change in the air caught her attention. A shadow passed over the sun, and an inexplicable chill ran down her spine.

"Is everything alright, dear?" Agnès asked, noticing the girl's sudden discomfort.

"Yes, thank you. I should hurry back home." Merona masked her unease with a smile, reminding herself that the potion required precise timing.

As she turned to leave, the feeling of being watched crept over her. Something was approaching. Something dark and large, she thought, quickening her pace.

At the edge of the village square, a tall, dark-haired stranger appeared. His presence was as jarring as thunder on a bright day. Merona's heart raced as his obsidian gaze locked onto hers, unraveling the calm of her morning.

"Who is that?" she whispered to herself, a mix of embarrassment and fear tightening in her stomach.

He walked toward her, moving with an unnatural fluidity. As he drew closer, the air around him seemed to shimmer with an energy that felt both powerful and malevolent.

"Good day, young one," he said, his voice smooth but cold, like the last breath of winter. "I'm looking for a child with... unique talents. Might you be able to assist me?"

Merona's brow furrowed, confusion mixing with her unease. "I'm not sure I understand, sir. There are many talented children in our village."

The man's smile didn't reach his eyes. It felt like a shadow falling over her heart. "Oh, but I'm looking for someone very special. Someone who can speak to plants and animals, perhaps?"

A dark weight pressed down on her, and she felt a sudden, primal urge to flee. The air thickened, heavy with dread, as her instincts screamed that danger was near.

"That talent sounds almost too specific," she said, trying to cover her fear with a hint of bravado. "It sounds like something from a twisted fairytale."

The stranger leaned closer, and the temperature seemed to drop. "Fairytales often hold secrets and truths, don't they, Merona?" His voice was low, laced with sinister intent.

Her breath caught in her throat. He knows my name. This is wrong. Every instinct told her to run, but she stood firm, recalling her mother's teachings about facing one's fears.

"I'm sorry, but I don't believe we've met," she replied, steadying her voice. "And I really must be getting back to my duties."

As she turned to leave, he grasped her arm, his touch cold and invasive.

"You can't run from your destiny, child," he hissed. The charm in his voice vanished, replaced by something darker. "The powers you possess are meant for greater things than this pitiful village."

A wave of panic washed over Merona. The village, once her safe haven, suddenly felt unfamiliar. The bustling square twisted into a place of shadows. She searched for a familiar face, a sign of normalcy, anything to ground her. But everything around her seemed to fade, and the only reality became the stranger's cold grip.

"Let go of me!" she cried, her heart pounding as if trying to break free from its cage.

He loosened his hold slightly, but his gaze remained fixed on hers, cold and unyielding. "You belong to something greater,

Merona. A legacy whispered by ancient forest spirits, carried by the touch of a falling leaf. You must embrace it."

Merona's mind raced, recalling childhood stories of witches driven by destiny into dark paths. Could that be her fate? She yanked her arm free, thinking of Murdach, who had taught her to weave magic like a tapestry: something to create with intention, not to be controlled.

"I refuse to become a pawn in anyone's game," she declared, feeling a spark of courage deep inside her.

Shadows flickered around them, dark tendrils curling like smoke, but she felt a wave of determination wash over her.

"Ah, but you misunderstand," the man said, leaning back as if considering her with a mix of curiosity and annoyance. "I'm offering you a chance. Power beyond your wildest dreams. All you need to do is accept it."

"Power? At what cost?" she shot back, clenching her fists as she remembered the stories of souls lost to the dark gifts they had eagerly grasped. She would not fall for that trap.

"Everything has a cost, child," he replied, stepping closer, his breath like ice. "But you will find it a fair trade for your true potential."

"And what if I don't want that?" Merona challenged, her eyes burning with fierce resolve.

The stranger took a step back, a glint of something strange flickering in his dark eyes.

"You've always wanted more, haven't you? The village surrounds you like a cage, and you've always known it."

Merona hesitated, a ripple of doubt stirring within her. Reality began to blur with the darkness that seemed to grow with the stranger's presence. She could see the flickering forms of the villagers, distant and unaware, blissfully ignorant of the dangerous exchange unfolding before them.

"Let go of me," she commanded, gathering all the courage she had. "You don't belong here, and you definitely don't know anything about my destiny."

The stranger's grip tightened, and his eyes flared with barely controlled anger. "You have no idea what forces you're dealing with, little witch. Come with me now, and I'll show you the full extent of your powers."

Merona's heart raced as she fought against his strong hold. The air around them buzzed with tension, and she could feel the plants nearby pulsing with nervous energy, reflecting her own fear.

"I said, let go!" she shouted, surprised by the strength in her own voice.

Just then, a familiar voice rang out across the village square. "Merona! There you are!"

A wave of relief washed over her as she turned to see Murdach walking toward them, his silver hair shining in the sunlight. The distraction gave her the chance she needed. In that brief moment, Merona yanked her arm free and stumbled back.

"Murdach!" she cried, her voice a mix of relief and warning.

The stranger's face twisted with rage, and for a moment, his human disguise faltered, revealing something dark and horrifying beneath. "This isn't over," he growled, his voice barely a whisper.

Merona blinked, and in that instant, he was gone. No puff of smoke, no grand gesture; he was simply gone, as though he had never been there at all.

"Merona, are you alright?" Murdach asked, quickly reaching her side and placing a protective hand on her shoulder. "Who was that man?"

She shook her head, still trying to process what had just happened. "I... I don't know. But Murdach, there was something wrong about him. Something... not human."

Murdach's eyes narrowed as he scanned the square. "Tell me everything," he said, his voice low and urgent.

As Merona told him everything that had happened, she couldn't shake the feeling that this was just the beginning of something far bigger and more dangerous than she had imagined.

Days turned into weeks after the unsettling encounter. The village went on with its usual routine, but Merona could sense a change in the air; a strange tension that made her skin crawl. Whispers of fear spread among the villagers, talking of odd things happening in the woods nearby: animals rushing back to their dens, villagers disappearing on their way to gather herbs, and strange lights flickering at the edge of the forest during the night.

Determined to uncover the truth, Merona sought counsel from her mother and Murdach. They met beneath the towering oaks outside an elder's cottage, an ancient place filled with the smells of herbs and earth.

"I can feel that something is coming," Merona said, her voice trembling. "That man…he was here for me. I can't shake the feeling it has to do with... my past, things I don't know."

Murdach's face softened with sympathy. "There are many mysteries surrounding your family history, Merona. The ancient blood in your veins is both a gift and a curse. It holds great power, but it also brings great danger. That man was just a tool of Armaeus, who seeks to take your power for himself."

Mairead suggested they gather with the village elders to help uncover the shadows that were troubling Merona. Their journey led them through winding paths, where soft light filtered through the leaves, casting an ethereal glow. The forest felt alive, whispering secrets that only Merona could hear; a language of rustling leaves and the earth's gentle breath.

When they reached the sacred grove where the Elders held council, the air grew thick with the weight of ancient magic. A circle of old stones stood watch around a small clearing. The Elders sat on thrones made of earth and roots, their faces hidden in shadows, but their eyes shone with wisdom.

"Merona," one Elder spoke, his voice deep like distant thunder, "you have walked a path entwined with fate. The one who confronted you is from the Night realm, a title for those who have been corrupted by power and darkness."

"What do they want from me?" she asked, fear tightening around her heart.

"They seek to claim your essence, to use your unique powers for their own dark purposes. You must learn to control your abilities, or darkness will swallow your future."

Merona shuddered, but inside, a spark of resolve flickered. "What do I need to do?"

"Embrace your heritage," said the eldest Elder, his eyes glinting with a sharpness that cut through the dim light. "Only then will you be ready to face the shadow that follows you."

Merona began intense training under the watchful eyes of the Elders, Murdach, and her mother. Days turned into nights as she learned to master spells, call upon the elements, and deepen her connection with nature. Murdach was always by her side, guiding her through moments of doubt, helping her grow stronger in her abilities.

Yet, even as her power grew, Merona could feel the presence of darkness lurking, patient and still, waiting for its chance.

One evening, as twilight fell and the world grew quiet, she felt the air shift. Shadows twisted and stretched around her, and once again, the stranger appeared. His cold laughter echoed in the silence.

"Little witch," Armaeus mocked, "you think your training will protect you? Your powers are nothing compared to mine."

"I'm not afraid of you," Merona said firmly, her voice steady. Flames flickered at her fingertips, a clear sign of her growing strength and unshakable determination.

"Brave words," Armaeus said, amusement flickering in his eyes. "But courage alone won't protect you from the truth of your blood."

"Show me then!" Merona shouted, her fear replaced by a fire that burned deep inside her.

The ground shook beneath them, and the shadows writhed, blurring the line between reality and nightmare.

The confrontation erupted into a battle of will and power. Armaeus twisted shadows into weapons, striking with ruthless force, while Merona fought back, weaving her magic with newfound strength. The energy of the earth surged through her, urging her to stand tall, to not back down. Her courage grew as she embraced the magic in her veins, the power of her lineage.

"Your true destiny is in the darkness!" Armaeus hissed, but Merona responded with a shield of light, pushing the shadows away. The forest around them trembled with the force of her will.

"Only I choose my destiny!" she shouted, releasing a wave of energy that shattered the darkness surrounding them.

For the first time, Armaeus faltered, a flicker of fear in his eyes. It was enough to drive Merona forward. "You? How can this be?" he snarled, retreating into the shadows, disappearing into the very threads he had woven around them.

"Not today," she whispered, drawing on everything she had learned. With one final incantation, Armaeus vanished.

As Merona recounted the battle, she couldn't shake the feeling that this was just the beginning. Something much larger and more dangerous than she had ever imagined was unfolding.

Chapter 9

The guards roughly grabbed her arms, dragging her through the cobblestone streets. The crowd was filled with hate, their voices raised together as they jeered and threw rotten vegetables at her. "Die, witch, die!" they yelled, while, in the middle of the chaos, a lone priest whispered prayers for her soul.

Merona's heart pounded loudly in her chest, but deep down, she knew: God had abandoned her. The woodpile was in front of her now, and fear twisted in her stomach as they tied her to the stake. The fire was set. Flames eagerly danced around the kindling, reaching hungrily for her. As the heat began to burn her skin, she drew strength from her prayers, refusing to scream. She closed her eyes, accepting her fate.

The darkness that surrounded her slowly faded, replaced by a soft gray light. "Where am I?" she croaked; her voice unfamiliar. Merona awoke in her bed, pain shooting through her chest, her lungs feeling as though they had just woken from centuries of sleep.

Merona sat up quickly, the bitter smell of smoke still lingering in her nose, the memory of the flames vivid in her mind. "Not again," she whispered, her voice hoarse with fear. The dreams had been coming more often; vivid, terrifying visions of her execution.

Through the fog of confusion, Merona spotted the red wolf, gently nudging her awake with soft paws. "Is this some kind of bad dream?" she muttered, feeling disoriented. The peacefulness of the scene felt like a stark contrast to the nightmare she had just experienced, leaving her unsure of what was real.

With effort, she pushed the furs off and stumbled out of bed, checking her hands. They were pale, unscarred; no burn marks from the fire. Could it have all just been a vivid nightmare? But deep in her heart, a whisper of unease lingered.

"By the gods," she gasped as her eyes met the amber gaze of the wolf. A deep connection surged between them, something she couldn't explain. The wolf stood tall and proud amidst the quiet sounds of the village, its regal presence drawing Merona in completely.

"Are you here for me?" she whispered, her voice barely above a breath. The wolf's tail swished softly, as if to answer her. An energy radiated from the creature, filling her with an overwhelming sense of safety. It was a feeling she had never known, so different from the whispers and sidelong glances that had followed her all her life.

"What secrets do you hold?" she asked quietly, feeling the pull of fate mixed with curiosity. Merona stepped closer, captivated by the wolf's fiery coat that shimmered in the sunlight.

As Merona studied the wolf, a rush of fear ran through her veins, made stronger by the weight of the day. It was Samhain. Her twelfth birthday, a day rich with ancient customs and foreboding prophecy. This day was said to be a turning point for those touched by magic, and Merona had always known that her life was different.

The wolf moved closer, as if it sensed her fear. "Will you protect me?" she asked, her breath catching in her throat. The wolf lifted its gaze, and for a brief moment, Merona saw beyond the creature, into a world of shadows and stone. She felt a strange pulse, as though the Labyrinth itself was calling to her, a maze of ancient power waiting to be explored.

With another gentle nudge, the wolf urged her to follow. "I'm not ready," she stammered, uncertainty battling with a growing sense of curiosity. But the wolf's calm patience and silent confidence sparked a bit of courage inside her.

As if understanding her hesitation, the wolf let out a soft, melodic whine. The sound resonated deeply within her, speaking of companionship, of navigating dark paths, and of battles yet to come. Feeling the strength of the creature beside her, Merona finally took a step forward.

Nearby, the villagers carried on with their usual tasks, preparing for Samhain, unaware of the special bond growing between Merona and the wolf. As she moved forward, everything else seemed to disappear, leaving only her and the creature.

"I will find a way to understand these dreams," she promised, gazing into the wolf's glowing eyes. "I will face my past."

A wave of protective energy surrounded her, as if the wolf was wrapping her in a shield of warmth. She felt safe, safe from the whispers and suspicious glances that had always followed her.

"You are here for me…I understand." Merona whispered, her voice soft but full of wonder. The wolf's tail swished, as though answering her.

Turning to face the wolf, her heart pounded with a mix of nervousness and awe. It stood before her, its fur a rich red that shimmered in the sunlight. Its amber eyes shone with both intelligence and power, but strangely, she felt no fear. Instead, she was captivated by its beauty and strength. What secrets could those eyes hold? And why had the wolf appeared today, on Samhain, and on her twelfth birthday? The mysterious dream only deepened her curiosity.

"Come on, girl," Merona called to the wolf, her new, loyal companion trotting beside her as they walked through the quiet streets. The sun shone brightly, and the leaves fell in a cascade of colors that made her smile.

As they walked, Merona's thoughts drifted back to her dream. She had always known that being accused of witchcraft was a possibility, given the superstitions of her time, but she never imagined she would actually be burned at the stake. The hatred and fear in the eyes of the crowd from her dream still haunted her, making her heart heavy.

She looked at the simple wooden huts that made up the village, their thatched roofs giving the place a timeless feel. Smoke curled lazily from a central fire pit, blending with the scent of woodsmoke and damp earth. The sounds of livestock and children's laughter filled the air, the contrast between life here and in the city she remembered from her dream striking her deeply.

"Is everything alright?" Mairead asked, concern in her eyes.

"Where I come from... it's so different," Merona whispered, her mind struggling to make sense of the stark contrast between the bustling city in her dream and this peaceful, rustic village.

"Perhaps you should sit down," Mairead suggested gently, guiding Merona to a nearby bench. "You look like you could use a moment."

Merona let out a relieved sigh as she sank onto the rough, wooden bench. Her companion, the wolf, settled at her feet. She rubbed her temples, trying to make sense of the strange dream that had woken her so abruptly.

"By the gods," Mairead whispered, her eyes locked on the red wolf. "The Morrigan herself has graced us with her presence."

Merona furrowed her brow. "The Morrigan? I thought she was just a legend."

Mairead smiled knowingly. "Many truths are hidden behind the veil of legend, child. The Morrigan is as real as you and I. Her appearance here is no mere coincidence."

The wolf's ears twitched at the mention of the name, and her golden eyes shifted to focus on Mairead.

"She's here as your guardian, Merona," Mairead continued, her voice low and urgent. "Just as Murdach has been."

At the mention of her mentor's name, Merona felt a pang of longing. "Murdach? What does he have to do with this?"

Mairead placed a hand on Merona's shoulder, her touch warm and comforting. "Murdach is more than just your teacher, child. He is bound to you by fate and ancient magic, just as the Morrigan is now."

As Mairead spoke, Merona felt a surge of energy flow through her body. Her fingertips tingled, and the air around her seemed to hum with invisible power.

"What's happening to me?" Merona gasped, her voice trembling with a mix of fear and excitement.

Mairead's eyes shone with a mix of pride and concern. "You're awakening to your power, Merona. The Morrigan's presence has stirred something deep within you."

Merona glanced down at her hands, astonished by the faint blue glow that seemed to pulse from her skin. She could feel the shift, not just in her body, but in her very being. It was as though a veil had been lifted, revealing a world of possibilities she had never imagined.

"It's... overwhelming," Merona admitted, her voice barely a whisper. "I feel like I could move mountains or control the tides. But what if I can't control it?"

The Morrigan stepped closer, her presence silent but comforting. Mairead gently squeezed Merona's shoulder. "That's why you have us, child. We are here to guide you, to protect you, and to help you embrace your destiny."

Without realizing it, Merona muttered, "How did I end up here?"

Mairead's voice softened. "Merona, I've told you the story of how you arrived in Septimania many times. Are you alright?"

Merona's mind raced as memories flooded back. "Just a bad dream that felt so real?" she echoed, her thoughts flashing to the trial, the whispers of the crowd, the fire; centuries into the future from now.

"Who am I?" Merona asked aloud, more to herself than to Mairead. Her voice wavered with frustration, revealing the deep, unrelenting need for answers that tugged at her very soul.

"The dreams have returned?" Mairead asked, her hazel eyes sharp in the bright morning light.

Merona nodded. "They feel so real, Mother. I can smell the smoke, feel the heat of the flames. And the Labyrinth... it calls to me, but I don't understand why."

Mairead's brow furrowed as she processed Merona's words. "These are not mere dreams, child. They are echoes of your past and glimpses of your future. The burning... it's a memory of your past life, a warning of the dangers that still threaten our kind."

"And the Labyrinth?" Merona whispered, her voice barely audible, as though afraid to speak the question aloud.

"It is your destiny, though its true purpose remains hidden," Mairead replied, her voice serious. "You must learn to face these visions without fear, for they hold the key to your path ahead."

Merona closed her eyes, trying to steady her breath. "How can I not be afraid when I feel the flames consuming me every night?"

Mairead's expression softened. "By remembering that you are no longer that helpless woman tied to the stake. You are Merona, the Reborn Witch, and your power grows with each day."

"Maybe it would help if we spoke to a village elder in Narbonne," Mairead suggested. "She has lived through many things and may have insights that can help you."

"Perhaps," Merona agreed, though she doubted the elder could truly understand the weight of her situation. Still, she was desperate for any guidance that might help her uncover the truth about who she was and why she had memories of being burned at the stake.

"Please, take me to her," Merona urged, her piercing blue eyes filled with determination. "I cannot rest until I find the truth."

"Of course," Mairead agreed, offering her arm for support. "I feel this is a journey you must take alone. Just follow the forest south until you reach the next town. I trust that the Morrigan will guide you on your quest." She hugged Merona and gave her a quick kiss on the cheek.

Lost in her thoughts, Merona didn't realize how far she had walked until she reached the edge of the forest. She paused and took a deep breath, enjoying the cool air and the peaceful silence.

Morrigan nudged Merona's leg, urging her deeper into the woods. Almost as if pulled by some unseen force, she followed the wolf until they reached a clearing with a small pond.

There was something about this place that felt different, almost timeless. The trees seemed to whisper secrets, and the water shimmered in the sunlight like it held magic.

Merona sat down on a nearby stump and let out a content sigh. For the first time, she felt free from judgment and persecution. She closed her eyes, letting herself be wrapped in the calm embrace of nature.

Suddenly, Morrigan began barking frantically at something behind them. Startled, Merona turned around to see what had caused the commotion.

Standing before her was an elderly woman with wild gray hair and piercing blue eyes. She wore a tattered cloak and carried a staff decorated with feathers and bones.

The woman approached Merona with a warm smile and extended her hand. "Hello, child. My name is Gwendolyn," she introduced herself.

Merona hesitated, still in shock from the unexpected encounter, but slowly shook her hand. "I-I'm Merona," she stammered.

"I know who you are, child," Gwendolyn said, her voice full of understanding. "You have been troubled by memories of your life as a witch in the future."

Merona's eyes widened in disbelief. How could this stranger possibly know something so personal and secret about her?

"Come, let us sit by the water," Gwendolyn suggested, motioning toward the peaceful pond nearby.

They sat on the soft grass by the water's edge, and Morrigan settled herself at their feet, as if standing guard.

"I'm sure you have many questions," Gwendolyn said gently.

Merona nodded, her curiosity bubbling over. "Who was I? Why do I remember being burned at the stake?"

Gwendolyn's gaze grew serious as she answered, "You were Anna Koldings, a powerful witch who lived in a future time when our kind was hunted and persecuted."

Tears welled up in Merona's eyes as she listened to Gwendolyn's words. It all made sense now the memories, the strong pull towards magic, even Morrigan's presence in her life.

"But why do I remember it now?" Merona asked, wiping the tears from her cheeks.

Gwendolyn took Merona's hand in hers, her touch warm and comforting. She looked deeply into Merona's eyes, filled with compassion. "The universe works in mysterious ways, my dear. Your memories have resurfaced for a reason. Perhaps it's time for you to embrace your true self and continue your journey as a witch."

"Who am I?" Merona whispered, the question lingering in her heart.

Gwendolyn's eyes sparkled with understanding. She smiled softly; her gaze steady as she studied Merona. "Ah," she murmured. "You are the one everyone speaks of the mysterious baby who appeared out of nowhere."

Merona nodded, her eyes searching the elder's face, hoping to find some clue or understanding. "Yes. I've been told I was found as a baby at the labyrinth on Samhain, but I have no memory of my past life. It's as if I've been reborn, and yet…"

"Go on," Gwendolyn prompted gently, her gaze unwavering, encouraging Merona to share her thoughts.

"Even though I can't remember anything, I feel this unshakable sense of destiny," Merona said softly. "As if I'm meant to be here for a reason." She paused, taking a deep breath, trying to sort through her swirling thoughts. "But who am I? What is my purpose?"

"Sometimes the answers we seek are not easily found," Gwendolyn replied, her voice calm and soothing. "What you do know is that you are strong, resourceful, and driven by a need to understand. Perhaps these qualities will guide you on your journey."

Merona looked down at her hands, feeling the weight of her emotions. "Yet I cannot shake the feeling that something dark lingers within me," she admitted, her voice trembling slightly. "A shadow from my past life that I cannot escape, no matter how hard I try."

"Darkness and light exist in all of us," Gwendolyn said gently, her eyes reflecting both understanding and mystery. "It is up to you to reconcile these forces and choose your path."

Merona's heart pounded. She leaned forward, desperate for any answers. "Is there any way for me to recover my memories?" she asked, her voice full of urgency. "I need to know who I was before, so I can understand who I am now."

"The journey has only just begun," Gwendolyn said cryptically, her gaze distant. "There are many paths you may take, but only one will lead you to the truth."

Merona's breath caught in her chest. "Which path should I choose?" she asked, her voice barely more than a whisper.

"Only you can decide," the elder said, her voice calm yet filled with weight. She gestured toward a bundle of ancient scrolls nestled in her bag. "However, this prophecy may hold the key to unlocking your past."

Merona hesitated, her heart racing with anticipation. She reached out slowly, her fingers trembling as she neared the parchment. But before she could touch it, a sudden gust of wind swept through the forest, rustling the leaves and causing the air to grow colder.

"Untold secrets lie within these pages," the elder warned, her voice now echoing through the forest in an unsettling way, as if the wind itself carried her words. "But beware: some truths may be too dangerous to reveal."

Merona paused, the weight of the elder's words pressing on her chest. She steadied her breathing and asked, "Will you help me find my answers?" Her hand hovered just above the scroll, uncertainty still lingering in her heart.

"Of course," the elder replied, her expression unreadable. She then added, almost as a warning, "But remember, the path to the truth may be treacherous. Once you begin, there is no turning back."

Merona frowned, confusion clouding her thoughts. "What does this have to do with me?" she asked, her voice shaky. "What truth could be so dangerous?"

"Patience, child," the elder said softly, offering a small smile. "All will be revealed in due time."

As Merona continued reading the scroll, a strange sense of familiarity washed over her. It felt as though these words had been written just for her, meant to guide her on this journey. Yet, as she read deeper, a cold chill crept up her spine. The prophecy spoke of darkness consuming light, of betrayal and destruction. With each line, Merona couldn't shake the feeling that this was truly her destiny.

"Do you believe this prophecy?" Merona asked, her voice trembling with fear.

The elder's face grew serious as she nodded slowly. "I have seen many prophecies come true in my time. And I fear this one may be no different."

"But why would I be connected to it?" Merona asked, feeling overwhelmed by the weight of everything being revealed to her.

"You are connected to it because you are connected to everything," the elder replied gently. "Your past lives and future lives may hold many secrets, both good and bad. But in the end, it is up to you how you choose to use your knowledge and power."

"I don't even know who I was before," Merona whispered, the uncertainty settling heavily in her chest.

The elder smiled reassuringly. "You may not remember, but your past life still lives within you. You just need to tap into it."

Merona nodded, trying to calm the fluttering nerves in her stomach. She knew she needed to embrace this journey and uncover the truth about herself and the prophecy.

"How do I do that?" Merona asked, her eyes focused on the elder, waiting for guidance.

"It will not be easy," the elder warned. "But you must begin by looking within yourself; into your memories, your dreams, and your emotions."

Merona took a deep breath and closed her eyes, trying to focus on her inner self. Images and feelings flooded her mind; blurry faces, a sense of warmth and safety, followed by waves of fear and pain.

"Good," the elder said, encouraging her. "Now go deeper."

With each new memory that surfaced, Merona felt like pieces of a puzzle were slowly falling into place. She glimpsed fragments of her past life, but they were unclear.

Then, suddenly, her heart skipped a beat. She saw a figure cloaked in darkness, radiating immense power, its presence so intense that it sent shivers down her spine.

"Who is that?" Merona asked, her voice shaky.

"That is a powerful demon," the elder answered solemnly. "It represents the darkness that seeks to steal your power and stop you from fulfilling your destiny."

Merona's shock was clear in her wide eyes as the realization hit her. Not only was she connected to the prophecy, but she was also its central figure.

"You must learn to control both light and darkness within yourself," the elder continued. "Only then can you fulfill your destiny and bring balance to our world."

Merona nodded, her expression serious. She knew this would not be easy, but she also understood that it was essential for the greater good.

"Where do I start?" she asked, determination in her voice.

The elder smiled softly. "You've already begun. Along your journey, you'll meet others who will help you unlock your powers. Keep the Morrigan close! There is an evil force watching you."

As they left the cozy cottage and began their journey back to Septimania, the sun sank lower, casting long shadows across the path. The crispness of autumn began to settle in, and the once-bright blue sky shifted to shades of orange and pink, creating a peaceful glow among the trees. The great red wolf walked beside Merona, his steady presence a comforting reminder that she was not alone. Every rustle of the bushes or crack of a branch was met with a sense of calm, knowing that a powerful protector was right beside her.

"I wish you could speak to me," Merona murmured, her hand instinctively reaching out to brush the Morrigan's fur. "There's so much I don't understand."

The wolf's amber eyes locked with hers, filled with an intelligence that seemed almost human. Though no words were exchanged, Merona felt a sense of reassurance wash over her, as though the wolf understood her confusion.

As they passed the village square, Merona's steps slowed. For a brief moment, the peaceful morning scene faded, and she saw herself standing before a jeering crowd, flames licking at her feet.

The Morrigan pressed against her leg, grounding her back in the present. Merona took a deep breath, pushing the haunting vision away.

"Thank you," she whispered to her silent guardian. "I'm beginning to understand why you're here. It's not just to protect me from outside threats, is it? You're here to help me face the battles within myself, too."

The Morrigan's tail flicked once, as if in agreement. They continued walking together, the wolf a constant companion by her side as Merona navigated both the physical world and the storm of thoughts swirling in her mind. She barely noticed the townsfolk gathered in the heart of the village square.

"Happy birthday, Merona!" the villagers cheered in unison, their faces lit with warm affection.

Merona's eyes widened in surprise, a blush creeping onto her cheeks. The square was decorated with wildflowers and colorful ribbons, a stark contrast to the dark visions that had haunted her dreams.

Mairead hurried over, wrapping her in a tight, loving hug. Old Marta hobbled forward, pressing a small, cloth-wrapped bundle into Merona's hands.

"For you, child," she croaked, her rheumy eyes sparkling. "A charm to ward off evil spirits."

"Thank you, Marta," Merona whispered, her voice thick with emotion. She pressed the gift close to her chest, feeling the weight of the villagers' kindness and their expectations settle on her heart.

As more gifts were handed to her; a woven bracelet, a carved wooden figurine, and a pot of honey. Merona's heart swelled with gratitude. Yet beneath the warmth, a sense of unease stirred within her.

"I don't deserve all this," she murmured, more to herself than anyone else.

The Morrigan nudged her leg gently, as if in disagreement.

Forcing a smile, Merona addressed the crowd. "Your kindness overwhelms me. I... I hope I can live up to the faith you've placed in me."

She embraced her mother tightly, her voice soft. "I'll be home soon, and we can talk about the elder and our conversation. Don't worry, I'll be safe with Morrigan. I love you so much!"

As the villagers began to disperse, Merona walked quietly to a peaceful spot beneath an ancient oak tree. She sank to the ground, the weight of the day settling around her like a heavy cloak. The

Morrigan curled up beside her, offering comfort in the stillness. Together, they sat in silence, letting the world continue on around them as Merona gathered her thoughts.

"Twelve years old," Merona mused, absentmindedly stroking the wolf's fur. "In the eyes of many, I'm a woman now. But how can I be when there's so much I don't understand about myself?"

The weight of her newly acquired powers pressed down on her, as tangible as the gifts in her lap. Merona closed her eyes, feeling the hum of magic stirring within her, a current that both excited and frightened her.

"I have a destiny to fulfill," she whispered, her voice growing stronger with each word. "Whatever it may be, whatever challenges lie ahead, I must face them. For the sake of those who believe in me, and for those who may come after."

The Morrigan's amber eyes locked with hers, reflecting a fierce determination that sparked something deep inside Merona, a fire that seemed to rise within her own heart.

Her moment of quiet reflection was broken by the sound of soft footsteps on the grass. Mairead approached, her presence calm and steady. Her mother sat beside her; hazel eyes gleaming with a knowing light.

"Your thoughts weigh heavy, young one," Mairead said softly, her voice rich with wisdom. "The prophecies trouble you?"

Merona nodded, her fingers still tangled in the Morrigan's fur. "I feel... unprepared. Like I'm standing at the edge of a vast chasm, expected to leap."

Mairead smiled gently, a look of understanding in her eyes. "All great journeys begin with a single step, Merona. You need not cross the chasm in one bound."

"But the challenges ahead..." Merona began, her voice trembling slightly.

"Will be faced as they come," Mairead interrupted, her tone firm yet reassuring. She reached out and took Merona's hand in hers. "Listen well, child. The path before you is treacherous, yes, but you do not walk it alone."

A warm current of energy passed between them, and Merona gasped, visions flashing behind her eyes…battles yet to be fought, alliances forged in fire and blood.

"The eclipse at Tolbiac," Merona whispered, her voice a mixture of awe and fear. "I saw it, Mother. The darkness... the fear..."

Mairead's face grew solemn, her gaze steady. "It will be a turning point, one that may tip the balance against our kind. But remember Merona, in darkness, your light will shine brightest."

Merona swallowed hard, her eyes locking with Mairead's steady gaze. "How can I prepare? What must I do?"

"Trust in your instincts," Mairead advised, her voice unwavering. "The elements bend to your will, you must learn to harness them, to weave them into a shield against those who would harm you. And above all, remember that knowledge is power. Your destiny awaits, Merona. Embrace it, for it is both your burden and your greatest strength."

With those final words, her mother, departed, leaving Merona alone with the Morrigan and her swirling thoughts. Together, they made their way to the village's edge, where the Labyrinth lay ahead.

"I am the Reborn Witch," Merona whispered, tasting the words as they left her lips. They felt right, as if she were speaking a fundamental truth about herself for the first time.

The Morrigan's amber eyes met hers, reflecting the fading light of the setting sun. In that moment, Merona felt the weight of centuries upon her shoulders, the lives lost, the battles fought, and the magic that coursed through her veins. She stood at the precipice, ready to face whatever lay ahead, knowing she was not alone.

"Whatever comes," she vowed, her voice growing stronger with each word, "I will face it. For those who came before, and those yet to come. This is my purpose, my calling."

As darkness settled around them, Merona stood tall, the Morrigan a silent sentinel by her side. The path ahead was shrouded in shadow, uncertain and foreboding, but for the first time, she felt a deep sense of readiness. With a steady breath, she took that first, crucial step into the unknown, knowing she was prepared to face whatever lay ahead.

ACT II

THE AWAKENING

"Once the soul awakens, the search begins and you can never go back."

John O'Donohue

Chapter 10

Battle of Soissons

At the age of 20, King Clovis I of the Franks was determined to expand his kingdom and conquer the Gallo-Roman Domain in Soissons. This region, nestled between the Somme and Loire rivers in Gaul, had been fiercely defended by Syagrius for 16 years. But Clovis could not ignore the allure of the territory. He brought together the Salian Frankish tribes of Tournai and Cambrai to prepare for battle against Syagrius.

The town of Soissons was alive with the sounds of clashing metal and shouted commands, the tension of the approaching battle spreading everywhere. Clovis stood on a hill overlooking the scene, his golden cloak, adorned with bees, swirling in the wind. The reflection of the fiery red sky shimmered on the Aisne River below. His dark eyes moved across the chaos; his heart filled with both pride and unease.

A quiet voice of doubt lingered in his mind, hidden beneath his confident demeanor. At 20, the weight of his responsibilities felt immense. His bloodline demanded greatness, and the stories of his ancestors echoed in his thoughts. Tales of a witch's return and the struggles that awaited him. He wondered if this moment would shape his legacy.

Near the edge of the battlefield, Chararic stood tall in shining armor, his sons at his side. Their horses stomped and snorted, ready for the fight ahead. Both armies, with 6,000 soldiers each, stood poised, swords in hand, waiting for the signal to charge.

Clovis nodded, his jaw tightening. "Numbers mean little when the fates have already decided." His fingers brushed the intricate bee embroidery on his cloak, a symbol of the Merovingian legacy. "Our victory was foretold long before this day."

Clovis' eyes swept across the battlefield, lingering on the Roman legionaries. Known for their fierce discipline, they were a force to be reckoned with, embodying courage and tactical skill. They never backed down from a fight, their resolve unshaken even against the Franks; a name that struck fear into many. Clad in heavy mail and gleaming helmets, the Roman soldiers carried rectangular shields that stretched from shoulder to knee, creating a nearly impenetrable wall against enemy attacks.

Each legionary was equipped with a gladius, a short sword deadly in close combat, and javelins designed for both throwing and thrusting. A dagger hung at their sides, ready for unexpected clashes. Their formation reflected their tactical brilliance. Shield-bearers in the front crouched on one knee, forming a defensive wall that protected their lightly armed comrades within the ranks. The second line raised their shields overhead, creating a protective canopy, while the third rank mirrored the same stance to guard those in front of them. This layered defense showed their unity and determination, standing firm against the chaos of battle.

At the core of this formidable Roman force stood the four most esteemed legionaries in the entire land, marked each distinguished by unique insignias that displayed their bravery and accomplishments. On the left flank, the legion from Gaul advanced with their sky-blue cloaks flowing in the wind, their shields adorned with the emblem of an eagle; a symbol of Roman power, alongside the image of a galloping winged horse.

These soldiers appeared like statues of polished bronze, their faces firm and unyielding, showing no fear or hesitation in their mission. The rear ranks of shields formed an unbroken wall, hiding the legionaries behind them and adding a sense of mystery and anticipation to the force ready to strike.

Clovis understood the gravity of this moment. This was a battle of giants; the disciplined Roman legionaries facing the fierce Franks. It promised to be a legendary clash, where courage would meet ferocity, and careful planning would battle against brute strength. Both armies stood prepared, waiting for the signal that would decide the outcome of this historic confrontation.

"My king," one of his tribal leaders broke through his thoughts, "shall we sound the advance?"

Clovis hesitated, his hand instinctively gripping the hilt of his sword. The cool metal pressed against his palm, anchoring him in the moment. He could feel the weight of his men's gaze, their anticipation thick in the air, waiting for the command that would unleash the battle.

"Not yet," he said, his voice low and carrying a strange depth that startled even him. "There is power gathering here, beyond what we can fully grasp."

He closed his eyes, reaching into the senses sharpened by generations of Merovingian magic. On the edge of his awareness, he felt it. A stirring of something ancient, a blend of fate and choice coming together.

When he opened his eyes, his voice rose, steady and commanding, carrying across the ranks of his army. "Men of the Franks! Today we fight not just for land or glory, but for destiny itself!"

A deafening roar erupted from the soldiers as they raised their weapons in salute. Clovis felt a surge of pride, though it was shadowed by the sobering knowledge of the blood price that would soon be paid.

The air hung heavy with anticipation, the soldiers standing rigid, awaiting the final command to charge into battle. The sun slipped behind a veil of darkness, casting the sky into a deep and foreboding black. At the forefront, the young king stood tall, his piercing dark eyes scanning the determined faces of his men. His hand moved absently through his long, midnight locks: weight of his kingdom pressed on his shoulders, the fate of all resting on this single day.

"Your Majesty," one of his leaders said, stepping forward and bowing deeply. "The men are ready."

"Good," Clovis replied, his voice calm and steady, even as unease coiled in his chest. "We must be ready for anything."

The air vibrated with tension as the Roman force advanced. Their rectangular shields interlocked to form an impenetrable barrier, a fortress of steel and discipline. Clovis could hear the rhythmic thunder of their march, a sound that had struck terror into countless foes before.

"Hold fast!" Clovis bellowed to his men, feeling their restlessness rise. "Let them come to us!"

As the Romans drew closer, Clovis' eyes caught sight of the four elite legionaries at the heart of their formation. Each one displayed a unique insignia, marks of honor and skill that set them apart from the others.

"Those four," Clovis thought, tightening his grip on the hilt of his sword. "They'll be the key to breaking their line."

His gaze shifted to the left wing, where the legion of Gaul stood tall, their sky-blue cloaks flowing in the wind. The winged horse on their shields seemed to come to life in the fading light, a symbol of speed and power.

"Gods of my fathers," Clovis whispered, a prayer and a plea. "Grant me the strength to lead my people to victory. Let the Franks show these Romans the true meaning of fear." The blue flag with three golden toads was held by the Frankish warrior next to Clovis, fluttering in the wind.

With a deep breath, he raised his sword high, ready to signal the charge that would forever change the fate of Gaul.

Clovis lowered his sword, his eyes sweeping over the battlefield. At the front of his army, a small group of calvary emerged, their presence almost lost among the sea of foot soldiers. The king's heart swelled with pride at the sight of his elite horsemen.

"Behold, our vanguard!" he shouted, his voice cutting through the ranks. "The Romans think us mere barbarians, but we shall show them the power of Frankish steel!"

The cavalry were armed to the teeth. Angons glinted in the fading light, their long shafts promising death from a distance. Shields hung at their sides, painted with intricate designs that told the story of their clan and heritage. But it was their axes that drew the most attention – double-edged, wickedly sharp, and with short handles for brutal close combat.

Clovis studied his men, noting their varied appearances. Most rode with bare heads, their long hair whipping in the wind. A few wore helmets, their metal surfaces catching the last rays of sunlight. Their upper bodies were exposed, showing their Frankish bravery, while leather or linen protected their legs from the cold.

"They look fierce," Clovis thought to himself. "But will it be enough to match Roman discipline?"

As if answering his silent doubt, a rustling sound came from behind the front lines. Clovis turned, his eyes widening as he saw a sight that made his heart race with excitement.

"By the gods," he whispered, a smile spreading across his face. "Our secret weapon reveals itself."

From behind the ranks of foot soldiers appeared a group of women, their presence as surprising as it was impressive. These were not ordinary camp followers, but warriors in their own right.

Shield maidens, trained in the ways of war, ready to fight alongside the men.

Their long hair was intricately braided and tucked beneath hooded cloaks, giving them an air of mystery. But it was their armor that truly set them apart. Covered with ancient symbols of war - stylized wolves, ravens, and spiraling knots - each piece spoke of battles fought and victories earned.

Clovis turned to his closest advisor, his voice low but filled with pride. "The Romans think they know what awaits them. But this... this will break their expectations. Our shield maidens will be the key to our victory."

The advisor nodded, his eyes shining with intensity. "Yes, my king. The element of surprise is a weapon sharper than any blade."

As the shield maidens took their positions, a powerful energy surged through the Frankish army. Clovis could feel it, a force that spoke of ancient magics and forgotten powers. He raised his voice once more, addressing his entire force.

"Men and women of the Franks! Today, we fight not just for land or glory, but for our very future. Let the Romans feel the weight of our combined might!"

A roar erupted from the assembled warriors, a sound so loud it seemed to shake the very earth beneath them. As the roar faded, Clovis turned his gaze back to the approaching Roman lines, his mind already working through strategies and possibilities.

"Now," he thought, "let the true battle begin."

The thunderous sound of hooves filled the air as Clovis looked past the shield-maidens. Emerging from the mist like ghostly figures, the horse archers rode forward. Their horses, muscular and wild-eyed, snorted plumes of steam into the chilly air. The riders' faces were set in grim determination, their bows already nocked and ready.

Clovis felt a rush of pride course through his veins. These mounted archers were his secret weapon, a force that could strike the Romans from a distance with deadly precision. He watched them take their positions, moving smoothly and confidently, their actions practiced and in sync.

"By the gods," he thought, his dark eyes narrowing, "the Romans won't know what hit them."

Raising his voice, Clovis spoke to his army again, his words carrying across the battlefield like the beat of a war drum. "My loyal Franks! Behind you stand our deadly horse archers, ready to strike at the Romans from the shadows!"

A loud cheer rose from the ranks. Clovis could feel the energy building, like a storm ready to break. He spoke again, his voice growing stronger with every word.

"We fight not just for land, but for our very souls! For the honor of our ancestors and the future of our children!"

His gaze swept across the assembled warriors, taking in their fierce expressions, watching how their grips on their weapons tightened at his words.

"Let every Roman soldier know!" Clovis roared, his voice booming across the battlefield. "They will not defeat us! We will fight to expand our land and our honor until our last breath!"

As the cheers of his army rang out, Clovis felt the heavy weight of destiny on his shoulders. He thought of the prophecies, the witch who was yet to come, and the labyrinth birthmark that marked him as chosen. This battle, he knew, was just the beginning.

"May the Morrigan guide our blades," he whispered to himself, his hand instinctively brushing the hidden mark on his shoulder. "And may our enemies tremble before the strength of the Franks."

Clovis' words hung in the air, thick with the promise of blood and glory. The echo of his declaration rippled across the field and reached the Roman lines, where it was met with a wall of silence.

Sygarius, the Roman commander, stood unmoving, his weathered face showing calm determination.

"They do not waver," Clovis thought, his dark eyes narrowing as he saw Sygarius raise a steady hand. "Perhaps they do not understand the storm that is coming for them."

The Roman army moved as one, their shields locking together with a loud clang that sent a chill through the air. The sound of metal scraping against metal filled Clovis' ears as he spurred his horse forward, the hooves pounding the earth beneath them.

"For the glory of the Merovingians!" Clovis roared, his voice rising above the noise of preparation. He could feel the ancient power rushing through his veins, a gift from his mysterious bloodline. "Let them feel the wrath of our ancestors!"

As he galloped toward the front line, Clovis glanced over his shoulder. Chararic's forces stood proud, their shields raised in defiance, but they made no move to join the fight.

"My brothers in arms," he murmured, his words meant only for himself. "May the gods smile upon us this day."

The distance between the armies closed, the tension growing tighter with each passing moment. Clovis took a deep breath, the scent of sweat, leather, and steel filling his nose. He could taste the metallic tang of blood already in the air.

"This is but a step," Clovis thought, his mind racing as he led his forces forward. "A step toward the destiny that awaits me... that awaits us all."

With a final, determined breath, Clovis urged his horse onward, charging headfirst into the heart of the battle. The clash of armies erupted around him, a storm of war cries and clashing steel that would be remembered through history.

As the chaos of battle surrounded him, Clovis' sharp eyes caught a flicker of movement behind the Frankish front lines. From the third row, like shadows given life, the shield-maidens appeared. Their black hooded robes billowed in the wind; faces hidden except for eyes that burned with an otherworldly fire. A cold shiver ran down Clovis' spine, mixing with the heat of the fight.

"By the gods," he whispered, frozen by their eerie presence. "I've never seen them like this."

The shield-maidens moved with graceful precision, their bows singing a deadly song as arrows struck their targets with deadly accuracy. Roman soldiers fell in waves, their tight formations breaking under the relentless assault.

Clovis watched, entranced, as one shield-maiden smoothly switched from bow to sword. Her blade flashed in the fading light, slicing through Roman armor like it was paper.

"Incredible," he breathed, ducking instinctively as a javelin whistled past his ear. "Their skill... it's beyond mortal."

The battle raged around him, but Clovis found himself captivated by the shield-maidens' deadly movements. They moved together as one, a dark wave sweeping over the Roman forces, leaving only destruction behind them.

"Could this be the power spoken of in the prophecies?" Clovis thought, his mind racing even as he blocked a Roman soldier's thrust. "The strength that will lead us to glory?"

As if in response, a shield-maiden turned her fiery gaze upon him. For a moment, everything seemed to freeze, and Clovis felt the weight of destiny pressing on him.

"We fight for you, King of the Franks," her voice rang out in his mind, though her lips never moved. "As was foretold."

Clovis nodded, a grim smile creeping across his face. "And I for you, daughters of the Morrigan," he murmured. "Together, we will forge a new future for our people."

With renewed strength, Clovis threw himself back into the fight, the shield-maidens' deadly precision driving him to fight harder. The tide of battle had shifted, and the future of Gaul rested on the edge of a blade.

The air crackled with an otherworldly energy as the shield-maidens formed a tight circle, their black robes swirling in an invisible wind. Their voices rose in unison, a haunting melody that sent a chill down Clovis' spine.

"Goddess of the Battle and Raven Queen, hear the words we ask of thee. Grant us vision, grant us power. Keeper of the Shield, this land falls under your protection."

The chant echoed across the battlefield, drowning out the clash of steel and the cries of the wounded. Clovis could feel his heart pounding in his chest, the beat matching the rhythm of their words.

"By the power of the gods," he whispered, his eyes wide with awe. "This is true power."

As the last word faded, an electric surge shot through Clovis' body. His sword, once heavy in his hand, now felt light as a feather. Without thinking, he raised the blade high, his voice joining the shield-maidens' in a primal roar.

"For the Morrigan! For Gaul!" he cried, his deep voice ringing across the battlefield.

The connection to the goddess was clear, a force both terrifying and thrilling. Clovis' mind raced with visions of victory, of a united Gaul under his rule. He saw the golden bees of his cloak spreading across the land, a symbol of immortality and divine right.

"This is it," he thought, a fierce grin spreading across his face. "The sign I've been waiting for. The Merovingian destiny unfolds before us!"

With new strength, Clovis charged back into the fray, his sword cutting through the air with unnatural speed. Each strike seemed guided by an unseen hand; each parry perfectly timed.

"Come, my warriors!" he shouted to his men. "The goddess favors us today. Victory is within our reach!"

The clash of steel on steel rang out across the battlefield, a loud symphony of death. Clovis watched as the once-proud Roman formation crumbled before him. Legionaries who had stood side by side now fought alone, their discipline broken by the unrelenting Frankish attack.

"They break!" Clovis roared, his voice cutting through the noise of battle. "Press on, my brothers! Show no mercy!"

As he fought, Clovis felt a strange sensation surround him. A fine mist, almost invisible, began to gather around his body. It shimmered with an unnatural light, deflecting blows that should have struck him.

"What sorcery is this?" he wondered, his sword slicing through a Roman shield as if it were paper.

The chanting of the hooded women grew louder, their voices carried by an unnatural wind. With each word, Clovis felt his mind grow sharper, his muscles filled with a strength he had never known.

"By the ancient gods," he muttered, blocking a thrust from a desperate legionary. "I've never felt such power."

As he fought, Clovis felt himself drawn to the chanting, as if an invisible force tied him to the mysterious women. Their words, though he couldn't understand them, rang deep within his soul.

"Is this the true power of the Merovingians?" he thought, his dark eyes scanning the battlefield. "The magic our ancestors spoke of in whispered tales?"

A Roman centurion, his armor splattered with blood, charged at Clovis with a roar of defiance. Without thinking, Clovis raised his hand, and a surge of energy shot from his palm, sending the man flying backward.

"By all that is holy," Clovis gasped, staring at his hand in disbelief. "What am I becoming?"

The mist swirled around him, growing thicker until it hid the battle from view. A faint light shone through the haze from above, and as it faded, Clovis found himself face to face with a massive raven. Its black feathers gleamed with an unnatural shine, and its eyes held the weight of centuries.

"The Raven Queen," Clovis whispered, his voice filled with awe and fear.

The goddess's voice rang in his mind, calm yet powerful. *"Clovis, King of the Franks, I have heard your prayers for protection."*

Clovis felt a shiver run down his spine. "Great Morrigan, I am honored by your presence. But why choose me?"

"You stand at a crossroads, young king. Your actions today will shape the fate of nations." The Raven Queen's beak remained still, but her words echoed deep within his soul. *"I offer you my blessing: Go now, my chosen one. Be bold in battle."*

Clovis nodded solemnly, gripping his sword tighter. "I will strive to be worthy of your favor, Raven Queen."

As the vision faded, Clovis found himself back on the battlefield. The Roman soldiers, seeing their chance, hurled a barrage of javelins. Clovis braced for impact, but the weapons seemed to change direction at the last moment, as if an invisible shield had pushed them away.

"The Morrigan's protection," he realized, his eyes widening.

The hooded women behind him drew their arrows, their movements smooth and synchronized. As they released, Clovis watched in disbelief as the arrows struck the ground, spreading a sickly green mist that crept across the battlefield.

"By the gods," Clovis muttered, watching the mist cover the fallen Roman soldiers.

The battlefield exploded into chaos, a storm of blood and steel. Clovis charged forward, his golden bee-adorned cloak flowing behind him like a banner of destiny. The clash of metal on metal rang out, mixed with screams of pain and the sickening thud of bodies hitting the blood-soaked earth.

"For the Franks!" Clovis roared, his voice cutting through the noise of battle. He swung his sword in a wide arc, slicing through a Roman legionary's armor as if it were paper. The man's eyes widened in shock before the light faded from them.

As Clovis fought, his mind raced. The Morrigan's words echoed in his thoughts: *"Be brave in battle, but never forget mercy."* He struggled with the contradiction, but his sword arm never wavered.

"How can I show mercy in this slaughter?" he wondered, ducking beneath a Roman javelin. *"Is this the crossroads she spoke of?"*

A nearby Frank cried out in pain as a Roman blade found its mark. Clovis spun, decapitating the attacker with a single, fluid motion. The Frank nodded gratefully, but Clovis barely registered it, his eyes scanning the chaos around him.

"My king!" A voice shouted. "The Romans are faltering! Victory is within our grasp!"

Clovis nodded grimly. "Press the advantage, but remember. We are Franks, not butchers. Offer quarter to those who surrender."

Chararic's brow furrowed in confusion. "But sire…"

"Do as I command," Clovis interrupted, his voice leaving no room for debate. "There has been enough death today."

As the last Roman soldier fell, a wave of relief washed over Clovis. He looked around at his army, seeing their exhaustion and injuries. But he also saw the fire in their eyes, driven by adrenaline and a sense of victory.

"We have won the day," Clovis announced, his voice carrying across the battlefield. "But at what cost?" he added softly, more to himself than anyone else.

As the echoes of battle faded, an ethereal chant rose from the edges of the bloodstained field. The hooded women, their faces still hidden, moved among the fallen Franks with calm purpose. Clovis watched, transfixed, as their hands began to glow with a soft, warm light.

"By the gods," he whispered, his eyes widening in awe. "The Morrigan's blessing goes beyond the carnage."

A wounded soldier near Clovis stirred, his groans of pain fading as one of the women placed her glowing hands on his chest. The King knelt beside the man, witnessing the miraculous healing.

"How do you feel, brave warrior?" Clovis asked, his voice thick with emotion.

The soldier blinked, disbelief spreading across his face. "The pain... it's gone, my King. I feel... renewed."

Clovis nodded, a mix of gratitude and unease stirring within him. He stood, surveying the battlefield as more of his men were brought back from the brink of death.

"This power," he thought, "it's both terrifying and beautiful. Like the Morrigan herself."

As night fell, Clovis led his victorious army into Soissons. The newly claimed castle buzzed with celebration, the air thick with the scent of roasted meat and the sound of laughter. Yet Clovis found himself drawn to a secluded balcony; his eyes fixed on the darkening sky.

"You seem troubled, my King," came a voice from behind him. It was one of his advisors, his weathered features showing clear concern.

Clovis sighed, keeping his gaze on the heavens. "We won a great victory today, old friend. But at what cost? And what does it mean for our future?"

As if in answer, the moon began to darken, an eerie eclipse casting long shadows across the land. Clovis felt a chill run down his spine, remembering the prophecies whispered in the dark corners of his childhood.

"By the gods," the man whispered, "an eclipse? On this night of all nights?"

Clovis gripped the balcony railing, his knuckles white. "It's a sign, of what, I'm not sure yet. But change is coming, as surely as the darkness now covers the moon."

His eyes remained fixed on the darkening sky, his mind racing with thoughts of what the eclipse meant. The ancient prophecy, passed down through generations of Merovingians, echoed in his mind.

"The witch," he murmured, his voice barely audible above the sounds of celebration below. "She will come when the sky turns black as night."

The man leaned in closer, his brow furrowing. "My King, surely you don't believe in such old tales?"

Clovis turned to face his trusted advisor, his dark eyes shining with an otherworldly knowledge. "I've seen too much today to dismiss the power of the old ways, Chararic. The Morrigan's blessing, the shield-maidens' chants... They are as real as the sword at my side."

He ran a hand over the hilt of his weapon, feeling the familiar curves of the golden bees embroidered there. "Our family's magic, the power that flows through our veins... it all leads to this moment."

A gust of wind swept across the balcony, carrying the scent of smoke and something else; something ancient and powerful. Clovis inhaled deeply, his senses sharpened by the growing darkness.

"Can you feel it?" he asked, his voice low and intense. "The air itself seems to tremble with anticipation. The witch is coming, and with her, a destiny that will shape the future of our kingdom.

Chapter 11

The Pyrenees Mountains had lost their charm as the last of the leaves were carried away by the wind. Winter was approaching quickly, bringing with it the bitter cold. As the sun sank behind the horizon, an eerie aura surrounded the forest. The mystical energy seemed to wrap itself around the landscape, growing stronger in the soft embrace of twilight. The warm sunlight bathed the ancient oaks and towering pines, casting a golden glow over the scenery and creating a dance of shadows in the gentle breeze. Amid the rustling leaves, haunting melodies from centuries past could be heard.

In the depths of the forest, Merona stood in a secluded clearing, her heart racing with excitement and curiosity. With the sun setting behind her, she was a striking sight. Her dark, shiny hair flowing down her back, and her piercing blue eyes capturing the last of the daylight. She wore layers of tunics, woolen pants, and a thick cape fastened with a brooch.

Merona's determination and ingenuity had carried her this far, but she knew the challenges ahead were ones she couldn't face alone. She knelt and petted Morrigan, who stood out against the muted shades of green and brown with her vibrant red fur. Her amber eyes gleamed in the fading light, and her strong, sturdy build exuded both strength and loyalty.

As Murdach stepped from the shadows, an ancient power seemed to fill the air, crackling around him. In the dim light, his eyes shone with intensity, cutting through the twilight. Merona's breath caught in her throat as she stood frozen, her heart pounding in her chest. She couldn't tear her eyes away from the imposing figure before her, even though she had seen him many times during her childhood. But now, there was something different about him that held her attention.

Murdach's voice was deep and powerful, like distant thunder, vibrating through the room. "You have a grand destiny before you, one that will change the course of history," he said. His long silver hair flowed down his broad shoulders, adding to his commanding presence. He wore a heavy cloak over his indigo blue shirt and tight trousers.

Merona swallowed hard, gathering her courage. "I do," she said, her voice steady despite the turmoil inside. "And you're here to test me, aren't you?"

A ghost of a smile touched Murdach's lips. "Perceptive. Show me your power, Merona."

Merona's mind raced. *What if I fail? What if I'm not strong enough?* But she pushed the doubts aside, focusing on what she had to do. She closed her eyes, reaching deep inside to tap into the wellspring of magic flowing through her veins.

The air around Merona began to shimmer, and leaves swirled in an unseen wind. Her eyes snapped open, glowing with an otherworldly blue light. She raised her hands, and tendrils of elemental energy danced between her fingertips.

"Impressive," Murdach murmured, his gaze fixed on her. "But can you control it?"

Merona gritted her teeth, focusing harder. The magic surged, threatening to overwhelm her. Morrigan pressed against her leg, a calm presence amid the chaos.

"I can," Merona gasped, her voice strained. "I must."

She held up her wand and spoke the incantation, "Aether, Domhan, Uisce, Dóiteáin, Aontacht! Air, earth, water, fire, unite."

She wove the energies together, creating intricate patterns in the air. Fire and water intertwined, earth and air danced in harmony. The display was beautiful, but Merona could feel her grip slipping.

Murdach's voice sliced through her concentration. "Enough."

The magic dissipated, leaving Merona breathless and trembling. She looked up at Murdach, hoping for any sign of approval or disappointment.

"You have potential," he said finally, his voice unreadable. "But potential alone will not save you from what's to come."

Merona's heart sank. "Then teach me," she whispered, her voice barely audible. "Help me become who I'm meant to be."

Murdach's expression softened, just slightly. "That, young one, is exactly why I'm here."

He settled himself on a moss-covered log, his eyes reflecting the fading light. He motioned for Merona to sit across from him. As she did, the air around them seemed to grow heavy with anticipation.

"To understand your destiny," Murdach began, his voice deep and steady, "you must first understand our history."

Merona leaned forward, eyes wide with curiosity. Morrigan curled up at her feet, ever watchful.

"Long ago," Murdach continued, "when the world was young, magic flowed freely. Witches were respected, not feared. We fought alongside great warriors, battled mythical beasts, and shaped the very fabric of reality."

As he spoke, the air shimmered, and Merona gasped as ethereal images began to form before her eyes. She saw fierce battles, magnificent creatures, and witches wielding incredible power.

Murdach's voice, once full of confidence and strength, became somber as he spoke of their people's past. "But with great power comes great envy," he said, his eyes showing the weight of centuries of struggle. "And with envy comes fear. The tides turned against us, and we were forced into hiding." He paused, his mind heavy with memories of the Witch Hunts that had ravaged Europe and reduced their numbers under the reign of King James. "That was after your previous life ended, before you were reborn in the land of Septimania." His words hung in the air, a reminder of the endless cycle of persecution and survival that had defined their existence.

Merona's heart clenched as she remembered her past life as Anna. "How can I change this?" she asked, her voice shaking with emotion. "How can I prevent such suffering?"

Murdach's eyes locked onto hers, intense and unblinking. "By fulfilling your destiny, Merona. You are the key to changing the course of history."

Merona's mind raced, her questions coming faster than she could speak. "But how?" she finally managed. "What must I do?"

"You must master your powers," Murdach replied, his voice carrying the weight of centuries. "Learn to control the elements, bend reality to your will. And most importantly, you must deal with the treacherous waters of faith and those in power."

Merona's brow furrowed. "Power? Faith? I thought this was about magic."

The sound of Murdach's laughter echoed like thunder, sending shivers down her spine. "My dear," he said with a chilling grin, "everything is connected. King Clovis' decisions will affect our kind in ways you cannot yet understand. And you must be ready for whatever comes." His voice carried a dark warning, making her heart race and her blood run cold.

As the sun sank below the horizon, Merona felt the weight of her fate growing heavier on her shoulders. She straightened up, her eyes filled with determination. "Then teach me," she said, her voice firm and resolute. "Show me how to change the world."

Murdach's eyes gleamed in the twilight, a hint of pride crossing his weathered face. He raised his hand, and the air around them shimmered, revealing an intricate pattern of glowing lines that pulsed with an otherworldly energy.

His chant in an ancient tongue, "Labyrinth Eternal, Lána Cuimhne. Aontaíonn sé an síoraí, an t-am atá caite, agus an todhchaí

Eternal Labyrinth, Maze of Memories. It unites the eternal, the past, and the future."

The words wove through the air, summoning the labyrinth's structure as glowing lines form an intricate web of possibilities.

"Behold, Merona," he said, his voice deep with ancient power. "The Labyrinth of Time."

Merona gasped, it was unlike anything she had ever seen, a complex web of intertwining paths that seemed to shift and change as she watched.

"What... what is it?" she breathed, reaching out to touch the glowing lines, only to have her hand pass right through them.

Murdach's voice was solemn as he explained, "This is the destiny you must face, child. The Labyrinth is a mystical place where past, present, and future meet. It is here that you will confront the echoes of your past lives and shape the path to our future."

Merona's mind spun with the meaning of his words. "My past lives? You mean... Anna?"

"And others," Murdach nodded. "Each twist and turn represents a choice, a moment that could change history. Your task is to move through this maze, to fix the wrongs of the past and protect the future of our kind."

Merona's heart raced, a mix of fear and excitement rushing through her. She clenched her fists, preparing herself for the challenges ahead.

"I won't let you down," she declared, her voice full of determination. "I'll face whatever trials come in the Labyrinth. For the sake of all witches, past and future."

Murdach's expression softened, and a rare smile appeared on his lips. "Your courage is admirable, Merona. Know that you do not walk this path alone. I will be here, guiding and supporting you every step of the way."

He placed a comforting hand on her shoulder, his touch warm and steady. "The road ahead will be full of danger, but I believe in you. Together, we will change the course of history."

Merona gave a small nod, her determination unwavering. As she looked out at the mysterious Labyrinth, a sense of resolve washed over her. Morrigan stood close by, offering her silent support as Merona prepared for the training Murdach was about to give her.

The air crackled with energy as Murdach raised his hands, his fingers moving through the air, tracing intricate patterns. "Watch closely, Merona," he said, his voice calm but intense. "The elements are not just forces to control, but allies to welcome."

Merona's eyes widened as tendrils of fire and water twisted around Murdach's outstretched palms. The two opposing elements danced together in perfect balance, neither extinguishing nor overpowering the other.

"How is that possible?" she whispered, her eyes wide, reflecting the mesmerizing display.

Murdach's gaze met hers. "Balance, child. True power does not come from control, but from understanding and respecting each element."

He gestured for Merona to step forward. "Now, you try. Reach out with your senses. Feel the fire's passion and the water's flow."

Merona closed her eyes, her brow furrowed in deep concentration. She could feel the heat of the fire, the cool touch of the water, but when she tried to bring them together, they sputtered and hissed.

"I can't do it," she groaned, frustration clear in her voice. "They're too different, too opposed."

Murdach's voice was gentle but firm. "Do not force them, Merona. Remember your purpose, the strength inside you. You are the bridge between worlds, between elements."

Merona took a deep breath, pushing away her doubts. She thought of the witches who had suffered, and of the destiny waiting for her in the Labyrinth. As she focused, she felt a warmth spreading from her core, reaching out to the elements around her.

Slowly, almost without noticing, wisps of fire and drops of water began to swirl around her fingertips. They merged and parted, a delicate dance of opposing forces brought together by her will.

"I... I'm doing it," she whispered, her voice filled with wonder.

Murdach nodded in approval. "Well done, Merona. This is just the first step on a long journey, but you've shown great promise."

As the sun set, casting long shadows across the clearing, Merona kept practicing. Her determination grew with each small success, but with each failure, each time the elements slipped from her control, doubt began to gnaw at her resolve.

"What if I'm not strong enough?" she murmured, more to herself than to Murdach. "So many lives depend on me. What if I fail them all?"

Murdach's hand settled on her shoulder, his touch warm and comforting. "Doubt is natural, Merona, but don't let it take over. Remember, you are not just Merona of Septimania. You are the reborn witch, destined to change the course of history."

His words echoed in the deepening twilight, a reminder of the power and purpose that lay inside her. When Merona looked up at her mentor, she saw not only the fierce dragon warrior, but also a source of hope and strength in the world she had entered.

"You're right," she said, her voice steadying. "I can't afford to falter. Not when so much is at stake."

With renewed determination, Merona turned back to her practice. The elements responded more willingly to her touch. As night fell, the clearing glowed with the ethereal light of her magic, a sign of the potential that lived within the young witch, who would soon face the trials of the Labyrinth.

As the night grew darker, Murdach's eyes seemed to glow with an otherworldly light. He sat on a moss-covered log, his silver hair flowing over his shoulders like moonlight. Merona felt an unspoken pull toward him, sensing that something very important was about to happen.

"Come, child," Murdach called, his voice heavy with the wisdom of ages. "There is a something I must tell you."

Merona moved closer, her heart racing. She sat down cross-legged in front of him, Morrigan curling up protectively at her side. The forest around them felt alive, as if it too was waiting to listen.

Murdach reached out and gently took her hand. "Our paths are connected, tied together by both fate and choice. The love I have for you goes beyond time."

Merona squeezed his hand, feeling the strength of their connection. "Murdach, I... I don't know what to say. Your guidance, your protection…they've meant everything to me. Without you, I would be lost in this world of magic and destiny."

A smile touched Murdach's lips, warm and reassuring. "You are stronger than you realize, Merona. My role is simply to remind you of the power that has always been inside you."

As they sat there, bathed in the light of the stars, Merona felt a deep change in their relationship. The connection between them, once that of a mentor and student, had grown into something far stronger. An alliance built from ancient battles and strengthened by their unbreakable bond of love.

"Thank you," Merona whispered, her voice thick with emotion. "For everything. For being here, for believing in me when I doubt myself. I couldn't face what's coming without you."

Murdach's eyes shone with unshed tears. "I will always be here, Merona. Our destinies are one. Whatever challenges come our way; we will face them together."

As the night stretched on, mentor and student, warrior and witch, sat in peaceful silence, their hands still clasped. The forest around them seemed to hum with the energy of their new understanding, a sign of what was to come in the mystic Labyrinth.

Merona stood up, her eyes shining with new determination. The cool night air brushed against her skin, carrying the scent of ancient magic and untold possibilities. She took a deep breath, feeling the fresh forest air fill her lungs and the power of the elements moving through her.

"I'm ready," she declared, her voice steady and unwavering. "Whatever lies ahead, I'll face it head-on."

Murdach nodded, "You've come so far, Merona. The challenges ahead will test you in ways you can't imagine, but I believe in you."

Merona's hand moved to the labyrinth birthmark on her forearm, her fingers tracing its detailed pattern. "The labyrinth," she whispered, her voice soft. "It's more than just a symbol, isn't it? It's a doorway to our past... and our future."

"Yes," Murdach replied, his voice heavy with the weight of centuries. "It is where the past and present come together, where destinies are shaped, and where even fate itself can be changed."

As they spoke, the forest seemed to pulse with a strange energy. Shadows danced at the edges of Merona's sight, and she thought she heard whispers in the wind; echoes of lives long gone and battles yet to come.

"I won't let them down," Merona said, her voice full of fierce determination. "All the witches who came before me, all those who will come after. I'll change their fate. I have to."

Murdach placed a comforting hand on her shoulder. "And you won't face this alone. Remember, Merona, your strength is not just in your magic, but in your heart. Your compassion, your courage…these are your true powers."

As the first light of dawn began to stretch across the horizon, painting the sky with soft pinks and golds, Merona felt a sense of peace settle over her. She was no longer afraid of the unknown; instead, she embraced it, ready to carve her own path through the twisting halls of destiny.

Unseen by them, deep in the shadows of the forest, a pair of crimson eyes watched with dark, quiet rage. Armaeus, cloaked in shadow, saw the tender moment between mentor and student and barely contained his fury. His claws dug into the bark of an ancient oak, leaving deep marks as he struggled to control his anger.

"Enjoy your moment of peace," he hissed silently, his words lost in the wind. "Because when the time comes, I will destroy you both and watch as your precious prophecy turns to dust."

A twisted smile spread across Armaeus' face as he melted back into the darkness. He would wait, gathering his strength and planning his revenge. For now, he would watch, knowing that soon, very soon, he would have his chance to tear down everything Merona and Murdach held dear.

Chapter 12

The mist clung to the water's edge, swirling and undulating like restless spirits in the pale moonlight. Merona's heart raced as she and Murdach neared the shore, their footsteps muffled by the damp, yielding earth beneath them. A crackling energy filled the air, making the hairs on the back of her neck stand on end.

"Can you feel it, Murdach?" Merona whispered, scanning the ethereal shoreline. "The veil between worlds feels thin here."

Murdach's gaze sharpened as he surveyed their surroundings. "Aye, I feel it too. Be cautious, Merona. The Seer's wisdom rarely comes without a cost."

As if summoned by their words, the mist ahead began to shift and solidify, its swirling tendrils merging into the shape of a human figure. Merona's breath hitched as an old woman emerged, her face deeply lined with the weight of countless years. The Seer's eyes, milky yet unnervingly piercing, locked onto Merona with an intensity that made her feel exposed, her very soul laid bare.

"Welcome, child of prophecy," the Seer intoned, her voice resonant and timeless, like the steady hum of the earth. "I have awaited your arrival for a long time."

Merona swallowed hard, resisting the instinct to retreat. The weight of destiny bore down on her, a heavy, unrelenting force threatening to crush her resolve. Yet she stood firm, drawing quiet strength from Murdach's steadfast presence at her side.

"I am here, as foretold," Merona said, her voice steadier than the turmoil churning within her. "What truth do you bring, Seer?"

The old woman's lips curved into a faint, enigmatic smile. "Truth child, not wisdom. Are you prepared to confront the shadows of your past and endure the trials of your future?"

Merona's thoughts raced, vivid memories clawing at the edges of her mind: flames licking at her skin, the agony of a life lost. She clenched her fists tightly, banishing the fear that threatened to consume her. "I have to be," she said, her voice firm and unyielding. "Too much depends on it."

The Seer's milky gaze softened, her tone carrying a thread of quiet empathy. "Your path is veiled in darkness, Merona. But remember, the brightest light often emerges from the deepest shadows."

Murdach stepped forward, his protective instincts bristling. "And what of the dangers lurking in those shadows? How do we know this isn't a trap?"

The Seer turned her sightless eyes to him, her expression inscrutable. "Certainty, Dragon, is a luxury none of us can afford. Fate's threads are tangled, and even my sight cannot discern all their ends."

Merona placed a steadying hand on Murdach's arm, feeling the tension coiled in his muscles. She shared his unease; his fears reflected her own. Yet a pull deep within her, insistent and unrelenting, urged her forward; a call she could neither deny nor fully understand.

"What must I do?" she asked, her voice soft but resolute.

The Seer extended a gnarled hand, her fingers curled as though clutching an unseen thread. "Follow the path that only your heart can see, child. Embrace the magic coursing through your veins. It is both your greatest strength and your most dangerous vulnerability."

As the Seer's words fell, the mist around them seemed to shimmer, pulsing with an eerie, otherworldly light. A surge of power welled up within Merona, ancient and familiar, yet overwhelming in its intensity. She closed her eyes, letting the sensation flow through her like a rushing tide. With each heartbeat, she felt herself drawn closer to the essence of who she truly was and to the destiny that loomed before her.

The Seer's voice softened to a whisper, her words drifting on the wind. "Come, child of prophecy. The answers you seek are hidden in the heart of the forest."

Merona hesitated, searching the treeline ahead. The woods seemed to shift and ripple, alive with secrets waiting to be uncovered. She took a steadying breath, squaring her shoulders under the ever-present weight of destiny, and stepped forward.

"I'm ready," she whispered, more to herself than to anyone else.

As they stepped into the shadowy embrace of the forest, a presence emerged beside Merona. The Morrigan, in her form as a great red wolf, padded silently at her side. The goddess's amber eyes burned with ancient wisdom, a silent reminder of the immense powers that now accompanied them.

"Does she always appear so... unexpectedly?" Merona murmured to the Seer, her fingers twitching with the urge to touch the Morrigan's crimson fur.

The old woman chuckled, her laughter dry and brittle, like the rustling of autumn leaves. "The Phantom Queen answers to no one, child. She comes and goes as she wills. Be thankful for her protection, dark forces gather at the edges of your destiny."

A chill ran through Merona as her heart quickened. "What forces? What am I truly up against?"

The Morrigan let out a low, resonant growl, a sound that was both a warning and a reassurance. Her voice filled Merona's mind, rich and layered with the echoes of untold centuries. *"Fate is not a path laid out before you, little witch. It is a tapestry you weave with every choice, every breath."*

Merona turned the goddess's words over in her mind as they moved deeper into the forest. The trees grew denser, their ancient roots and twisted branches weaving a labyrinth of shadow. The air itself seemed alive, crackling with primal magic that made her skin tingle and her senses sharpen.

"I feel... something," Merona murmured, her brow furrowing as she focused. "It's as though the forest is whispering to me."

The Seer nodded; her unseeing eyes fixed on some distant point. "The old powers recognize their own. Listen well, Merona. The trees remember the songs of your past lives."

As they ventured deeper into the forest, Merona felt an uncanny sensation that each step carried her not just through the woods, but through time itself. The weight of countless centuries seemed to press down on her, and for a fleeting moment, the enormity of her task threatened to crush her resolve.

But the Morrigan's steadfast presence at her side and the Seer's sure guidance ahead kept her grounded. Whatever secrets lay hidden in her past, whatever challenges awaited her, Merona knew she must face them with courage. Within the mysteries of her soul, she held the power to reshape the threads of history itself.

Ahead, an ancient wooden door groaned as it swung open, revealing a dimly lit interior thick with the scent of herbs and smoke. The Seer shuffled a gnarled table at the center of the room, her gnarled fingers tracing the edge as she moved.

"Come, child," she beckoned, her voice rustling like dry leaves caught in the wind. "The answers you seek are within."

Merona stepped inside, scanning the cramped cottage with a mix of curiosity and unease. Bundles of dried herbs dangled from the rafters, their shadows swaying gently in the dim light. Shelves crowded with vials and strange, arcane objects lined the walls, each one whispering of untold mysteries. Behind her, the steady warmth of the Morrigan's presence served as a quiet reassurance against the chill that permeated the air.

The Seer reached for a small, earthenware cup resting on the gnarled table before her. "This brew," she began, her milky eyes locking onto Merona, "is the key to unlocking the vault of your memories. It will unveil the truths of your past lives, the essence of who you truly are."

Merona's heart thudded in her chest, a wild rhythm of anticipation and dread. Her thoughts strayed to Anna, to the searing flames of Copenhagen, and to the torment etched into her soul. Would she relive that agony? What other buried horrors might rise to the surface?

"Is it... safe?" Merona asked, her voice barely above a whisper.

The Seer's lips curved into a cryptic smile, both tender and foreboding. "Safe? No, child. Truth is rarely safe. But it is always necessary."

Merona's hand trembled as she reached for the cup. The liquid inside shimmered with a strange, otherworldly glow, pulsing faintly as if alive, as if it recognized her.

"Remember," the Seer said, her voice low and resonant, "you are more than the sum of your past lives. You are Merona, the Reborn Witch. Your destiny awaits."

Merona took a steadying breath and raised the cup to her lips. A scent both grounding and ethereal, like earth kissed by starlight filled her senses. She hesitated, a fleeting moment of doubt rippling through her, before tilting the cup back. The cool liquid flowed down her throat, leaving a trail of warmth that unfurled in her chest like a flickering flame.

As the heat spread through her body, a single thought anchored her resolve: *And so, the journey truly begins.*

The Seer's voice resonated, an unbroken thread of guidance weaving through the thickening air. "Follow the path, child. It will lead you to the truth hidden within."

Merona's feet moved without conscious thought, as though drawn by an unseen force. The labyrinth walls writhed and shifted, their ancient stones radiating a pulsing, bluish light. Reaching out, she brushed her fingertips against the cool surface, the sensation both grounding and strange.

"What am I supposed to find here?" she asked, her voice trembling as the enormity of the moment pressed down on her.

The Seer's response came, calm yet heavy with meaning. "Not what, but who. You are here to find yourself, Merona."

The deeper she ventured, the denser the air became, vibrating with raw, unyielding power. It wrapped around her like a living thing, pressing against her skin, filling her lungs, and seeping into her very bones. Her steps faltered, her breath quickening in shallow gasps as the weight of the journey bore down upon her.

"I feel it," Merona whispered, her words meant more for herself than the Seer. "It's as if... the very stones are alive with magic."

"The labyrinth remembers, child," the Seer replied, her voice like a distant echo. "It holds the memories of all who have walked its paths. Can you sense them? The echoes of the past?"

Merona closed her eyes, letting the sensations envelop her. Whispers in long-lost tongues brushed against her ears, their meanings just out of reach. Phantom touches grazed her skin, featherlight yet undeniable. When she opened her eyes again, the labyrinth seemed to ripple and shimmer, its form shifting before her.

"It's changing," she murmured, her voice strained with a blend of awe and unease. "The labyrinth... it's transforming."

The Seer's voice returned, calm and resolute, cutting through the surreal haze. "You are entering the heart of the maze, where time and reality weave together. Trust in yourself, Merona. The answers you seek await just ahead."

Suddenly, Merona's vision blurred, and a flood of images surged through her mind. She gasped, her body reeling as memories not her own overwhelmed her like crashing waves.

"What's happening to me?" she cried out, her voice trembling and echoing in the surreal space.

The Seer's voice resonated inside her, calm yet powerful. "You are remembering, Merona. These are the lives you've lived before."

Merona found herself in ancient Gaul, her hands deftly weaving spells beneath a moonlit sky. Then, she was a fierce warrior, leading armies into battle against encroaching darkness. Each vision grew more vivid, filling her with a deep, overwhelming sense of purpose.

"I... I remember," Merona whispered, her voice awe-struck. "I've always been here, fighting this fight."

But as the memories began to fade, new images replaced them. Merona's heart clenched as she watched scenes of horror and injustice unfold. Men and women, accused of witchcraft, dragged from their homes, tortured, and executed. Kings and clergy stood over the carnage; their faces twisted with righteous wrath.

"No," Merona breathed, her tears streaming down her face. "This can't be the future. We can't let this happen."

The Seer's voice was heavy with warning. "This is what awaits if you fail, child. The persecution of our kind, sanctioned by both crown and cross."

Merona's fists clenched at her sides, her horror shifting into unwavering determination. "Then I won't fail. I can't. Tell me, Seer, what must I do to prevent this future?"

"Your path is treacherous, Merona," the Seer warned. "To change the course of history, you must face those who would see our kind eradicated. Are you prepared to bear such a burden?"

Merona stood tall, "I am. Whatever it takes, I will not let this future unfold. Our people deserve to live without fear, without persecution."

As the visions faded, leaving her in the twisting passages of the labyrinth once more, Merona felt the weight of her destiny press firmly upon her shoulders. The path ahead was shrouded in uncertainty, fraught with peril, but now, she knew she carried the strength of countless lives before her.

"Guide me, Seer," Merona said, her voice steady and resolved. "Show me the way forward, so that I may forge a new future for us all."

Merona's eyes flew open, her chest rising and falling as she gasped for air. The cottage's dim interior swam into focus, the scent of herbs and incense thick in the visions still heavy in her mind. Her heart pounded against her ribs, each beat echoing the weight of the visions that still clung to her mind like cobwebs.

"By the gods," she whispered, her voice shaking. She pressed a trembling hand to her forehead, feeling the cold sweat that had gathered there. "It's all so clear now. The past, the future... our fate."

The Seer's weathered face loomed before her, eyes glinting with ancient knowledge. "What you've seen, child, is but a glimpse of what may come. The path you walk is fraught with danger, but it is not unchangeable."

Merona swallowed hard, her throat parched. "I saw so much death, so much suffering. How can I possibly stop it all?"

"You cannot save everyone," the Seer replied, her voice soft yet resolute. "But you can change the course of history. Your choices, your actions, will send ripples through time."

Merona struggled to grasp the magnitude of her task, a heavy weight pressing on her chest. A sudden chill crept up her spine. She turned toward the small window into the gathering gloom of twilight. For a moment, she could have sworn she saw a pair of eyes gleaming in the shadows, red as fresh blood.

"Armaeus," she whispered, her body tensing with unease. "He's here, isn't he?"

The Seer nodded, her expression grave. "The demon never strays far when destiny is in motion. Be cautious, Merona. He will stop at nothing to see you fail."

Outside, hidden among the twisted trees, Armaeus watched the cottage with a predatory focus. His lips curled into a cruel smile, revealing sharp teeth that gleamed in the fading light.

"So," he murmured, his voice a low growl that seemed to darken the very air, "the little witch thinks she can change the future. How quaint."

His clawed hand curled into a fist, shadows writhing around him like living things. "Let her try," he growled. "I've waited centuries for this moment. I won't let some upstart, reborn witch ruin everything I've worked for."

As night descended, Armaeus vanished into the darkness, his thoughts already weaving a web of deceit and destruction. The game had begun, and the fate of countless lives teetered on a knife's edge.

Murdach walked alongside Merona and the Morrigan as they made their way back to Septimania. Merona's fingers trembled around the rough-hewn pendant the Seer had given her. Its weight was a constant reminder of the burden she now carried. She inhaled deeply, fighting the surge of emotions that threatened to overwhelm her.

"I won't let him win," she murmured, her voice gaining strength with each breath. "I can't."

Murdach's voice was gentle, yet firm. "Remember, child, your strength lies not only in your magic, but in your heart. Armaeus may have centuries of malice, but you carry the power of rebirth and renewal."

Merona knelt beside the wolf, her fingers gently combing through the Morrigan's thick red fur. "How can I possibly stand against such darkness?" she murmured, fear and doubt creeping into her voice.

Murdach placed a steady hand on her shoulder. "By embracing the light within you. Your past lives, the knowledge of what's to come. These are your weapons. Use them wisely."

With a deep breath, Merona stood tall. Her gaze drifted toward the darkening forest, where Armaeus undoubtedly lurked, plotting her downfall. The weight of centuries pressed upon her, but with it came a fierce surge of resolve.

"I won't merely stand against the darkness," Merona said, her blue eyes burning with determination. "I'll push it back. For those who will suffer if I fail, for the innocent lives at stake. I will fight with everything I have."

As she spoke, Merona felt the elements stirring around her, earth trembling beneath her feet, air whispering through her hair, fire igniting in her heart, and water flowing through her veins. The

Seer's words echoed in her mind, a roadmap guiding her through the battles that awaited.

"Then let us begin," Merona said, a fierce smile curving her lips.

The forest thickened around them, shadows stretching like dark fingers, eager to entrap them. Merona's heart hammered in her chest, each beat a reminder of the heavy burden she carried. She stole a glance at the Morrigan, drawing strength from the goddess's unwavering presence.

"Do you feel it?" Merona whispered, her voice barely rising above the rustling leaves. "The air... it's thick with foreboding."

The Morrigan nodded, her gaze sharp as she surveyed the surrounding darkness. "Armaeus' influence is spreading. He seeks to twist the very essence of this land."

A twig snapped somewhere in the distance. Instinctively, Merona summoned a protective barrier of shimmering air around them, feeling the tingling pulse of magic surge through her fingers.

"He won't succeed," Merona said, more to reassure herself than anything else. "We can't let him."

As they continued, the trees seemed to close in, their branches reaching out like gnarled fingers. Merona's thoughts raced, the weight of the Seer's warnings pressing on her mind. *What if I'm not strong enough? What if I fail and* condemn *thousands to death?*

The Morrigan's voice cut through Merona's doubts, steady and commanding. *"Remember who you are, Merona. You carry the strength of countless generations within you."*

Suddenly, a cold laugh echoed through the forest, sending an icy shiver down Merona's spine. Armaeus' voice, dripping with malice, seemed to come from every direction at once.

"Ah, the little witch with her pet goddess and dragon," he sneered. "How touching. Do you really think you can change the course of history?"

Merona's fists clenched, blue flames flickering between her fingers. "I don't think, Armaeus. I *know*."

As the words left her lips, the forest erupted into chaos. Shadows twisted into monstrous shapes, lunging at them from every angle. Merona and the Morrigan stood back-to-back, magic and divine power intertwining as they fought off the onslaught.

With a fierce roar, Merona unleashed a blast of fire, pushing the shadows back. Her eyes blazed with determination. The Morrigan fought alongside her, her claws slashing through the demons, leaving them lifeless in her wake.

As she fought, a new voice echoed in her mind. It was the Murdach's voice, ancient and wise. *Use your gifts, child. The elements are yours to command.*

Merona closed her eyes and took a deep breath, focusing on the elements within her. The earth groaned beneath her feet, and with a thought, tendrils of vines from the ground, ensnaring their attackers. The air howled as she summoned gusts of wind, knocking the enemies off balance.

Then it happened. Something deep inside Merona shifted, unlocked by Murdach's words. A powerful surge of energy coursed through her, filling her with overwhelming strength.

With a cry that echoed through the forest, Merona unleashed her true potential. Flames blazed around her like a fiery shield as she soared into the sky on a gust of wind.

The Morrigan watched in awe as Merona transformed into a formidable warrior, wielding her powers to fend off the demons. Meanwhile, Murdach morphed into a dragon, his wings of fire and scales gleaming like precious gemstones.

Together, they fought back against Armaeus' army with renewed strength, their fierce determination driving them forward. Murdach breathed fire upon their enemies, while the Merona called down lightning from the sky.

As they emerged victorious from the battle, Merona let out an exhilarated roar before she returned to her human form. She collapsed onto the ground in exhaustion, panting heavily but grinning triumphantly.

"I couldn't have done it without you," she gasped, glancing at Murdach and Morrigan, still catching her breath.

Feeling a sense of fulfillment and newfound strength, Merona stood up and gazed out at the peaceful forest. Armaeus may still be out there but I am coming for him."

Chapter 13

Leaving Septimania, the trio's footsteps echoed on the worn cobblestones, a stark reminder of the dangers ahead. Merona's heart was heavy with conflicting emotions; excitement for the journey, fear for what lay ahead, and grief for leaving behind the woman who had raised her as her own. As they bid their final goodbyes to Mairead, Merona felt torn between her duty as the chosen one and her love for her mother and the village she called home.

"I can't help but wonder if we'll ever return," Merona murmured, her eyes fixed on the distant horizon.

Murdach's voice rumbled beside her, deep and reassuring. "Our path leads forward, Merona. We must trust in the journey."

The lush countryside of southern Gaul unfolded before them, a tapestry of rolling hills and sun-dappled forests. As they walked, Merona's thoughts turned inward, contemplating the enormity of their quest. Could she truly change the course of history? Could she save countless lives from the flames of persecution?

Beside them, Morrigan's red fur gleamed in the sunlight as she padded silently along, her piercing gaze sweeping over their surroundings. The wolf goddess spoke; her voice carried on the wind. *"The land remembers, child. It whispers of battles long past and prophecies yet unfulfilled."*

Merona shivered, despite the warmth of the day. "I can feel it," she whispered, her voice barely audible. "It's as if the very air has changed, thick with intensity."

As they neared the foot of the Pyrenean mountains, the landscape shifted. Beech groves and fir plantations stretched endlessly, their branches reaching toward the azure sky. Merona paused, allowing the beauty and tranquility of the land to wash over her.

"It's breathtaking," she murmured, her eyes wide with wonder.

Murdach nodded, a small smile playing at the corners of his mouth. "Aye, it is. But we must remain vigilant. Beauty often hides danger."

No sooner had the words left his lips than a chill wind swept through the trees, carrying with it sense of foreboding. Merona's skin prickled, her magical senses suddenly on high alert.

"Do you feel that?" she asked, her voice tense with unease.

Morrigan's hackles rose, a low growl rumbling in her throat. *"Darkness approaches,"* the wolf goddess snarled. *"The horde draws near."*

In the distance, the first faint sounds of the approaching enemy reached them, carried on the wind. Merona's heart raced, a blend of fear and determination swirling within her. She turned to Murdach, seeing her own resolve reflected in his eyes.

"We knew this moment would come," Merona said, straightening her spine and drawing her magical energy around her like a cloak. "Are you ready?"

Murdach's hand found hers, his grip firm and reassuring. "Together, we can face any darkness," he replied, his voice brimming with unwavering faith.

As the distant sounds of their foes grew louder, Merona took a deep breath, bracing herself for the battle ahead. The once-beautiful land now felt suffused with hidden menace, the shadows between the trees darker, more threatening.

"May the gods be with us," Merona whispered, her voice barely audible, as the trio prepared for the oncoming storm.

The first of the demonic creatures erupted from the tree line, their twisted forms a mockery of nature. Merona's breath caught in her throat as she took in their nightmarish features…limbs bent at unnatural angles, joints protruding unnaturally beneath sickly, mottled skin. Their eyes glowed an infernal red, piercing the air with a malevolent, suffocating presence. Razor-sharp claws scraped against the tree bark and earth as they advanced.

Merona's heart pounded in her chest, but she forced herself to stay calm. "Murdach," she called, her voice steady despite the terror that threatened to overwhelm her. "We need to act quickly."

Murdach nodded, his silver hair whipping around him in the unnatural wind that heralded the horde's arrival. "I'll take to the skies," he said, his voice deepening as the transformation began. "You and Morrigan guard the ground."

As Murdach's form shifted and scales began to shimmer into existence across his skin, Merona turned to Morrigan. "We'll funnel them through the ravine," she said, pointing to a narrow passage between two jagged rock formations. "It'll limit their numbers and give us the chance to pick them off."

Morrigan's fierce eyes gleamed with approval. *"A solid strategy, young one,"* the wolf goddess growled. "I'll harry their flanks and keep them from spreading out."

Merona closed her eyes for a brief moment, centering herself and drawing upon the magic that Mairead and Murdach had taught her. She felt the earth's energy thrumming beneath her feet, the air crackling with potential around her.

"Ready yourself," she murmured, her eyes opening to face the oncoming horde. The demons were much closer now, their twisted forms becoming clear in the dimming light. Merona raised her hands, feeling the power surge within her.

Beside her, Murdach completed his transformation. Where the man had stood moments before, a magnificent dragon now towered, its scales glittering like precious gems in the fading light. With a thunderous roar that shook the very ground, he launched himself into the air.

"Now!" Merona cried, releasing a blast of pure energy that slammed into the front ranks of the demonic horde. As the creatures reeled from the impact, giving Morrigan the opening she needed to dart forward, teeth bared and claws flashing.

The battle had begun, and Merona knew that the fate of everything she held dear hung in the balance.

Her heart pounded as she wove intricate patterns in the air, channeling the elemental forces at her command. A wall of flame erupted before her, incinerating a group of demons that had slipped through Morrigan's defensive line.

"They just keep coming!" she shouted to Murdach, who swooped low, his massive dragon form casting an enormous shadow over the battlefield.

The dragon's voice rumbled in her mind. *"Your strength is greater than you know, Merona. Trust in yourself!"*

Merona nodded, gritting her teeth as she summoned a whirlwind that tore through the demonic ranks. She could feel the magic coursing through her veins, more potent than ever before. With each spell she cast, her confidence grew.

"Murdach, behind you!" she cried out, spotting a particularly large demon leaping towards the dragon's exposed flank. Without hesitation, Merona thrust her hands forward, sending a barrage of ice shards hurtling through the air. They struck the creature mid-leap, shattering its grotesque form.

As Murdach wheeled around, his eyes met Merona's. "Well done, my love," he projected, his mental voice filled with pride.

Merona allowed herself a brief smile before turning her focus back to the battle. She could sense the tide turning in their favor, but the fight was far from over. With renewed determination, she reached deep within herself, drawing upon reserves of power she had never known she possessed.

"For Mairead, for Septimania, for all of Gaul," she whispered, her voice rising to a shout as she unleashed a devastating burst of energy that sent demons flying in all directions. "We will not fall this day!"

Morrigan, her red fur bristling with otherworldly energy, leapt into the fray with savage grace. Her razor-sharp teeth gleamed in the dim light as she tore through the demonic horde, each bite accompanied by an unearthly growl that sent shivers down Merona's spine.

"By the gods," Merona breathed, momentarily transfixed by the sight of the goddess in battle. Morrigan's eyes, blazing with ancient power, locked onto hers for a fleeting moment.

"Remember, child," Morrigan's voice echoed in her mind. *"We are the trinity of fate. Our strength lies in unity."*

Merona nodded, a deep understanding flooding through her. She turned to Murdach, who was using his massive dragon form to create a barrier between them and the advancing demons.

"Murdach," she called out, "we need to form a triangle! It's the only way!"

The dragon's head swiveled towards her, comprehension dawning in his eyes. With a mighty roar, he began to move, positioning himself at one point of an invisible triangle.

Merona sprinted to the next point, her hands already weaving intricate patterns in the air. The magic crackled around her, responding to her will with an intensity that both thrilled and terrified her.

"Morrigan!" Merona shouted above the chaos. "Complete the formation!"

The wolf-goddess bounded across the battlefield, her movements a blur of red fur and flashing fangs. As she took her place, Merona felt a surge of power unlike anything she had ever experienced.

"Now," she whispered, her voice carried by the wind to her companions, "let us show these demons the true meaning of fear."

The air crackled with raw energy as Merona, Murdach, and Morrigan formed their triangle; a bastion of strength against the surging horde of demonic creatures. Merona's heart pounded in her chest, each beat quickening as she channeled her magic through her fingertips.

"They're coming!" Murdach's voice boomed, his dragon form poised and ready for battle.

Merona's eyes darted across the writhing mass of twisted limbs and glowing red eyes. She gritted her teeth, summoning a wall of shimmering energy before her. "Hold the line!" she shouted, her voice brimming with strength she didn't know she possessed.

The first wave of demons crashed against their defenses like a dark tide. Merona felt the impact reverberate through her body, nearly buckling her knees. She pushed back, her magic flaring bright against the encroaching darkness.

"Murdach, on your left!" She cried, spotting a group of creatures attempting to flank the dragon.

Murdach pivoted, his tail lashing out and scattering the demons like leaves in a gale. "Well spotted, love," he growled, his voice filled with both affection and fierce determination.

Suddenly, a group of grotesque creatures broke through Merona's magical barrier. She stumbled back, her eyes wide with fear as their razor-sharp claws reached for her. Time seemed to slow, and panic gripped her as she realized she couldn't react fast enough.

"Merona!" Murdach's roar split the air. In a blur of scales and fury, he was there, interposing his massive form between her and certain doom. His claws ripped through the demons, turning them into wisps of acrid smoke.

Breathing heavily, Merona locked eyes with her protector. "Thank you," she whispered, her voice barely audible over the chaos of battle.

Murdach's gaze softened for a moment, and then he nodded. *"Always. Now, let's finish this."*

With renewed determination, Merona turned back to the fray, her magic surging with newfound power. The battle was far from over, but in that moment, she knew that together, they could face anything the darkness threw at them.

Merona's eyes narrowed as she focused on the writhing mass of demonic creatures before her. Her chest heaved with exertion, sweat beading on her brow. Reaching out with her empathic abilities, a cacophony of emotions slammed into her senses.

"They're... afraid," she murmured, her voice barely audible over the roar of battle.

Murdach, still in his dragon form, turned his massive head toward her. *"What do you mean?"*

Merona's brow furrowed as she probed deeper. "It's not just fear. There's pain, confusion... desperation." She locked eyes with a particularly grotesque demon, its red gaze burning with malice. Beneath that, she sensed something darker. "They're being driven by something. Or someone."

"Can you use that?" Morrigan's voice, low and urgent, sliced through Merona's concentration.

Merona nodded slowly, a plan forming in her mind. "I think so. Cover me!"

As Murdach and Morrigan moved to shield her, Merona closed her eyes and reached out with her magic. She sought the threads of fear and pain that bound the demons together, following them back to their source.

"You don't have to do this," she whispered, her words carrying the weight of her empathy. "You're being used. Fight it!"

For a moment, nothing happened. Then, a ripple of confusion passed through the horde, and several demons hesitated, their attacks faltering.

Murdach's voice rumbled with surprise. *"It's working!"*

Merona pushed harder, sweat beading on her brow as she poured all her energy into the connection. "You have a choice!" she called out, her voice now resonating with power. "Break free!"

A piercing shriek tore through the air as the first demon crumbled, its form dissolving into mist. One by one, others followed, the horde thinning as more succumbed to Merona's influence.

As the last demon faded away, Merona stumbled, her knees buckling beneath her. Murdach was there in an instant, catching her before she could fall.

"I've got you," he murmured, in his human form, cradling her gently.

Merona looked up at him, her eyes heavy with exhaustion. "Did we... did we do it?"

Morrigan padded over, her red fur matted with blood and ichor. *"We did it, child. Thanks to you."*

As the adrenaline of battle faded, Merona became acutely aware of the ache in every part of her body. Her limbs felt heavy, and her head throbbed from the strain of her magical exertion.

"I didn't know I could do that," she whispered, her voice hoarse.

Murdach's eyes softened as he looked at her. "You're stronger than you realize, but even the strongest need rest."

Merona nodded weakly, letting her eyes drift closed. As unconsciousness began to pull her under, she couldn't shake the feeling that this battle, though harrowing, was only the beginning of their journey.

The silence that followed was deafening. Merona's ears rang in the absence of demonic shrieks and the clash of weapons. She opened her eyes, scanning the blood-soaked battlefield, littered with the fading remnants of their otherworldly foes.

"It's over," she breathed, her voice barely audible.

Murdach, still holding her, nodded. "For now, at least." His usually fierce eyes shimmered with concern. "Are you alright?"

Merona tried to stand, wincing as pain shot through her body. "I'll live," she said, forcing a weak smile. "What about you?"

Murdach's silver hair was matted with sweat and grime, and a deep gash marred his forearm. "Nothing that won't heal," he reassured her.

Morrigan approached, her red fur darkened to a grim crimson, sticky with the ichor of fallen demons. *"We've won this battle,"* she growled, her voice low and foreboding, *"but the war is far from over."*

Merona nodded, her eyes clouded with exhaustion and concern. "I know. But for now..." She trailed off, glancing at her companions. "For now, we rest."

They limped toward a nearby clearing, collapsing onto the soft grass. Merona closed her eyes, feeling the earth's energy pulsing beneath her. She drew strength from it, letting the grounding power seep into her.

"We should assess our injuries," Murdach said, breaking the silence. "The Buragach won't wait for us to heal."

Merona opened her eyes, meeting his gaze. "You're right," she sighed. "But Murdach... what we just faced... I've never seen anything like it."

"Few have," Morrigan interjected, her wolfish features grave. *"The darkness is growing stronger. We must prepare for worse to come."*

As Merona tended to Murdach's wounds, her mind raced with possibilities. What other horrors awaited them on their journey? Would they be strong enough to face them?

"We will be," Murdach said softly, as if reading her thoughts. "Together, we're stronger than any demon horde."

Merona managed a genuine smile this time. "Together," she agreed, her voice gaining strength. "Now, let's get patched up. The Buragach awaits, and with it, our destiny."

Chapter 14

The wind howled relentlessly, tugging at Merona's cloak as she gazed up at the imposing silhouette of Bugarach Mountain. Its jagged peak pierced the sky, shrouded in mist and mystery. She shivered, not from the cold, but from the palpable energy that seemed to pulse from the very earth beneath her feet.

"The Mountain of God," Murdach murmured beside her, his voice barely audible over the howling gale. "A fitting place for your training to begin, young one."

Merona nodded, eyes fixed on the daunting climb ahead. "I can feel it," she whispered, more to herself than her companions. "The power here... it's unlike anything I've ever experienced."

As they began their ascent, Merona's thoughts raced. Would she be able to harness the elemental forces as Murdach believed? Or would she fail, condemning countless future witches to persecution and death? The weight of her destiny pressed down on her like a tangible burden.

"Stay alert," Morrigan's voice sliced through her reverie. *"This mountain holds many secrets, not all of them benign."*

No sooner had the goddess spoken than Merona felt a shift in the air. The wind seemed to pause for an instant, and a hushed silence enveloped their small group. To their left, barely visible through the swirling mists, a secluded grove beckoned.

"Do you feel that?" Merona asked, her voice tight with anticipation.

Murdach nodded grimly. "Aye, child. A presence most potent. We'd be fools to ignore it."

"Or fools to investigate," the Morrigan countered, her amber eyes narrowing. *"This mountain is not known for its hospitality to mortals."*

Merona stood frozen, caught between curiosity and caution. The grove seemed to pulse with an otherworldly energy, both alluring and terrifying. She closed her eyes, reaching out with her fledgling magical senses. The power she sensed was neither malevolent nor benign, just ancient.

"We must go," she said finally, her voice stronger than she felt. "Whatever awaits us in that grove, I believe it's connected to why we're here."

As they cautiously approached the tree line, Merona's heart pounded in her chest. What secrets would this hidden sanctuary reveal? And, more importantly, was she truly ready to face them?

The beech trees loomed before them, their silvery bark shimmering in the ethereal light. As Merona stepped into the grove, a hush fell over the world, as if nature itself held its breath. The wind, ever present on the mountain, died to a whisper.

Then, out of the mist, a majestic stag emerged, its antlers branching toward the sky like living sculptures. Merona's breath caught as recognition dawned.

"Cernunnos," she whispered, awe and reverence mixing in her voice.

The stag's eyes, deep pools of ancient wisdom, fixed on her. Merona felt exposed, as if her very essence lay bare before the Horned God.

Murdach's voice was low and urgent. "Bow your head, child. Show respect."

Merona complied, her companions following suit. As she lowered her head, a surge of wild, untamed energy coursed through her.

"Lord of the Wild," the Morrigan intoned, her usual bravado tempered with deference, *"we seek passage through your domain."*

The stag regarded them in silence, its presence suffusing the grove with palpable power. After what felt like an eternity, it dipped its massive antlers in quiet acknowledgment.

As they slowly raised their heads, Merona's eyes locked once more with those of Cernunnos. In that brief moment, she felt a deep, unspoken connection to the land itself; its eternal cycle of life, death, and rebirth embodied in the god's gaze.

"We must press on," Murdach said softly, his voice breaking the spell. "The summit awaits, and our time grows short."

Merona nodded, her voice thick with emotion. "Yes, we should continue. But... I feel different, somehow."

The Morrigan in her human form placed a hand on her shoulder, her touch firm yet reassuring. "The touch of a god is not easily forgotten, young one. Carry this moment with you."

As they stepped away from the grove, the wind returned, its intensity growing stronger, as though eager to reclaim the space. The path ahead steepened sharply, and Merona noticed caves dotting the mountainside like gaping wounds in the earth.

"This will not be an easy ascent," Murdach warned, his eyes scanning the treacherous terrain. "The Mountain of God guards its secrets jealously."

Merona squared her shoulders, resolve firming her features. "Then we'll prove ourselves worthy of those secrets."

As they began their arduous climb, an unsettling sensation gripped Merona; a feeling that unseen eyes watched their every move. Her encounter with Cernunnos had awakened something deep within her, a primal connection to the elements she was destined to master. With each labored step, a mix of exhilaration and fear surged within her, the dormant power waiting to be unleashed.

Further up the mountain, Merona's breath caught as a breathtaking sight unfolded before them. A vast field of vibrant flowers stretched out, their red and orange petals swaying gently in the mountain breeze.

"Pyrenean lilies," Murdach whispered with reverence. "A sign of hope in these troubled times."

Merona took a cautious step forward, breathing in deeply. The musky scent enveloped her, rich and intoxicating. She reached out to brush a delicate petal, marveling at its silken texture.

"They're beautiful," she murmured, her voice filled with awe. "But why do they grow so tall here?"

Murdach's eyes narrowed, scanning the horizon with caution. "The mountain's magic nurtures them. But we must remain vigilant. Beauty often conceals danger in these lands."

A chill ran down Merona's spine, and she spun around, her heart pounding in her chest. "Did you feel that?" she hissed; her voice sharp. "We're not alone."

The Morrigan nodded grimly, her expression dark. "We're being watched. Perhaps followed."

Instinctively, Merona's hand went to the hilt of her dagger. "Should we confront them?"

"No," Murdach said firmly, his tone resolute. "We press on. Our goal is too important to risk a needless confrontation."

As they continued their ascent, Merona couldn't shake the feeling of unseen eyes fixed on her. The sun dipped lower in the sky, painting the mountain in hues of gold and crimson.

"We're running out of time," Murdach murmured, his voice tight with concern.

Merona gritted her teeth, forcing herself to push through the exhaustion. "We'll make it," she said, determination hardening her voice. "We have to."

With one final, grueling effort, they crested the summit just as the last rays of sunlight kissed the horizon. Merona collapsed to her knees, gasping for breath, her wide eyes drinking in the breathtaking view.

"We did it," she whispered, a blend of relief and unease swirling inside her. "But what happens now?"

The wind howled around them, tugging at her hair and cloak. Murdach placed a weathered hand on her shoulder, his eyes gleaming with a purpose that set the air humming.

"Now, young one," he said, his voice carrying over the whistling gusts, steady and sure, "you must call upon the wind as your first element."

Merona's heart quickened in her chest. "The wind? But how?"

Murdach's silver hair swirled in the breeze as he spoke, his gaze unwavering. "Feel its power, its unpredictability. It is wild, yet it can be tamed by one who understands its nature."

The Morrigan, in her red wolf form, padded silently to Merona's side. Her amber eyes locked with the girls, and a voice resonated in Merona's mind, soft yet commanding. *"Trust in your instincts, child. The wind has been waiting for you."*

Excitement bubbled inside Merona, mingled with a sharp twinge of fear. She stood, her legs still shaky from the climb. "I'm ready," she declared, her voice steadier than she felt.

Murdach nodded approvingly. "Come. There's a place where the wind speaks louder than anywhere else on this mountain."

As they made their way to a secluded outcropping, Merona's thoughts raced. What if I fail? What if I'm not strong enough? But beneath the doubts, a fierce determination flickered. I was reborn for this. I can do this.

They reached a narrow ledge where the wind howled with untamed fury. Merona's cloak billowed around her, soaring like great wings.

"Here," Murdach said, gesturing toward the precipice. "This is where you will begin."

Merona swallowed hard, her gaze fixed on the vast expanse before her. "What do I do?"

"Close your eyes," the Morrigan's voice whispered softly in her mind. *"Feel the wind's embrace. Become one with it."*

Taking a deep breath, Merona obeyed, her eyes shutting as the wind's song filled her ears, its touch cool against her skin. She spread her arms wide, surrendering herself to its wild rhythm.

"That's it," Murdach encouraged. "Now, reach out with your spirit. Call to the wind. It has been waiting for you to guide it."

Her heart raced as she stood at the precipice; her arms outstretched. The wind whipped her raven hair around her face, its force both exhilarating and terrifying. She took another deep breath, grounding herself in the earth beneath and the vast sky above.

With renewed determination, Merona raised her arms higher, her voice ringing out across the mountaintop. "Cailleach! Goddess of the winds, hear me!"

The words felt ancient, like they had been waiting for centuries to be spoken. For a brief, breathless moment, all was still. Then, a gust of wind so powerful it almost knocked her off her feet, rushed around her.

Murdach's voice cut through the howling gale. "Focus, Merona! Channel the wind's power through you!"

Merona gritted her teeth, struggling to maintain her balance. *Is this how it ends?* she thought frantically. *Blown off a mountain before I've even begun my training?*

But then she felt it…a presence, ancient and wild, brushing against her consciousness. The Morrigan's voice whispered in her mind, *"She's here, child. Cailleach hears you. Now, show her your strength."*

Merona's eyes flew open, blazing with newfound resolve. "I am Merona!" she cried into the tempest. "Reborn witch and master of the elements. Cailleach, lend me your power!"

For a moment, the wind seemed to pause, as if considering her words. Then, like the rustle of a thousand whispers, it swirled around her, no longer fighting her, but moving with her.

A laugh, pure and unrestrained, escaped Merona's lips as she felt the wind bend to her will. She was terrified, exhilarated, and utterly alive.

Merona closed her eyes, surrendering to the raw energy coursing through her veins. The wind's whispers became a symphony, each gust a note in an ancient melody only she could hear. Her raven hair whipped around her face as she extended her arms, palms upward.

"I am one with the world," she murmured, her voice barely audible above the howling wind. "I am the world."

As the words left her lips, Merona felt a profound shift. The ground beneath her seemed to pulse with life, its rhythm matching her heartbeat. Rivers of energy flowed through her body, as tangible as her own blood.

She took a deep breath, feeling the very essence of the air fill her lungs. "My breath is the wind that blows through the trees," she whispered, a smile playing on her lips as a playful breeze tugged at her hair.

Exhaling slowly, Merona raised her arms higher, her eyes fluttering open. The world around her seemed to come alive, sharper, more vibrant. The wind responded to her movements, swirling and dancing around her like a living thing.

But as the exhilaration faded into focus, Merona's brow furrowed. The gusts grew stronger, their ferocity intensifying as they whipped around her. She struggled to control the maelstrom she had summoned, panic tightening in her chest.

"I can't..." she gasped; her voice lost to the wind. "It's too much!"

The Morrigan's voice sliced through her fear, a calm presence in the storm. *"Focus your mind, Merona. You are not separate from the air. You are one with it. Visualize yourself as part of the wind itself."*

Merona closed her eyes again, trying desperately to follow the Morrigan's guidance. But the howling gale raged around her, its force threatening to overwhelm her thoughts.

Merona's heart raced as she struggled against the tempest, she had unwittingly summoned. The wind howled around her, a furious symphony of nature's power. But as she stood, arms outstretched and eyes squeezed shut, something inside her began to shift.

"I am the wind," she whispered, her voice barely rising above the roar of the gale. "I am not its master, but its partner in this dance."

At her acknowledgment, the wind's intensity began to fade. Merona sensed a new connection; an unspoken bond between her spirit and the air itself. She opened her eyes and marveled at the change. The currents now moved around her, no longer a force to be resisted but an ally, flowing in harmony with her intentions.

Murdach's deep voice cut through her reverie. "Well done, Merona. You're beginning to understand. Now, let's see what else you can do with this newfound connection."

He gestured to a pile of autumn leaves nearby. "Try to create a small whirlwind. Focus on the air's natural movements and guide them, don't force them."

Merona bit her lip, concentrating on the task at hand. "How do I start?" she asked, uncertainty creeping into her voice.

Murdach's eyes sparkled with encouragement. "Feel the currents around you. Imagine them as extensions of your own body. Now, reach out with your mind and coax them into a circular motion."

Taking a deep breath, Merona extended her hand toward the leaves. At first, nothing stirred. Then, gradually, a few leaves began to flutter, caught in a delicate eddy that slowly formed into a spiral.

"I'm doing it!" Merona exclaimed, her face lighting up with joy and wonder.

"Indeed, you are," Murdach replied, his voice full of pride. "Now, try to guide that whirlwind. Move it to your left."

Merona focused harder, furrowing her brow in concentration. The small vortex wavered, then drifted slowly to the left as she had willed it. A surge of confidence filled her.

"This is incredible," she breathed, her eyes wide with awe. "I never imagined I could connect with the elements like this."

Murdach nodded, a knowing smile on his face. "This is just the beginning, Merona. With practice, you'll harness the wind's power in ways you've never dreamed possible."

As Merona continued to manipulate the whirlwind, a thought stirred within her. "Murdach," she asked, her voice laced with both curiosity and a hint of trepidation, "how will this help me fulfill my destiny? To prevent the deaths of thousands of witches in the future?"

The ancient warrior's expression turned solemn. "The path ahead is fraught with danger, my dear. Mastery over the elements will be essential in the battles to come. But remember, true power lies not in domination, but in harmony and understanding."

Merona nodded, her determination growing with each passing moment. As her attention back to the swirling leaves, she couldn't help but wonder what other challenges lay ahead on this perilous journey through time.

The howling wind tugged at Merona's cloak as she stood at the edge of a narrow ledge carved into the mountainside. Her raven hair whipped around her face, obscuring her vision. The path ahead was treacherous; a thin strip of rock hugging the cliff face, with a sheer drop to jagged rocks below.

"You must cross, Merona," Murdach's voice carried over the gale. "Use what you've learned."

Merona swallowed hard, her heart pounding. *I can do this,* she thought. *I am one with the wind.*

Taking a steadying breath, she stepped onto the path. Instantly, a powerful gust threatened to pull her off her feet. Instinctively, she raised her hands, reaching out to feel the air currents swirling around her.

"That's it," the Morrigan's voice resonated in Merona's mind. *"Feel the wind's rhythm. Become part of its dance."*

Merona closed her eyes, tuning into the ebb and flow of the air. With each step, she moved in perfect harmony with the gusts, her body fluidly redirecting their force.

Halfway across, a violent updraft hit her unexpectedly. For a heart-stopping moment, she teetered on the edge.

"Focus, Merona!" Murdach's voice sliced through the chaos.

In that instant, Merona drew upon her training. She didn't fight the wind; instead, she surrendered to it, using its power to steady herself. What had threatened to throw her into the abyss now became her ally, guiding her back to solid ground.

When she finally reached the other side, her legs trembled from exertion and relief.

"Well done," Murdach said, "but we're not finished yet."

The Morrigan, in her majestic wolf form, padded forward. *"Now, young one,"* her voice echoed in Merona's mind, *"you must face the true fury of the elements."*

Without warning, Murdach raised his arms, and the wind around them exploded into a violent maelstrom, carrying debris and a biting cold.

"Protect yourself!" he commanded.

Merona's eyes widened in panic. *How could I possibly…?* Her thoughts were cut short as a branch hurtled towards her face.

Merona's instincts took over. She raised her hands, palms outward, and focused on the air surrounding her. The wind responded to her will, forming an invisible barrier. The branch glanced off, harmlessly falling to the ground.

A surge of exhilaration coursed through her veins. "I did it!" she exclaimed, her eyes shining with newfound confidence.

Murdach nodded approvingly. "Good. Now redirect it."

Merona furrowed her brow, fully concentrating on the swirling vortex before her. She visualized the currents, feeling their flow and pressure. With a sharp, deliberate gesture, she guided the wind away from her, sending it spiraling off to the side.

The Morrigan's voice echoed in her mind. *"You're beginning to understand, child. The wind is not just a force to be controlled, but an extension of yourself."*

Merona's chest swelled with pride. For the first time since her rebirth, she felt truly connected to her powers. "It's... incredible," she breathed, her voice filled with wonder. "I can feel every gust, every breeze. It's like the air itself is alive."

Murdach approached, his silver hair dancing in the wind. "That's because it is, Merona. And now, you must learn to harness this life force in combat."

Merona's excitement faltered. "Combat? But I thought…"

"Your destiny demands more than mere control," Murdach interrupted, his tone grave. "You must become one with the wind, using it to enhance your every movement."

He demonstrated, his body flickering with impossible speed. "The wind can make you faster, more agile. It can strengthen your blows and shield you from harm."

Merona watched in awe, her mind racing with possibilities. Could I really become that powerful? she wondered. And if I do, will it be enough to face what's coming?

Taking a deep breath, Merona centered herself. She faced Murdach and the Morrigan, the wind whipping around them, tugging at her raven hair and whispering secrets in her ears. She closed her eyes and let the air's energy flow through her veins.

"Ready yourself," Murdach called, his voice carried by the breeze.

Merona's eyes snapped open, her gaze sharp with focus. She could feel the shift in the air as Murdach lunged forward, his movements a blur. Instinctively, she called upon the wind, propelling herself to the side with startling speed.

"Good!" Murdach praised, spinning to face her. "Now, attack!"

Merona hesitated for a fraction of a second before pushing off, letting the wind carry her forward. She aimed a strike at Murdach's chest, but he deflected it with ease.

"You're thinking too much," the Morrigan's voice echoed in her mind. *"Let the wind guide you."*

Gritting her teeth, Merona tried again. This time, she didn't overthink her movements. Instead, she surrendered to the air currents, allowing them to dictate her path. She weaved around Murdach, her strikes coming from unexpected angles.

Murdach grinned, "Now you're getting it!"

For what felt like hours, they sparred. Merona learned to use gusts of wind to amplify her punches, to create walls of air to deflect attacks, and to ride currents to outmaneuver her opponents. With each passing moment, her confidence grew, her movements more fluid, as if she were becoming one with the air around her.

As the sun dipped below the horizon, Murdach called a halt to their training. "You've done well, Merona," he said, his voice a mix of pride and concern. "But now comes your final test."

Merona followed his gaze to the dense forest ahead. The trees were so tightly packed that no path was visible, their branches tangled in a chaotic embrace. Her heart sank. "You want me to... clear a path?"

The Morrigan padded forward, her red fur gleaming in the fading light. *"This is more than simply moving trees, child. It's about understanding the true depth of your power."*

Doubt crept into Merona's chest. *Can I really do this? What if I fail?*

"Trust in yourself," Murdach said gently, placing a hand on her shoulder. "Remember, you are one with the wind."

Taking a steadying breath, Merona stepped forward. She raised her arms, feeling the wind respond to her call. Closing her eyes, she focused, visualizing the path she needed to create, imagining the wind as an extension of her will.

I am the wind, she thought. I am unstoppable. She raised her arms and chanted *"Cailleach na gaoithe, éist le mo ghuth, Tugaim dom do gaoithe, a thiarna na gaoithe!*

Féach ar na scamaill, ag gluaiseacht le mo ordú,
Gabh mo dhóchas, mar a thagann an gaoith!"

With a cry that seemed to shake the very mountains, Merona unleashed her power. A massive gust of wind erupted from her hands, roaring through the forest. Trees groaned and branches snapped as the gale tore them aside, carving a wide path through the dense growth.

When it was over, Merona opened her eyes, her breath coming in ragged gasps as she took in the sight before her. A clear path now stretched into the forest, wide enough for them to travel with ease.

"By the gods," Murdach whispered, awe in his voice as he gazed at the destruction.

The Morrigan's amber eyes gleamed with approval. *"Well done, child. You've taken your first true step toward your destiny."*

Merona stared at her hands, still tingling with the aftershocks of power. But for the first time since her journey began, she felt ready for whatever lay ahead.

As twilight settled over Bugarach, Merona stood at the mountain's peak, her raven hair whipping in the wind she now commanded. She gazed out over the sprawling landscape, lost in thought.

"You've come far," the Morrigan's voice broke through her reverie. *"But this is only the first step on a long and treacherous path."*

Merona turned, her eyes glinting with determination. "I feel... different. Stronger. As if the very air around me is an extension of my will."

The goddess nodded, her wolf form shimmering in the fading light. *"The element of Air has accepted you, child. But remember, with great power comes great responsibility and greater danger."*

Murdach approached, his weathered face etched with concern. "Armaeus will not rest. He'll sense your growing power and redouble his efforts to stop you."

A chill ran down Merona's spine at the mention of the demon's name. She closed her eyes, feeling the wind caress her face. "Then I must be ready," she whispered, more to herself than to her companions.

Murdach's voice was grave. "There are still three elements to master, and time is growing short. The balance of power in Gaul hangs by a thread."

Merona's mind raced, the weight of his words settling heavily on her. "Where do we go next? What challenges await us?"

"To the heart of the old forests," Murdach replied. "There, you will face trials that will test not just your newfound abilities, but the very core of who you are."

As darkness fell, Merona gazed at the stars emerging above. She thought of Ane Koldings, of the fire that had consumed her past self. *I won't let that future come to pass,* she vowed silently. *Whatever it takes, I'll change our fate.*

The wind picked up, as though responding to her resolve. Merona took a deep breath, savoring the crisp night air. "Then let's not waste another moment," she declared, her voice ringing with newfound confidence. "The journey ahead may be long, but I'm ready to face whatever comes our way."

As they prepared to descend the mountain, Merona cast one last look at the majestic peak of Bugarach. She knew that whatever trials lay ahead, whatever dark forces Armaeus would throw at her, she would face them with the strength of the wind at her back and the fire of determination in her heart.

Chapter 15

The merciless weather ravaged the landscape, each passing season etching its mark of destruction. For months, the determined trio braved the treacherous journey toward their goal: the harsh and unforgiving expanse of Gascogne. Each step tested their resolve, as biting winds and numbing cold waged a constant battle against them. Yet, harsh winds and biting cold, but they pressed on with dogged determination fueled by their mission. Along the way, they sought food and brief refuge in scattered villages, though true rest remained elusive until they reached their ultimate destination, Paris.

Merona wrestled with the labyrinth of her mind, she couldn't escape the dark demon, Armaeus. He haunted her dreams and tormented her thoughts, whether she was awake or asleep. His sinister intent threatened not only to strip her of her power but to endanger the lives of those she loved most.

Before them stretched the ancient forest, its twisted branches clawing at the dimming light like skeletal fingers. Merona's heart raced as her gaze fixed on the foreboding tree line, searching for any sign of movement within the shadows.

"We must press on," Murdach's deep voice rumbled beside her, his silver hair catching the last rays of light. "Gascogne lies just beyond this forest. There, we will finally confront Armaeus."

Merona inclined her head, her raven hair shifting softly in the evening breeze. "I can feel his presence growing stronger," she murmured, a shiver rippling through her. "The air itself seems thick with his malevolence."

The Morrigan padded silently at their side, her amber eyes alert and watchful. Her voice echoed in Merona's mind, calm yet foreboding: *"Be wary, young one. The path ahead is fraught with danger."*

As they ventured deeper into the forest, the towering trees seemed to draw closer, their branches intertwining overhead to block out what little light remained. Merona's fingers twitched, ready to call upon her elemental magic at a moment's notice.

A sudden, bone-chilling howl shattered the oppressive silence, followed by the snap of twigs and the rustling of unseen movement. Merona spun, her heart pounding as grotesque forms began to emerge from the gloom, their twisted features illuminated by the faint light seeping through the canopy.

"Armaeus' minions," Murdach growled, his eyes blazing with a fierce determination. He gripped his weapon tightly. "Stand ready, Merona. We must fight our way through."

The earth beneath Merona's feet shuddered as if, the sky overhead a tapestry of violent hues, echoing the chaos that swarmed before them. With each breath, she tasted the acrid stench of malevolence, the demonic horde an undulating mass of corruption, thick with malevolent energy.

"Circle formation!" she shouted, her voice cutting sharply through the cacophony of snarls and screams.

Murdach, now a towering dragon whose sea-toned scales rippled with an otherworldly sheen, responded with a thunderous roar that shook the battlefield. The Morrigan, sleek and agile, moved swiftly to secure their flank, her fiery red fur gleaming defiantly amidst the shadowy onslaught.

"Merona, above you!" Murdach bellowed, his draconic power entwined with his human voice.

Reacting instantly, Merona rolled to the side, narrowly evading the razor-sharp claws of a beast plunging from the smoke-choked sky. Her heart thundered in her chest, but her focus remained sharp, her movements deliberate. With a surge of energy, she thrust her palms forward, releasing a spear of radiant light that pierced the creature, reducing it to a cloud of ash that scattered in the wind.

"Good call," she acknowledged, casting a quick glance at Murdach.

He met her gaze with a nod, his emerald eyes alight with unyielding determination, already scanning the battlefield for their next threat.

"To your left, goddess!" Murdach's voice boomed, this time a warning meant for Morrigan. The wolf reacted instantly, her movements fluid and precise as she sprang forward, intercepting a demon that had crept dangerously close.

"Thank you," Morrigan's voice echoed softly in Merona's mind, a fleeting connection between their bonded souls. Her amber eyes flickered with a hint of gratitude before she lunged back into the battle, her fangs glinting like silver blades against the dark forms of their enemies.

"Stay close!" Merona commanded, her voice steady despite the chaos. She could feel the pull of her magic, the primal force of the earth flowing through her like a roaring current. Every spell she cast was more than a defense; it was a lifeline, binding their survival to the strength of their unity. "Cover me!"

Murdach descended in a powerful arc, his massive wings beating with enough force to send waves of wind crashing into their foes. The gusts staggered the demonic horde, buying Merona the crucial moments she needed.

Drawing on every ounce of her will, she raised her hands, and a radiant barrier of light erupted around them. Its brilliance pushed back the encroaching darkness, repelling the demons that dared approach. For a brief moment, the battlefield fell silent, as if the barrier itself had commanded even the chaos to pause.

"Never falter. Never yield," Merona reminded herself, the mantra a steady flame stoking her resolve.

"Behind you, Murdach!" she shouted, the warning more than sight; it was instinct, a pulse through the bond they shared. The dragon spun swiftly, his tail sweeping the ground in a crushing arc, scattering the fiends attempting to ambush him.

"Your vigilance honors me, Merona," Murdach rumbled, his voice carrying a deep, resonant respect. *"Together, we stand against this tide."*

"Always," she replied, her tone fierce with unshakable conviction.

The battle roared on, an unrelenting storm of claws and spells. Merona felt the strain of her magic, the weight of responsibility pressing heavy on her shoulders. Yet she moved with precision and grace, her spells flowing like rivers, her steps calculated and steady.

Trust in your strength. Trust in theirs, she repeated inwardly, grounding herself in the wellspring of her power. She was no longer the hesitant girl shadowed by doubt, no longer frozen by fear. Now, there was only the fight, only the unwavering certainty that she would not let the darkness prevail.

Morrigan surged forward, tearing through another enemy with feral intensity, though Merona could feel the wolf's growing fatigue; a subtle yet undeniable echo in their bond. *"Hold on, Morrigan. Just a little longer,* she urged, her thoughts laced with quiet determination."

Second by second, they pushed back the tide. Their combined might became a relentless symphony of destruction, each movement orchestrated to protect the other. They fought as one. A tempest against the legion of shadows, each covering the blind spots that could mean the difference between survival and ruin.

"Almost there," Murdach said, his voice heavy with exhaustion but steadfast in its resolve.

"Let's finish this," Merona declared, summoning every ounce of strength for a final assault. She closed her eyes briefly, envisioning the perfect harmony of their trio; dragon, witch, and wolf. They pressed forward with renewed determination.

Merona inhaled deeply, grounding herself as the remnants of the horde surged toward them. Her voice, soft yet resolute, carried over the chaos. "I'm ready, Murdach. We've come too far to fail now."

With a united effort, they unleashed their power, and one by one, the minions fell. When the last shadow dissolved into nothingness, Merona leaned heavily against a tree, her chest heaving with each ragged breath. "They're growing stronger," she said, her voice edged with worry. "Armaeus knows we're close."

Murdach, now returned to his human form, stepped forward and rested a steady hand on her shoulder. "You fought with courage, Merona. Your command of the elements is becoming formidable."

Merona's lips curved into a faint smile, the gratitude in her eyes unmistakable. "I couldn't have done it without you both," she replied, glancing between Murdach and the Morrigan, who stood vigilant and alert despite her weariness.

As they moved onward, the dense forest began to thin, its oppressive shadows giving way to the rolling hills and open plains ahead. On the horizon, the faint outline of Gascogne's walls emerged; a beacon of hope amid the encroaching darkness.

With each step closer to their destination, an oppressive weight pressed down upon them. The air grew dense and stifling, laced with the acrid stench of brimstone and decay.

Merona's voice wavered as she broke the silence. "Can you feel it? It's as if the land itself is crying out in agony."

Murdach's expression hardened, his jaw clenched in grim resolve. "Armaeus' influence is stronger here. We must be ready for anything."

When they reached the crest of the final hill before Gascogne, the scene that unfolded stole the breath from their lungs. Above the city, the sky churned with dark, roiling clouds, pulsating with an eerie, unearthly glow.

"By the gods," Merona whispered, her voice tinged with both shock and despair. "What has he done?"

The Morrigan's voice echoed in their minds, solemn and foreboding. *"The battle is upon you, young ones. The fate of all rests in your hands."*

Merona straightened her posture, steeling herself against the fear clawing at the edges of her resolve. Once a simple village girl, she now stood as a symbol of defiance, a beacon of hope against the consuming darkness.

With Murdach by her side, his strength unwavering, and the Morrigan's wisdom guiding their steps, Merona felt a spark of certainty ignite within her. They had come too far to falter now. Together, they would face whatever lay ahead. Together, they had a chance.

"Then let us face it together," she declared, her voice clear and steady, infused with newfound resolve. "For those who have fallen and all those yet to come, we must not fail."

As they began their descent towards Gascogne, the air crackled with anticipation, charged with the tension of an impending clash that would decide their fate and that of countless others.

The ground beneath their feet suddenly lurched, throwing Merona off balance. She stumbled, catching the rough bark of a nearby tree just as the world around them began to shake violently.

"Earthquake!" Murdach shouted, his powerful voice straining to rise above the deafening roar of the land splitting apart.

Merona's heart raced as she took in the chaos around them. Trees crashed to the ground, their roots exposed like gnarled, skeletal fingers, while massive boulders careened down the hillside. The earth itself seemed to scream in agony, breaking apart under unseen forces.

"We need to find shelter!" Merona yelled, her eyes scanning desperately for any sign of safety amidst the destruction.

Before they could move, a thunderous crack split the air, a sound so piercing it felt as though the world itself was being torn in two. Merona turned just in time to see the ground beneath Murdach collapse, swallowing him in a choking plume of dust and debris.

"Murdach!" she screamed, her voice raw with panic and disbelief as she rushed toward the gaping void where he had stood only moments before.

"Be cautious, child," the goddess cautioned, her voice steady yet heavy with concern. *"The earth is unstable."*

Merona's thoughts raced, a tide of panic threatening to engulf her. *I can't lose him...not now, not after everything we've been through."*

As the quake subsided, leaving an unsettling silence cloaked the landscape. Merona edged closer to the jagged rim of the newly formed chasm, her pulse hammering in her ears. She peered into the void, her breath catching as the abyss stretched into shadowy depths.

"Murdach?" she called out, her voice quivering with a mix of fear and hope. "Can you hear me?"

A faint groan echoed back, faint but unmistakable. Relief flooded her, igniting a spark of hope within her chest He was alive...barely, but for how long?

"Hold on, my love," she murmured, her voice steadying as determination steeling her voice. "I'm coming for you."

Turning to the Morrigan, Merona's eyes burned with resolve. "I have to save him. No matter what it takes."

The goddess inclined her head in solemn acknowledgment. "Then waste no time. The earth's fury may not yet be spent."

As if the land itself heeded the warning, another tremor rippled beneath her feet, shaking the ground with renewed ferocity. Merona clenched her fists, her resolve hardening.

The man who had stood beside her through endless battles, who had guided and shielded her when all seemed lost, now needed her. And she would not fail him.

Taking a deep breath, Merona steeled herself for the challenge ahead. She had faced trials and tribulations before, but this; this would be her greatest test yet.

Closing her eyes, she reached out with her senses, feeling the rhythmic pulse of the earth beneath her feet. The connection she had nurtured throughout their perilous journey surged within her, a potent force waiting to be unleashed. Yet, never had she attempted something so monumental. Murdach's life depended on her success.

"Earth, hear me," she murmured, her voice steady but imbued with urgency. "I am your daughter, your guardian, your ally."

The ground trembled faintly, a subtle acknowledgment of her plea. Merona's eyes flew open, glowing with a fierce, ethereal light. Her hands lifted, fingers spreading wide as she summoned her strength.

"Glaoim ar an talamh, ar anamacha an domhain, ar mo thiarnas! Open the way to him," she commanded, her voice resonating with ancient power.

The earth groaned in response, its deep voice rumbling through the chasm. Rocks scraped and shifted, and slowly, a narrow fissure began to take shape, winding its way into the depths.

Sweat trickled down Merona's brow as she pushed her energy further, her focus unwavering. Each heartbeat felt like an eternity, but she would not falter. She couldn't. For Murdach, she would move the very earth itself.

"It's working," the Morrigan remarked, her voice touched with awe.

Merona didn't reply, her entire focus locked on the task before her. As the fissure widened, a glimpse of silver hair caught her eye amid the wreckage.

"Murdach!" she called, her heart skipping a beat. "Can you move?"

A faint cough reached her ears. "Merona... be careful..."

His warning only fueled her determination. She inhaled deeply, steadying herself as she prepared to channel even more power into the incantation. The earth's raw, vibrating energy coursed through her veins.

"Mother Danu," she intoned, her voice rich with ancient power, "lend me your strength..."

Her words trembled with emotion, but her resolve was unwavering. Her eyes blazed with fierce determination as she continued, "Here and now, I call upon Danu, mother of the earth. I summon you to aid me in moving mountain, stone, and dust."

The air hummed with raw energy, her raven hair stirring in a wind no one else could feel. Her hands trembled slightly as she reached out toward the rubble that imprisoned Murdach.

"Earth, I call thee forth," she chanted, her voice gaining strength with each syllable. "Grant me the power of the Mother

Earth and invoke the elements to release Murdach from this tomb. So mote it be."

As the final syllable left her lips, Merona felt a powerful surge ripple through her body. The earth beneath her feet trembled, and she could almost feel the very soul of the land answering her call.

"Murdach," she whispered, her voice tight with urgency. "Hold on, my love."

With a strained grunt, Merona raised her hands, summoning all her will to move the heavy debris. Slowly, agonizingly, the stones and earth shifted. Sweat beaded on her brow as she poured every ounce of her energy into the task.

"I won't lose you," she muttered through clenched teeth. "Not now. Not ever."

As she worked, memories of their time together flashed through her mind; Murdach's wisdom, his steadfast support. The thought of losing him spurred her on, driving her beyond what she thought possible.

Then, a flicker of silver caught her eye. Murdach's hand broke free of the rubble, reaching towards her. With a final, desperate surge of power, Merona cleared the remaining debris, revealing Murdach's battered but breathing form.

"Merona," he gasped, his eyes locking onto hers. "You did it."

She collapsed to her knees beside him, tears of relief streaming down her face. "We did it," she whispered, her voice trembling. "Together." Gently, she cradled his head in her lap, the weight of their shared victory settling over her.

The Morrigan, her fur bristling, stood as a vigilant sentinel. Her amber eyes scanned the horizon, her immense wolf form casting long shadows in the dying light. Merona could feel the goddess's tension, the low growl rumbling from her chest, a warning of the danger still lurking.

"We're not safe yet," the Morrigan's voice echoed in Merona's mind. *"Armaeus' minions are out there."*

Merona nodded, her fingers intertwined with Murdach's as he slowly regained strength. She watched his chest rise and fall, each breath a precious, steady reminder of his survival. "How do you feel?" she asked softly, her concern evident.

Murdach's lips curved into a weak smile. "Like I've been crushed by a mountain," he rasped, then chuckled, wincing at the pain. "But I'm alive, and it's all thanks to you."

Merona's heart swelled with emotion. "I couldn't bear to lose you," she whispered, her voice thick with unshed tears. "When I saw you buried beneath the rubble, I..."

"Shh," Murdach soothed, reaching up to gently cup her cheek. "You were magnificent, Merona. Your control over the earth... it's growing stronger."

As the dust settled around them, Merona allowed herself a brief moment to breathe. The air was thick with the scent of disturbed soil and lingering magic. She closed her eyes, feeling the pulse of the earth beneath her, a connection that had deepened in the crucible of their crisis.

"This ordeal," Murdach said, his voice growing stronger, "it's brought us closer to our goal to each other."

Merona nodded, warmth spreading through her chest. "I felt it too," she admitted softly. "As if the earth itself recognized our bond."

But the peaceful moment shattered like brittle glass. A bone-chilling screech tore through the air, sending a spike of fear through her. Merona's eyes snapped open, and her heart sank as she saw a horde of grotesque creatures emerging from the horizon. Their twisted forms; nightmarish blends of shadow and decay; advanced with unnatural speed.

"Armaeus," Merona hissed, venom lacing her words. She rose swiftly, positioning herself between Murdach's vulnerable form and the oncoming threat. "He's sensed our weakness."

The Morrigan's voice rang out in Merona's mind, sharp and urgent. *"Prepare yourselves! They come in numbers!"*

Merona's heart pounded in her chest, but she steeled herself, drawing upon the raw power of the earth that now thrummed through her veins. With a swift motion, she thrust her hands toward the ground, channeling her will into the soil beneath her feet.

"Earth, heed my call," she intoned, her voice resonating with newfound authority. "Rise and protect us!"

The ground before them erupted as massive slabs of stone shot upward, forming a protective barrier. Merona's brow furrowed in concentration as she commanded the earth to obey.

"Murdach," she called without turning, her eyes fixed on the advancing horde, "can you stand?"

He grunted in effort, slowly rising to his feet. "I can fight," he assured her, though his voice was strained.

Merona's mind raced, calculating their odds. *We're outnumbered,* fear gnawed at her, but then her thoughts shifted to the lives at stake, to the destiny she was bound to fulfill. *No, she whispered to herself. I won't let Armaeus win. Not now. Not ever.*

"Mother Earth, i do chumhacht, dún na sléibhte agus na gleannta don namhaid! Mother Earth, in your power, enclose the mountains and valleys around my foes!"

With a fierce cry, she thrust her palms outward, sending a wave of stone spikes hurtling toward the first wave of attackers. As the creatures fell, impaled by the earth itself, Merona felt a surge of power unlike anything she'd ever experienced before.

"Come then, minions of darkness," Merona challenged, her voice carrying across the battlefield. " Tabhair aghaidh ar fhearg an domhain féin! Face the wrath of the earth itself!"

The air shimmered with otherworldly energy as Murdach's form began to shift. His silver hair rippled like liquid moonlight, his body elongating and expanding. In moments, where the man had stood, a magnificent dragon now towered, scales gleaming with iridescent hues of emerald and sapphire.

Merona's heart swelled with a mix of awe and fierce pride. "Murdach," she breathed, her voice barely rising above the chaos of battle.

The dragon's eyes locked onto hers, a familiar intelligence burning within their depths. With a deafening roar that shook the earth beneath them, Murdach launched himself into the air, his massive wings casting dark shadows over the battlefield.

"By the gods," Merona thought, mesmerized as Murdach dive-bombed the oncoming horde, his razor-sharp claws cutting through their ranks. "He's magnificent."

Snapping herself out of the momentary stupor, Merona refocused on the battle. She raised her arms high, channeling her energy into the earth once more. "Mother Danu, lend me your strength," she whispered, feeling the power surge through her veins.

The ground trembled, then split open, swallowing a group of Armaeus' minions whole. Above, Murdach's fiery breath lit the darkening sky, incinerating waves of enemies.

"Merona!" Murdach's voice boomed in her mind, their bond stretching beyond his draconic form. *"To your left!"*

She spun just in time to see a grotesque creature lunging toward her. Without hesitation, she thrust her palm forward, and a pillar of stone erupted from the earth, impaling the beast mid-leap.

"Thank you, Murdach," she called, both aloud and through their mental link. The endearment slipped out unbidden, but in that moment of shared peril and triumph, it felt right.

As they fought side by side, Merona and Murdach moved with flawless synchronicity. Where her earthen barriers rose, his wings swept low, herding enemies into her traps. When his flames drove foes to retreat, her stone spikes lay in wait.

"We can do this," Merona realized, a fierce joy swelling within her heart. "Together, we're unstoppable."

Her eyes blazed with newfound determination as she surveyed the battlefield. The air crackled with energy, thick with the scent of scorched earth and acrid smoke. The earth's power pulsed through her, more potent than ever before.

"Murdach," she called out, her voice unwavering despite the chaos. "I can feel it. The earth... it's responding to me like never before."

The dragon's massive head swung toward her, his intelligent eyes gleaming. "Then use it, Merona. Show them the true power of the earth element!"

With a deep breath, Merona plunged her hands into the soil. The ground beneath her fingers seemed to hum with life, vibrating with untapped potential. She closed her eyes, visualizing the landscape around her, feeling every contour, every stone.

"Mother Danu," she whispered, "guide my hands."

Suddenly, the earth erupted. Massive columns of stone shot up from the ground, impaling and crushing Armaeus' minions. Fissures split open beneath their feet, swallowing entire groups whole.

Merona's eyes snapped open, glowing with an ethereal light. "This ends now," she declared, her voice carrying across the battlefield. "*Domhain, éist liom! Lúbfaidh mé agus cosnaíonn mé, an ríocht i mo lámha!* Earth, hear me! Bend and protect, dominion in my hands!"

As she spoke, the mountains themselves seemed to answer her call. Boulders broke free, rolling down to crush the remaining enemies. The ground trembled, undulating as it threw the dark creatures off balance.

Murdach roared in approval, unleashing a torrent of flame to complement Merona's earthen assault. "You're doing it, Merona!" he cried out in her mind. "Your power... it's incredible!"

Merona allowed herself a small smile, even as she continued to channel the earth's energy. "I never knew I was capable of this," she thought back to him. "But with you by my side, I feel invincible."

As the last of Armaeus' minions fell, silence settled over the ravaged landscape. Merona slowly lowered her arms, her breath coming in ragged gasps. She surveyed the aftermath of the battle, a mixture of awe and disbelief washing over her.

"We... we did it," she murmured, her voice barely above a whisper.

The acrid scent of smoke and dust filled the air as Merona stood amidst the aftermath. Her raven hair, streaked with dirt, whipped around her face in the eerie stillness. She turned to Murdach realizing that he too was exhausted but exhilarated.

"We've weathered this storm," Merona said, her voice hoarse yet resolute. "But I fear it's only the beginning."

Murdach nodded, his silver hair catching the last of the light. "You've grown stronger, Merona. Your connection to the earth... it's unlike anything I've ever witnessed."

The Morrigan padded silently to Merona's side, her amber eyes reflecting ancient wisdom. *"The path ahead is shrouded in shadow, young one,"* she said, *her voice carrying the weight of prophecy. "But remember, even in the darkest of times, the earth beneath your feet remains constant."*

Merona knelt, placing her palm flat against the ground. She could feel the pulse of the earth, its rhythm syncing with her own heartbeat. "I won't forget," she murmured. "This power... it's both terrifying and exhilarating."

Rising to her feet, Merona's gaze swept over the ravaged landscape. "What if Armaeus sends more?" she asked, the hint of fear creeping into her voice. "What if next time, I'm not strong enough?"

Murdach's hand found hers, his touch a steady reassurance. "Doubt is the seed of failure, Merona. You must believe in yourself, as I believe in you."

The Morrigan's voice broke through the silence, sharp and commanding. *"The wheel of fate turns, and with it, your destiny unfolds. Each challenge faced is a step towards your true potential."*

Merona squared her shoulders, drawing strength from their words and the solid earth beneath her feet. "Then we press on," she declared with unwavering determination. "Gascogne awaits, and with it, the next chapter of our journey."

As they prepared to move forward, Merona cast one final glance at the battlefield. In her mind, she made a silent vow, "Whatever comes next Armaeus, know this! I am ready."

Chapter 16

As the sun dipped below the horizon, casting amber and violet hues across the sky, the town of Burdigala rose before them, its ancient stone walls resiliently standing resolute against the encroaching night. Merona's weary eyes traced the contours of the formidable ramparts and elegant towers, offering a moment of respite in their relentless journey. It had been a grueling three years since they first set out, crossing rugged terrains, verdant valleys, and snow-capped mountains; each step pushing them closer to places where the elemental energies pulsed most vibrantly. These energies were crucial to Merona, who sought to harness their power for a purpose that felt both monumental and daunting. At sixteen, she had grown not only in maturity but in her abilities.

Murdach's voice cut through her reverie, resonating with a calm authority that was both reassuring and practical. "We'll rest here tonight," he announced, eyes scanning the horizon with the vigilance. "The gates will close soon." His words roused Merona from her contemplative haze, awakening her senses to the reality that they were approaching safety, even if only for the night.

Merona nodded in acknowledgment, the weight of fatigue settling heavily on her shoulders like a leaden cloak. Her raven hair, tangled and windswept from days of relentless travel, danced in the cool evening breeze, carrying with it the familiar yet jarring scents of the town; acrid wood smoke blending with the earthy aroma of livestock. It was a stark reminder of her home in Septimania, the path they traveled a crossroads between the life she once knew and the quest she now pursued. The journey was both familiar and alien, bridging the ordinary world and the extraordinary forces they sought to control.

As they neared the massive wooden gates of Burdigala, a voice pierced the quiet; a voice that was ethereal yet grounding, belonging to Morrigan in her human form. "Be wary, child," she warned, her voice laced with a haunting melody that sent a shiver down Merona's spine. "Even in sleep, darkness may find you."

The words struck a chill in Merona, a stark reminder that danger lurked not only in the physical challenges of their journey but also in the unseen realms threading through the very fabric of reality. She understood that the pursuit of elemental energies carried a price, and that vigilance was essential, even in moments of apparent calm.

As the trio drew closer to the gates, the town stirred to life: laughter echoed from nearby taverns, the clatter of hooves against cobblestones resonated in the air, and lanterns flickered to life, casting warm pools of light on the street. The sounds of humanity welcomed them, a stark contrast to the solitude of the wilderness they had left behind. This blend of noise and scent stirred something deep within Merona a flicker of hope mingled with a persistent unease.

Entering Burdigala felt like both a return home and a step into the unknown. What adventures, what dangers awaited them within the town's ancient stone walls? Merona straightened her shoulders, her resolve hardening. They would find shelter, rest, and gather strength for the trials ahead. But even in moments of reprieve, Morrigan's warning echoed in her mind. The quest was far from over, and the darkness trailing them was not yet finished.

Once inside the town, they secured lodgings with a kind villager. The room was simple but clean, a welcome reprieve from the long journey. As night fell, Merona sank onto the straw-filled mattress, her muscles aching from the strain of the road.

"Rest now," Murdach murmured, his voice soothing and steady. "I'll keep watch."

With the faintest flutter of her eyelids, Merona surrendered to exhaustion, slipping into a deep, dreamless sleep. As she drifted off, her surroundings blurred and twisted, taking on a dreamlike quality. Morrigan was there, offering warmth and comfort by her side.

Flames licked at the edges of her vision, the acrid smell of smoke filling her lungs. Merona found herself standing in a crowded square, the heat from a towering pyre searing her skin. Panicked screams echoed through the air as a woman was led to the stake.

"No," Merona whispered, her heart pounding in her chest. "Not again."

She tried to move, to intervene, but her feet remained rooted to the ground. The crowd pressed in around her; a sea of faces contorted with hate and fear. And then, the chaos, she saw him.

Murdach stood at the edge of the square, his silver hair shimmering in the firelight. Their eyes met across the distance, a fleeting moment of recognition amidst the horror.

Merona jolted awake, her breath coming in frantic gasps. The room was shrouded in darkness, save for a sliver of moonlight spilling through the window. She sat up, her mind reeling from the intensity of the dream.

"Murdach," she whispered, her voice shaky.

He emerged from the shadows; his face marked by concern. "What troubles you, my love?"

Merona closed her eyes, the images from her dream still vivid in her mind. "I saw Copenhagen," she murmured. "The fire, the crowd... and you. You were there, weren't you?"

Murdach's expression softened, a mixture of sorrow and ancient wisdom in his gaze. He sat beside her, taking her hand gently in his. "Yes," he admitted. "I was there."

Merona's mind swirled with questions, but before she could voice them, exhaustion overtook her once more. She sank back into a restless sleep, the memory of dancing flames still flickering behind her eyelids.

Merona's eyelids snapped open, her heart racing as she found Murdach still by her side. His eyes locked onto hers, and the intensity of his gaze tightened a knot in her throat. The fervor with which he looked at her made her feel the heat radiating from his body, sparking a fire deep within her own.

"You were there," she whispered, her voice hoarse with raw emotion. "In Copenhagen. Why didn't you save me?"

Murdach's fingers intertwined with hers, his touch both familiar and ancient. "My love," he began, his voice carrying the weight of countless lifetimes, "our souls have danced together across the ages. We've been lovers, warriors, and guardians of secrets long forgotten by mortal men."

Merona's heart raced, memories of other lives flickering just beyond her reach. "But why..." she started, her words faltering.

"Mo ghrá, I couldn't interfere with destiny," Murdach continued, his eyes shimmering with unshed tears. "In Copenhagen, as in every life, your path was yours to walk. To intervene would have unraveled the very fabric of time."

Merona sat up, her raven hair spilling over her shoulders. "Tell me," She demanded, her voice firming with resolve. "Tell me about our beginning."

"Long ago," Murdach began, his voice taking on a rhythm as though woven from the fabric of time itself, "in an age before time, I knew you. We fought side by side against a great evil, a creature of nightmare; the Minotaur."

Murdach's gaze grew distant, as if lost in the mists of forgotten memories. "It was in the Labyrinth," he continued, his voice taking on a melodic cadence. "I was a mortal warrior, sent to face the Minotaur. And you... you were Ariadne, a goddess in human form. You were breathtakingly beautiful, pale skin and deep piercing eyes the color of the sea. You wore a dress made of hessian and leather, adorned with gold and pearls woven into your braided hair and crown."

Murdach's fingers gently caressed Merona's forearm as she lay in his arms, his touch tender yet laden with the weight of the past. "You granted me immortality, transformed me into a mighty sea dragon, to defeat the Minotaur."

Merona's heart clenched at the bitterness in his voice. "But why?" she asked, her voice trembling. "Why would you choose to live forever if it meant losing me?"

Murdach's cruel smile faded, replaced by an expression of deep sorrow. "I was selfish," he confessed, his eyes filled with regret. "I thought I could win your love by proving myself in battle. But when I saw the pain in your eyes as I emerged from the Labyrinth, I realized my mistake too late."

Tears welled in Merona's eyes as she reached for his hand again, her voice a whisper of comfort. "But we found each other again," she said softly.

Murdach nodded solemnly, his gaze heavy with the weight of untold histories. "Yes, my dear. Across countless timelines and worlds, we have met. In some, we were mortal enemies; in others, allies fighting for a common cause. But regardless of the form our relationship took, there was always a profound connection between us. I have treasured every moment we shared."

Merona's breath caught in her throat. "But... how is that possible?"

Murdach's eyes softened with the depth of ancient sorrow and enduring love. "You were different then, a goddess incarnate. And I... I was a warrior, sworn to protect you."

As he spoke, images flickered in Merona's mind; flashes of battles long past, the clash of steel, the roar of a monstrous creature. She saw herself, yet not herself, wielding unimaginable power.

"We loved then," Murdach whispered, his voice barely audible. "And I love you still, my dear Merona. It is why I have watched over you, why I will always stand by your side."

Merona's mind reeled at the realization of other lives she had lived with this man by her side. "But why don't I remember any of it?"

"Your memories are sealed," Murdach explained gently. "They will resurface when the time is right, and the circumstances demand it."

Despite the comfort of his words, one question still gnawed at Merona's thoughts.

Murdach's expression darkened, his tone grave. "Armaeus wants to use your power for his own gain. He believes that with your immortality and divine abilities, he can conquer and rule over all the lands."

Merona shivered at the thought of being used as a weapon by someone like Armaeus. "But why me?" she asked, her voice trembling with growing fear.

"Because you were chosen to stop the evil and darkness in the world and restore balance. "Murdach answered with unwavering certainty. "Your powers are unmatched, even among the gods and goddesses."

Merona's mind spun as she tried to process everything she had just learned. "So what do we do now?" she asked, her voice thick with overwhelm.

"We must prepare for battle," Murdach said, his tone resolute. "Armaeus will stop at nothing to control you."

Merona shrugged her shoulders, the weight of doubt pressing on her. "I'm not skilled in battle. I'm no warrior."

Murdach's gaze softened with a mixture of pride and sorrow. "You may not remember it now, but in our past lives, you were a fierce warrior," he said gently. "It's in your blood, my dear."

Merona's eyes widened in disbelief. She couldn't imagine herself as a fierce fighter, let alone a goddess of war.

"But even so," Murdach continued, "I will train you to awaken your dormant powers and help you channel them in battle."

Merona nodded slowly, feeling both afraid and determination swirling inside her. She knew Armaeus was a formidable foe, but she also knew she couldn't let him win.

Murdach's expression darkened at the mention of Armaeus' name. "Armaeus is consumed by his thirst for power and control. He wants to harness your abilities to become unstoppable."

Merona's brow furrowed. "How do you know this?"

"We've faced him before," Murdach replied, his voice heavy with the weight of the past. "In another lifetime, where he succeeded in bringing you under his sway."

A chill crept through Merona's chest at the thought of being controlled by someone as merciless as Armaeus. But the fear was quickly replaced by a surge of resolve. "I won't let him succeed," she said, her voice unwavering.

Murdach's eyes softened, his heart racing as he remembered the passion they had shared across countless lives. He continued to tell her about their shared history, Merona felt the weight of eons settling upon her shoulders.

She closed her eyes, the enormity of their past overwhelming her. "And now?" she asked, her voice barely above a whisper. "What are we now?"

Murdach cupped her face in his hands, his touch igniting a fire deep within her. "Now, my love," he said, his voice filled with the power of the elements he commanded, "we are the guardians of a destiny far greater than this single lifetime. Together, we will confront the darkness that threatens to consume us all."

Merona leaned into his touch, feeling the strength of their bond surge through her.

"Will you hold me?" she asked, her voice trembling with longing, her heart and body aching for his embrace. Murdach's eyes closed in anguish before he took a deep breath and replied, "I have longed for this moment, my love."

As they melted into each other's arms, the world around them blurred into a soft haze. Time seemed to stand still as their bodies intertwined, lost in an ethereal realm of pure passion. The heat of his touch set her soul ablaze, igniting a wildfire of desire that consumed her whole.

In that moment, memories of past lives flooded her, overwhelming her with the depth of their love and connection. They clung to one another, tears streaming down their faces as they mourned the time lost.

"Hold me until dawn breaks," she whispered, unable to bear the thought of being apart again. "Your touch is all I need," she sobbed, clutching him with every fiber of her being. In that moment, nothing else mattered except for the warmth and safety of his embrace, a sanctuary from the chaos of the world.

"For eternity, we are bound together," he declared fiercely, determined never to let her go again. And as they clung to each other, they both knew that even at their very last breaths, they would be together.

As the first rays of sunlight spilled across the floor, Merona knew that no matter what challenges lay ahead, they would face them together, as they always had.

Merona's gaze lingered on his form, stretched out before her in all his breathtaking beauty. His chest rose and fell with each steady breath, a testament to the strength and resolve he carried. In that moment, she understood the immense responsibility he had shouldered to guide her and help her fulfill her destiny. Every line of his face, every scar on his skin, spoke of the sacrifices he had made for her. Deep in her heart, she knew she loved him more than words could ever convey.

"Maidin mhaith, Good morning," Murdach murmured, his eyes fluttering open to meet hers. "Did you sleep well?"

"Better than I have in a long time," Merona admitted, comforted by the security of his presence. She leaned into his embrace, clinging to him as if afraid she might vanish again. Their connection felt like a thread woven through time and space, binding them together for eternity.

Murdach held her close, his heart aching at the raw pain in her voice. He had missed her just as much, if not more, during their time apart. Yet, he knew they couldn't remain lost in each other forever.

"We have to face our destiny," he said softly, breaking the silence between them.

Merona nodded against his chest, knowing he was right. The looming threat of Armaeus and the darkness he carried couldn't be ignored.

With a heavy sigh, she pulled away and met his gaze. "What do we do now?" Her voice trembled with emotion.

"We train," Murdach replied firmly. "We need to awaken your powers and prepare for battle."

Merona took a deep breath and nodded once more. She knew the path ahead wouldn't be easy, but with Murdach by her side, she felt a quiet confidence. His guidance and unwavering support gave her strength, and together, she believed they could overcome any obstacle.

For countless hours, they trained with Morrigan, honing Merona's dormant powers. Murdach pushed her to her limits, yet always made sure to offer her moments of rest. As they worked side by side, their bond only grew stronger and deeper.

Even so, despite their intense training, Merona often felt the weight of their destiny pressing down on her. There were moments when she found herself lost in thought, wondering if they were truly ready for the challenges that lay ahead.

One day, while meditating in a quiet corner of the forest, Merona sensed an unsettling presence creeping up on her. Slowly, she opened her eyes, and there stood Armaeus, a malevolent grin twisting his features.

"So this is where you've been hiding," he sneered.

Merona rose to her feet, her heart pounding as a mix of fear and anger surged through her. "What do you want?" she demanded; her teeth clenched in defiance.

Armaeus' voice dripped with malice. "Join me," he urged. "Together, we can rule the world. Or continue down this futile path of resistance and face your inevitable destruction."

Merona's eyes flashed with defiance as she stared at him. She knew that she would never join forces with someone like him, and that they were destined to defeat him.

"I will never join you," she said firmly, her voice trembling not with fear, but with determination.

Armaeus chuckled darkly, taking a step closer, his shadowy aura encircling her. "Stubborn to the end," he mused. "But it doesn't have to be this way. Think of the power and glory that could be yours as my partner."

Merona felt the weight of Armaeus' words pressing against her, attempting to crack her resolve. But she stood firm, drawing on everything Murdach had taught her about resisting evil.

"You may have power," she said boldly, "but I possess something stronger."

"Love," she added, her voice unwavering.

Armaeus scoffed at her declaration, yet Merona noticed a brief flicker of doubt in his eyes. She knew then that he had never truly known love; it was a concept foreign to him, something he could never grasp.

Before he could respond, Merona felt a surge of energy building up within her. It was unlike anything she had ever felt before – raw power pulsating through every fiber of her being.

With a fierce cry, she unleashed it toward him. The blast hit Armaeus head-on, sending him hurtling backward into the trees.

Breathing heavily, her body trembling from the exertion, Merona watched in awe as Armaeus slowly rose, his fury unmistakable but tinged with something else; perhaps a grudging respect for her strength.

"So be it," he growled, his voice dark with menace, before vanishing in a swirl of smoke.

Merona stood there, feeling the pulse of triumph in her chest. Though the battle was far from over, she had stood her ground and for that, she felt a sense of victory.

She hurried back to Murdach and Morrigan, eager to share what had happened. As soon as Murdach saw her, he pulled her into a tight embrace. "Don't face him alone," he pleaded. "I need you with me for this."

She hugged him tightly, then turned to Morrigan, making a vow to keep them both by her side, no matter what. Together, they would continue their journey to Rennes Gaul, determined to master the element of fire.

Chapter 17

The wind howled through the twisted branches, whipping Merona's raven hair across her face as she pushed up the rocky incline. Her allies trailed closely behind, their cloaks snapping in the fierce gale. The path to Rennes lay before them; a treacherous ribbon twisting through the jagged terrain.

"We must press on," Merona called over her shoulder, her voice steady despite the exhaustion threatening to overtake her. "Rennes awaits, and with it, our destiny."

As they crested the hill, the full fury of the storm hit them. Rain lashed against their faces, sharp as icy needles. Merona squinted into the downpour, her eyes scanning the horizon. A flash of lightning illuminated the sky, revealing the distant silhouette of Rennes.

Murdach, his weathered features etched with concern, moved to her side. "The elements conspire against us, my love. Perhaps we should find shelter and wait for the storm to pass."

Merona shook her head, her resolve firm. "No, Murdach. We cannot afford to delay. Every moment we waste gives Armaeus more time to prepare."

She pressed on, each step sinking her boots deeper into the mud. Her companions followed, their loyalty to her outweighing their discomfort. As they descended into a narrow valley, Merona's thoughts turned inward, the weight of their mission settling heavy on her shoulders.

How many more obstacles would they face before this journey's end? Merona wondered, the weight of her destiny pressing down on her like an unbearable burden. It was heavier than any physical load, yet she refused to falter, drawing strength from the very earth beneath her feet.

Suddenly, the air shifted. The wind ceased, replaced by an unnatural stillness that sent a chill through her. Merona froze, her senses sharpening at the shift in atmosphere. Dark clouds, tinged with an eerie green, began to gather overhead.

"Do you feel that?" she whispered to Murdach. her voice tight with apprehension.

The old mentor nodded grimly. "Aye, my love. The very air crackles with malevolence. Armaeus is near."

As if on cue, a bolt of crimson lightning sliced through the sky, followed by a deafening thunderclap. The clouds swirled ominously, twisting into a vortex directly above them.

Merona's heart raced, but she fought against the fear threatening to overwhelm her. "We knew this wouldn't be easy," she said, her voice strong and steady, carrying to all her companions. "But we are stronger together. Whatever Armaeus throws at us, we will face it head-on."

She raised her hand, feeling the elemental energies coursing through her veins. The air hummed with power, both light and dark, as two great forces prepared to collide. Merona took a deep breath, readying herself for the battle to come.

"For the future," she murmured, her eyes fixed on the storm-tossed sky. "For all those who will come after us. We cannot fail."

With those words, Merona steeled herself and led her allies forward into the heart of the gathering darkness. The fate of Rennes and perhaps the world hung in the balance as they marched on, undeterred by the storm that loomed ahead.

Without warning, the ground beneath them trembled violently, and the air thickened with the acrid scent of sulfur and smoke. In an instant, a perfect circle of hellfire erupted around them, its flames reaching greedily for the sky. Merona's eyes widened in terror as the fire consumed their only escape routes, turning them into an inferno of blazing orange and deep crimson. The roar of the flames was deafening, drowning out all other sounds and sending waves of heat crashing over them. It felt as if they had been swallowed by the very depths of hell.

"We're trapped," she breathed, her voice barely audible over the deafening blaze.

From the dark recesses of the inferno, Armaeus appeared, as though materializing from the very shadows. His piercing crimson eyes gleamed with a malevolent victory. Behind him, his horde of demons loomed, grotesque and contorted, their bodies pulsating with eager anticipation. Their claws clicked together in a rhythmic, unsettling pattern as they awaited their master's command. The air around them grew colder, the flames flickering in uneasy response to their presence. The stench of sulfur and decay filled the air, a tangible aura of evil and malice that weighed heavily on all who stood before it.

"Did you truly believe you could challenge me, little witch?" Armaeus' voice echoed, dripping with contempt. "Your journey ends here."

Merona's fists tightened at her sides, her resolve battling the fear that threatened to overwhelm her. She met the eyes of her companions, seeing the same blend of determination and terror reflected in their faces.

"We won't go down without a fight," she declared, her voice more confident than she felt.

A low growl echoed in her mind, and Merona turned to see Morrigan, the majestic red wolf, padding towards her. The goddess's amber eyes locked with hers, filled with centuries of wisdom and power.

"Merona," Morrigan's voice resonated in her thoughts, *"you must have faith in yourself now. Draw upon the element of Fire. It lies within you, waiting to be unleashed."*

Merona furrowed her brow in confusion. "But how? The flames surround us, threatening to consume everything."

"The very force he uses to trap you can be your salvation," Morrigan replied. *"Remember your training. Remember who you are."*

As Armaeus and his demons closed in, Merona closed her eyes to center herself amidst the chaos. She felt the searing heat of the flames, heard their crackling fury. But instead of succumbing to fear, she focused on drawing strength from the raw power around her.

'I am Merona,' her inner voice grew steadier, fiercer. 'I am the one foretold. I will not be defeated here.'

Her eyes snapped open, blazing with newfound determination. The air around her shimmered, the oppressive heat of Armaeus' fire transmuting into a different kind of warmth; one that radiated from the depths of her soul.

"I feel it," she whispered, her voice almost lost in the roar of the flames. "The fire... it's calling to me."

Murdach, his weathered face etched with worry, moved closer. "Focus, lass. Let it flow through you, but don't let it consume you."

Merona nodded, her raven hair whipping wildly in the wind as she extended her hands, palms outward. The fire, which had moments before threatened to engulf them, now seemed to respond to her, curious tendrils of flame licking her fingertips without burning.

"Goddess Brigid," Merona intoned, her voice gaining strength with each word. "Goddess of Fire, I call upon your strength."

The air hummed with raw energy, and for a brief, dizzying moment, Merona thought she glimpsed a flash of red hair and fierce, fiery eyes within the heart of the flames. Was it her imagination, or had Brigid herself answered her call?

"What's happening?" one of her companions asked, their voice trembling with a mixture of awe and fear.

Merona didn't respond. She couldn't. Every fiber of her being was focused on the fire flowing through her veins; a torrent of raw power that threatened to consume her. But she held firm, drawing strength from Murdach's teachings and Morrigan's unwavering faith in her.

"I am the vessel," she thought, her inner voice calm and resolute amidst the storm of energy swirling around her. "I am the conduit between the old world and the new. And I will not fail."

As the flames danced and crackled around her, Merona felt a subtle shift in the air; a disruption in the very fabric of reality. The fire was no longer merely an element; it had become an extension of herself; a force she could command to shape the world according to her will.

In that moment, with Armaeus and his demonic horde before her, Merona knew she was ready to fight back.

Her eyes blazed with an inner fire as she raised her hands, palms outward. The flames responded to her command, swirling with newfound intensity, her voice cutting through the roar of the inferno. *"Bríde, tine agus beatha, tabhair an chumhacht dom an lasair a rialú.* Brigid, of fire and life, grant me the power to command the flames!"

Morrigan's voice resonated in her mind: *"You are the spark of change, Merona. Let your will be known."*

"Flame of passion, of life, and of new beginnings," she intoned, her words imbued with power. The fire formed intricate patterns around her, moving with purpose, as though alive.

Merona inhaled deeply, the heat of the flames surging through her veins. She fixed her gaze on Armaeus, his twisted demonic form snarling in hatred and fear.

"I call upon you to destroy and burn away anything that hinders my true will," she commanded, her voice resolute and unwavering.

The fire responded instantly, surging forward in a brilliant wave. Merona felt its raw power, a force brimming with both destruction and renewal.

This is it, she thought, her heart pounding. This is what I was born to do.

As the flames raced towards their targets, Merona steeled herself for what was to come. The battle was far from over, but for the first time since this nightmare began, she truly believed victory was within reach.

"Spirit of Fire, Spirit of Force, I call upon you now! *A Spioraid Tine, Spiorad na Fórsa, glaoim ort anois."* Merona cried out, her voice resonating with a power that seemed to shake the very earth beneath her feet.

The air around her crackled with energy, sparks dancing at the edges of her vision. Then, a surge of heat unlike anything she had ever felt washed over her, and her raven hair whipped around her face as an unseen force lifted her from the ground.

This is it, she thought, a mixture of awe and terror coursing through her. *The true test of my destiny.*

Flames erupted from nowhere, engulfing her entire body. Yet, miraculously, they did not burn. Instead, they seemed to caress her skin, like the touch of a lover; warm, comforting, and all-consuming.

"Merona!" Murdach's voice broke through, thick with concern. "Are you alright?"

She wanted to reassure him, but the words wouldn't come. The fire consumed her, not in a physical sense, but spiritually. It felt as though every fiber of her being was being reforged in the heat of its crucible.

I am the flame, Merona realized with wonder.. *And the flame is me.*

As she hovered above the ground, wrapped in her fiery cocoon, she saw Armaeus and his demons' recoil. Their eyes, once gleaming with malevolent glee, now held the first glimmers of fear.

Good, she thought, a grim smile tugging at her lips. *Let them know what true power feels like.*

With a deep breath, Merona extended her hands, palms facing outward. The flames surrounding her responded instantly, gathering into a swirling vortex between her outstretched fingers. She focused her will, shaping the fire into a pulsing sphere of blinding heat and light.

"By the goddess Brigid," she whispered, her voice steady and resonant with newfound power, "I will not falter."

The fireball swelled, feeding on Merona's determination. Sweat beaded on her brow as she poured more of herself into the blazing orb. Its core blazed white-hot, surrounded by writhing layers of orange and red flames that danced like living things.

Murdach's voice cut through her concentration, filled with concern. "Merona, be careful! Don't lose yourself to the fire's hunger!"

She gritted her teeth, fighting to maintain control. "I won't, Murdach. This is my destiny. I can feel it."

The heat intensified, becoming almost unbearable. Merona's arms trembled, straining to contain the raw power she had summoned. In her mind's eye, she saw the faces of those who had suffered at the hands of Armaeus and his minions; the innocent victims of witch hunts yet to come.

For them, she thought fiercely. *For all of us who have been persecuted and misunderstood.*

The fireball pulsed in sync with her emotions, growing ever brighter. She infused it with her purpose, her unwavering desire to protect the vulnerable and alter the course of history. The destructive potential within the sphere built with each passing second, ready to be unleashed at her command.

"This ends now," Merona declared, her voice ringing with authority. The fireball crackled ominously, a harbinger of the devastation to come.

Armaeus' eyes narrowed, their crimson depths flickering with a mixture of rage and unease. His demons shifted uneasily, their shadows elongating in the flickering firelight, sensing as they sensed the growing threat. The air crackled with tension, thick with the acrid scent of brimstone and fear.

"You dare challenge me, child?" Armaeus snarled, his voice a guttural rumble that shook the very earth beneath them. "I am eternal. I am darkness incarnate!"

Merona stood her ground, the fireball pulsing between her palms. Her raven hair lashed around her face, whipped by the unseen currents of power swirling around her. "No more, Armaeus. Your reign of terror ends here."

The demon lord's laughter rang out, an eerie sound that sent a chill deep into the bones of mortals. Yet Merona remained unmoved, her eyes blazing with an inner fire that mirrored the inferno she commanded.

I am not afraid, she thought, steeling herself for the battle ahead. *I am the flame that burns away the darkness. I am the hope of generations yet unborn.*

With a primal cry that seemed to rip from the depths of her soul, *"Bríde, tine agus beatha, tabhair an chumhacht dom an lasair a rialú!* Brigid, of fire and life, grant me the power to command the flames!"

Merona thrust her arms forward. The fireball launched from her hands, a comet of vengeance streaking toward its target. Time slowed as the projectile arced through the air, bearing the heavy weight of destiny.

Armaeus' smirk faltered, his eyes widening in growing realization. "Impossible," he breathed, as the fireball hurtled inexorably towards him and his demonic horde with unstoppable force.

The fireball streaked through the night, a blazing meteor of retribution. Its searing heat left the air shimmering in its wake, warping the very fabric of reality around its incandescent form. Merona watched, heart pounding, as her creation illuminated the darkness, casting long, dancing shadows across the battlefield.

"By the gods," Murdach whispered beside her, his eyes wide with awe. "You've done it, Merona. You've harnessed the power of Fire itself."

Merona couldn't respond, her focus fixed entirely on the fireball's trajectory. Time seemed to stretch, each second an eternity, as the blazing sphere closed in on Armaeus and his demonic legion.

Please, she prayed silently. *Let this be enough.*

The moment of impact came with a deafening roar. The fireball collided with the demons, exploding in a cataclysmic burst that lit the night like a second sun. Flames engulfed Armaeus and his minions, their agonized screams rising above the inferno.

"No!" Armaeus howled, his voice nearly lost in the roar of the flames. "This cannot be!"

Merona stood transfixed, watching as the flames consumed her enemies. The heat was intense, even from a distance, and sweat beaded on her brow.

"Is it over?" she whispered, more to herself than anyone else. "Have we won?"

Murdach placed a comforting hand on her shoulder. "Not yet my dear. But you've struck a mighty blow. Armaeus won't soon forget this night."

As the screams faded and the flames began to die down, Merona felt a mixture of exhilaration and exhaustion. wash over her. She had done it. She had faced her greatest fear and emerged victorious. But deep down, she knew this was only the beginning of her journey.

As the inferno subsided, Merona stood amidst the charred remnants of their enemies, the acrid scent of burnt flesh stinging her nostrils. Her heart raced as she surveyed the devastation, a mix of triumph and trepidation weighing heavily on her.

"Murdach," she called, her voice hoarse from the smoke. "We must contain this fire before it spreads."

The silver-haired warrior nodded, his eyes reflecting the dying embers. "Indeed. Your mastery over fire is impressive, but we mustn't let it harm the innocent."

Without hesitation, they moved swiftly. Merona extended her hands, focusing on drawing the flames back into herself. She could feel the heat pulsing through her veins, a constant reminder of the raw power now at her command.

"The forest," Murdach warned, pointing to where sparks threatened to ignite the dry underbrush.

Merona's brow furrowed in concentration. "I see it."

With a graceful sweep of her arm, she gathered the errant flames, pulling them away from the trees and condensing them into a tight ball of fire hovering above her palm. The effort left her breathless, but she refused to falter.

"How are you feeling?" Murdach asked, his concern evident.

Merona managed a weak smile. "Alive. More alive than I've ever felt before." Her expression shifted to something more serious. "But also... scared. This power, Murdach. It's overwhelming."

As they worked to extinguish the last of the flames, the ring of fire that had trapped them began to flicker and fade. Merona watched in awe as the barrier dissolved, leaving only smoldering embers and the faint scent of victory in the air.

"You've done it, Merona," Murdach said softly, pride lacing his voice. "Your mastery over fire is complete."

Merona nodded, her raven hair catching the fading light. "But at what cost?" she wondered aloud, her eyes sweeping over the scorched earth. "And what battles still lie ahead?"

She slumped against a nearby tree, heavy with exhaustion. The adrenaline from the battle was ebbing away, leaving her limbs leaden and her mind racing. She took a deep breath, the scent of ash and burned earth filling her lungs.

"We should rest," Murdach said, his weathered face marked with concern. "You've expended much energy."

Merona nodded, her gaze fixed on the horizon. "Just... just for a moment," she agreed, her voice barely a whisper. As her eyes closed, the weight of their journey pressed upon her. "Murdach," she began, hesitation coloring her words, "do you think we're ready for what's to come?"

Murdach settled beside her, his presence a comforting anchor. "Ready or not, destiny marches on," he replied, his tone gentle but firm. "But you, Merona, have shown tremendous growth. Your control over fire today was... remarkable."

A small smile tugged at Merona's lips, though it didn't reach her eyes. "It felt... right. Like the flames were an extension of myself. But also terrifying. So much power, so much potential for destruction."

As they rested, the landscape around them seemed to breathe a sigh of relief. The charred earth softened, tiny shoots of green pushing through the ash. Merona watched in awe as nature began to reclaim what had been lost.

"Look," she whispered, pointing to a delicate fern unfurling nearby. "Life finds a way, doesn't it?"

Murdach nodded with quiet wisdom. "The world is resilient, Merona. As are you. Remember that in the trials to come."

Merona stood, brushing off her clothes. The weight of destiny settled on her shoulders once again, but this time it felt less like a burden and more like a purpose. "We should move on," she said, her voice stronger now. "Rennes awaits, and with it, our next challenge."

As they resumed their journey, Merona marveled at the transformation around them. Where there had once been devastation, now there was renewal. It filled her with hope, a flickering flame in the uncertainty ahead.

Merona's raven-black hair shimmered in the fading light as she crested a small hill. The path ahead stretched long and winding, disappearing into the mist where Rennes awaited. A cool breeze brushed her face, carrying with it the scent of damp earth and possibility.

"We're close now," she murmured, more to herself than to her companions. "I can feel it."

Murdach stepped up beside her, his weathered face marked with concern. "Aye, but remember, lass. The closer we get, the greater the danger."

Merona turned to her mentor, a spark of defiance in her eyes. "I'm ready for whatever comes, Murdach. The fire within me burns brighter than ever."

She paused, her gaze drifting inward as she reflected on the journey that had led her here. From the flames of her execution in Copenhagen to her rebirth in this ancient time, every step had brought her closer to this defining moment.

"Do you think..." she hesitated, her voice faltering for a moment, "do you think I can truly change the course of history? Save all those witches from persecution?"

Murdach's expression softened with a quiet understanding. "I believe you have the power to reshape the very fabric of time,

Merona. But remember, with great power comes great responsibility."

Merona nodded, her jaw set with unwavering determination. "I won't let fear hold me back. Not when so much is at stake."

As they continued their journey, the landscape seemed to echo Merona's growing resolve. The earth, once scorched, was now bursting with new life, delicate wildflowers marking the path ahead. It was as though nature itself was cheering them on, offering a quiet, persistent hope in the face of darkness.

"Each step brings us closer to our destiny," Merona said, her voice steady with quiet strength. "And with it, the chance to bring about a new era of peace and renewal."

Chapter 18

Before Merona stood the mighty Rhone River, its waters a deep, ink-black expanse that churned and roared with a power all its own. The current surged relentlessly, carrying with it the weight of ancient secrets and untold stories from centuries past. She stood at the precipice, her eyes reflecting the tumultuous flow below. The burden of destiny pressed heavily upon her shoulders, a mantle she had borne ever since that fateful Samhain night when her mysterious arrival had set everything into motion. As she gazed out at the river, its immense power and deep history seemed to pulse through her, reminding her that she was part of something much larger than herself.

Her midnight-black hair whipped wildly around her face, tangled by the fierce gusts of wind. Despite the chaos of the elements, Merona remained resolute, her gaze unwavering as she stared into the river's dark depths. "Water," she murmured, her voice almost lost to the roar of the current. "You are the element of life and death, invoked by my ancestors for generations untold." Her words mingled with the rushing water, blending as if the river itself was listening. The air crackled with unseen energy as she raised her arms, calling upon the power of ancient rites.

Standing at the water's edge, arms lifted high in supplication, the air around her hummed with potent magic. Her body tingled with the charge of unseen forces, a reminder of the immense power that flowed through her veins. With her eyes closed, Merona focused on the deep well of magic within her, drawing upon its vast reserves to fuel her next move. Her body tingled with anticipation as she prepared to wield this extraordinary power over the water.

"Am I truly ready for this?" A fleeting doubt flickered in her mind, threatening to undermine her focus. She quickly dismissed it. "No," she whispered inwardly. "I must be. Too much depends on it."

With a steady breath, Merona's voice rose, ancient and commanding, weaving through the air. The words flowed from her lips like a river, steeped in the power of countless generations of witches. Each syllable carried the weight of her ancestors, a direct link to the very fabric of reality, bridging the divide between the mortal realm and the realm of magic.

"*Tiarnas Uisce*! Dominion of Water, I command thee! By the Cauldron of Dagda, source of plenty," she intoned, her voice gathering strength with each word. "I call upon the spirits of water to heed my will."

As she spoke, energy crackled around her, swirling like a storm summoned by her command. The air itself seemed to hum with power, responding to her summoning, bending to her will.

The river's gentle flow stilled, as if the very waters were drawn in by Merona's invocation. A surge of raw, untamed energy coursed through her veins, electric and alive. Her thoughts flickered to Anna, to the image of her past self-consumed by the flames in Copenhagen. A fire ignited within her, burning with fierce resolve. "Never again," she whispered, the words lost in the rush of water, but her intent was clear. "I will alter our destiny." The air around her seemed to vibrate with magic possibility, as if the very forces of nature themselves had rallied to her side.

As Merona's chant reached its powerful crescendo, her eyes fluttered open. The world around her shimmered and twisted, bending to the strength of her magic. No longer standing on the muddy riverbank, she was now poised upon the surface of the water itself. Her feet hovered just above the flowing current, supported by a faint blue aura, as though the river itself had chosen to bear her weight. Gentle ripples lapped at her ankles, sending electric shivers up her spine. The power coursing through her veins was undeniable, connecting her to the very elements and giving her dominion over them. This was only a glimpse of her potential, and she longed to explore the full extent of her abilities.

The words slipped from her lips in a soft exhale, tinged with awe and determination. "It's working," she whispered, her voice thick with emotion. "Now, to truly master this element and carve the path to our destiny."

As she spoke, Merona sensed a shift in the water around her, responding to the magic within her. With every powerful word, with every movement of her hands, she felt her connection to the element deepen. The road ahead would be fraught with peril, filled with challenges both visible and hidden. Yet, standing on the mighty Rhone, Merona knew she was closer than ever to fulfilling the prophecy that had brought her back through time.

The sun kissed the river's surface, casting shimmering reflections onto the trees that lined its banks. A gentle breeze stirred the leaves, carrying the faint scent of moss and wildflowers. In this moment, surrounded by the elements and the forces of destiny, Merona felt truly alive; empowered, and ready for whatever lay ahead.

The once-calm surface of the Rhone began to churn, its placid waters transformed into a wild, swirling dance of eddies and rippling waves. Merona's raven-black hair whipped violently around her face as the river responded to her summons, its essence seeming to reach out to her like a living creature. The sound of rushing water grew louder as Merona's voice carried over it, her words an ancient incantation that echoed through the surrounding mountains.

With commanding and powerful voice, Merona intoned the ancient pact that bound her to the elements. " *Eirigh agus éist le mo thoil, uiscí na Rón.* Rise and heed my will, waters of the Rhone," she called, her words reverberating like a spell. In response, the river surged, crashing against the banks, and sending sprays of water high into the air.

She stood at the center of it all, her dark hair whipping wildly as she harnessed the raw power of the elements. The air crackled with electricity, and she felt the pulse of energy rushing through her veins. Though she had never attempted such a feat before, Merona felt an undeniable connection to something greater than herself; the very forces of nature. It was both intoxicating and terrifying, but her focus remained sharp as she wielded the raging waters with effortless grace.

"Is this what true mastery feels like?" she thought, her eyes wide with awe.

Unaware of the danger lurking in the shadows, Merona continued to command the waters with confidence. But hidden from her sight, Armaeus watched intently, his eyes burning with a fury that could not be contained. His hatred simmered beneath the surface, and with a feral snarl, he spoke in a voice laced with a guttural rasp that seemed to freeze the air around him. "This cannot be allowed," he growled, his eyes glowing with an otherworldly intensity. With a swift, menacing gesture, he raised his clawed hand, and dark magic began to gather, swirling around him like a malevolent storm, ready to unleash its wrath upon the world. The energy crackled and swirled around him, like a malevolent storm gathering strength.

As though summoned from the depths of the Rhone, twisted and grotesque shapes emerged from the water, their forms writhing and pulsing with an unholy energy. With a hiss and gurgled as they surged toward Merona, their fluid bodies contorting into monstrous forms that seemed to defy logic. An eerie blue-green glow emanating from them, casting an otherworldly light upon the surrounding waters, and deepening the terror of their presence. Like creatures from a nightmare, they oozed and slithered toward her, leaving a trail of slimy residue in their wake. Merona could only watch in horror as these abominations, formed from the very element she sought to control, closed in on her. Their intentions were unclear but one thing was certain, they were malevolent.

"What in the name of the Morrigan?" Merona gasped, her concentration faltering as she caught sight of the approaching monsters. She could feel the taint of Armaeus upon them, a dark corruption that twisted the very element of water she had sought to master.

A quickening pulse thudded in Merona's chest, but she refused to let fear weaken her resolve. She shut her eyes, drawing deeply from the wellspring of power within her, feeling it surge through her veins like liquid fire. When she opened them again, her gaze burned with unyielding determination.

"I will not falter," she whispered, her voice carrying the ancient weight of prophecies and legacies. "Water, heed my call. Rise and protect!" Her words became tangible, a force of energy that manifested as her outstretched hand glowed with a pulsating blue light. The air around her crackled with electricity, and the sounds of roaring waves could be heard in the distance. Merona stood tall, fierce and resolute, ready for whatever challenge lay ahead.

With graceful, fluid movements, Merona commanded the river to bend to her will. The Rhone responded immediately, its once gentle waters now surging upward in a great, swirling dome that encased her completely. The powerful barrier shimmered with an otherworldly light, pulsing, and rippling like a living entity. Armaeus' monstrous creations crashed against it with all their might, but they were no match for the force of the river under Merona's command. The sound of rushing water filled the air, mingling with the cracking of bones and the roars of frustration from the defeated creatures.

From within her aqueous sanctuary, Merona watched as the creatures clawed and gnashed at the barrier, their efforts futile against her newfound mastery. A small, satisfied smile played at the corners of her lips.

"Is this the best you can muster, Armaeus?" she thought, her inner voice laced with defiance that even surprised her. "I've faced worse in my nightmares."

In a split second, the peaceful night air was shattered by an ear-piercing howl that sent chills down their spines. The Morrigan, her crimson fur gleaming like molten lava in the moon's pale light, erupted from the shadows in a frenzy of feral energy. Her powerful wolf form moved with lethal grace, lunging at Armaeus' water creatures, her sharp teeth bared in a menacing snarl. Another ferocious roar tore through the air. Her eyes, glowing with divine amber fire, radiated fury and power as she unleashed her wrath upon her enemies.

Merona watched in awe as the Morrigan fought alongside her, their combined strength creating a devastating force against Armaeus' minions. Together, they were unstoppable.

The goddess's power crackled through the air, manifesting as lightning bolts that streaked down with pinpoint accuracy, striking Armaeus' creatures one by one. The ground trembled under the weight of her fury as wave after wave of energy erupted from her, searing through the night like a comet blazing across the sky.

It was a sight that both terrified and awed anyone who witnessed it; a true display of the goddess's fearsome might. Merona felt her own power surge, strengthened by the Morrigan's presence, their energies intertwining and amplifying each other in a storm of unstoppable force.

With a final surge of strength, Merona summoned every last drop of power within her, channeling it into one last wave of magical energy. The barrier around them exploded outward in a brilliant burst of light and sound, sending Armaeus' minions flying back with a deafening roar.

In that fleeting moment, time seemed to slow. Merona and the Morrigan stood side by side amidst the chaos they had wrought, upon their enemies. For what felt like an eternity, they locked eyes and shared an unspoken understanding that went beyond words or mortal comprehension.

But even as their victory seemed imminent, Armaeus emerged from the shadows once more, his form now towering over them. He let out a blood-curdling laugh that reverberated through the night air like a death knell.

"You may have defeated my minions," he sneered, "but you are no match for me."

As the storm raged around them, Merona and the Morrigan braced themselves for the final showdown. The god of water had bent the elements to his will, and it seemed their victory was slipping from their grasp.

But Merona would not relent. She gathered the last of her energy, unleashing a powerful beam of light that struck Armaeus with blinding force, temporarily weakening him. The Morrigan seized the opportunity, pouncing with deadly speed, her claws tearing through his watery form.

Just when it seemed they were gaining ground, Armaeus let out a roar that shook the very earth beneath them. A powerful surge of water rushed towards them, threatening to engulf Merona and the Morrigan in its icy, suffocating grip.

With no time to hesitate, Merona called upon the last of her strength, conjuring a shield of pure energy around herself and the Morrigan. Together, they braced against the rushing tide, pushing back against it with all their might.

As they fought back against Armaeus' onslaught, Merona felt the bond between her and the Morrigan deepen, an unbreakable unity born from their shared purpose. They were unwavering in their resolve, determined to defeat this god of water.

Finally, after what felt like an eternity, Armaeus' strength faltered. With a final, defiant roar, he vanished into thin air, defeated by the combined might of Merona and the Morrigan.

Exhausted but victorious, Merona collapsed to her knees, allowing her power to fade. The storm dissipated as quickly as it had arrived, leaving only an eerie silence in its wake.

The Morrigan in her human form, approached Merona slowly, extending her hand to help her rise. As Merona took the goddess's hand, they both stood for a moment in quiet solidarity, their gazes sweeping over the devastation they had wrought. The air, still heavy with the remnants of magic, hummed with the weight of their victory. In that instant, they both knew they had triumphed.

Merona's eyes glimmered with newfound determination as she stretched her arms wide, her palms facing downward. She felt the pulse of the river beneath her feet, the rhythmic heartbeat of the Rhone calling to her. With a deep, steadying breath, she began to weave the currents into a complex, deliberate pattern.

"Flow with me, *Sreabhadh liom*" she murmured, her voice carrying the weight of ancient incantations. "Show me the way."

The water responded with a graceful dance, swirling and churning until it formed a shimmering path that stretched across the surface of the river. Merona took a tentative step forward, her breath catching as the liquid solidified beneath her feet like solid stone.

"Impossible!" Armaeus' voice thundered from the shadows, seething with venom. "You cannot master the elements so quickly!"

Merona allowed herself a small, triumphant smile. "Perhaps you underestimate me, demon," she called out, her voice steady even as her heart raced in her chest.

With each cautious step, Merona moved farther across the river. But even as the water held her, her mind raced. *Is this truly my destiny? To walk upon water and face such ancient evil?*

Without warning, the air grew thick, pressing down with an oppressive darkness. Armaeus materialized from the shadows, his crimson eyes blazing with unrestrained fury. A guttural roar rumbled from his chest as he thrust his hands toward the river.

"You think you've won, witch?" he snarled, his voice dripping with malice. "Let's see how you fare against the very forces you claim to control!"

The water beneath Merona's feet began to writhe and churn violently, as if enraged by the god's command. In an instant, a massive whirlpool formed, its spiraling maw threatening to pull her under. Merona's eyes widened in alarm as the force of the vortex clawed at her.

"No," she whispered, barely audible above the furious roar of the waters. "I will not be defeated so easily."

With a swift, graceful motion of her hand, Merona channeled her power into the violent waters. " An t-oighear, Glacies!" she commanded, her voice sharp and full of authority. The air crackled with energy as the whirlpool, once a liquid deathtrap, began to crystallize. Slowly, it transformed into a towering pillar of ice, its jagged edges gleaming in the dim light.

Armaeus howled in frustration, his demonic features contorting with rage. "You little witch!" he bellowed. "How dare you defy me?"

Merona stood atop the frozen column. She felt the raw power coursing through her veins, a testament to her growing mastery over the elements. "I dare because it is my destiny, Armaeus," she replied, her voice calm yet resolute. "Your darkness cannot overcome the light within me."

As she spoke, Merona raised her arms once more, her palms facing the turbulent river. Closing her eyes, she drew deeply from the well of ancient knowledge that Murdach had imparted to her. The incantation flowed from her lips, each syllable resonating with power and purpose.

"*Uisce na beatha, uisce íon,*" she intoned, her voice growing stronger with each word. "Cleanse this river, restore its spirit. Let the waters flow free and untainted by evil."

The air around her shimmered as the river responded to her call. For a moment, doubt flickered in Merona's mind. *Is this truly happening?* she thought, a mix of awe and determination in her heart. *Am I really capable of such feats?*

As if in response to her unspoken question, the waters of the Rhone began to glow with an ethereal light. The once murky depths cleared, revealing sparkling sand and smooth river stones beneath. Fish darted through the newly purified currents, their scales shimmering in the moonlight.

Armaeus, still seething with fury, spat, "This isn't over, Merona. Your little tricks won't save you from what's to come!"

Merona opened her eyes and met the demon's glare with steady resolve. "Perhaps not," she replied, her voice a blend of weariness and determination. "But your threats will not deter me from my path. This river now stands as a testament to the power of renewal, Armaeus. Remember that."

The Rhone River, once a churning maelstrom of Armaeus' fury, now flowed with a tranquil grace that belied its recent turmoil. Moonlight danced across its surface, casting rippling silver patterns that seemed to whisper ancient secrets. Merona stood at the water's edge, her raven hair billowing in the gentle breeze, her cerulean eyes reflecting the newfound serenity of the river.

"It's beautiful," she murmured, her voice barely above a whisper. A sense of accomplishment washed over her, mingling with a deep exhaustion that threatened to overwhelm her senses.

Taking a tentative step toward the riverbank, her legs trembled beneath her. The magnitude of her achievement crashed over her like a wave. *Have I truly mastered this element?* she wondered, her mind reeling with the weight of it.

"Well done, child," came Murdach's gruff voice from behind her. "You've shown remarkable control."

Merona turned to face her mentor, a small smile playing at the corners of her lips. "I couldn't have done it without your teachings, Murdach. But tell me, will this be enough to face what's coming?"

His eyes darkened, his weathered face etched with concern. "The path before you is treacherous, Merona. Your mastery of water is but one step on a long journey."

She nodded, her gaze drifting back to the calm waters. "I understand. But for now, let us appreciate this moment of peace. It feels like a lifetime since we've known such tranquility."

As she stepped onto the riverbank, her connection to the water element hummed within her veins, a constant reminder of the power she now wielded. The weight of her destiny pressed heavily upon her shoulders, yet she stood tall, ready to face whatever challenges awaited on the road to Paris and beyond.

A guttural roar of rage echoed through the night, causing Merona to whirl around. Armaeus' demonic form flickered, at the edge of her vision, his crimson eyes burning with hatred.

"This isn't over, witch," he snarled, his voice dripping with venom. "Your destiny will crumble, and I'll be there to watch you fall."

Merona's heart raced, but her voice remained steady. "Your threats are as empty as your soul, Armaeus. Retreat now, while you still can."

The demon's form began to dissipate, melting into the darkness. "I'll find another way," he hissed. "Mark my words, your journey ends in flames."

As Armaeus vanished, Merona let out a shaky breath. The Morrigan, still in her wolf form, padded silently to her side.

"He grows desperate," Merona murmured, her fingers trailing through the wolf's fur. "What do you think his next move will be?"

The Morrigan's amber eyes locked with Merona's, and a voice echoed softly in her mind. *"The desperate are often the most dangerous. We must remain vigilant."*

Merona nodded, turning her gaze back to the now-calm Rhone. Moonlight danced on its surface, casting a serene glow that contrasted sharply with the chaos of the battle they had just endured. She closed her eyes, feeling the gentle pulse of the water element flow through her veins.

"It's beautiful," she whispered, more to herself than to the Morrigan. "To think, just moments ago, this river was a maelstrom of chaos."

The young witch's thoughts drifted to the long road ahead. How many more battles would she face? How many more elements would she need to master before she could truly fulfill her destiny?

"We've come so far," Merona said, her voice tinged with both pride and weariness. "Yet, I can't shake the feeling that our greatest challenges still lie ahead."

The Morrigan's voice resonated once again in her mind. *"The path of destiny is never easy, child. But remember, you do not walk it alone."*

Merona smiled softly, drawing strength from the words. She took a deep breath, savoring the moment of peace while steeling herself for the trials ahead. The tranquil river before her was both a testament to her growing power and a reminder of the delicate balance she sought to maintain.

"Come," she said to the Morrigan, her voice now laced with renewed determination. "We have much ground to cover, and time waits for no one – not even a witch born out of time."

The winding road stretched before Merona, a serpentine path cutting through the heart of Gaul. Six long years had passed since she first left Septimania, each step drawing her closer to an uncertain destiny. The weight of time pressed heavily upon her, but she pressed forward, the Morrigan a silent guardian at her side.

"Paris," Merona murmured, letting the name roll on her tongue. "To think, we journey to meet a king."

The Morrigan's eyes glinted in the fading light. *"Clovis is more than a king, child. He carries the blood of the Merovingians, touched by ancient magic."*

Merona's brow furrowed. "And what of his conversion to Christianity? Will that not conflict with the old ways?"

A low growl rumbled in the goddess's throat. "That remains to be seen. The threads of fate are tangled, and even I cannot see their full design."

As they crested a hill, Merona paused, her eyes sweeping across the landscape. The setting sunbathed the sky in hues of crimson and gold, casting long shadows across the rolling fields. In the distance, wisps of smoke rose from scattered villages; reminders of the human lives teetering in the balance of her quest.

"Sometimes," Merona confessed, her voice barely a whisper, "I wonder if I'm truly ready for what lies ahead. Six years of training, and still I feel... incomplete."

The Morrigan's form shimmered, transforming into that of a raven perched on a nearby branch. *"Doubt is the shadow cast by courage, Merona. It is not weakness to question, but strength to persist in spite of those questions."*

Merona nodded, absentmindedly tracing the labyrinth birthmark on her shoulder. "And what of Armaeus? I can feel his presence, like a storm gathering on the horizon."

The raven's eyes gleamed with an ancient knowing. "He bides his time, gathering his strength. But so too have you grown stronger. Remember the Rhone, child. Remember the power that flows through your veins."

With a deep breath, Merona squared her shoulders and resumed her journey. The road to Paris stretched before her, long and uncertain, each step drawing her closer to Clovis, to destiny, and to the looming confrontation that would shape the fate of Gaul itself.

ACT III

THE LABYRINTH AWAITS

"Things outside you are projections of what's inside you, and what's inside you is a projection of what's outside. So when you step into the labyrinth outside you, at the same time you're stepping into the labyrinth inside."

Haruki Murakami

Chapter 19

Merona stood atop the windswept hill, her raven hair whipping around her face as she gazed at the distant silhouette of Paris. The city loomed on the horizon, a dark promise of intertwined destiny and danger. Six long years had passed since she and Murdach began their journey, tracing the points of the pentacle etched across the land of Gaul. Fire, air, earth, and water; she had embraced them all, their elemental powers now coursing through her veins.

"We're almost there," Murdach's deep voice rumbled beside her. His eyes met hers, a tempest of emotions swirling in their depths.

Merona's heart quickened. "So much has changed since we began," she murmured, her voice laced with both wonder and trepidation.

She thought back to the frightened girl she had been, thrust into a world of magic and prophecy. Now, she stood tall, a woman grown, her eyes holding the wisdom of ages past and the weight of futures yet to unfold.

Murdach's hand found hers, his touch igniting the familiar spark that danced along her skin. "You've come so far, mo chridhe," he said softly. "Your strength never ceases to amaze me."

Merona leaned into him, savoring his warmth. "It's because of you," she whispered. "Your guidance, your protection... your love."

The word lingered between them, heavy with unspoken longing. Merona felt heat rise in her cheeks, her body acutely aware of Murdach's closeness. She knew their time together was fleeting, a cruel twist of fate that bound their hearts to a collision course with destiny.

"Murdach," she began, her voice thick with emotion, "I know we can't…"

He silenced her with a gentle finger to her lips. "Shh, mo ghrádh. Let us not dwell on what cannot be. We have this moment, here and now."

Merona nodded, blinking back tears, and turned her gaze back to Paris, steeling herself for the trials ahead. "Do you think we're ready?" she asked, voicing the doubt that had plagued her throughout their journey.

Murdach's arm tightened around her waist. "You are more ready than you know," he assured her. "The elements have blessed you with their power, but your true strength comes from within."

As if in response to his words, Merona felt the magic stir inside her, a living thing pulsing with the rhythm of the earth itself. She closed her eyes, reaching out with her senses to the world around them.

The wind whispered ancient secrets in her ears. The ground beneath her feet thrummed with hidden power. In the distance, she could hear the faint lapping of water against distant shores. And deep within, a fire burned, fueled by determination and love.

Opening her eyes, Merona met Murdach's gaze once more. "Whatever comes," she said, her voice steady and resolute, "we face it together."

As the first rays of dawn crept into their room, Merona stirred from her slumber. A smile tugged at her lips as she felt Murdach's arm draped protectively over her waist, pulling her closer to his bare chest.

The night before had been a blur of passion and tenderness, their bodies melding in a dance as old as time. Merona had lost herself in him, surrendering to the overwhelming love and desire that coursed through her veins.

Now, lying in his embrace, she felt a peace settle over her; peace she had never known before. As if sensing her thoughts, Murdach stirred behind her, pressing a soft kiss to the nape of her neck.

"Good morning, mo chridhe," he murmured against her skin.

Merona turned to face him, tracing the lines of his face with delicate fingertips. "Good morning," she whispered. "Last night… it was everything."

Murdach's eyes shone with emotion as he leaned in to capture her lips in a tender kiss. "It was only a taste of what our forever could be," he whispered against her mouth.

A pang of longing shot through Merona's heart at his words. She knew they had only this fleeting moment together before their paths would diverge once more. But for now, she pushed those thoughts aside and reveled in the warmth of his touch.

They spent the rest of the day exploring the small town outside of Paris, admiring its grand architecture and bustling streets. Murdach shared his favorite spots with Merona, pointing out hidden gems and regaling her with stories from his past.

As they walked along the Seine River at sunset, Murdach took Merona's hand in his and pressed a gentle kiss to her palm. "I cannot thank you enough for showing me your world," he said softly. "I will carry these memories with me always."

Merona's heart swelled with both love and sadness at his words, knowing that their time together might be fleeting. The future they dreamed of could be cut short by the cruel echoes of time.

Standing there, silhouetted against the fading light, Merona realized that no matter what challenges awaited them in Paris, the bond they shared would give her the strength to face them all.

As the sun dipped below the horizon, Merona and Murdach sought refuge in their secluded campsite. The air around them grew heavy, thick with the promise of a warm night ahead. As they settled by the flickering fire, shadows danced across Merona's features, her bright blue eyes reflecting the flames like twin stars. Morrigan nestled close to her, offering warmth and protection for the night.

Murdach's fingers traced the curve of her cheek, his touch igniting a spark that coursed through her veins. "My love," he murmured, his voice low and resonant, "these years have been both a blessing and a torment."

Merona leaned into his touch, her heart quickening. "How so?" she asked, though she already sensed the answer.

"To be near you, to watch you grow into your power," Murdach said, drawing her closer, "has been the greatest honor of my long existence. And yet..."

"And yet?" Merona prompted, her breath catching in her throat.

Murdach's eyes smoldered with an intensity that made her knees weak. "And yet, every moment, I've longed to hold you like this."

As their lips met, Merona felt the elements surge within her, responding to the passion that threatened to consume them both. Fire, air, earth, and water; all paled in comparison to the overwhelming force of their love.

"Murdach," she whispered against his lips, "I don't care what fate has in store. This moment, here and now, is ours."

Miles away, in the opulent halls of Paris, a figure cloaked in shadows watched the flames dance in a gilded hearth. Armaeus, masquerading as the Bishop, allowed a cruel smile to twist his human features.

"Soon, Clovis," he murmured to himself, his voice a silken caress laced with malice. "Soon you will embrace the cross, and with it, seal your fate."

He paced the room, his steps measured and predatory. "And when you do, when you relinquish your pagan powers," Armaeus continued, his eyes glowing with an unholy light, "I will be there to claim what is rightfully mine."

The demon paused, sensing a disturbance in the air; a ripple of power that could only belong to Merona. His smile widened, revealing teeth too sharp to be human.

"Come to me, witch," he hissed. "Your power, and your protector, will be no match for what awaits you here."

As if in response to his dark thoughts, the fire in the hearth flared, casting monstrous shadows across the walls. Armaeus laughed, the sound reverberating through the empty chamber, a chilling promise of doom.

Chapter 20

Armaeus' claws scraped against the frozen stone as he paced his chamber, each breath forming a cloud of vapor in the frigid air. The ice-encrusted walls seemed to close in around him, a prison of his own making, deep within the Grotte du Mas-d'Azil.

"The time draws near," he growled, his crimson eyes flashing in the dim light. "I can feel it in my bones."

For countless lifetimes, he had waited, plotted, and schemed, preparing for this moment. The prophecy burned in his mind like a brand, its promise of revelation both a torment and a temptation. Three days of darkness, and then...

Armaeus clenched his fists, feeling the raw power surge through his veins. He was the Daemon, the bringer of nightmares, and yet this mere girl threatened everything he had built.

"The Morrigan," he spat, the name bitter on his tongue. "That meddlesome goddess thinks she can protect the child from me."

He pictured the Phantom Queen in his mind's eye, her presence a shield around the girl; impenetrable, but not invincible. Even the strongest defenses had their weaknesses, and Armaeus was nothing if not patient.

"I will find a way," he vowed, his voice a low, menacing rumble. "I must end her before she comes into her power. The fate of this realm hangs in the balance."

Armaeus paused in his pacing, his gaze settling on his reflection in a sheet of ice. His demonic visage glared back at him, a reminder of the dark power he commanded. With a thought, he shifted, his form rippling and changing until a handsome man with piercing black eyes stood in his place.

"Soon," Armaeus murmured, running a hand through his raven hair. "Soon, I will walk among them, and they will never suspect the danger lurking in their midst."

"Let the darkness come," he whispered, his words echoing through the icy chamber. "For in the shadows, I reign supreme."

"Blood from the heavens," Armaeus murmured again, his crimson eyes fixed on the frost-covered walls. Ancient texts and forgotten prophecies flooded his mind; incantations he had studied over lifetimes.

He clenched his fist, feeling the dark energy surge within him, crackling through his veins. The cold air seemed to vibrate with malignant power. "She may have the Morrigan's protection," he snarled, "but I have the strength of ages."

Armaeus strode toward a frost-covered mirror, his reflection shifting between his demonic form and human guise. "The eclipse approaches," he mused, tracing a clawed finger along the glass. "Three days of darkness... the perfect cover for what must be done."

He turned, pacing the chamber with predatory grace. "The girl thinks she's safe," he spat. "Protected by her goddess, revered by the fools who fail to see the danger she represents."

Armaeus paused, his eyes closing as he focused on the wellspring of power pulsing within him. "I've waited centuries for this moment," he whispered, his voice thick with dark conviction. "I won't let some child with borrowed strength stand in my way."

His eyes snapped open, blazing with unyielding determination. "The ancient magics are mine to command," he declared, his voice unwavering. "I'll use every dark art, every forbidden ritual, to ensure her defeat."

A cruel smile spread across his face. "Let the Morrigan try to shield her," he sneered. "I'll tear through that protection like parchment. And when I'm done, there will be nothing left of the girl but ashes and shattered dreams."

The cold air grew heavier, thick with the weight of his malevolent intent. He stood motionless, savoring the anticipation of his imminent triumph, when a hesitant voice broke the silence.

"Are you ready, my lord?"

Armaeus turned, his crimson eyes locking onto Varis, who stood uncertainly in the doorway. A wicked grin curled the demon's lips, relishing the concern on his loyal follower's face.

"Ah, Varis," he purred, his voice a smooth blend of malice and charm. "Come, join me in this moment of... anticipation."

Varis stepped forward, his eyes nervously darting around the frost-covered chamber. "My lord, I-I couldn't help but overhear. Are you certain about confronting the witch directly? The risks…"

"Risks?" Armaeus interrupted, a low, menacing chuckle rumbling in his throat. "What are risks to one who has walked the earth for eons? Who has tasted the blood of countless sacrifices?"

He moved closer to Varis, each step deliberate, exuding a predatory air. "Tell me, my faithful servant, do you doubt my power?"

Varis swallowed hard, shaking his head vigorously. "N-no, my lord. Never. It's just... the prophecy speaks of her great potential."

Armaeus' eyes flashed dangerously. "Potential?" he spat. "Potential is nothing compared to the raw power I command. I've toppled empires, Varis. I've whispered in the ears of kings and watched civilizations crumble. What is one girl against such might?"

Armaeus turned away from Varis, his gaze drawn to the icy window overlooking the misty valleys of Gaul. The land stretched out before him; a shadowed tapestry ripe for the taking. His fingers traced the frost-etched glass, leaving smoldering trails in their wake.

"More than ready," Armaeus replied, his voice laced with venom. Each word lingered in the air; a death sentence sealed with malice. "The time has come for the final battle. I will end her quest in the Labyrinth, and with it, her very destiny."

The demon's eyes gleamed with an unholy light as he pictured Merona's life force draining away, her powers twisting into his control. The thought sent a shiver of dark pleasure through his being.

Varis hesitated for a moment, his loyalty battling against the primal fear clawing at his chest. The weight of Armaeus' words pressed down on him, heavy with the promise of bloodshed and chaos. He knew the consequences of failure all too well; he had seen the fate of those who dared disappoint his master.

Finally, steeling himself, Varis nodded. "As you command, my lord."

Armaeus turned back to his servant, a cruel smile playing on his lips. He savored the fear emanating from Varis, drinking it in like a fine wine. *Yes,* he thought, *let them all tremble before me. Soon, the witch's power will be mine, and with it, the very fabric of this world.*

Armaeus' claws scratched against the cold stone as he paced, each step leaving smoldering imprints on the floor. His mind raced with ancient incantations, dark whispers from forgotten realms echoing in his thoughts. The air around him crackled with malevolent energy, a testament to the immense power he was about to unleash.

"The Cauldron of Dagda," he murmured, his voice a low growl. "Its power will be crucial." His burning eyes fixed on Varis. "Bring it to me."

As Varis hurried away, Armaeus closed his eyes, channeling the dark energies swirling within him. He could feel the strength of countless souls he had consumed over the centuries, their essence feeding the infernal might coursing through him.

"Merona," he hissed, the name tasting like ash on his tongue. "Your light will soon be extinguished."

Varis returned, struggling under the weight of attaining the ancient cauldron. He feared the wrath of Armaeus if he failed.

His voice dropped to a sinister whisper. "We strike when she is most vulnerable. Only then can we snuff out her light."

Varis nodded, his face a mask of grim resolve. "And the Morrigan, my lord? How do we deal with her protection?"

Armaeus' eyes glittered with dark amusement. "Leave that to me. I have plans for the Raven Queen."

Varis bowed his head, his voice a reverent whisper. "Understood, my lord."

Armaeus turned away, his claws scraping against the cold stone as he paced. The weight of centuries pressed upon him, each step reverberating with the urgency of his mission. The prophecy; the cursed foretelling. loomed in his mind like a malignant shadow.

"Time," he growled, his voice a guttural rumble that seemed to shake the very foundations of his underground lair. "It slips through our grasp like sand."

He whirled to face Varis, his eyes blazing with hellfire. "Do you grasp the magnitude of what we face? This isn't just about the girl. The fate of our entire realm hangs in the balance."

Varis nodded, a flicker of fear crossing his face. "Yes, my lord. But surely, with your power…"

"Power?" Armaeus snarled, cutting him off. "Power is useless without proper application. We must be swift, decisive." He clenched his fist, dark energy crackling around it. "One misstep, one moment of hesitation, and everything we've fought for will crumble."

The demon's mind raced, calculating every possible outcome. He could almost taste victory; sweet and tantalizing just beyond his reach. Yet the path to triumph was fraught with peril, lined with traps that could spell their undoing.

"Prepare the others," Armaeus commanded, his voice dropping to a deadly whisper. "We move at nightfall. And Varis?"

"Yes, my lord?"

A wicked grin spread across Armaeus' face, revealing rows of razor-sharp teeth. "Failure is not an option. Remember that."

Varis swallowed hard, his throat constricting with a mix of fear and admiration. He gazed upon his master, shrouded in shadows that seemed to writhe with a life of their own. Armaeus' eyes glowed with an otherworldly light, a testament to the ancient power that surged through his veins.

"Are you certain we can defeat her, my lord?" Varis asked, his voice barely more than a whisper. Despite the confidence emanating from his master, a flicker of doubt gnawed at him. "The Morrigan is said to be guarding her."

Armaeus turned, his movements fluid, like smoke unfurling in the air. A low, menacing chuckle escaped his lips, sending an icy shiver down Varis's spine.

"Difficult, yes," Armaeus acknowledged, his voice a silken purr that belied the deadly undertones. "But not impossible." He raised a hand, dark energy swirling around his fingers. "Her bloodline gives her power, but in the end, it will not save her."

As Armaeus spoke, his mind churned with possibilities. The witch's strength was formidable; her lineage and the Morrigan's protection had made her nearly invincible. But Armaeus had waited lifetimes for this moment, perfecting his dark craft, delving into forbidden magics that would make even the bravest tremble in fear.

"The Phantom Queen may believe herself untouchable," Armaeus murmured, more to himself than to Varis. "But even gods can bleed. And I intend to make rivers flow with their essence."

Varis leaned forward, his eyes gleaming with a mixture of fear and eager devotion. "Then what do you propose, my lord?" he asked, his voice thick with anticipation to serve his dark master.

Armaeus' crimson eyes narrowed as he paced the cold stone floor, each step resonating ominously through the chamber. His claws scraped against the ancient walls, leaving faint traces of sulfur in their wake. His mind raced, weighing centuries of forbidden knowledge against the Morrigan's formidable protection.

"The old ways," Armaeus murmured, his voice a dark caress. "We must tap into magics so ancient, even the Phantom Queen will tremble." He paused, a wicked grin spreading across his face, revealing rows of razor-sharp teeth. "The Cauldron of Dagda, the Spear of Lugh, the Sword of Nuada; these artifacts hold power beyond mortal comprehension."

Varis's eyes widened in disbelief. "But my lord, those relics are lost to time. How can we?"

Armaeus silenced him with a raised hand, dark energy crackling ominously between his fingers. "Not lost, my faithful servant. Merely hidden." He turned to face Varis, his gaze burning with malevolent intent. "We will use the girl's very bloodline against her. The power that courses through her veins will be the key to unlocking these ancient weapons."

As Armaeus spoke, his demonic form began to shift, melting away to reveal the handsome, charming facade he used to deceive the unsuspecting. "The prophecy speaks of blood from the heavens," he mused, his voice now smooth as silk. "We shall make it rain crimson, and in doing so, reveal the path to our victory."

He paced the chamber, his footsteps echoing ominously against the cold stone floor. He turned to Varis; his eyes gleaming with dark purpose.

"I will continue to use my power to infiltrate King Clovis' advisers and as the Bishop," he declared, his voice dripping with malice. "The king's mind is already torn between the old ways and the new. I will ensure he follows his wife's wishes and converts to Christianity."

Varis tilted his head; confusion etched across his face. "But my lord, how will the king's conversion aid our cause?"

Armaeus chuckled, a sound that sent a cold shiver down Varis's spine. "The witch draws strength from the old gods, from the very earth itself. As Christianity spreads, it will sever her connection to these ancient powers."

He clenched his fist, dark energy swirling around it. "While I work to undermine her from within the court, you and the others will have a crucial role to play."

"What would you have us do, my lord?" Varis asked, eager to serve.

Armaeus' gaze hardened. "You will keep the Morrigan occupied. Distract her, challenge her; do whatever it takes to draw her attention away from the girl. I need her unprotected, vulnerable."

As he spoke, Armaeus' mind raced with possibilities. The Morrigan was formidable, but even she had weaknesses. He would exploit every one of them.

"And the witch?" Varis asked hesitantly.

A cruel smile twisted Armaeus' lips. "Leave her to me. When the time is right, when her guardians are distracted and her powers at their weakest, I will strike. Her destiny will be snuffed out like a candle in the wind."

Varis shifted uneasily, his eyes darting to the cold stone walls of Armaeus' chamber, as though seeking an escape from the weight of his master's words. The chill in the air seemed to deepen, mirroring the growing unease in his heart.

"Is it wise for you to face her alone?" Varis questioned, a hint of concern in his voice. His hand instinctively moved to the hilt of his sword, as if preparing for an unseen threat.

Armaeus turned, his crimson eyes blazing with infernal light. For a moment, his human guise flickered, revealing the grotesque demon beneath. The sight made Varis flinch, but he held his ground.

"Her powers are formidable," Armaeus conceded, his voice a low growl that seemed to reverberate through the chamber. "But I have waited lifetimes for this moment. I have honed my skills, studied her weaknesses. I know I can defeat her."

As he spoke, Armaeus' mind raced, revisiting centuries of preparation, countless sacrifices made in the darkness of his underground lair. The blood of innocents had fueled his power, each drop bringing him closer to this pivotal moment.

"You doubt me, Varis?" Armaeus asked, his tone dangerously soft.

Varis swallowed hard, choosing his words carefully. "Never, my lord. I merely... I fear for your safety. The witch's power grows stronger with each passing day, and the Morrigan's protection is not easily overcome."

Armaeus laughed, a sound devoid of mirth. "Your concern is noted but misplaced. I am no feeble mortal to be felled by a mere girl, prophecy or not."

Varis bowed his head, his long hair falling forward to obscure his face. "Very well, my lord," he said, his voice barely above a whisper. "We shall do as you command."

Armaeus nodded, satisfaction glinting in his obsidian eyes. The air around him seemed to thicken, shadows coalescing at his feet like writhing serpents. He clenched his fist, feeling the raw power surge through his veins.

"Good," he growled, determination burning in his gaze. His lips curled into a cruel smile, revealing teeth that gleamed unnaturally sharp. "Her destiny will be snuffed out like a candle in the wind."

As he spoke, Armaeus' mind raced with visions of his impending victory. He imagined the witch's lifeless body at his feet, her power flowing into him, making him invincible. The thought sent a thrill of dark pleasure coursing through his being.

"Prepare the others," Armaeus commanded, his voice resonating with unholy authority. "We move at nightfall."

Varis hesitated for a moment, his loyalty warring with an instinctive fear. "And what of the Morrigan, my lord? Her wrath will be terrible if we succeed."

Armaeus laughed, the sound echoing off the cold stone walls. "Let her come. When I'm done, even the gods will tremble before me."

The first drops of rain pattered against the ancient stone, each one a harbinger of the storm to come. Armaeus stood at the mouth of his cavernous lair, his eyes gleaming with malevolent anticipation as he gazed upon the darkening sky. The air crackled with electric tension, mirroring the excitement coursing through his veins.

"Can you feel it, Varis?" he murmured, his voice a low, menacing rumble. "The very elements bend to our will tonight."

Varis shifted uneasily beside him. "My lord, the power gathering here... it's unlike anything I've ever sensed."

Armaeus chuckled, the sound cold and void of warmth. "Of course it is. The magic of ages converges on this moment." His eyes gleamed crimson as he continued, "The Tuatha De Danann, the Dragon Kings of Anu, the Davidic house – their power will soon be mine to command."

He clenched his fist, feeling the ancient energies swirl around him. The thought of Merona's impending doom sent a rush of dark pleasure through his veins. Soon, her light would be snuffed out, and all that was rightfully his would be claimed.

"My lord," Varis ventured cautiously, "what of Murdach? His devotion to the girl is unwavering."

Armaeus sneered, contempt dripping from his words. "That lovesick fool? He's no match for what I've become." He turned to face his subordinate, eyes burning with unholy fire. "Prepare the others, Varis. The final battle awaits us. I won't let anything stand in my way – not Murdach, not the Morrigan, and certainly not some prophesied child."

As Varis hurried away to carry out his orders, Armaeus allowed himself a moment of quiet reflection. Centuries of planning, of patiently biding his time, had led to this. He could almost taste victory on his tongue, as sweet and intoxicating as the finest wine.

"Soon," he whispered to the gathering storm, "all will tremble before me."

Chapter 21

The ancient gates of Paris loomed ahead, weathered stone sentinels guarding secrets as old as time itself. A chill ran down Merona's spine as she passed beneath their shadow, the weight of history pressing heavily on her. The city's narrow streets twisted like serpents, buildings leaning close as if to whisper dark prophecies.

At the edge of a cramped square, a familiar figure awaited. Mairead's piercing hazel eyes locked onto Merona's, a flicker of relief crossing the elder witch's face before her expression steeled once again.

"You've arrived at last," Mairead said, her voice low and urgent. "Come quickly. We mustn't linger in the open."

Merona rushed toward her. "Mother, I'm so glad to see you. How did you know we'd be here?"

"The Raven Queen, in all her dark and foreboding glory, sent word of your impending arrival," Mairead explained, her voice tight with urgency. "I've crossed treacherous lands and endured endless trails to reach you before the ultimate battle you prophesied at Tolbiac." Her grip tightened on Merona's hand, the bond between them feeling unbreakable in that moment.

"Please, come with me," Mairead urged, her voice lowering even further. "We need to find a place where we can speak without being overheard." Her eyes flicked nervously around them, a silent warning that they were not alone, and that caution was paramount.

The winding alleys twisted like a maze of shadows and whispers, and with every step, Merona's skin prickled, charged with the anxious energy of the city. She could feel the weight of history pressing down on her, the dark prophecies swirling in the air like a palpable current. The conflicting energies of the inhabitants clashed and churned, creating a charged atmosphere that pulsed against her skin like waves crashing on the shore.

"What has happened, Mairead?" Merona asked, matching the elder witch's hurried pace.

Mairead's lips pressed into a thin line. "The balance has shifted, child. The Christians grow bolder each day, their influence spreading like a plague. Our people are being forced further into the shadows."

Merona's heart tightened. She had known this day would come, had glimpsed its shadow in her visions, but the reality stung, nonetheless. "And what of our allies within the city?"

"Few and far between," Mairead replied grimly. "Those who haven't fled outright are walking a razor's edge, terrified of being discovered. We must tread carefully, Merona. A single wrong word could bring ruin upon us all."

As they ducked into a small cottage, Merona's mind raced. The task ahead seemed more daunting than ever, the weight of destiny pressing heavily upon her shoulders. How could she hope to change the course of history when the tide was already turning against them?

Mairead seemed to sense the turmoil swirling within Merona. The elder witch's expression softened ever so slightly as she placed a reassuring hand on Merona's arm. "Do not lose heart, child. Our people have endured worse. The old ways are not so easily forgotten."

Merona nodded, drawing strength from Mairead's unshakable resolve. "What would you have us do?"

"For now, we wait," Mairead replied. "But tonight... tonight, we remind ourselves of who we are and where we come from. There is a gathering in the forest beyond the city walls. Will you join us?"

Merona's pulse quickened at the thought. Despite the danger, the pull of her heritage was undeniable. "Of course," she answered without hesitation.

As darkness descended, Merona felt the ancient forest enfold her. The towering trees loomed like silent sentinels, their twisted branches reaching up toward the starlit sky. The air was thick with the heady scent of earth and herbs, a tangible reminder of the magic that still coursed through the land.

Figures moved silently through the shadows, cloaked in secrecy. Merona felt the power building, a rising current of energy that made the hairs on the back of her neck stand on end. When they reached a moonlit clearing, her breath caught in her throat.

A circle of ancient standing stones rose before them, their weathered surfaces seeming to pulse with an inner light. At the center stood an altar of rough-hewn stone, adorned with flowers, fruit, and intricate carvings that stirred something deep within Merona's soul.

Mairead stepped forward, her voice clear and strong, carrying through the air. "Brothers and sisters, we gather here in defiance of those who seek to scatter us to the winds. Tonight, we honor the old gods and reaffirm our bond with the land beneath our feet."

A murmur of assent rippled through the gathered crowd. Merona felt a surge of belonging, an undeniable sense of rightness that nearly brought tears to her eyes. This was her heritage, her birthright; no matter the trials that awaited.

As the ritual deepened, Merona lost herself in the rhythms of ancient chants and the movement of swaying bodies. The beat of drums matched the pounding of her heart, and she felt the barriers between herself and the world around her begin to fade.

Power surged through the circle, raw and primal. Merona's skin tingled as she absorbed it, feeling it mix with her own magic. Visions flashed before her eyes; glimpses of past and future entwined, possibilities branching like the roots of a great tree.

In that moment of connection, Merona understood with crystalline clarity why she had been sent back to this time and place. The path ahead would be fraught with danger, but she was not alone. The strength of her ancestors flowed through her veins, and the hopes of generations yet unborn rested on her shoulders.

As the ceremony reached its crescendo, Merona raised her voice in a wordless cry of affirmation. The sound rippled through the air, echoed by those around her; a defiant chorus against the encroaching darkness.

When the energy began to subside, Merona stood trembling, both from exertion and emotion. Mairead appeared at her side, fierce pride shining in her eyes.

"You felt it, didn't you?" Mairead asked softly. "The true power of our people, undiminished by time or persecution."

Merona nodded, still struggling to find the right words. "It was... overwhelming. I've never experienced anything like it."

Mairead's expression grew solemn. "Remember this feeling, child. In the days to come, when doubt and fear threaten to swallow you, let the memory of this night be your anchor."

As they made their way back toward the city, Merona's mind raced with everything she had just experienced. The enormity of her task still loomed large, but now, for the first time, she felt a spark of hope stirring within her.

"What comes next?" she asked Mairead, as the first light of dawn began to paint the eastern sky.

The elder witch's eyes gleamed with determination. "We gather our allies, both old and new. The Christians may seek to stamp out our ways, but among them, there are those who remember the old truths. We must find them, forge alliances where we can."

Merona nodded, her resolve hardening. "And what of the king? Clovis must be made to see reason."

"All in due time," Mairead cautioned. "We must tread carefully, laying the groundwork before making such a bold move. For now, we focus on building our strength and staying hidden from those who would harm us."

As they slipped back into the awakening city, Merona's thoughts turned to the challenges that lay ahead. The path was treacherous, but now she knew she had the strength to walk it. Whatever trials awaited, she would face them with the power of her people behind her and the fire of destiny burning in her heart.

The cobblestone streets of Paris echoed with angry voices as Merona and her companions rounded a corner. A group of Christian zealots, their faces twisted with righteous fury, blocked their path.

"Heathens!" one man shouted, brandishing a crude wooden cross. "Your kind brings nothing but sin and corruption to our holy city!"

Merona's heart raced, but she kept her voice steady. "We seek only peace and understanding. There is room for all beliefs in this world."

"Lies!" A woman spat at Merona's feet. "The devil speaks through you, witch!"

The crowd surged forward, hands reaching and fists flying. Merona raised her arms, calling upon the elements to shield them. A gust of wind swept through the street, momentarily disorienting their attackers.

"Run!" Mairead hissed, pulling Merona by the arm.

As they fled, Merona's thoughts spun. *How can we hope to change minds when hatred runs so deep?*

They ducked into a narrow alley, breathless. "We must reach the palace," Merona insisted. "King Clovis must hear us out."

Mairead shook her head. "It won't be that simple, child. The Bishop wields too much influence."

Undeterred, Merona pressed on toward the towering spires of the royal residence. At the gates, a guard eyed them warily.

"I seek an audience with King Clovis," Merona declared, standing tall.

The guard sneered. "His Majesty has no time for peasant rabble."

"Please," Merona pleaded, "This is a matter of utmost importance."

A shadow fell across them as a portly figure in ornate robes approached. The Bishop's cold gaze swept over Merona and her companions.

"The King cannot be bothered with such nonsense," he drawled. "Run along now, before I have you removed."

As they were ushered away, a chill crept down Merona's spine. Something in the Bishop's voice, the glint in his eye, hinted at dangers yet to come.

"We cannot give up," she whispered to Mairead. "The very fate of our people hangs in the balance."

The parchment arrived in the dead of night, slipped silently beneath their door by an unseen hand. Merona's fingers trembled as she unfurled it, quickly scanning the carefully penned script.

"A sympathetic Bishop," she murmured, her brow knitting in confusion. "He wishes to meet."

Mairead glanced over her shoulder, skepticism lacing her voice. "It could be a trap."

Merona closed her eyes, reaching out with her senses. A faint trace of magic lingered on the parchment, a whisper of truth. "No," she replied softly. "This feels genuine."

"Even so," Mairead cautioned, "we must be cautious."

At the break of dawn, they made their way to the agreed meeting place; a small chapel on the outskirts of Paris. Merona's heart raced, caught between hope and apprehension.

The Bishop, a slender man with compassionate eyes, greeted them warmly. "I am Father Lucien," he said, ushering them inside. "I have long believed our faiths must find a way to coexist."

Merona studied him closely, sensing no dishonesty. "Why take the risk to reach out to us?"

Lucien's sigh was heavy with weariness. "The growing divide, the violence; it contradicts everything I stand for. But there are those in the Church who seek to stoke the fires of hatred."

As they conversed, Lucien revealed whispers of a plot, plans to frame the pagan community for horrific acts. Merona's blood turned cold.

"We must expose this," she said, her voice hardening with determination.

Lucien nodded grimly. "I can provide you with evidence but using it will be perilous."

As they left the chapel, the documents securely hidden, Merona's mind raced with possibilities. "If we can gather enough support, show the people the truth..."

Mairead squeezed Merona's hand. "It's a risk, but one we must take."

Merona gazed out over the city, feeling the weight of destiny settling heavily on her shoulders. "For the sake of all our people," she whispered, "we cannot fail."

As twilight fell over Paris, Merona felt the Morrigan's presence grow stronger. In her wolf form, the goddess prowled silently beside her, amber eyes gleaming with a watchful, otherworldly intensity. A chill ran down Merona's spine.

"She won't leave your side," Murdach murmured, his eyes flicking between Merona and the Morrigan. "The air is thick with the scent of doom."

Merona nodded, her voice barely a breath. "I feel it too. A darkness closing in."

They moved quickly through the shadowed streets, Mairead leading the way toward the city's outskirts. The high priestess's auburn hair caught the last light of day, glowing faintly as her steps quickened with purpose.

"There's an abandoned farmhouse not far from here," Mairead explained, her tone tight with urgency. "We can rest there and plan our next move."

As they walked, Merona's mind raced. "How are we to reach Clovis?" she asked, frustration creeping into her voice. "The Bishop's interference has made it nearly impossible."

Murdach's hand landed gently on her shoulder, a steadying presence. "We'll find a way. We always do."

The farmhouse loomed ahead, a dark silhouette against the dimming sky. Once inside, Mairead wasted no time securing the perimeter with protective wards, her tattoos glowing softly as she worked.

Merona sank into a rickety chair, exhaustion settling over her like a heavy cloak. "The Labyrinth," she muttered, mostly to herself. "It's the key to everything. I'm sure of it."

The Morrigan's voice reverberated in her mind, a whisper both eerie and urgent. *"The catacombs beneath Paris hold many secrets, young one. But beware, for they also harbor great danger."*

Merona's eyes widened in realization. "The catacombs! Of course!" Her fatigue momentarily lifted as excitement surged within her. She turned to the others. "The Labyrinth must be hidden there. If I can find it! If I step into it..."

Mairead's expression darkened with concern. "It's a perilous path, Merona. The catacombs are a maze of death and forgotten history."

"But it might be our only chance," Murdach spoke up, his voice resolute, carrying the weight of certainty. "To reach Clovis, to change the course of history…we must take risks."

As night fully claimed the sky, Merona gazed out of the grimy window, the weight of her destiny pressing heavily on her chest. The Morrigan's presence lingered in her mind, a constant reminder of the darkness that threatened to consume them all.

"Tomorrow," she said softly, her eyes catching the starlight. "Tomorrow, we gather our allies and make our plans. Then, we descend into the heart of Paris and pray we find the path that will save us all."

Chapter 22

The air pulsed with malevolent energy as a monstrous shape emerged from the mist-shrouded forest. Merona's heart hammered in her chest, eyes widening at the grotesque creature Armaeus had summoned. Its twisted form; a writhing mass of shadows and bone, towered over her and her companions at the outskirts of Paris.

"Stand firm," Murdach growled, his eyes flashing with resolve. "We face this abomination together."

Merona nodded, gathering the elemental forces she had only recently learned to command. The earth beneath her feet thrummed with power, responding to her unspoken summons. As the creature lunged, she thrust out her hands, willing the ground to rise up and ensnare its misshapen limbs.

Without hesitation, Morrigan sprang into action, her crimson wings unfurling as she shot toward the creature with blinding speed. A piercing cry split the air, striking fear into the abomination as Morrigan swooped in, her talons tearing into its shadowy form.

Merona watched in awe as she fierce bravery bought them precious time. She focused her own energy, summoning the elements to bolster Morrigan's assault. The earth trembled, rocks tumbling down upon the creature, weakening it even further.

Just when victory seemed within reach, Armaeus' voice rang out, dripping with malice. "You dare challenge me?" he sneered; his dark eyes gleaming with deadly intent.

In an instant, the creature grew larger and more powerful, its roars deafening. A wave of unease gripped Merona as she felt herself being overwhelmed by its malevolent energy.

Morrigan let out another piercing cry, her wings beating furiously against the creature's face, but it wasn't enough. Merona could feel her control over the elements slipping away, and panic began to take root within her.

Then, in the darkest moment, a powerful force surged through her; pure and unbridled magic. It coursed through her like fire, consuming every part of her being, and she knew instinctively that this power was unlike anything she had ever felt before.

With a cry, Merona released the newfound power, a wave of light radiating from her body. It pushed back the darkness that had threatened to swallow them. Armaeus' control over the creature faltered, and with a deafening roar, it collapsed into a lifeless heap on the ground.

Murdach rushed forward to help Morrigan land safely, while Merona stood frozen, still reeling from the surge of magic she had just unleashed. The air around them had shifted, now filled with a profound sense of peace; a testament to the immense power Merona had tapped into.

"Your newfound abilities serve you well, young one," Mairead called, her aged face a mix of pride and concern. "But do not overextend yourself. Remember, your strength lies not just in your magic, but in the bonds we share."

The creature howled, a sound that pierced the very air and sent a chill through Merona's core. She faltered, doubt creeping into her thoughts. Was she truly ready to confront such horrors? Could she bear the weight of the destiny thrust upon her?

Morrigan's voice broke through her spiraling thoughts. *"Focus, Merona! You are more than capable. Trust in yourself, as we trust in you."*

Steeling herself, Merona reached out with her senses, feeling the currents of energy swirling around her. The air shimmered with raw potential, and she drew upon it, weaving a protective barrier around her companions. The creature's claws scraped against the invisible shield, sending a cascade of ethereal sparks into the air.

"Well done!" Murdach shouted, his silver hair whipping wildly in the wind as his form shifted. Emerald and sapphire scales erupted across his skin. "Now, let us show this abomination the true power of unity!"

As Murdach soared into the sky, unleashing torrents of flame upon their foe, Merona felt a surge of confidence. She wasn't alone in this battle. With her companions at her side, perhaps they could change the course of history.

But their fleeting triumph was shattered by a bone-chilling laugh that reverberated across the battlefield. The air thickened with dread, and Merona's blood turned to ice as she turned to face the looming figure of Armaeus. His crimson eyes glowed with a malice that burned through the darkened air.

"Did you truly think a single victory would be enough, little witch?" Armaeus sneered, his voice laced with disdain. "Your journey ends here, at the very gates of your precious Paris."

Merona's mind raced, fear threatening to consume her. But as her gaze swept over her companions; Murdach's fierce resolve, Mairead's calm strength, Morrigan's unwavering presence; her resolve returned.

"You're wrong, Armaeus," she said, her voice steady despite the tremor in her chest. "This is not our end. It's only the beginning."

As Armaeus unleashed his hellish power, Merona braced herself for the battle ahead. The fate of countless lives hung in the balance. With her allies at her side and the elements at her command, she would not falter now.

The true test of her destiny had only just begun. The air crackled with dark energy as Armaeus raised his arms, his fingers tracing eldritch symbols in the air. The ground beneath them trembled, and from a widening fissure, a monstrous creature emerged; its form a grotesque fusion of shadow and bone.

Merona's heart hammered in her chest as she stared at the abomination. Its hollow eyes glowed with an eerie light, and its mouth dripped with a viscous, inky substance that hissed and smoked on contact with the earth.

"By the gods," Murdach whispered, his voice taut with fear. "What kind of beast is this?"

Merona swallowed, her mouth dry. "A manifestation of Armaeus' darkest powers," she replied, her gaze fixed on the creature. "We must stand together."

The beast lunged with terrifying speed, its claws slashing the air where Merona had stood just moments before. She rolled aside, calling upon her newfound abilities to summon a gust of wind that carried her out of its reach.

"Mairead, flank it!" Morrigan's command rang out, the red wolf darting between the creature's legs, her teeth snapping at its shadowy form.

As Mairead circled around, her hands weaving intricate patterns of protective magic, Merona focused on the elements surrounding them. She felt the pulse of the earth beneath her feet, the whisper of the wind in her ears, the latent heat of fire in her blood.

"Murdach, we need your strength!" Merona shouted, her voice rising above the creature's unearthly howls.

The warrior nodded grimly, hefting his axe. "Aye, lass. Let's send this demon back to the hell that spawned it."

While her companions engaged the beast, Merona closed her eyes and reached deep within herself. The raw power of the elements surged through her veins, a symphony of creation and destruction at her fingertips.

"Elements of earth and sky, of fire and water, *"Aether, Domhan, Uisce, Dóiteáin, Aontacht!"* She intoned, her voice carrying ancient power, "I call upon you now. Lend me your strength to vanquish this evil! "

The air around Merona shimmered with energy as the elements responded to her call. With a sweeping motion, she unleashed a torrent of elemental fury at the creature, each blast stripping away its shadowy form.

As the battle raged on, Merona's resolve solidified. This was what she had trained for, what destiny had prepared her to face. With her allies at her side and the elements at her command, she would not falter.

"Your end approaches, Armaeus," Merona declared, her eyes blazing with unshakable determination. "Your darkness cannot stand against our light!"

The acrid stench of defeat hung thick in the air as Armaeus, his demonic form battered and broken, retreated from the battlefield. His once fiery crimson eyes now simmered with barely contained rage, the malevolent fury that had once burned bright dimming under the weight of his defeat. His claws dug into the earth, leaving deep gouges as he dragged his monstrous form away from Merona and her victorious companions.

Armaeus' thoughts seethed with dark purpose. This was but a temporary setback, a fleeting stumble in the grand scheme of his design. As he slunk back into the shadows, his form began to twist and warp. The blackened skin and razor-sharp claws faded, replaced by the facade of a pious Bishop, his face an immaculate mask of benevolent wisdom.

"You may have won this battle, witch," he muttered under his breath, his voice venomous, "but the war for Gaul's soul has only just begun."

With renewed determination, Armaeus made his way toward the castle where King Clovis awaited. The weight of his robes felt foreign after the freedom of his demonic form, but he wore this guise as if it were his own skin. Each step brought him closer to his true objective; the corruption of the Frankish king.

Arriving at the castle gates, Armaeus carefully schooled his features into an expression of false piety. "I must speak with King Clovis at once," he declared to the guards, his voice resonating with feigned urgency. "The fate of his immortal soul hangs in the balance."

The guards, awed by the presence of a holy man, quickly ushered him inside. Armaeus allowed himself a small, cruel smile as he was led through the torch-lit corridors. Soon, he would stand before Clovis once again, and then, the true game would begin.

Chapter 23

The spires of Paris pierced the twilight sky like ancient spears, their jagged silhouettes casting long shadows over the cobblestone streets. As Merona and her companions neared the city's heart, the air grew thick with whispers of change, carried on a chill wind that wove through her raven locks.

Mairead's voice broke the silence, sharp and resolute. "Remember, child, you carry the hopes of our people. Do not falter."

Merona nodded, eyes fixed on the imposing palace ahead. Murdach's presence at her, Murdach radiated a steady warmth, his gaze sweeping the dim alleys, ever watchful for unseen threats.

From the shadows, a figure stepped forward, bowing low. "My lady, King Clovis has sent me to guide you."

Wordlessly, they followed the silent guide through a maze of winding corridors. Merona's thoughts churned, the weight of destiny settling heavily on her shoulders. It was a burden she had never sought, but one she could not escape.

When the grand hall doors swung open, a sea of faces turned to her. For a moment, Merona faltered, her breath catching as she took in the opulence of the chamber; a world apart from the humble village where her journey had begun.

The Bishop sat upon his throne, his dark eyes locking onto Merona's with piercing intensity. The air between them seemed to hum with unspoken tension, dense and sharp as a drawn blade.

"Welcome, Merona of Septimania," his voice rang out, deep and commanding, echoing through the grand hall. "We have long awaited your arrival."

Merona stepped forward, her posture resolute despite the relentless pounding of her heart. "I am honored by your summons," she replied, her voice steady, "but I was told King Clovis would be here to meet me."

A ripple of unease swept through the gathered crowd. Murmurs of "witch" and "pagan" floated to her ears, their venom thinly veiled. Fear clawed at the edges of her resolve, but she forced her face into an unyielding mask.

"Tell me, witch," the Bishop said, leaning forward as his penetrating gaze bore into her, "do you understand why you are here?"

Merona's thoughts raced, grappling for the right response. She drew a steadying breath before speaking. "I believe I am here to unite what is divided," she said, her tone firm yet measured. "To forge a path that honors both the old ways and the new."

The Bishop's expression remained inscrutable, his stillness unsettling. Yet something in the air shifted; an almost imperceptible crack in the tension, though its meaning was unclear.

Rising from his throne, the Bishop loomed larger, his shadow stretching across the polished stone like an omen. As he approached, Merona caught the turmoil in his eyes: curiosity entangled with mistrust, reverence warring with wariness. His gaze settled heavily on her, a weight that made her skin prickle, as if the storm she had stepped into was just beginning to unfurl.

"Merona," the Bishop began, his deep voice reverberating through the hall like the toll of a solemn bell. "Your arrival has ignited both hope and fear within our kingdom. Tell me? How do you reconcile the ancient ways with the tide of change sweeping across our lands?"

Merona inhaled slowly, steadying herself as countless eyes bore into her. Though her heart thundered, her voice emerged calm and resolute. "True strength," she replied, "lies not in forsaking our roots but in discovering harmony between the old and the new."

The Bishop's brow knit in thought, his fingers tracing the intricate stitching of his cloak in a subconscious rhythm. "And yet," he said, his tone weighted with uncertainty, "the Church grows stronger with each passing day. How can we uphold our bond with the old gods without inviting conflict into our midst?"

A wave of understanding swept through Merona. The Bishop's struggle mirrored her own; an endless balancing act between expectation and destiny. "Perhaps," she ventured, her voice gentle but firm, "the answer does not lie in choosing one path over another, but in weaving them together. The wisdom of our ancestors need not be lost as we embrace new truths."

As their words echoed in the grand hall, the atmosphere shifted with an almost tangible energy, like the first gust of wind before a brewing storm. The opulent chamber, draped in tapestries depicting the kingdom's storied past, became a silent battlefield of emotions. Some courtiers leaned forward eagerly, their eyes glinting with curiosity and hope, as if captivated by the possibility of unity. Others drew back, their faces hardening with indignation. Lines of disapproval etched deeper into their features as they exchanged furtive, disapproving glances.

The division was undeniable; a growing chasm threatening to fracture the once-unified kingdom. The air crackled with tension, heavy with the unspoken fear that the balance Merona sought might already be slipping beyond reach.

Merona stole a glance at the Bishop, whose narrowed eyes held a glimmer of something indecipherable. Was it hope flickering in their depths, or a shadow of something darker; something more sinister? The uncertainty made her heart race. "You speak of a difficult path, witch," he said, his voice low and measured. "One that may satisfy neither the old gods nor the new. Such a choice teeters on the edge of ruin. Can you bear the weight of such a choice?"

"Indeed," Merona replied, her voice growing steadier, each word cutting through the fraught silence like tempered steel. "Because it is a path that could lead us to a future where your people can flourish, where the chains of the past are broken once and for all. Is that not a cause worth risking struggle and sacrifice?" Her chest rose and fell with the force of her resolve, the pounding of her heart driving her forward.

The Bishop's lips twisted into an unsettling smile that sent a shiver down Merona's spine. "You are wise beyond your years, Merona," he said, his eyes glinting with a hint of admiration and something more lurking underneath. "But tell me, why do you think you possess the power to fulfill your destiny? What makes you believe that you are the one to lead this grand endeavor?"

As their conversation deepened and flowed like a river winding through desolate terrain, Merona could feel the delicate threads of understanding beginning to weave between them, forming an intricate tapestry of possibility. Here were two figures, both burdened with the fate of their people's future, grappling with their responsibilities while trying to find common ground amid insurmountable odds. Yet, despite their burgeoning connection, a chill crept up the nape of her neck, raising her hair as acute awareness of danger gnawed at her. Panic unfurled within her gut, eclipsing the sense of calm she had momentarily embraced, and whispered doubts invaded her mind: *What if the cost of this path was far greater than anyone could foresee?*

Merona's heart seemed to stop in her chest as the Bishop's gaze intensified, pinning her with a penetrating stare. The heavy doors to the throne room had closed behind her with an ominous thud, cutting off any means of escape. The weight of destiny pressed down on her shoulders like a heavy cloak, pressing down on her with each passing moment.

As the Bishop spoke, his voice carried an eerie resonance, each word laced with foreboding. "You speak of sacrifice and struggle," he said, his lips curving into a twisted smile that sent a chill through her. "But tell me, are you truly prepared for what such a path demands?"

For a moment, Merona stood frozen, her thoughts a whirlwind of uncertainty. Was this some elaborate trap? The man before her; was he truly the compassionate Bishop she had addressed only moments ago?

Then she saw it, a flicker, subtle but unmistakable. His features shifted ever so slightly, and a faint, unnatural glow began to emanate from within him. The truth struck her like a bolt of lightning.

"You are not the Bishop," she whispered, stepping back as realization dawned.

The figure before her let out a low, guttural laugh that reverberated through the chamber, chilling her to the core. "How perceptive," he sneered, his voice now a gravelly echo of its former self.

Merona felt fear grip at heart as she recognized him for who he truly was – Armaeus.

"How dare you come here and deceive our people!" she shouted, her voice quivering with both fear and fury. Anger surged through her, igniting a fire within that pushed back against her rising dread. "What is it you want from us?"

Armaeus began to circle her slowly, his presence thick with malice, each step deliberate and predatory. "What I *want*," he hissed, his tone dripping with disdain, "is what I am owed. Power, loyalty, dominion; you cannot deny me these things."

Merona's jaw tightened, her voice steadying as she faced him head-on. "You will never have our power," she said, her words resolute. "We will not be pawns in your schemes."

His laughter filled the room, a cruel and mocking sound that seemed to echo endlessly. "Such bold words from one so young," he said, his eyes burning with a fiery determination. "You think you can stand against me? I have seen the future, Merona. And in it, I am victorious."

Merona held her ground, the fire in her eyes matching his. The air between them crackled with tension, the battle of wills as fierce as any war fought with steel.

"We will fight back," Merona declared, her voice fierce and unwavering as she stood tall before him, unyielding despite the darkness surrounding them.

Armaeus' lips curled into a smirk; his expression laced with cruel amusement. He stepped closer, his presence cold and oppressive, and raised a hand to caress her cheek with icy fingers. "Oh, my dear witch," he drawled, his tone dripping with mockery. "Do you truly believe there is anything you can do to stop me? My powers are far beyond your imagination."

But Merona refused to cower under his touch or his threats. She knew that their powers were strong enough to resist him – they just needed to stand together.

Suddenly, a loud commotion outside the throne room shattered the tense silence. The grand doors burst open, and Murdach stormed in, flanked by a squad of guards. His eyes immediately found Merona!" he exclaimed in relief upon seeing her safe and sound.

But his relief was short-lived. as Armaeus turned them, his features twisting with an angry snarl on his face.

"You dare interrupt me?" he roared, his voice echoing like a thunderclap. With a sweep of his arm, he unleashed a surge of dark energy, the blast crackling through the air like a tempest. "You cannot hide behind your protectors forever, witch," he sneered, his tone venomous. "I will have what I came for."

Merona acted swiftly. She seized Murdach's hand, pulling him toward the rear of the throne room as Armaeus' deadly attacks tore through the space around them. They darted through the chaos, narrowly evading his strikes, and fled the castle and reached safety with Mairead and Morrigan.

Armaeus seethed with frustration at missing his chance to kill Merona and absorb her powers. He had successfully lured her away from the others, but the dragon arrived too soon and thwarted his plans. In a low, menacing whisper.

"It is only a matter of time," he murmured, his tone filled with ominous certainty. "Her power will be mine. Their fragile unity will shatter, and the path will be cleared for Clovis to fall." His lips twisted into a sinister grin. "This is far from over."

Chapter 24

Merona stood at the village's edge beside the Morrigan, staring out at the horizon. At mid-day on Samhain, her 18th birthday; the sky became black as night, a stark contrast to the joyous laughter and dancing behind her. The air carried a strange mix of scents; woodsmoke and roasted chestnuts mingled with the earthy dampness of approaching rain.

"Can't you feel it?" she murmured; her voice barely audible over the festivities. Her hands clenched into fists, trembling with tension. "The storm…it's coming." As the first drops began to fall, a chill swept through her, whispering of the chaos that lay ahead, and she knew that the merriment would soon give way to a reckoning far darker than anyone could imagine. With a heavy heart, Merona turned back to the revelers, their carefree spirits oblivious to the ominous shadows gathering on the horizon, unaware that the very laughter that filled the air might soon be silenced by the tempest of fate.

As if her words summoned it, a vision struck her with the force of a tidal wave. Merona gasped, her body folding as her knees gave way beneath her. Horror surged through her mind in vivid, unrelenting images. Screams pierced her consciousness, each cry laced with agony. The acrid stench of burning flesh filled her senses, suffocating her. Faces twisted with fury and fear, their expressions lit by the glow of torches, as they hunted their prey through the shadows of a dark, forbidding forest.

"No," she whimpered, shaking her head violently in a futile attempt to dispel the haunting visions. "This can't be."

But the images refused to relent, growing sharper, more visceral. Demonic figures skulked in the darkness, cloaked in the guise of piety and virtue. Their whispers slithered into the ears of the fearful, spreading venomous lies and igniting flames of hatred and suspicion.

Merona's breath came in ragged gasps, her heart pounding like a war drum. A bone-deep certainty settled over her, chilling her to the core: these were not idle nightmares. They were glimpses of a future teetering on the brink of reality; a future she had been reborn to stop.

"I won't let it happen," Merona whispered, her voice barely audible above the sounds of celebration. "I can't."

With a final glance at the oblivious villagers, Merona slipped away into the gathering darkness. Her movements were swift and deliberate, each step guided by an instinct as old as time itself.

As she descended into the underground catacombs, the air around her began to shimmer with an otherworldly energy. Each stone seemed to pulse with a hidden light, reflecting the power that coursed through this sacred place.

Merona stopped in her tracks, pressing her hand against the chilly and moist wall. The magic here was palpable in the air, a physical energy that sent a shiver rippling down her spine; a mixture of exhilaration and dread.

"Morrigan," she murmured, her voice hushed but urgent. "Do you feel it? The power…it's overwhelming."

"Goddess Danu," she whispered, her voice echoing softly in the tunnel. "Guide my steps. Show me the way to change what I have seen."

The stones seemed to respond to her plea, their faint glow intensifying to illuminate a hidden path deeper into the catacombs. Merona exhaled slowly, steadying the storm of emotions within her.

"I am ready," she said, her voice resolute despite the fear coiled tightly in her chest. "I am the Reborn Witch, and I will not falter."

With Morrigan at her side, she pressed forward, the narrow passage giving way to a grand, cavernous chamber. Soft, golden light bathed the room, revealing towering stone pillars etched with the intricate visages of ancient deities. The air hung heavy with the scent of incense, its ethereal tendrils weaving around her like ethereal fingers.

Merona's heartbeat thundered in her ears as she stepped into the chamber, each footfall reverberating through the sacred space. She felt the weight of the moment settle upon her; a collision of destiny and determination.

He stood like a figure plucked from the pages of legend, his presence regal and unyielding. The piercing intensity of his gaze seemed to cut straight through her, unraveling every layer of her defenses. Draped over his broad shoulders, a cloak embroidered with golden bees gleamed faintly in the chamber's light; a symbol of ancient power and unyielding authority. His dark, untamed locks and beard lent him an air of wild mysticism, as though he were both king and enigma.

"Welcome, Merona," he intoned, his deep voice reverberating through the vaulted chamber like the toll of a great bell. "I have awaited your arrival."

A shiver ran down her spine, the sensation as fleeting and profound as a ghostly whisper brushing against her skin. She swallowed, her voice barely escaping her lips. "You… know who I am?" she asked, disbelief and cautious curiosity mingling in her words.

A smile played at the corners of Clovis' lips, a knowing expression that only deepened the intrigue. "I've known of you since before you were reborn. The stars themselves heralded your coming twinkling with anticipation since the dawn of time." His words carried the weight of prophecy, wrapping around her like a silken thread.

With a deliberate grace, Clovis extended his hand, gesturing toward the chamber's stone floor. There, etched into the ancient surface, was an intricate labyrinth of swirling designs and twisting patterns. Each line and curve seemed to pulse faintly, hinting at mysteries buried deep within its core.

"Come," he said, his voice low and resonant, carrying the cadence of the ancients. "The Labyrinth awaits. Within its heart lie the secrets of our lineage." The command was undeniable, his words echoing against the chamber walls, pulling her forward with an irresistible gravity.

Merona hesitated, her thoughts swirling in a storm of doubt and anticipation. This moment, the fulcrum of everything she had prepared for, weighed heavy on her. Fear clawed at her resolve, threatening to anchor her where she stood.

But she refused to succumb. Taking a deep, steadying breath, she stepped forward, her eyes locking onto Clovis' with a newfound determination. "Teach me, Your Majesty," she said, her voice quivering yet layered with an unexpected strength. "I'm ready to embrace my destiny."

Clovis' expression shifted, his voice lowering into a reverent timbre that resonated through the stillness of the chamber. "Behold," he began, his tone imbued with an almost sacred weight. "The mark of my lineage; the symbol of the Merovingian bloodline."

He rolled back his sleeve, revealing an intricate labyrinth birthmark on his forearm. It glimmered faintly, a mesmerizing red glow that seemed to pulse with a life of its own.

Merona's fingers instinctively grazed her own birthmark, an intricate design that throbbed faintly beneath her skin. "I don't understand," she whispered, her voice breaking as the enormity of the revelation pressed down on her. "Why me?"

Clovis inclined his head solemnly and turned toward the entrance of the Labyrinth. The arched threshold shimmered with a living energy, its ancient aura both inviting and foreboding. "The path ahead is fraught with peril, Merona," he said, his tone a mixture of caution and encouragement.

"The ancient power of the Merovingians courses through your veins. It is your birthright, as sacred as it is dangerous. You are descended from the Tuatha Dé Danann and the dragon kings. Reborn countless times, you carry fragments of memory from your past lives. You are the chosen one, blessed by the Gods themselves to bring aid to those in their darkest moments." His words were both a blessing and a great burden, echoing like the tolling of a distant bell.

The weight of his proclamation settled heavily on her shoulders as they approached the entrance to the winding maze. She felt the hum of magic vibrating in the air, beckoning her forward into the vast unknown. In that moment of truth, despite the fear coiling within her, she understood without a doubt that she was destined for this task and would face whatever challenges awaited her with the courage and determination that surged in her heart.

As they descended into the mystical maze, Merona felt the atmosphere shift. The air crackled with ancient energies, eager to be unleashed. The weight of history, prophecy, and untold legacies pressed down on her, but she stood tall, resolute, ready to confront the trials that awaited.

The runic tattoos that adorned her skin; each one earned through mastering the elements began to glow softly. With each pulse of the runes, Merona could feel the surge of her newfound powers shifting within her, an invigorating force that stirred her spirit. Each symbol was more than just ink on her skin; they thrummed with the echoes of ancestors long passed and promises yet to be fulfilled. She could feel their presence deep in her soul.

King Clovis stood before her, his gaze both piercing and wise, radiating a fierce strength tempered with unyielding kindness. Merona's heart raced as the enormity of her transformation settled into her very bones. Flexing her fingers, she watched faint sparks dance between them like tiny stars caught in a whirlwind. With a quiet murmur, she murmured, "It's... overwhelming." The tremor in her voice betrayed her vulnerability she tried so hard to hide.

Clovis' dark eyes softened, a flicker of understanding crossing his rugged face. "The power of the Merovingians is not easily borne, Merona. It is both a blessing and a burden, a sacred trust you must learn to bear."

"These bees," he continued, running his fingers along the embroidery, of his cloak "represent more than mere decoration. They are a testament to our divine right to rule, a connection to powers beyond mortal comprehension, and provide immortality."

Merona reached out, her fingers brushing the delicate bees. She nodded, swallowing hard as she steadied herself. "I feel them, Clovis. The ancestors. Their voices... they're so clear." The connection overwhelmed her, a mixture of awe and trepidation flooding her chest.

"They speak through you now," he replied, his deep voice resonating in the stillness of the chamber, echoing the weight of ages past. Stepping closer, he added, "Merona, the powers you now possess are not merely a gift, they are a responsibility. For generations, the Merovingians have upheld the balance between this world and the next. Now, it is your turn to walk this ancient path."

Merona met his gaze, determination and anxiety swirling within her. "How can I be sure I'm ready for such a task?" she asked, her voice barely more than a whisper. The question hung in the air, fragile and uncertain.

Clovis placed a reassuring hand on her shoulder, his touch warm with encouragement. "You were chosen, Merona. Reborn for this very purpose. The road ahead will be fraught with danger, but within you flows the strength of countless generations." His belief in her filled her with newfound courage.

She closed her eyes, taking a deep breath. The weight of destiny pressed on her, yet a surge of resolve ignited within her. "I won't let them down," she vowed, her voice gaining strength. "I won't let you down, King Clovis."

A rare smile tugged at the corners of the king's lips, a blend of pride and hope. "I have no doubt, Merona. The trials ahead will test you but remember, you are never truly alone. The spirits of our ancestors walk with you, their light illuminating even the darkest corners of this labyrinth."

As Merona absorbed his words, an unfamiliar sensation washed over her. The chamber around her seemed to ripple and shift, as if reality itself were bending, revealing hidden layers. Visions of the Labyrinth unfolded before her eyes; a vast web of countless paths, each shimmering with infinite potential and fraught with peril, beckoning her to explore their depths.

"I see it," she whispered, awe and trepidation mingling in her voice. "The paths... they're endless." In that moment, she understood her journey had just begun, a voyage that would lead her to the heart of her legacy, where the destinies of those in darkness awaited her guiding light.

He nodded solemnly. "What you see, Merona, are the myriad possibilities of your journey. Each twist and turn represents a choice, a potential future. Not just for you, but for all those above us."

Merona's heart raced as glimpses of her village flashed before her eyes; its inhabitants unaware of the darkness closing in. She saw faces twisted in fear, heard echoes of screams yet to be uttered. "The village," she gasped. "They're in danger, aren't they?"

"Tonight," Clovis continued, his eyes reflecting the ethereal glow of the chamber, "is not just Samhain. It marks a convergence of energies, where the veil between worlds is at its thinnest. The storm brewing above is a dark omen, but it could also be a catalyst for profound change. In two days' time, the battle of Tolbiac will be fought, and many lives will be lost. May the Gods grant us victory."

He paused, his gaze lingering on the With, a flicker of admiration passing across his features. "Your courage is commendable, Merona. Perhaps... perhaps there is a way forward that doesn't require us to be enemies."

Merona's brow furrowed, her mind racing. "You mean a path that embraces both our beliefs? Is such a thing even possible?"

The Frankish king turned, his cloak of golden bees shimmering in the dim light. "Our world stands at a crossroads. Christianity spreads like wildfire, yet the old ways still pulse in the earth beneath our feet. Why must we choose one over the other?"

Merona's heart quickened at the implication. "A new era... one of unity and acceptance?"

"It won't be easy," Clovis cautioned, his deep voice heavy with the weight of his words. "Many on both sides will resist. But imagine the strength we could wield if we were to combine the power of your ancient magic with the fervor of this new faith."

As he spoke, Merona envisioned it; a land where the sacred groves stood alongside Christian churches, where the Rite of Veils was celebrated with the same reverence as Easter mass. The vision was as intoxicating as it was daunting.

"It would require immense change," she mused, her fingers absently tracing the labyrinth birthmark on her shoulder. "Not just in laws or customs, but in the very hearts of our people."

Clovis' eyes gleamed with resolve. "Change is the very essence of power, young witch. And it is a power we must wield with care."

A chill ran down Merona's spine as she recalled the ominous clouds gathering over the village. "The storm... I felt its approach earlier. But how can we use it?"

Clovis' voice sharpened with urgency. "Together, we shall harness its energy. The power within you, combined with the ancient magic of this night, can turn the tide against the encroaching darkness."

Merona clenched her fists, feeling the runic tattoos pulse with newfound strength. "I'm ready," she declared, her voice steady despite the fear gnawing at her insides. "Whatever it takes to protect my people, to fulfill this destiny thrust upon me, I'll do it."

As thunder rumbled overhead, Merona steeled herself for the challenges to come, knowing that the fate of many rested upon her shoulders.

Clovis' gaze deepened with ancient wisdom as he swept his arm toward the floor. With a swift motion, he gestured to a glowing sigil, its intricate runes pulsing with an otherworldly light.

"Step into the Labyrinth," Clovis intoned, his voice rich with power, "and let your heart guide you. The spirits will reveal the paths that are meant for you."

Merona's breath caught in her throat as she gazed at the mystical design. Her fingers trembled, the weight of her newfound powers thrumming just beneath her skin.

"Trust in the power you've awakened," Clovis urged, his words a blend of encouragement and caution.

Merona swallowed hard, her mind racing. "And if I lose my way?" she asked, her voice barely a whisper.

Clovis' expression softened with understanding. "The Labyrinth is a reflection of your inner self, Merona. It will test you, but it cannot harm you. Remember who you are. The witch reborn, destined to change the course of history."

Drawing a deep breath, Merona took her first step forward. Fear and exhilaration intertwined in her chest as she neared the sigil. The air around her thickened with anticipation, pressing against her like an unseen force.

"I'm ready," she whispered, more to herself than to Clovis.

With a final, determined step, Merona crossed the threshold. The instant her foot touched the glowing runes, a surge of energy coursed through her body. The chamber around her began to dissolve, stone walls melting away like mist.

Merona's heart pounded as the world shifted around her. In the blink of an eye, she was plunged into the ethereal realm of the Labyrinth, surrounded by swirling mists and shimmering pathways that stretched endlessly into the unknown.

"Remember," Clovis' voice echoed from somewhere near, yet impossibly distant, "trust in yourself, and in the magic flowing through your veins."

As his words faded, Merona stood alone at the entrance of the mystical maze, on the precipice of a journey that would test her resolve and shape her destiny.

Shadows danced at the edges of her vision, their whispers like ghostly fingers brushing against her mind. The labyrinth stretched before her, its paths twisting in impossible patterns that shifted with every blink of her eyes.

"What secrets do you hold?" Merona murmured, her voice barely audible over the pulsing energy of the runes coursing through her veins.

As she took her first tentative steps, the shadows grew bolder. Faces flickered in the darkness; men and women long forgotten, their eyes filled with a mixture of fear and hope.

"We were like you once," a wispy voice echoed. "Hunted. Feared."

Merona's heart raced. "And what became of you?"

The labyrinth answered by shifting, unveiling a new path. As she rounded the corner, a vision struck her like a physical blow. Men in clerical robes, their faces contorted with righteous fury, dragged a screaming woman toward a pyre.

"No!" Merona cried, instinctively reaching toward the scene. But her hands passed through the illusion as if it were smoke.

The woman's agonized screams echoed through the maze, intertwining with Merona's ragged breaths. She pressed a hand to her chest, feeling the frantic pounding of her heart.

"Is this my fate?" she whispered, fear clawing at her. "To burn, like so many other witches?"

Even as the horrific vision began to fade, Merona felt a surge of defiance rise within her. The runes on her skin pulsed with renewed energy, responding to her determination.

"No," she declared firmly, clenching her fists. "I won't let it end that way. Not for me. Not for anyone else."

As if in response to her resolve, the labyrinth shifted again. This time, the shadows receded, revealing glimpses of ancient forests and towering trees. A gentle warmth radiated from these visions, a stark contrast to the cold fear that had gripped her moments before.

A deep, resonant voice seemed to rumble from the very earth beneath her feet. "We stand with you, daughter of the earth. Remember, even in the darkest night, hope still grows."

Merona nodded, drawing strength from the ancient spirits. "Thank you," she whispered, feeling her courage grow with each step she took deeper into the labyrinth's unknown depths.

Her footsteps echoed through the twisting passages as she pressed onward. The air crackled with unseen energy, sending shivers down her spine, making the fine hairs on her arms stand on end. Then, a familiar voice cut through the eerie silence.

"Remember, Merona," Clovis' voice echoed softly in her mind, "you are not alone. The spirits will temper your resolve and bolster your spirit."

She stopped, "King Clovis?" she whispered, a mixture of relief and uncertainty in her voice.

There was no response, but Merona felt a surge of warmth flood through her, as if the very essence of the labyrinth was embracing her. She closed her eyes, drawing in a steady breath.

"I hear you," she murmured, her fingers tracing the intricate runic tattoos on her arms. "And I will not falter."

As if in response to her renewed resolve, the labyrinth shifted again. The walls pulsated with energy, stone and shadow dancing in a mesmerizing display. Merona's heart raced as she watched the impossible rearrangement of reality unfold before her eyes.

"By the gods," she breathed, her raven hair whipping around her face as unseen currents of air swirled through the maze.

When the movement ceased, Merona found herself in a circular chamber. At its center stood a shimmering well of light, its radiance casting long shadows across the ancient stones. She approached cautiously, drawn by an inexplicable pull.

"What secrets do you hold?" Merona wondered, kneeling before the well. As she drew closer, the tattoos on her arms began to glow more intensely, responding to the well's energy. Hesitantly, she extended a hand, feeling the warmth surge through her body.

"Is this... is this the magic within me?" she asked aloud, awe filling her voice as she marveled at the connection she felt to the ethereal light. "The power of the Merovingians, passed down through generations?"

Merona closed her eyes, surrendering to the flow of energy. In that moment, flashes of the past and glimpses of possible futures swirled before her, weaving a tapestry of time into the very core of her being.

The realization struck her like a bolt of lightning, and her eyes flew open, flooded with understanding. She wasn't merely a conduit for ancient power; she was its guardian, its protector.

"The visions," she whispered, her voice trembling with newfound purpose. "They weren't nightmares. They were warnings."

The well of light pulsed in response, as though affirming her epiphany. Merona's gaze hardened, her jaw set with unshakable determination.

"I won't let it happen," she vowed, her words echoing through the chamber. "I will fight against the darkness that threatens to bind us all."

With a steadying breath, Merona plunged her hands into the shimmering well. The surge of energy hit her like a tidal wave, raw and overwhelming. She gritted her teeth, forcing herself to remain grounded.

"I am Merona," she declared, her voice growing stronger with each word. "The Reborn Witch, guardian of the ancient ways."

Above her, she felt the storm's fury, its rage mirroring the tempest within her own heart. But here, fear had no hold. With each pulse of her heart, the magic of her ancestors coursed through her veins, blending with her very being.

"I am not afraid," Merona spoke with unwavering clarity. "For I carry the strength of those who came before me, and the hope of those who will follow."

As the power surged within her, her thoughts turned to her village, to the people she had sworn to protect. Their faces flashed in her mind's eye, their joys and sorrows intertwining with her own.

"I will be their shield," she promised, her resolve unbreakable. "Against the coming darkness, against those who would bind our hearts and minds."

The well's light began to fade, its energy now fully absorbed into Merona. She stood tall, the weight of her newfound responsibility settling firmly upon her shoulders.

"So it begins," Merona murmured, her eyes glowing with an inner fire. "The true test of a guardian's strength."

The Labyrinth shuddered, its walls pulsing with otherworldly energy. Merona's raven hair whipped around her face as the maze began to twist and reform before her eyes. In the distance, a warm golden light called to her, growing brighter with each passing moment.

"King Clovis," Merona whispered, recognizing the unmistakable aura of the Merovingian king.

"The way is clear," a deep voice echoed through the Labyrinth. Clovis' words wrapped around her like a comforting cloak. "Come, Merona. It is time."

With every step she took, Merona felt the weight of her destiny grow heavier. The visions of torture and hunts flashed through her mind, but now, they fueled her determination rather than sowing fear.

"I'm ready," she called out, her voice steady, resolute. "Ready to face what lies beyond."

As she reached the outer chamber of the Labyrinth, Clovis' imposing figure came into view. His dark eyes gleamed with a mix of pride and concern.

"You've changed," he said, extending his hand. "The Labyrinth has left its mark on you."

Merona grasped his hand, feeling the unspoken bond of their shared bloodline. "As it should," she replied. "For now, I understand the true weight of our legacy."

Clovis nodded solemnly. "And with that understanding comes great responsibility. Are you prepared for what lies ahead?"

Merona turned back to face him, her eyes shimmering with unshed tears. "And Armaeus? The prophecy speaks of his role, but how can I hope to stand against such darkness?"

A shadow passed over Clovis' face. "Armaeus is but one piece in this cosmic game. Your destiny, the prophecy, the fate of our people; they are all intertwined in ways we have yet to fully comprehend."

As their conversation drew to a close, Clovis' expression grew solemn. He placed a hand on Merona's shoulder, his touch surprisingly gentle for a warrior king. "Know this, Merona," he said, his voice steady but grave. "You have my unwavering support in the trials to come. I pledge to protect you and aid you in fulfilling your destiny. Even if it means challenging the very foundations of the order I've built."

Merona's breath caught in her throat, the weight of his offer settling over her. "Your Majesty, I…"

"The path ahead is treacherous," Clovis interrupted, his voice low and urgent. "But together, we may yet forge a future that honors both the old ways and the new. Are you prepared for what that might entail?"

"We part ways now," Clovis continued, his deep voice resonating in the cavernous space. "But our paths will remain intertwined. May the wisdom of your ancestors guide you, Merona."

"And may your God watch over you, King Clovis," Merona replied, her head bowing slightly in respect.

Her thoughts flashed to her village, to the storm raging above, to the shadows creeping ever closer, threatening all she held dear. A fierce protectiveness surged within her. "Tonight, we celebrate Samhain, but we also kindle the flames of resistance. The dormant spirit of our people will awaken, and I will lead them."

A smile crossed Clovis' face, bittersweet with pride and sorrow. "Then let us return to the surface, for your tale is only beginning, Witch of the Merovingians."

Chapter 25

The flickering torchlight cast shifting shadows across the damp stone walls as Merona emerged from the yawning mouth of the Labyrinth. Her raven hair clung to her sweat-slicked brow, and her eyes blazed with an unearthly light. She stumbled forward, her legs trembling beneath her, the ancient magic coursing through her veins like liquid fire. Her cloak, intricately woven with bees sewn into the fabric by golden thread, shimmered in the dim light. Morrigan stood silently by her side.

"By all the gods," Murdach breathed, his voice barely a whisper.

Merona's gaze locked with his, and in that instant, she saw the weight of generations reflected in his dark eyes. The prophecies, the bloodlines, the fate of nations. It all converged in this single, breathless moment.

"It's done," she said, her voice hoarse but steady. "The power of the Labyrinth... it's a part of me now."

Murdach stepped closer, his broad form casting a shadow over her. His hand reached out, pausing for a heartbeat before resting gently on the shimmering cloak of bees draped across her shoulders.

The insects hummed softly, their wings vibrating in perfect harmony with the pulse of the ancient magic.

"I can feel it," he murmured, his fingers tracing the intricate patterns formed by the living mantle. "The magic of your ancestors, the very essence of the earth itself."

Merona closed her eyes, savoring the warmth of his touch. In her mind's eye, flashes of the future flickered battles yet to be fought, lives hanging in the balance. The weight of her destiny pressed down upon her, a burden so immense it threatened to crush her beneath its sheer gravity.

"We stand at a crossroads, Murdach," Merona said, her eyes meeting his once more. "The old ways and the new. Paganism and Christianity. The magic that flows through our veins, and the faith that seeks to deny it."

Murdach's jaw tightened, the internal conflict clear in the furrow of his brow. "How can we bridge such a divide? His people look to him for guidance, but it feels as if he is torn between worlds."

Merona reached up, cupping his cheek with her hand. "We must find a way," she said, her voice unexpectedly steady, filled with a determination that surprised even her. "For the sake of all who come after us. The witch hunts, the persecutions; we can stop them. We can shape a future where magic and faith coexist in harmony."

As she spoke, the bees on her cloak buzzed with renewed energy, their collective hum rising in a chorus that reverberated through the cavernous space. It was a sound of affirmation, of ancient powers stirring, awakening to a new purpose.

Murdach closed his eyes, leaning into her touch. When he opened them again, the depths of his gaze had changed. There was a newfound resolve burning within him. "Then let us forge that path together, Merona. Whatever challenges lie ahead, we will face them as one."

A low, rumbling growl vibrated through the air, sending a shiver down Merona's spine. She turned to see the Morrigan, now in her wolf form, circling them with predatory grace. The goddess's amber eyes gleamed with pride and fierce protectiveness, her red fur bristling as she positioned herself between them and the shadowy recesses of the Labyrinth's entrance.

Merona's breath caught in her throat as she watched the Phantom Queen silently patrol their perimeter. "She's guarding us," she whispered, more to herself than to Murdach.

In the shadows of the ancient trees, Armaeus lingered, his demonic form shimmering with barely contained rage. His dark eyes blazed with fury as he watched Merona and Murdach, the air around him crackling with dark energy.

"Unthinkable!" he hissed, his hands balled into tight fists, sharp claws piercing his palms, drawing crimson drops of blood. "The Labyrinth was supposed to annihilate her, not make her stronger. A three-day shroud of darkness has commenced, and on her 18th birthday, she will harness her full powers. As the shadows thickened around him, it dawned on him that the very energies intended to keep her at bay were instead amplifying her abilities. With every fleeting second, she was becoming more powerful than he could have ever conceived."

In the darkness, Armaeus' fury reached its boiling point. He would not allow these mortals, no matter how powerful, to stand in the way of his ambitions. The time for waiting had passed. Now was the moment to strike.

Merona replayed her conversation with Clovis in her mind; the labyrinth, their shared destiny, and the bloodline that bound them.

A cool breeze whispered through the trees, carrying the scent of damp earth and the hint of approaching autumn. Merona closed her eyes, letting the wind caress her face, grounding herself in this fleeting moment of peace before the storm.

"We stand at a crossroads, Murdach," she said softly, her eyes meeting his intense gaze. "The path ahead is treacherous, filled with sacrifices we can scarcely comprehend. But we must walk it for the sake of all who will come after us."

Murdach pulled Merona into his arms, his deep voice steady and filled with resolve. "Together," he said, his words resonating with unwavering conviction. "Whatever trials we face; we will face them as one."

A surge of warmth bloomed in Merona's chest, a flicker of hope that cut through the looming darkness. "Together," she echoed, her voice barely a whisper.

The air around them suddenly thickened, heavy with an oppressive darkness that seemed to rise from the very earth beneath their feet. Merona's skin prickled as her newfound powers pulsed beneath the surface, sending a warning through her. Her heart raced as she turned, eyes widening at the monstrous figure that emerged from the shadows.

Armaeus stood before them, his true form revealed in its horrific splendor. Twisted horns sprouted from his skull, curling like blackened branches reaching into the night. His crimson eyes burned with fury, reflecting the seething rage that distorted his demonic features.

"Did you think you could escape me?" Armaeus snarled, his voice a guttural growl that sent chills down Merona's spine. "Your little prophecy ends here!"

With a roar that rattled the very air around them, Armaeus unleashed a torrent of dark magic. The malevolent energy crackled and writhed, surging toward Merona and Murdach like a tide of liquid night.

Merona's heart thundered in her chest, fear threatening to paralyze her. But deep within, something ancient and powerful stirred. *I am more than this moment,* she thought, her resolve hardening. *I am the culmination of countless lives, countless struggles.*

"Spirits of the ancients, hear my call!" Merona's voice rang out, surprising her with its strength and resonance. "Elementals of earth and sky, lend me your power!"

As the words left her lips, Merona felt a surge of energy unlike anything she had ever known. It flowed through her, a confluence of fire and water, earth and air, life, and death itself. In her mind's eye, the faces of those who had come before her appeared witches who had suffered, fought, and died for their beliefs.

A shimmering barrier sprang to life before them, iridescent and pulsing with otherworldly power. Armaeus' dark magic crashed against it, the force of the collision sending shockwaves through the air.

Murdach gripped his sword tightly, his knuckles turning white. "By all the gods," he breathed, eyes wide with awe and fear.

Merona stood firm, her arms outstretched as she poured every ounce of her being into holding the shield. "This ends now, Armaeus," she declared, her voice carrying the weight of centuries. "Your reign of terror will not continue into the future I've seen!"

The darkened sky blazed with an otherworldly light as Merona, Murdach, and the Morrigan stood their ground, their silhouettes stark against the maelstrom of clashing energies. Before them loomed Armaeus in his demonic form, his crimson eyes burning with hatred as he unleashed wave after wave of dark magic.

Merona's raven hair whipped around her face. She turned to the Morrigan, her voice steady despite the chaos surrounding them. *"Together, united in power, we can overcome this evil."*

With a shared resolve, they pushed forward. Merona channeled the elemental forces, weaving them into a tapestry of raw power that surged toward Armaeus. At the same time, Murdach transformed into a dragon, his immense form joining their collective strength to bring an end to Armaeus.

Armaeus sneered, his twisted horns casting grotesque shadows. "You cannot hope to defeat me, children of dust!" he roared, his voice dripping with malice. "I am eternal!"

Merona's mind raced, flashes of future witch trials filling her vision. *No,* she thought fiercely, *I won't let that future come to pass.* Aloud, she shouted, "Your time is over, Armaeus. The world is changing, and there is no place for your darkness in it!"

Suddenly, a blood-chilling howl pierced the air. The Morrigan, in her red wolf form, was a blur of motion as she leapt from the shadows. Her amber eyes gleamed with ancient wisdom and fierce protectiveness as she lunged at Armaeus, her powerful jaws sinking into his demonic flesh.

Armaeus screamed in fury and pain, his anguished cry reverberating through the dense forest. The dark magic he wielded with such confidence faltered, flickering like a dying candle flame as he struggled against the brutal, unexpected attack. The Morrigan, her eyes alight with predatory brilliance, bore down on him with an intensity that was both terrifying and awe-inspiring. Her teeth sank into his flesh with savage ferocity, a move that even the goddess herself had not anticipated. Every growl from her throat carried the weight of a thousand battles fought and won, a chilling reminder of her power and wrath.

In a sudden flash, Armaeus vanished, leaving behind only a lingering trace of darkness that slowly dissolved into the cool night air.

The scene shifted abruptly, and they stood in stunned silence, their hearts racing as they took in their surroundings. Above them, the night sky stretched out, clear and pristine, finally free from the swirling tides of dark magic that had consumed it moments before. The stars twinkled brightly, indifferent to the chaos that had unfolded. The air was still, serene, and the only sound was the gentle rustling of leaves in the light breeze, as if nature itself were exhaling in relief.

"What happened?" Murdach's voice broke the stillness, shaking with disbelief as his gaze swept the area. His expression was a mix of confusion and awe.

Merona stepped forward cautiously, her heart pounding in her chest as her shaky steps led her across the clearing. Her eyes darted around, searching for any sign of Armaeus' lingering presence. But there was nothing. The remnants of his demonic form had vanished without a trace, swallowed by the very shadows that had once marked his dominion.

As silence settled over them again, Merona's voice emerged, barely a whisper, laden with both relief and uncertainty. "It's over for now," she murmured, a wave of conflicting emotions crashing over her. A bittersweet sense of relief washed over her, soothing her frazzled nerves, but a nagging doubt lingered in the air. *How could they be certain they had truly defeated him? Was the end of Armaeus even possible?*

The Morrigan let out a soft sigh, her fierce demeanor softening for the first time. With a slow, knowing nod, she affirmed Merona's words, signaling an unspoken acknowledgment of their victory, however temporary it might be.

Murdach, brimming with uncontainable excitement, let out a triumphant roar that echoed through the clearing, blending with the sounds of the night. The primal joy surged through him as he shifted back into his human form, the tension in his body melting away.

He turned to Merona, his eyes alight with pride and admiration, and pulled her into a warm embrace, pressing a soft kiss to her lips. "We did it!" he exclaimed, his voice booming with exhilaration, the thrill of victory coursing through him.

Despite the exhaustion that weighed heavily on her, Merona felt a radiant smile spread across her face, pride swelling within her at their shared victory. "Let's go find Mother," she suggested, her voice laced with determination as she took a step back to steady herself. "We need to tell her about the Labyrinth and our battle with Armaeus."

Elsewhere, Armaeus sat in the solitude of his cave, deep in thought as he prepared for the upcoming battle at Tolbiac. The sting of his defeat at the hands of Merona and Murdach still burned within him, fueling a fierce determination to crush them once and for all.

Armaeus knew that in order to achieve his goal, he would need more power. He required the four treasures of the Tuatha De Dannan; the artifacts that possessed unimaginable magical abilities. With them in his grasp, he was certain that no one could stand in his way.

He summoned Varis, his most trusted lieutenant, to his side. "I ordered you to find the four treasures before our next attack," he said, his voice thick with conviction.

Varis hesitated; his words laced with caution. "My lord, those treasures cannot be found. We have searched every realm, and they are not easy to locate," he warned, fear creeping into his voice. He knew the consequences of failure all too well.

Armaeus' eyes narrowed, his gaze cold and dangerous. "I care not for your excuses," he snarled. "Find a way to retrieve those treasures, or you will suffer my wrath."

Panicked, Varis nodded quickly and scurried off to carry out the order.

Alone again, Armaeus began plotting his next move, strategizing for the battle at Tolbiac and how best to wield the treasures' power against Merona and her allies.

Chapter 26

Battle of Tolbiac 496 AD

King Clovis of the Salian Franks stood unwavering against the chaos, his grip tightening on his sword until his knuckles turned white. He joined King Sigebert and the Ripuarian Franks on the battlefield, facing the Alemanni, a powerful confederation of Germanic tribes. The conflict had erupted from fears that the Alemanni would invade Sigebert's kingdom.

On each side of the battlefield, roughly six thousand soldiers clashed, and as the fighting intensified, Clovis couldn't shake the dread that gnawed at him, sensing an ominous outcome. The sound of steel against steel rang through the air, a cacophony of death and desperation. Each strike reverberated with the anguished cries of the wounded and the battle cries of the warriors. For three long days, a suffocating darkness had hung over the land, casting a shadow over the conflict and plunging it into a nightmarish realm where the line between friend and foe grew dangerously unclear.

The Franks, known for their ferocity, charged into the fray, their arms emblazoned with the distinct insignia of their identity: blue banners adorned with three golden toads, symbols of their courage and kinship. Each warrior carried the weight of their tribal legacy, fighting in unarmored splendor, a bold choice that spoke both of confidence and recklessness. While many chose to forgo heavy armor, a few wore rudimentary helmets, their faces set with fierce determination, ready to face the enemy. Others had vibrant red hair, twisted into warrior knots atop their heads, marking their heritage and strength. Their attire was practical and emblematic, with tight-fitting tunics that reached just above the knees for maximum mobility. Over these, some wore sleeveless vests made from durable fur, a testament to the harsh conditions they had endured and their deep connection to the wild lands they hailed from. Their feet were clad in caligae, laced up their calves for added agility.

Amidst the chaos, the varied weapons of the Franks became extensions of their very beings. The air was thick with the sounds of battleaxes cleaving through flesh, swords carving arcs of deadly precision, and angons (throwing spears) whistling through the air before finding their mark. Shields were raised in desperate defense as bows and arrows contributed to the symphony of destruction. Archers, strategically positioned, unleashed a rain of deadly projectiles, their arrows cutting through the dimness like streaks of vengeance.

As the battle raged on, the stench of sweat and blood thick in the air, Clovis couldn't help but wonder if fate had woven this conflict into the very fabric of his people's future. His heart raced, not just from the adrenaline of combat, but from the heavy weight of destiny that seemed to hang over the battlefield, threatening to reshape the Franks' future forever. With a rallying cry that cut through the din, Clovis urged his men onward, hoping that somehow, they would emerge from this darkness into a future of glory and unity.

"Hold the line!" Clovis bellowed, his voice hoarse from hours of shouting orders. "For the glory of the Franks!"

Yet, even as his men echoed his battle cry, a sickening dread coiled deep within him. This was no ordinary battle. The very air crackled with malevolent energy, and an acrid scent of sulfur permeated the field, thickening the atmosphere with a sense of impending doom.

Suddenly, the sky erupted in a dazzling display of dark lightning, forking across the inky clouds in unnatural patterns. Clovis watched in horror as bolts of purple-black energy rained down upon his forces, incinerating men where they stood.

"Armaeus," Clovis hissed, his eyes narrowing as he scanned the battlefield for the demonic figure.

As if summoned by the king's thoughts, a towering form emerged from the carnage. Armaeus, the Demon, stood cloaked in shadow, his crimson eyes gleaming with malice. With a swift gesture of his clawed hand, tongues of hellfire erupted from the earth, engulfing entire battalions of Frankish soldiers in a blaze of destruction.

Clovis felt the searing heat of the inferno, even from his position, the acrid smoke stinging his eyes and choking his lungs. A heavy sense of dread settled in his chest. Was this the end? Would all his ambitions turn to ash before the overwhelming force of dark magic?

"My lord!" A nearby soldier cried in panic. "What devilry is this? How can we stand against such magic?"

Clovis remained silent, his mind racing. The words of Bishop Remigius and his wife Clotilde echoed in his thoughts. They had spoken of the power of their Christian God; an all-encompassing force capable of overcoming even the darkest of evils. In that moment of despair, Clovis found himself considering a path he had long resisted.

"Perhaps..." he murmured to himself, "it is time to embrace a new faith."

As another wave of Armaeus' destructive magic swept across the battlefield, Clovis made his decision. He would convert to Christianity; not only to save himself, but to save his people from this hellish onslaught. With newfound resolve, he raised his sword high.

"Stand fast, men of Gaul!" Clovis roared, his voice booming over the chaos. "This demon may wield his dark arts, but we have something greater. We have hope!"

Even as he spoke, Clovis silently prayed to this new God, pleading for the strength to overcome the evil that threatened to devour them all. The battle raged on, a violent tempest of steel and sorcery; with the fate of Gaul hanging in the balance.

The defenders rallied around Clovis' cry, their shields locking together in a desperate formation against Armaeus' relentless assault. Swords clashed against the undead hordes, and the air was thick with the acrid stench of burning flesh and sulfur.

A young soldier, barely more than a boy, trembled beside Clovis. "Sire, I... I'm afraid," he whispered, his eyes wide with terror.

Clovis gripped the boy's shoulder, his voice steady despite the chaos. "We all are lad. But fear can forge us into something stronger." He thrust his sword skyward, deflecting a bolt of dark energy. "Channel it into your sword arm!"

As they fought, a deep, ominous rumble echoed across the battlefield. The sky, already darkened by Armaeus' foul magic, churned with angry crimson clouds. A cold dread settled in Clovis' stomach.

"By all the gods," he breathed, his voice tinged with disbelief. "What fresh horror is this?"

The air grew heavy, charged with an unnatural energy that sent chills down Clovis' spine. In the distance, he saw Armaeus, the demon's eyes gleaming with malevolent satisfaction.

"Do you see it, mortals?" Armaeus' voice boomed across the battlefield. "The blood rain comes! Your doom is at hand!"

Panic rippled through the ranks. Men faltered, their courage wavering in the face of this apocalyptic threat.

Clovis' mind raced. How could they stand against both Armaeus' magic and this impending disaster? The weight of leadership pressed down on him, heavier than any crown.

"We cannot flee," he thought grimly. "But how can we possibly survive this?"

Clovis watched in anguish as another wave of his men fell before Armaeus' relentless assault. The metallic tang of blood filled the air, mingling with the bitter scent of dark magic. His heart pounded painfully in his chest; each beat a harsh reminder of his failure to protect his people.

"My lord!" A voice cried out, desperate and pleading. "What are we to do?"

Clovis turned, his gaze locking with that of a young soldier, barely more than a boy. The fear in the lad's eyes mirrored the turmoil churning within him. For a fleeting moment, Clovis was pulled back to his conversation with Bishop Remigius, the holy man's words echoing in his mind.

"The old gods have abandoned us, Clovis," the Bishop had said. "Only the Christian God can save your people now."

Chlotild's gentle voice followed in his memory. *"My love, faith can move mountains. Perhaps it's time to embrace a new path."*

Clovis closed his eyes, his grip tightening around his sword. "Could it be true?" he wondered. "Have our ancient ways brought us to this doom?"

Opening his eyes, he surveyed the apocalyptic scene before him. The sky swirled with crimson clouds, foretelling the blood rain that would soon drown them all. In that moment, Clovis made his decision.

"Lord God of Heaven," he whispered, his voice barely rising above the chaos. "If you are truly as powerful as they say, grant us Your protection. Save my people, and I will forsake all others and serve only You."

As if in answer to his plea, a brilliant light suddenly burst forth from the far side of the battlefield. Clovis shielded his eyes from the blinding radiance. When the light faded, what he saw took his breath away.

There stood Merona, her raven hair whipped by an otherworldly wind. Her eyes burned with an undeniable power as she raised her arms to the turbulent sky.

"Spirits of the ancients, heed my call!" Merona's voice rang out, clear and commanding. "Elementals of earth and sky, of fire and water, lend me your strength! *Aether, Domhan, Uisce, Dóiteáin, Aontacht!*"

The ground beneath them trembled, and Clovis watched in awe as tendrils of earth snaked from the soil, wrapping around Armaeus' demons, and dragging them down. Fierce gusts of wind tore through the enemy ranks, scattering their formations.

"By the gods," Clovis breathed, his voice laced with awe. "Or by God... what manner of power is this?"

Merona's magic continued to unfold before them in a dazzling display of elemental fury. Flames danced at her fingertips, leaping outward to form a protective barrier around the Frankish forces. Streams of water coalesced midair, dousing the demon's hellfire, and washing away the taint of dark magic.

As Clovis watched Merona wield the very forces of nature against their foes, a glimmer of hope flickered in his chest. Perhaps, he thought, they stood a chance after all.

A deafening crack split the air, and the battlefield erupted in an eerie, otherworldly glow. Through the chaos, Merona's eyes widened as three figures materialized before her: Mairead, her auburn hair blazing like a fiery halo; Murdach, his eyes flashing with fierce determination; and, between them, the Morrigan herself, radiating an aura of ancient power.

"The cavalry has arrived, my love," Murdach called out, a hint of a smile playing on his lips despite the grimness of the moment.

Merona's heart swelled with relief and renewed strength. "I feared you wouldn't make it in time!" she shouted over the din of battle.

The Morrigan's voice, deep and resonant, reverberated in their minds, rich as fertile soil. *"We stand with you, child of prophecy. The fate of Gaul hangs in the balance."*

The three powerful Morigna; fierce warriors and allies of the Tuatha De Dannan stood united in a sacred bond. Badh, the embodiment of battle rage, and the Morrigan, the shape-shifting goddess of war, urged their comrades onward with a resounding battle cry. Their mere presence ignited a fiery passion in the hearts of their fellow warriors, driving them toward victory. With sword and shield raised high, they charged into the fray, fueled by unyielding determination and the divine protection at their backs.

Mairead stepped forward, her hazel eyes alight with arcane energy. "Merona, we must combine our powers. Only together can we hope to overcome Armaeus and his demons."

As if summoned by his name, a wave of demonic energy surged toward them. Merona instinctively raised her hands, unleashing a burst of elemental magic to meet the oncoming attack. Murdach's dragon form erupted into existence, his glittering scales reflecting the light as he unleashed a torrent of flame.

"Mother, to your left!" Merona cried out, spotting a group of demons flanking their position.

The Elder witch spun, her tattoos blazing to life as she chanted an ancient incantation. The earth split open beneath the demons, swallowing them whole.

Amidst the chaos, Merona's thoughts raced. *How can we possibly win against such darkness?* Her resolve wavered for a fleeting moment.

Sensing her doubt, the Morrigan's presence wrapped around her like a cloak. *"Remember who you are, Merona. The power of ages flows through your veins."*

Steeling herself, Merona nodded, her determination reigniting. "Then let's show Armaeus what true power looks like."

With a unified cry, the four of them unleashed their combined might. The very fabric of reality seemed to warp as their magic, both ancient and new, collided with the demonic forces in a spectacular clash of light and shadow.

The deafening roar of steel and sorcery filled the air as Merona scanned the battlefield. Her eyes narrowed, searching for any weakness in Armaeus' seemingly impenetrable line of demons.

"There!" she shouted, pointing to a slight depression in the terrain. "We can use that ravine to our advantage."

Murdach, still in his dragon form, swooped low. "A sound strategy, young one. What do you propose?"

Merona's mind raced, quickly formulating a plan. "We'll funnel them through the narrow pass. Mother, can you raise earthen barriers on either side?"

The Elder witch nodded, her hands already weaving intricate patterns in the air. "Consider it done."

As Mairead's magic began to reshape the landscape, Merona turned to the Morrigan. *"We need your ravens to harry their rear guard, drive them forward."*

The goddess's eyes sparkled with approval. *"My children hunger for battle. It shall be as you command."*

Merona felt a surge of confidence. "And I'll be waiting at the mouth of the ravine with a surprise."

As their allies took their positions, Merona closed her eyes, drawing deeply from the well of elemental power within her. The air hummed with rising energy.

Suddenly, a bone-chilling roar split the air. Merona's eyes snapped open to see Armaeus himself leading a charge, his demonic form radiating malevolence.

"Brace yourselves!" she shouted, her voice carrying across the battlefield.

The plan worked at first. Demons poured into the ravine, harried by shadowy ravens, and hemmed in by towering walls of earth. But as Armaeus drew nearer, the very ground beneath him seemed to wither and die.

Merona gritted her teeth, unleashing a maelstrom of elemental fury upon the trapped demons. Fire and lightning rained down, tearing through their ranks.

For a fleeting moment, victory seemed within grasp. But then Armaeus raised his clawed hands, dark energy pulsing from his form. The barriers Mairead had created began to crack and crumble.

"No!" Merona gasped, feeling the tide of battle shift once more.

Murdach's voice rang out from above. "Stand firm, Merona! Remember your training!"

As despair threatened to overwhelm her, Merona closed her eyes, grounding herself. *I am the Reborn Witch,* she reminded herself. *I will not falter.*

Opening her eyes, she saw Armaeus advancing, a cruel smile twisting his features. "Your tricks cannot save you, little witch," he sneered.

Merona stood tall, power surging through her veins. "Perhaps not," she said, her voice unwavering. "But my will might."

With that, she thrust her hands forward, channeling every ounce of her strength into one devastating blast of pure, elemental chaos.

The air crackled with raw energy as Merona's magic collided with Armaeus' dark power. Reality itself seemed to warp, the fabric of existence straining under the weight of their conflict. The battlefield fell eerily silent, all eyes drawn to the titanic struggle unfolding before them.

Merona's eyes blazed with an otherworldly light, her raven hair whipping around her face as she poured every ounce of her being into the conflict. Armaeus, now fully revealed in his demonic form, snarled in defiance, his crimson gaze fixed on her.

"You cannot hope to defeat me, witch," Armaeus growled, his voice resonating with infernal power. "I am eternal, forged in the depths of hell itself!"

Merona gritted her teeth, the strain of maintaining her assault evident. "I may not be eternal," she retorted, her voice sharp with determination, "but I carry the hopes and dreams of countless souls. Their strength is my strength!"

As she spoke, a surge of energy coursed through her. The spirits of the ancients, the elementals, and even the fading echoes of forgotten deities seemed to rally behind her. She could almost hear their whispered encouragements, urging her onward.

Armaeus' eyes widened in shock as he felt his power begin to waver. "Impossible!" he roared, redoubling his efforts. The ground beneath them cracked and splintered, dark tendrils of energy snaking outward.

But Merona stood firm, drawing on every lesson Murdach had taught her. She thought of the villagers who had raised her, of Clovis and his struggling people, of all those who would suffer if she failed. With a cry that seemed to shake the heavens, she unleashed a final, devastating surge of elemental fury.

"By the power of earth, air, fire, and water, *Aether, Domhan, Uisce, Dóiteáin, Aontacht!*" she intoned, her voice strong with authority, "I cast you out, Armaeus! Back to the depths from which you came!"

The world erupted in a blinding flash of light. When it faded, Armaeus was gone, leaving only a scorched patch of earth and the lingering scent of brimstone.

Merona swayed on her feet, exhausted but triumphant. As the weight of her victory settled in, a small, weary smile tugged at her lips. "It's over," she whispered, her voice barely audible. "We've won, but Armaeus isn't dead. He is just gone for now!"

The dust began to settle, and the eerie silence of the aftermath swept over the battlefield. Merona's legs buckled beneath her, and she sank to her knees, her raven hair matted with sweat and grime. She looked in horror at the devastation around her.

"Merona!" Murdach's voice cut through the haze of her exhaustion. He limped toward her, his weathered face a mixture of concern and pride. "By all the gods, you've done it."

She managed a weak smile. "We've done it, Murdach. All of us."

As if on cue, survivors began to emerge from the battlefield. Clovis, his armor dented and bloodied, approached with awe in his eyes.

"I... I've never seen such power," he stammered, his gaze flicking between Merona and the scorched earth where Armaeus had fallen. "Is it truly over?"

Merona nodded, her voice hoarse but resolute. "Armaeus is banished for now. I fear he lingers still in the darkness. The prophecy is fulfilled." She paused, her brow furrowing with a touch of concern. "But at what cost?"

As if in answer, a mournful wail rose from the battlefield. Merona's heart clenched as she witnessed the growing number of bodies being tended to by the survivors.

"So many lost," she murmured, her eyes welling with tears. "Was it worth it?"

Murdach placed a comforting hand on her shoulder. "You've saved countless more, lass. Don't forget that."

Clovis knelt beside her, his face etched with both gratitude and uncertainty. "I... I made a vow during the battle. To the Christian God." He swallowed hard; his voice thick with emotion. "I think it's time for a change, for all of us."

Merona felt a cold shiver run down her spine, a flash of the future she'd come from. "Change can be good, Clovis," she said carefully, choosing her words. "But remember, there's wisdom in the old ways too."

As they spoke, the Morrigan approached, her presence both regal and unsettling. "The wheel turns Witch," she intoned, her voice as soft as the whisper of ravens' wings. "One battle won, but the war. It's only just begun."

Merona's gaze shot up sharply. "What do you mean?"

The Morrigan's eyes gleamed with an ancient knowing. "The seeds of the future are sown in victory as surely as in defeat. Watch closely in the days to come."

As the goddess melted back into the shadows, Merona felt a shiver of foreboding. She looked out over the ruined landscape, her mind racing with questions. The prophecy may have been fulfilled, but her journey, she realized with a mix of anticipation and dread, was far from over.

Chapter 27

The flickering torchlight cast long shadows across the cathedral's cold stone walls, illuminating Merona's face as she stood before Armaeus. Her eyes burned with an inner fire, her raven hair stark against her pale skin. The air crackled with tension, thick with unspoken truths and ancient magics. The labyrinth maze on the floor seemed to glow in response.

"I know what you are," Merona declared, her voice steady, despite the rapid pounding of her heart. The power of the elements surged within her, echoing her rising emotions.

Armaeus, resplendent in his Bishop's robes, raised an eyebrow. "My child, whatever do you mean?" His voice was smooth as silk, but beneath it, Merona sensed a malevolent edge.

She took a step forward, her hand instinctively brushing the protective amulet at her throat. "You're no servant of God," she said, her words carrying the weight of centuries. "You're a demon, Armaeus, sent to destroy us all."

For a brief moment, the Bishop's facade cracked, a flash of red flickering in his eyes before he regained his composure. "Serious accusations, young one," he warned, his tone cold. "Be careful with your words."

Merona's mind raced, recalling all she had learned from Murdach about ancient magics and the world's true nature. She had to expose Armaeus, not only for her own survival but to save countless others from falling victim to his twisted plots.

"I've seen through your lies," she pressed on, her voice growing bolder. "The darkness around you, the evil seeping from your very being. You can't hide from me."

Armaeus' mask of benevolence faltered, his features twisting with barely contained rage. "You dare challenge me, witch?" he hissed, the illusion of his human guise cracking.

Merona stood her ground, drawing on the strength of her ancestors and the power of the elements. "I don't just challenge you, demon. I expose you for what you truly are."

As she spoke, the air around them shimmered, and the veil between worlds thinned. She could feel the weight of unseen eyes upon them, bearing witness to this confrontation between light and dark, good and evil.

Armaeus lunged forward, his human form melting away to reveal the monstrous creature beneath. "You think you can stop me?" he snarled, his voice now a guttural growl. "I am eternal, you foolish girl!"

Merona raised her hands, calling on the elements for protection. "You may be ancient," she replied, her voice unwavering despite the fear rising within her, "but I carry within me the power of rebirth. Your time is over, Armaeus. The truth will be known."

As the demon's true form emerged, gasps of horror rippled through the cathedral. Merona remained steadfast, a beacon of light against the encroaching darkness, ready to face whatever came next in her mission to fulfill her destiny and save the future from the horrors of the past.

Her voice rang out, clear and resolute, addressing the stunned crowd. "Look upon your so-called Bishop, people of Gaul! See the deceit that has been perpetrated against you!"

The onlookers, their eyes wide and mouths agape, recoiled as Armaeus' monstrous form became fully visible. Merona's heart raced, but she pressed on, her words imbued with an ancient power that seemed to resonate through the very stones of the cathedral.

"He promised you salvation but delivered only damnation. He spoke of love while sowing hatred. The miracles you witnessed were naught, but illusions meant to ensnare your souls!"

A murmur spread through the crowd. Doubt flickered in their eyes, replacing blind devotion. Merona felt the change in the air, like a tide turning.

To her left, King Clovis stood rigid, his expression a mask of inner turmoil. His dark eyes flicked between Merona and the demon-Bishop, his fingers absently tracing the golden bees embroidered on his cloak.

Merona's gaze held Clovis'. "Your Majesty," she said, her voice softening without losing its edge, "you stand at a crossroads between the old ways and the new. But ask yourself: what kind of faith demands the blood of innocents?"

Clovis' brow furrowed; his internal struggle written across every line of his face. "The Church offers stability," he muttered, though his words faltered, lacking the usual confidence. "A united faith for a united kingdom."

"At what cost?" Merona pressed. "The wisdom of our ancestors, the magic that runs through your veins, would you discard it all for empty promises?"

As Clovis wrestled with his conscience, Merona felt a shift beside her. The Morrigan, in her human form, stood silently; a reminder of the ancient powers still at play in this land of transition.

Merona closed her eyes and drew a deep breath. The air around her shimmered, charged with an otherworldly energy. When she spoke again, her voice rang out with a power that was not entirely her own.

"I call upon the essence of Merovech, the sea-born king," Merona intoned, her words resonating through the chamber. "And to the gods who have watched over these lands since time immemorial."

A surge of warmth coursed through her veins, and Merona felt herself becoming a vessel for something far greater than herself. Her raven hair whipped around her face as if caught in an invisible wind, and her eyes blazed with a light born of inner power.

"What sorcery is this?" Armaeus hissed, his human facade slipping as his eyes flickered to a menacing red.

Merona raised her arms, tendrils of golden light swirling around her. "This is the truth of our people," she declared, her voice carrying a blend of strength and compassion. "The magic that has sustained us, protected us, and guided us through the darkest of times."

The air crackled with energy, sparks of blue and gold dancing between her fingertips. She could feel the raw power swelling within her, a tempest barely contained.

Armaeus took an involuntary step back, his face twisted with a mixture of fear and rage. "You cannot stand against me, witch," he snarled, but the tremor in his voice betrayed his growing uncertainty.

Merona advanced, each step leaving a shimmering imprint on the stone floor. "I am more than just a witch, Armaeus," she said, her words weighted with centuries of knowledge. "I am the culmination of countless hopes and dreams, the answer to prayers whispered in the dark. And I will not let you destroy all that we hold dear."

As the power within her surged toward its peak, Merona realized with startling clarity that this moment, this confrontation, was the very reason she had been reborn. All the pain, the loss, and the centuries of waiting had led to this.

"Your reign of terror ends now," she declared, her voice ringing with finality as she prepared to unleash the full force of the ancient magic coursing through her veins.

The labyrinth began to pulse with an otherworldly energy, their surface rippling like water disturbed by an unseen force. Merona watched in awe as intricate patterns emerged, glowing with an ethereal blue light that seemed to dance across the stone.

By the gods," she whispered, "It's awakening."

Clovis, his face a mask of conflicting emotions, stepped forward. "What sorcery is this, Merona? What have you done?"

Merona turned to him, her raven hair swirling around her like a dark halo. "This is no sorcery, Your Majesty. This is the true power of our ancestors; the magic that flows through the very veins of this land."

She took a deliberate step toward the shimmering walls, her heart pounding with a mixture of excitement and apprehension. As she moved, she felt the weight of every gaze in the chamber. Clovis torn between loyalty to tradition and the pull of a new faith. The Morrigan stood ready to defend Merona and Armaeus, whose malevolent gaze seethed with hatred and fear.

"Can you feel it?" Merona asked, her voice barely above a whisper as she reached toward the labyrinth. "The pulse of the earth, the whispers of our forebears?"

Her fingers grazed the cool stone, and in an instant, a surge of power coursed through her. Merona gasped, overwhelmed by the sheer intensity of the sensation. It was as though every drop of blood in her veins had been replaced with liquid starlight.

"This," she said, her voice trembling with emotion, "is what you sought to destroy, Armaeus. This connection to our past; the very essence of who we are."

As she spoke, the magic of the labyrinth intertwined with her own, creating a tapestry of power that stretched back through the ages. In that moment, Merona understood with perfect clarity the weight of her destiny and the path that lay before her.

The air crackled with energy, and reality itself seemed to warp and bend around Merona. The labyrinth's walls pulsed with an otherworldly light, casting eerie shadows that danced across the chamber. Merona stood at the center of it all, as though caught in the eye of a storm, raw power swirling around her in dizzying eddies.

"This power..." Merona breathed, "It's beyond anything I ever imagined."

Armaeus snarled in frustration, his human facade slipping away to reveal the terrifying demon beneath. "You think you can wield forces beyond your understanding, witch?" His voice echoed unnaturally, thick with malice and desperation.

Merona turned to face him, her raven hair whipping around her face as if caught in an invisible wind. "I don't seek to wield it, Armaeus. I am a part of it, as are all of us. You're the one who sought to control what was never meant to be controlled."

The demon's eyes flashed crimson as he raised his clawed hands. "Then I'll tear it all down!" he roared, dark tendrils of energy beginning to coalesce around him, a stark contrast to the shimmering light pouring from the labyrinth.

As Armaeus launched his assault, Merona stood her ground, drawing strength from the ancient magic flowing through her. She thought of all those who had come before her, of the countless lives lost to fear and ignorance.

"No more," Merona whispered, her voice heavy with conviction, resonating as if it echoed through time itself. "This ends now."

As Armaeus' dark energy surged toward her, a blur of russet fur flashed across her vision. The Morrigan, now a fearsome red wolf, leapt through the air with otherworldly grace. Her amber eyes blazed with the fury of countless battles as she clamped her powerful jaws onto Armaeus' arm.

The demon's howl of pain and rage reverberated through the labyrinth, shaking its very foundation. "Insolent beast!" he snarled, thrashing to break free from the Morrigan's unyielding grip.

Merona's heart swelled with gratitude for her divine ally. "Thank you," she whispered, her thoughts reaching out to the goddess.

The Morrigan's voice rang in her mind, fierce and commanding. *"Now, child of prophecy. Strike while he is vulnerable!"*

Merona nodded, her pulse racing as she dug deep within herself, tapping into the wellspring of power that bound her to the ancient bloodlines. She thought of Murdach, whose unwavering love and support strengthened her even in this moment.

"This is for all you've hurt, Armaeus," Merona declared, her voice carrying the weight of centuries. "For the witches you've murdered, for the lives you've destroyed."

She raised her hands, channeling the combined might of the elements, the labyrinth, and her unbreakable will. The air crackled with energy as she prepared to deliver the final blow.

Still writhing against the Morrigan's grip, Armaeus turned his burning gaze toward Merona. "You cannot destroy me, witch," he hissed. "I am eternal!"

Merona's eyes narrowed, her resolve unshakable. "Nothing is eternal, Armaeus. Not even your malevolence."

With a cry that seemed to tear through the very fabric of reality, Merona unleashed the full force of her power.

The air crackled with an otherworldly energy as her magic collided with Armaeus. The demon's form began to waver, his edges blurring and dissolving like smoke caught in a fierce wind. His agonized scream echoed through the labyrinth, a sound of pure rage and desperation.

"No!" Armaeus howled, his voice warping as his body twisted and contorted. "This cannot be!"

Merona stood firm, hands outstretched, pouring every ounce of her strength into the magical onslaught. The labyrinth's walls pulsed with an eerie light, lending their ancient power to her cause.

Is this truly the end? Merona wondered, her heart pounding. After all we've endured, all we've sacrificed...

As though answering her unspoken thought, Armaeus' form continued to disintegrate at an accelerated rate. Flakes of darkness peeled away from his body, vanishing into nothingness.

"You may destroy this form," Armaeus sneered, his voice growing faint. "But my essence will endure. I will return, witch!"

Merona's eyes blazed with unwavering determination. "Not in this world, demon. Your time here is over."

With a final, ear-splitting shriek, Armaeus' form imploded, collapsing inward before vanishing entirely. An oppressive silence fell over the labyrinth, broken only by Merona's ragged breathing.

As the last echoes of Armaeus' malevolence faded, Merona turned to see the Morrigan shifting. The fearsome red wolf shimmered and stretched, its form elongating and transforming until a regal woman stood in its place.

The goddess's eyes gleamed with satisfaction as she surveyed the scene. "Well done, child," she said, her voice rich with approval. "You have fulfilled your destiny."

Merona's legs trembled, threatening to give way beneath her. She drew a shuddering breath, scanning the labyrinth's shimmering walls. The air still crackled with residual energy, a testament to the monumental battle that had just unfolded.

"Is it... truly over?" she whispered; her voice hoarse from exhaustion.

The Morrigan nodded solemnly. "You have altered the course of history, Merona. The future you once knew will never come to pass."

A wave of emotion washed over Merona; relief, triumph, and an overwhelming sense of purpose fulfilled. She closed her eyes, allowing herself a moment to process the enormity of what had transpired.

"Murdach," she murmured, her thoughts turning to her beloved. "Is he...?"

"Safe," the Morrigan assured her. "As are all those who would have fallen victim to Armaeus' machinations."

Merona's heart swelled with joy. She took a tentative step forward, her body aching from the magical exertion. As she moved, the labyrinth seemed to shift around her, its walls becoming translucent, allowing glimpses of the world beyond.

"What do you see, child?" the Morrigan asked, her tone gentle yet probing.

Merona gazed out at the landscape unfolding before her. Rolling hills of vibrant green stretched as far as the eye could see, dotted with ancient stone circles and lush forests. The air seemed cleaner, fresher somehow.

"I see... hope," Merona replied, her voice growing steadier. "A world where magic and faith can coexist, where the old ways are not forgotten but woven into the fabric of a new era."

The Morrigan smiled, a rare warmth crossing her usually stern features. "You have done more than save lives, Merona. You have preserved a legacy, ensuring that the wisdom of ages past will not be lost to time."

Merona nodded, feeling the weight of her accomplishment settle upon her shoulders. It was a burden, yes, but one she would gladly bear. "What happens now?" she asked, her gaze still fixed on the world beyond the labyrinth.

"Now," the Morrigan replied, "you step into that world and help shape it. Your journey is far from over, Merona. It has only just begun."

With those words, the labyrinth's walls began to fade away entirely, leaving Merona standing at the threshold of a new dawn. She drew in a deep breath, straightening her shoulders as she steeled herself for the challenges that lay ahead.

"I'm ready," she said, her voice filled with quiet determination. And with that, Merona took her first step into a future brimming with possibility, her heart filled with the knowledge that she had fulfilled her destiny, ushering in an era of peace and renewal.

Chapter 28

The ancient oak trees cast long shadows over the gathered villagers, their gnarled branches reaching like grasping fingers across the twilit clearing like grasping fingers. Merona stood atop a weathered stone dais, her raven hair whipping in the chill autumn wind. Beside her, Clovis exuded authority, his broad shoulders cloaked in a mantle embroidered with golden bees. As Merona surveyed the sea of expectant faces before her, the weight of destiny settled heavily upon her, a mantle she could not cast off.

She drew a deep breath, the scent of woodsmoke and fallen leaves filling her lungs. "People of Gaul," she began, her voice steady and resonant, "we stand on the brink of a new era. For too long, our land has been fractured by strife and division, our hearts poisoned by fear and mistrust."

A murmur rippled through the crowd, a low tide of unease. Merona could feel it; the resistance born of deeply rooted prejudices, nurtured over generations. How can I make them see? she wondered. How can I illuminate the path to unity when conflict has been their only truth?

"I have walked among you," she continued, "I have seen the scars that hatred and intolerance have left on our people. Yet, I have also witnessed kindness, fleeting moments of understanding that ignite hope for a better future."

She paused, allowing her words to sink in. The silence that followed was profound, charged with a palpable energy. In that moment, Merona felt the heartbeat of the crowd, the rhythm of their collective breath. The clearing seemed alive, thrumming with potential; the electric anticipation of change, the instant before the storm breaks.

"The time has come to cast aside our old ways of thinking," Merona urged, her voice rising with passion. "We must embrace a new vision of acceptance and understanding. No longer can we allow the prejudices of the past to dictate our future. Each of us, regardless of our beliefs or origins, has a place in the tapestry of Gaul."

As she spoke, Merona felt a surge of power coursing through her veins. It was not the raw, elemental magic she had learned to harness, but something deeper, more profound. This is my true purpose, she realized. Not just to wield magic, but to heal the wounds that divide us.

"I stand before you not as a savior," she declared, "but as a beacon of hope. The path ahead will not be easy, but if we walk it together, there is no challenge we cannot overcome."

Merona turned to Clovis, seeing the fire of inspiration kindled in his dark eyes. He stepped forward, his presence commanding instant attention from the crowd.

"My people," Clovis began, his deep voice resonating across the clearing, "I have long grappled with the question of faith and its place in our kingdom. I have seen the power of belief, both to unite and to divide."

He paused, his gaze sweeping across the assembled villagers. Merona could sense the tension in the air, the collective intake of breath as they waited for his next words.

"Today, I make this solemn vow," Clovis declared. "From this day forward, the people of Gaul shall be free to worship as they choose. No longer will we seek to impose one faith upon all. The old ways and the new shall coexist in harmony, each accorded the respect it deserves."

A hushed silence fell over the crowd. Merona could feel the weight of centuries of conflict and persecution in that moment of stillness. Will they accept this change? she wondered. Or are the wounds of the past too deep to heal?

Clovis continued, his voice growing stronger with each word. "I renounce any attempt to force Christianity upon those who do not freely choose it. Let it be known throughout the land that all faiths shall be protected, all beliefs honored. No one shall live in fear of persecution for their spiritual practices."

As he spoke, Merona watched the expressions of the villagers begin to shift. Doubt gave way to hope, suspicion to cautious optimism. Pride swelled in her chest for Clovis, as she recognized the courage it took to make such a proclamation.

"This is not a decision I make lightly," Clovis added, his gaze locking with Merona's for a brief, intense moment. "But it is one born of wisdom and necessity. Our strength lies not in uniformity, but in the rich tapestry of our diverse beliefs and traditions."

Merona stepped forward, standing shoulder to shoulder with Clovis. "Let this be the first step on our journey toward a united Gaul," she said, her voice reaching the farthest corners of the clearing. "A land where acceptance triumphs over fear, where understanding vanquishes hatred."

She raised her hands, palms outward in a gesture of openness and peace. "I ask you now to look to your neighbors, to those you may have once viewed with suspicion or disdain. See them not as strangers or enemies, but as fellow travelers on this road we walk together."

As Merona's words lingered in the air, a palpable shift began to ripple through the gathering. The tension that had gripped the crowd started to dissolve, replaced by a burgeoning sense of possibility. Smiles began to break across faces that, moments ago, had been shadowed with doubt. Hands extended, clasping those of former adversaries in hesitant yet heartfelt gestures of reconciliation.

This is only the beginning, Merona thought, her heart swelling with equal parts hope and determination. The path ahead would undoubtedly be fraught with challenges. Centuries of mistrust and prejudice could not be undone in a single day. Yet, as she stood there, witnessing the fragile bonds of unity forming among her people, Merona felt a profound certainty take root within her.

We will prevail; she vowed silently. Together, we will forge a new destiny for Gaul, one built on the unshakable foundations of acceptance and understanding. And in doing so, we will alter the course of history itself.

The crowd's cheers rose like a tidal wave, sweeping over Merona and Clovis. Faces that had once borne the weight of worry now glowed with unbridled joy. Tears streamed down weathered cheeks, and hands reached skyward in jubilation. Merona felt the energy of their collective hope surge through her, a force as tangible and powerful as the magic coursing through her veins.

As the celebrations continued, Merona caught Clovis' eye. With a subtle nod, they slipped away from the jubilant throng, seeking a moment of solitude beneath the shadow of an ancient oak.

"We've come so far," Merona murmured, her eyes locking with Clovis' intense gaze. "There were times I feared we'd never see this day."

Clovis reached out, his calloused hand gently clasping hers. "It is you who has brought us here, Merona. Your courage, your vision…they've changed everything."

Merona felt a lump rise in her throat. "Not I alone," she insisted. "Your willingness to challenge the old ways, to risk everything for what is right. That has been the cornerstone of all we've achieved."

They stood in a brief, contemplative silence, the weight of their shared journey hanging heavily between them. Merona's thoughts drifted to the trials they had endured: the treacherous labyrinth beneath Paris, the blood-soaked fields of Tolbiac, the unrelenting threat of those who feared change.

"We've both sacrificed so much," Clovis said softly, his voice a blend of sorrow and pride. "Our old lives, our certainties…"

"And gained so much more in return," Merona interjected, her grip on his hand tightening. She felt the power of their shared destiny, their fates intertwined and symbolized by the matching labyrinth birthmarks they bore.

As they stood there, guardians of a new era dawning over Gaul, Merona allowed herself a moment of reflection. From the flames of her execution in a future yet to come, to this pivotal moment in history; her journey had been beyond imagining.

A sudden flash of red caught Merona's attention, drawing her gaze to the edge of the forest. There, half-hidden among the ancient oaks, stood the Morrigan in her wolf form. The goddess's amber eyes gleamed with an otherworldly light, fixed on Merona with an intensity that sent a shiver down her spine.

Merona's heart swelled with a bittersweet ache. "She's here," she whispered, her voice barely audible.

Clovis followed her gaze. "The Morrigan?" he asked, his tone reverent.

Merona couldn't look away from the wolf, its luminous form flickering as though it existed between two worlds. A deep certainty settled in her chest; her time under the Morrigan's watchful eye was ending.

"She looks proud," Clovis murmured, his tone reverent.

"And at peace," Merona replied, her voice thick with emotion. "It's as if she believes her purpose here is fulfilled."

The Morrigan's voice resonated softly in Merona's mind, filling her with a bittersweet warmth. *"You no longer need my guidance, child of two times. Your strength is forged, your purpose clear. Lead with wisdom and courage."*

Merona's vision blurred as tears welled in her eyes. "Thank you," she whispered into the crisp air. "For everything."

The wolf inclined its head in a gesture of acknowledgment before fading seamlessly into the shadows of the ancient forest.

Clovis tightened his grip on her hand. "There's still much to do," he reminded her gently. "The council is waiting."

Drawing a steadying breath, Merona nodded. "You're right. It's time to turn dreams into reality."

They walked together to the great hall, where a diverse assembly awaited. Druids crowned with oak leaves sat across from solemn Christian priests. Devotees of Mithras, their faces shadowed with the enigma of their faith, observed followers of Isis with measured curiosity.

When Merona and Clovis entered, silence enveloped the room. The weight of expectation, apprehension, and hope pressed against her. She embraced it fully; now certain she was ready to bear this mantle.

"Welcome," Merona began, her voice resonating with the authority of one who had traversed realms beyond their comprehension. "We stand on the threshold of a new era, one where unity…"

Her words, laden with promise, were abruptly cut short by a scornful laugh from the far corner of the hall.

"A new era?" a grizzled druid mocked, rising to his feet. His weathered face was etched with disdain, and his piercing gaze swept the room. "You mean an era where our ancient ways are discarded in favor of this... Christian god?"

A ripple of agreement murmured through the pagan assembly, their nods and murmurs underscoring his challenge. Across the room, Christian priests stiffened, their expressions hardening.

"Your 'ancient ways' have led us into darkness and ruin!" a young priest shot back; his cheeks flushed with fervent indignation. "Only through Christ can…"

"Enough."

Merona's calm but commanding voice cut through the tension, silencing the escalating exchange. She let her power subtly ripple through the air, the unseen forces stirring in response to her inner resolve.

Drawing a steadying breath, she met the room's divided gazes. "We are not gathered here to discard one faith or exalt another," she said, "We are here to forge a way forward, together."

As Merona spoke, she moved gracefully among the gathered representatives, her presence soothing the agitation in the room like a balm. She could feel their fears and doubts as vividly as if they were her own, each one a weight pressing upon her shoulders.

"I understand your concerns," she said, her tone softening yet steady. "Change is never easy. But consider this: does not the oak and the ash grow side by side in the forest? Does not the river and the stone coexist, each shaping the other over time?"

The druid who had challenged her earlier frowned, the lines of his face etched with skepticism. Yet Merona caught a fleeting flicker of consideration in his eyes, a crack in the wall of resistance.

"Our strength lies not in sameness," she continued, her voice warm and unwavering, "but in the tapestry we weave together. Each thread is unique, yet all are essential to the greater whole."

As she spoke, Clovis watched her with a mixture of pride and awe. He had known she was special from the moment he'd first laid eyes on her, but seeing her now, guiding these fractious factions with wisdom beyond her years, he felt a surge of hope for their shared future.

Later, Merona found herself alone, standing on the edge of a barren field. The once-fertile soil of Gaul stretched before her, cracked and lifeless under a restless sky. Her raven hair whipped in the wind as she closed her eyes, grounding herself in the pulse of the earth beneath her feet.

"Mother Goddess," she whispered, her voice carrying on the wind. "Guide my hands."

With a steadying breath, Merona knelt and pressed her palms against the cracked, lifeless ground. A soft blue light radiated from her fingertips, spreading like veins of hope into the parched earth. She felt the land's sorrow, its aching desire for renewal, resonating deep within her.

As the glow intensified, a farmer approached hesitantly, his weathered face a mix of fear and tentative hope. "What manner of witchcraft is this?" he asked, his voice trembling.

Merona lifted her gaze, her eyes shimmering with unearthly power. "Not witchcraft, friend," she replied, her tone calm and assuring. "Healing. The land hasn't forgotten its former strength; I'm merely helping it remember."

The farmer's eyes widened as green shoots began to push through the soil, unfurling like tiny miracles. "I... I've never seen anything like this," he murmured, awestruck.

Merona stood, brushing dirt from her hands as if shedding the doubts of centuries. "The old ways and the new can live side by side," she said gently. "Just as this field will soon hold both wild herbs and your cultivated crops."

As she spoke, more villagers gathered, drawn by the spectacle. Merona felt a familiar twinge of apprehension. How many times had such gatherings ended in accusations and violence? But she steeled herself, remembering her purpose.

"Your land will flourish again," she declared, her voice carrying across the field. "But it needs more than just my touch. It needs your care, your faith in its resilience."

A woman stepped forward, hope shining in her eyes. "Will you teach us? Show us how to nurture the land as you do?"

Merona smiled, feeling a warmth spread through her chest. This was why she had been reborn, why she had endured so much. To bring hope, to heal."

I will," she promised, her smile radiant. "Together, we'll restore Gaul to its former glory. And in doing so, we'll forge a new way forward; one of harmony, where all people and beliefs can coexist."

As the villagers crowded closer, eager to learn, Merona felt the weight of her destiny settle over her once more. But this time, it wasn't a burden; it was a calling. A purpose she was ready to embrace.

Merona stood atop the hill, her raven hair swept back by the restless wind, as her eyes roamed over the lush, reborn landscape of Gaul. Beneath the vibrancy of the scene, a bittersweet ache stirred within her chest. She turned to Murdach, whose silver hair gleamed like starlight in the fading glow of the sun.

"It's time, isn't it?" she asked softly, her voice carrying the weight of inevitability.

Murdach nodded, his eyes reflecting both pride and sorrow. "Septimania calls, my love. Mairead awaits our return."

Merona's fingers traced the intricate runes etched into the bracelet circling her wrist; a parting gift from Mairead. The cool metal pulsed faintly, as if alive with an otherworldly energy, a reminder of the destiny she could not ignore.

"I'm afraid to leave them," Merona admitted, her gaze sweeping over the distant villages dotting the horizon. "What if the darkness returns when I'm gone?"

Murdach stepped closer, resting a reassuring hand on her shoulder. "The seeds of change you've sown here will continue to grow," he said firmly. "Your work is not undone; it has only begun."

Closing her eyes, Merona attuned herself to the harmony of the elements surrounding her. The wind whispered encouragement, the earth beneath her feet promised steadfastness, the fire in her soul burned with purpose, and the waters within offered clarity. She had restored balance to the land, but the cost weighed heavily.

"Mairead's message was clear," Murdach said, his tone laced with quiet urgency. "The next phase of your journey awaits. We cannot tarry."

When Merona opened her eyes, her gaze met his, steady and resolute. The uncertainty that had shadowed her moments before was gone.

"You're right," she said, her voice firm with renewed purpose. "The path ahead may be perilous, but we will face it together."

As Merona prepared to depart, she cast a final glance at the land she had come to love. The weight of her destiny pressed heavily upon her, yet she found strength in the knowledge that her actions had already altered the course of history.

"Septimania," she murmured, "and whatever trials await us there."

Chapter 29

October 31, 511 AD

Merona, Murdach, and the Morrigan journeyed back to the place where it all began, their footsteps echoing on the ancient stones that paved their path. The Morrigan's steady presence at Merona's side was a comfort, a reminder of the bond they shared and the battles they had fought together. Fifteen years had passed since their victory at the bloody battle of Tolbiac, and they reveled in the peace and happiness that came with Armaeus no longer a threat. The love between them radiated, stronger than ever, yet they both sensed that change loomed once more.

The Morrigan's paws left no trace in the dew-kissed grass as they approached the village. Dawn's first light bathed the sky in hues of lavender and gold, casting long shadows across the familiar landscape. Merona's heart quickened, a mixture of anticipation and unease coursing through her veins.

"It seems both eternal and fleeting," Merona murmured, her eyes drinking in the sight of thatched roofs and winding cobblestone streets. The scent of freshly baked bread mingled with the earthy aroma of herbs from nearby gardens, carried by the morning breeze.

Murdach's deep voice rumbled beside her. "The village may seem unchanged, but you, Merona, have been forged anew in the crucible of your journey."

Merona nodded, her raven hair catching the soft light of the early morning. *How strange,* she thought, *to find both comfort and unease in these once-familiar surroundings.* The weight of her destiny pressed down upon her shoulders, heavier than ever before.

As they entered the village proper, the bustling marketplace came into view. Merchants were setting up their stalls, their voices a symphony of greetings and bartering. Merona's gaze lingered on a flower seller's booth, vibrant blooms reminding her of simpler times.

"I used to weave daisy chains here as a child," she said softly, a wistful smile tugging at the corners of her lips. "Now, I weave spells that could alter the very fabric of time."

The Morrigan's eyes met Merona's, a silent understanding passing between them. *The innocence of youth has given way to the weight of power,* Merona thought, her fingers absently tracing the outline of the Cauldron of Dagda hidden beneath her cloak.

"Merona," Murdach's voice cut through her reverie, grounding her. "Remember why we've returned. The fate of countless lives hangs in the balance."

She squared her shoulders, drawing strength from the elements that pulsed within her. "Yes, of course. The village may be my past, but it holds the key to our future." Her voice carried the gravity of prophecy, echoing the words spoken over her cradle on that fateful Samhain night.

In the center of the village stood Mairead, her long amber hair shining in the morning sun. The village's wise woman, Mairead carried the responsibility of teaching the villagers their traditions and preparing them for important events like Samhain.

The villagers gathered around her, hanging on her every word as she spoke about the significance of the evening's events. Mairead's voice was a soothing melody, her presence exuding a sense of calm and wisdom that was revered by all.

"This is no ordinary Samhain," Mairead began, her gaze sweeping over the faces before her. "It marks a turning point in our history. The Morrigan has returned, and with her comes great change."

A murmur spread through the crowd, some faces filled with fear, others with excitement. Many had only heard tales of the Morrigan, a powerful goddess said to hold dominion over fate itself.

"But fear not," Mairead continued, raising a hand to quiet the whispers. "For it is said that when change arrives, it brings both challenge and opportunity. And tonight, we will be given a chance to shape our own destiny."

Merona watched from the shadows, hidden from view, as the scene unfolded before her. A sense of pride swelled within her as she listened to Mairead's words.

Mairead then instructed the villagers on their preparations for the night's festivities. They were to leave offerings at their doorsteps for wandering spirits, gather around bonfires for protection from otherworldly creatures, and, most importantly, keep open mind and heart for whatever change may come.

As Mairead dismissed the gathering, Merona stepped forward from her hiding spot.

"Mother," she called softly.

Mairead's face registered surprise, which quickly transformed into a warm smile as she turned toward Merona. "My dear, you've returned!" she exclaimed, rushing toward her with open arms. The two embraced tightly, tears of happiness streaming down their faces as they reunited after what felt like an eternity apart. Their embrace spoke volumes of their unbreakable bond and the love that had kept them connected across time and distance.

As they walked toward Mairead's cottage, Merona couldn't help but take in the familiar sights and sounds of her childhood home. The scent of burning wood from nearby homes, the laughter of children playing in the distance, and the warmth that radiated from the community around her; it felt as though she had never left.

As they entered Mairead's cozy cottage, Merona was enveloped by a comforting warmth. The wooden furniture, colorful tapestries, and shelves lined with jars of herbs and potions brought back memories of helping her mother with their family's trade.

Mairead busied herself preparing a hearty meal, while Merona sat at the table, watching her mother's graceful movements. She couldn't believe how much she had missed these simple moments with her mother.

"So," Mairead said, placing a steaming bowl of stew in front of Merona and Murdach, "tell me about your journey."

Merona took a deep breath, then began recounting her tale. She spoke of losing track of time while exploring ancient ruins and stumbling upon an enchanted amulet that transported her to another time.

Mairead listened intently, interjecting with questions, or showing her disbelief at certain points in the story. Murdach also contributed to the conversation, but he mostly observed the dynamic between mother and daughter. The way they interacted filled him with a sense of hope and reassurance.

As the meal continued, Mairead's voice quivered when she revealed the details of the ritual. "It will take place at midnight, deep within the Labyrinth," she said. At the mention of the maze, Morrigan's heart quickened, memories of its dark corridors and twisted secrets flooding her mind. Merona's hand instinctively clutched her chest, a wave of fear and excitement washing over her. She knew that their fate would be sealed within those perilous walls. Despite their exhaustion, they knew they could not refuse Mairead's invitation. The stakes were too high, and their destiny was bound to the Labyrinth's mysteries.

As they made their way toward the sacred grove, Merona couldn't shake the feeling that every step brought her closer to a confrontation with destiny itself. The whispers of the wind seemed to carry ancient secrets, and the earth beneath her feet hummed with anticipation.

"I am ready," Merona declared, more to herself than to her companions. "Whatever trials lie ahead, I will face them with the strength of the elements and the wisdom of ages."

The Morrigan's low growl of approval mingled with the distant tolling of the village bell, heralding the dawn of a new day and perhaps, the dawn of a new era for all of Gaul.

Mairead fell into step beside Merona, her weathered hand reaching out to grasp the younger witch's. The High Priestess's touch was warm, her grip firm yet gentle. Merona glanced at her mother, noticing the mix of emotions etched across Mairead's face; pride battling with sorrow, hope tangled with resignation.

"My child," Mairead whispered, her voice thick with unshed tears. "The babe I found on that Samhain night has grown into a force of nature."

Merona squeezed her mother's hand in return, her throat tightening with emotion. "Because of you, Mother. Your guidance, your love..."

Their moment was interrupted by a collective gasp from the villagers. Heads turned, conversations stilled, and a wave of excitement rippled through the crowd. "It's her!" a child's voice rang out, clear and loud. "The witch has returned!"

Merona's heart raced as she watched recognition spread across familiar faces. Some villagers beamed with pride; others watched her with a mixture of awe and fear. The weight of their expectations pressed down on her, heavy and unfamiliar.

"They look at me as if I'm some sort of savior," Merona murmured to Mairead, her voice barely audible. "How can I possibly live up to that?"

Mairead's response was firm. "You already have, Merona. Every choice you've made, every trial you've faced. It's all led to this moment."

As the villagers gathered around them, their eyes wide with wonder, Merona took a deep breath. *I am no longer the child who left this place,* she thought. *I am the witch reborn, the one who must bridge the past and the future.*

With renewed determination, Merona lifted her chin and stepped forward to greet her people, ready to embrace whatever destiny had in store.

Her eyes glistened as she surveyed the sea of familiar faces. The weight of her journey, the trials she had endured, seemed to melt away in the warmth of their welcome. A lump formed in her throat as she struggled to find words.

"My friends," she began, her voice trembling with emotion, "I... I've come home."

An elderly woman stepped forward, her weathered hands reaching out to clasp Merona's. "You've always been home, child. In our hearts."

Merona squeezed the woman's hands, a tear slipping down her cheek. *This is what I've been fighting for,* she thought. *This connection, this love.*

As the villagers pressed closer, sharing words of welcome and pride, Merona felt a familiar presence at her side. The Morrigan, in her wolf form, emerged from the shadows, her amber eyes scanning the crowd with fierce intensity.

Be wary, young one, the *Morrigan's* voice echoed in *Merona's* mind. *Not all smiles hide friendly hearts.*

Merona glanced down at her protector, a mixture of gratitude and concern in her eyes. "They're my people," she whispered. "Surely there's no danger here?"

The wolf's ears twitched, her gaze never leaving the throng of villagers. *Danger wears many faces. Stay alert.*

As if on cue, a man's voice cut through the jubilant atmosphere. "And what magic do you bring back to us, witch? What price must we pay for your... protection?"

The crowd fell silent, tension rippling through the air like a storm about to break.

Merona's eyes narrowed as she scanned the crowd, seeking the source of the accusation. Taking a steadying breath, she squared herself before addressing the gathering.

"I bring no price, only purpose," Merona declared, her voice carrying across the hushed crowd of villagers. "The sacred grove calls to us. Will you join me?"

Without waiting for an answer, she turned and began walking toward the ancient trees that marked the grove's boundary, hand in hand with Murdach. The Morrigan padded silently at her side, a dark shadow against the vibrant green of the surrounding foliage.

As they approached the entrance, Merona felt the air with an almost tangible energy. The hairs on her arms stood on end, and she could taste the metallic tang of magic on her tongue.

It's stronger than I remember, she thought, her heart *racing* with anticipation and a *touch* of fear. *Or perhaps I'm just more attuned to it now.*

"Can you feel it?" she whispered to the wolf at her side. "The power here... it's alive."

The Morrigan's ears twitched in response, her amber eyes gleaming with ancient wisdom. *This place remembers you, child. It has been waiting.*

Merona stepped into the grove, the dappled sunlight filtering through the canopy above, casting an ethereal glow on the moss-covered earth. She closed her eyes, drawing in a deep breath, allowing the familiar scent of earth and magic to fill her lungs.

"It's just as I left it," she murmured, her voice thick with emotion. "And yet... everything has changed."

Opening her eyes, she took in the twisted trunks of ancient oaks, the rustle of leaves stirred by a breeze that seemed to exist only within the grove's boundaries. Memories flooded back; lessons learned, powers awakened, and a destiny revealed.

"What now?" Merona asked, her gaze sweeping the sacred space. "How do I fulfill what was promised?"

The Morrigan's form shimmered, shifting from wolf to woman, her dark eyes boring into Merona's. "You already know the answer, child. It lies within you, as it always has."

Merona nodded, her hand unconsciously moving to touch the pendant at her throat; a symbol of her journey, her power, and the choices that lay ahead.

Merona's footsteps were soft against the moss-covered earth as she approached the ancient altar. Her heart pounded, each beat echoing the pulsing energy of the grove. Kneeling before the weathered stone, her fingers trembled as they reached out to trace the familiar symbols etched into its surface.

"I was but a babe when last I lay here," she whispered, her voice barely audible above the rustling leaves. The grooves of the talismans hummed beneath her touch, sending waves of warmth up her arm in recognition.

Merona closed her eyes, overwhelmed by the rush of emotions that swept over her. *How far I've come,* she thought. *And yet, how much further I must go.*

Taking a deep breath to steady herself, she began to speak. Her voice was soft at first, then grew stronger with each word. "Great Goddess Danu, mother of all, I come before you with a heart full of gratitude."

The air around her thickened, as if the very essence of the divine was drawing near to listen.

"You have guided my steps, even when the path was shrouded in darkness," Merona continued, her eyes glistening with unshed tears. "You have given me strength when I faltered, purpose when I was lost."

She paused, her gaze sweeping across the grove, her eyes lingering on the shimmering form of the Morrigan standing sentinel at the edge of the clearing. "And you have blessed me with companions, protectors, and mentors who have shaped me into who I am today."

A gentle breeze brushed her face, carrying the scent of wildflowers and ancient magic. Merona smiled, feeling the loving embrace of the Goddess all around her.

"I stand ready to face what lies ahead," she declared, her voice ringing with unwavering determination. "Whatever trials await, whatever sacrifices must be made, I will not falter. For I am your chosen, reborn through time to fulfill a greater purpose."

As her final words lingered in the air, a sudden hush fell over the grove. Even the leaves stilled, as if nature itself was holding its breath in anticipation of what was to come.

Merona rose slowly, her legs trembling slightly as she turned to face her companions. Her eyes shimmered with a mixture of sadness and acceptance as they met Mairead's hazel gaze, before flicking to Murdach and the Morrigan in turn. The weight of the moment pressed heavily on her chest, a bittersweet ache threatening to overwhelm her.

"It's time," she whispered, her voice barely audible over the soft rustling of leaves.

Mairead nodded, her auburn hair catching the dappled sunlight filtering through the canopy. "You've come so far, my dear," she said, her voice thick with emotion. "The path ahead is yours alone to walk."

Merona's heart clenched at the words. She took a steadying breath, steeling herself for what she knew must come. With deliberate steps, she crossed the mossy ground toward her mother, her arms opening wide.

"Thank you," Merona murmured as she fell into Mairead's embrace. Their tears mingled as they held each other tightly, the fabric of Mairead's robes rough against Merona's cheek. "For everything."

Mairead tightened her arms around her. "You carry the hopes of so many, Merona. But never forget, you also carry our love."

Merona pulled back slightly, her eyes locking with Mairead's. "I promise," she whispered fiercely. "I will carry your teachings with me always. Your wisdom, your strength…they're a part of me now."

As they slowly separated, Merona thought; *This is truly the end of one journey and the beginning of another. How can I possibly be ready?* But even as doubt crept in, she felt the warmth of the Goddess's blessing, a silent reminder of her purpose.

"You've prepared me well," Merona said, managing a small smile despite the tears that continued to fall. "I won't let you down. I won't let any of you down."

Merona turned to Murdach, her heart quickening as their eyes met. A storm of emotions swirled within her gaze; love, determination, and a flicker of fear for the unknown path ahead. She reached out, her slender fingers intertwining with his calloused ones.

"Murdach," she breathed, her voice barely above a whisper. The air between them crackled with unspoken words and promises.

He squeezed her hand gently. "I know, mo chroí," he murmured, using the Gaelic term of endearment that always made her heart flutter.

Merona's thoughts raced. *How can I leave him behind? How can I not, when my destiny calls?* She searched his face, committing every line and curve to memory.

"I wish…" she began, but Murdach shook his head, silencing her with a gentle smile.

"No wishes, no regrets," he said firmly. "You carry my heart with you, Merona. Always."

She nodded, blinking back fresh tears. "And you have mine," she replied, her voice steadier now. "Guard it well."

They held each other tightly, fighting back the flood of emotions. Slowly, their fingers untangled, and Merona felt the loss keenly. Taking a deep breath, she squared her shoulders and turned toward her final farewell.

The Morrigan stood before her, regal and imposing even in her wolf form. Merona knelt, her hand reaching out to stroke the thick, red fur. The wolf's amber eyes, filled with ancient wisdom, met hers unflinchingly.

"Great Morrigan," Merona whispered, her voice filled with reverence and gratitude. "How can I ever thank you for your protection, your guidance?"

The wolf's voice echoed in her mind, rich and otherworldly. *Your journey is far from over. Our paths will cross again.*

Merona's fingers curled in the wolf's fur. "I'll carry the strength you've given me," she vowed. "Through all the battles to come, seen and unseen."

The Morrigan's tail swished once, a gesture of acknowledgment. *Remember, witch, in darkness or in light, in victory or defeat, you are never truly alone.*

As Merona rose to her feet, a profound shift stirred within her. The air hummed with potential, the promise of a destiny about to unfold. She looked at her companions one last time, her heart heavy with love, determination, and the bittersweet ache of farewell.

"It's time," she murmured, more to herself than to the others. With each breath, she felt the weight of her past lifting, her spirit preparing for ascension. The next chapter of her journey awaited with unknown challenges ahead, but also the promise of hope, and the true magic of understanding and acceptance.

The Morrigan, in her ethereal wolf form, gently nudged Merona's hand, a silent testament to their deep connection. As Merona knelt before the wolf at the entrance to the labyrinth, they shared one last gaze. The vibrant red cloak draped over Merona's shoulders, her hood falling gracefully over her raven hair, adding an air of mystique to the moment. The beautiful red wolf pressed her muzzle softly to Merona's forehead, a parting kiss, as if to seal their bond. The forest around them seemed to close in, the dusky embrace of the trees, while the moon's soft glow filtered through the canopy, casting an otherworldly light on the scene.

"Will I see you again?" Merona asked, her voice a whisper.

The wolf's response came not in words, but in a sensation; a deep certainty that their paths would cross when the need was greatest.

The labyrinth pulsed with light, as though calling to Merona. She reached out, her fingers brushing against its surface, feeling a surge of power course through her veins. She closed her eyes, surrendering herself to its energy, allowing it to guide her thoughts and intentions.

"I seek wisdom," she whispered, opening herself fully to whatever knowledge the labyrinth had to offer. "Beneath the sun and moon, I hear the labyrinth's call. I have the freedom to choose and claim my right to be reborn to maintain the balance between good and evil."

Images flooded Merona's mind – scenes of ancient battles, fierce creatures roaming untamed lands, and powerful deities watching over their devoted followers. Yet, one vision stood apart: a figure cloaked in shadows yet radiating with an undeniable power and grace.

Rising to her feet, Merona turned toward the west, where the full moon glowed bright. The magic of the land pulsed beneath her, intertwining with her own power, reinforcing her resolve.

"Chun an scáth agus an fhoirm a chloisteáil, i labyrinth an dorchadais, tar chugam!"
Hear me, shadows, and take form, come to me, labyrinth of darkness! My powers strengthen in the deep shadows,
My spirit guides me with every step I take,
Through the veil of darkness, my strength is revealed,
The stars above light my path.
Courage leads me through the labyrinth of shadows,

Guided by a secret flame and the moon's embrace.
I pray to Danu for her divine guidance."

"Remember," Merona's voice rang clear, carrying over the gathered crowd, "our strength lies not in isolation, but in unity. In understanding. In love."

With those words, Merona took her first step forward, leaving behind all she had ever known and venturing into the vast unknown that awaited. As she moved, the weight of the past lifted, and she felt her spirit ascend, ready to embrace the journey ahead.

Her heart was full, her spirit alight with purpose, for she carried not only magic, but the unbreakable bonds of family, friendship, and the village that would always be her home.

Chapter 30

November 27, 511 AD Paris

The flickering candlelight cast long shadows across the chamber, dancing on the weathered face of Clovis, King of the Franks. His once-imposing frame now lay fragile upon the ornate bed, each labored breath a stark reminder of his mortality. The golden bees embroidered on his cloak seemed to shimmer with an otherworldly energy, a striking contrast to the man who wore them.

Clovis' dark eyes, still intense despite his frailty, scanned the faces of those gathered around him. Loyal subjects, family members and advisors, all standing in solemn silence. Their expressions held a mixture of reverence and sorrow.

"My people," Clovis rasped, his deep voice barely more than a whisper, "the stars have spoken. This day... this November 27th... will mark the end of an era."

A collective gasp rippled through the room. Clovis felt a fleeting sense of pride at their reaction, even as a wave of melancholy washed over him. He had led them through tumultuous times, uniting tribes, facing down both mortal enemies and mystical forces. Now, he faced his greatest challenge alone.

"Do not weep for me," he continued, his words carrying the ancient wisdom of the Merovingians. "For in my passing, a new chapter begins."

As he spoke, Clovis' thoughts drifted to the countless battles he had fought, the alliances forged and shattered, and the weight of the crown he had borne for three decades. Every scar on his body told a story, a testament to the life he had lived.

"My lord," one of his advisors stepped forward, voice trembling, "surely there is more time. The kingdom needs you."

A wry smile tugged at Clovis' lips. "Time, my old friend, is a fickle creature. She has favored me for countless years, but now she beckons me to my final rest."

He closed his eyes, feeling the pull of something beyond this world. In his mind's eye, he saw the vast expanse of his kingdom, stretching from the misty forests of the north to the sun-drenched fields of the south. He had united these lands, but at what cost?

"I have walked between two worlds," Clovis mused, his voice taking on an otherworldly resonance. "Between the old ways and the new, between the magic of our ancestors and the power of the Christian God."

The room fell silent, every ear attuned to his words. Clovis felt the weight of his legacy pressing down upon him, a swirl of pride and regret his chest.

"Remember," he said, his voice growing stronger for a moment, "that true strength lies not in conquest alone, but in unity. In the bonds we forge with one another."

As he spoke, an unsettling sensation washed over Clovis, as if the very fabric of reality was bending around him. The candlelight flickered and dimmed, and the faces of those gathered began to blur.

"My time draws near," he whispered, a flicker of fear creeping into his voice. "But know this: the spirit of the Merovingians will endure. In each of you, in the land itself."

With these final words, Clovis, King of the Franks, closed his eyes, letting out a long, shuddering breath. The chamber fell into a hushed silence, broken only by the soft weeping of those who had loved and followed him.

As the last ember of life flickered within him, Clovis felt a strange peace settle over him. He had lived, he had ruled, and now, he would face whatever lay beyond with the same courage that had defined his reign.

The darkness behind Clovis' eyelids swirled and shifted, coalescing into a familiar form. There she stood, as vivid as the day he had first seen her; the Witch from his childhood. Her raven-black hair cascaded over her shoulders, framing eyes that seemed to pierce through time itself.

Clovis' breath caught in his throat. This was no mere memory, no fleeting dream. The Witch's presence felt tangible, as though she had crossed the veil between worlds to stand before him in this moment of transition.

"You... the Witch from my childhood," Clovis whispered, his voice barely audible in the stillness of his mind.

The Witch's lips curved into a gentle smile; her eyes filled with an ancient wisdom that both comforted and unsettled him. Clovis felt a wave of conflicting emotions; wonder, like a child witnessing the supernatural, tempered by the hard-earned skepticism of a battle-worn king.

Is this truly happening? he wondered, his thoughts spinning. Or have the shadows of death already begun to cloud my mind?

As if sensing his uncertainty, the Witch took a step closer. The air around her shimmered with an ethereal energy, reminiscent of the magic that had both blessed and burdened the Merovingian line.

"Clovis," she spoke, her voice carrying the weight of centuries, "you stand at the threshold between worlds. The path you've walked has been long, fraught with trials. But your journey is not yet complete."

The King of the Franks felt a tremor run through his form. "What more can there be?" he asked, weariness creeping into his voice. "I have united tribes, fought battles, wrestled with faith. What more does destiny demand of me?"

The Witch's eyes gleamed with an unnatural light, reflecting the countless souls she had guided over the ages. "Yes," she replied softly, her voice like a whisper on the wind. "It is time for you to move on."

Clovis felt a jolt course through him, as if struck by lightning. The finality of the Witch's words resonated deep within him, echoing across the vastness of his consciousness. He had faced death countless times on the battlefield, his sword singing with the blood of his enemies. But this... this was different.

"Move on?" he repeated, his voice faltering. The mighty King of the Franks, reduced to a trembling whisper in the face of eternity.

His mind whirled, memories flashing before him like leaves caught in a storm. The weight of the crown, the victories and betrayals, the unrelenting struggle between the old ways and the new faith that had swept across his lands.

A mix of fear and anticipation gripped Clovis. He had always been a warrior, never flinching in the face of death on the battlefield. But now, with it truly upon him, a sense of trepidation stirred within him. His hand reached instinctively for a sword that was no longer there, grasping at the fleeting remnants of his mortal form.

"I am not ready," he murmured, even as a part of him longed for the release from earthly burdens. "There is still so much to be done, so many challenges awaiting my people."

The Witch's gaze softened, a look of understanding crossing her timeless face. "Your reign has ended, Clovis. The time has come to entrust the future to those who will follow in your wake."

Clovis swallowed hard, his throat dry as parchment. The weight of her words settled over him like a heavy cloak. He gazed into her eyes, so familiar yet alien, grasping for one final thread of control.

"Will you guide me to the afterlife?" he asked, his voice barely a whisper.

The Witch nodded solemnly, her raven-black hair gleaming with an otherworldly light. "I will guide you to your next life."

A shiver ran through Clovis' essence. *Next life?* The concept both thrilled and terrified him. He had heard whispers of such beliefs; echoes of ancient traditions that had endured despite the church's best efforts to stamp them out.

"What do you mean, next life?" he asked, curiosity battling with apprehension. "I thought... I believed..."

The Witch's lips curved into a knowing smile. "There is much you have yet to learn, King of the Franks. The journey of a soul does not end with a single lifetime."

Clovis felt a surge of emotions; confusion, wonder, and a spark of hope. Perhaps this was not truly the end, but a new beginning. He straightened, feeling a shadow of his old regal bearing returning.

"Then lead on, Witch," he said, his voice strengthening. "I face this new battle as I have faced all others; with courage and determination."

As the Witch's ethereal fingers brushed against his spectral form, Clovis felt himself slipping away from the mortal realm. The world around him began to blur and fade, replaced by a kaleidoscope of memories flashing before his eyes.

He saw himself as a young prince, fierce and untamed, the golden bees on his cloak a symbol of destiny. The Battle of Soissons unfolded before him in vivid detail; the clash of steel, the coppery scent of blood, and the rush of victory that solidified his reign.

"By the gods," Clovis whispered, his voice echoing strangely in the void. "I had forgotten the fervor of those early days."

The Witch's voice drifted to him, seeming to come from everywhere and nowhere at once. "The tapestry of your life is rich with both triumph and tragedy, Clovis. Each thread has woven you into the king you became."

Another memory surged forth; the moment he had stood before the labyrinth beneath Paris, the witch Merona by his side. He once again felt the mix of fear and determination that had driven him to face the unknown.

"I was so certain then," Clovis mused, a hint of wistfulness in his voice. "So sure of my path, of the magic that flowed in my veins."

Suddenly, the memories vanished, plunging Clovis into an endless, consuming darkness. Panic gripped him, a primal fear unlike anything he had experienced in life. He tried to call out, but no sound escaped his lips.

"Witch!" he thought desperately. "Where are you? Do not abandon me to this void!"

For a moment that stretched into eternity, Clovis knew true, unrelenting terror. Then, as quickly as it came, the darkness was replaced by brilliant, all-encompassing light.

The light receded, revealing a vast expanse of wildflowers stretching as far as the eye could see. Tall grasses swayed gently in the breeze, their whispers carrying the echoes of forgotten songs. Clovis blinked, overwhelmed by the vibrant colors and sweet fragrances surrounding him.

Beside him stood the Witch, her raven-black hair dancing in the wind. She extended her hand, palm upward, as if offering the landscape before them.

"Where... where are we?" Clovis asked, his voice trembling with a mixture of awe and trepidation.

The Witch turned to him, her expression serene yet tinged with an ancient sadness. "This is the land of spirits, Clovis," she explained, her words carried on the breeze. "A place where souls come to rest and prepare for their next journey."

Clovis gazed at the rolling fields, a sense of peace washing over him. Yet beneath it, a current of unease stirred. "Rest? But I... I don't feel tired. I feel..."

"Unfinished," the Witch finished for him, nodding knowingly. "Your spirit carries the weight of a life filled with both triumph and regret. It is not uncommon."

He closed his eyes, inhaling deeply. The scent of wildflowers mingled with something else; a faint hint of smoke, of battles long past. "I thought the afterlife would be... different. Valhalla, perhaps, or the Christian heaven. Not this... limbo."

The Witch's laughter rang out, light and haunting, like the tinkling of distant bells. "Oh, Clovis. Always caught between worlds, weren't you? Pagan and Christian, conqueror and unifier. Your journey is far from over."

Epilogue

Echoes of time

The flickering candlelight cast long shadows across Dr. Emily Thompson's study, illuminating stacks of weathered tomes and glass cases filled with ancient relics. She hunched over her oak desk, wire-rimmed glasses perched on the bridge of her nose, her calloused fingers tracing the worn spine of a leather-bound book.

"This could be it," she murmured, her heart quickening. "The key to unlocking centuries of hidden truths."

Dr. Thompson's gaze darted around the cramped room, taking in the artifacts that hinted at a history long buried; a tarnished silver amulet, fragments of parchment covered in cryptic runes, a gnarled wooden staff leaning in the corner. Each item whispered of untold stories, of magic and mystery that defied conventional wisdom.

She reached for the book with trembling hands, its cracked leather cover cool against her skin. As she lifted it from the desk, a chill ran down her spine. Was it excitement or fear? Perhaps both, she mused, for knowledge could be as dangerous as it was enlightening.

"What secrets do you hold?" Dr. Thompson asked the tome, her voice barely above a whisper. She traced the faded gilt lettering on the cover, her mind racing with possibilities. Could this be the missing link in her research, the piece that would finally prove the existence of a powerful witch who had shaped the course of history?

The weight of potential discovery pressed down on her shoulders, a familiar but exhilarating burden. Dr. Thompson's fingers hovered over the book's clasp, her breath catching in her throat. She hesitated, suddenly aware of the magnitude of what she might uncover.

"No turning back now," she said, steeling herself. With a decisive click, she unlatched the book, the musty scent of aged parchment filling her nostrils as she opened it to the first yellowed page.

As her eyes scanned the faded text, Dr. Thompson's world narrowed to the words before her, the dim study fading away. She was no longer a respected historian in her cluttered office but a seeker of truth on the brink of revelation, poised to challenge everything she thought she knew about the past.

Dr. Thompson's breath caught as she read the first lines, her eyes widening with each word. "By the Goddess," she whispered, her voice trembling with excitement. "It's her. It's really her."

The pages revealed the tale of Merona, a witch reborn in 478 AD, her arrival heralded by a comet on Samhain night. Dr. Thompson's hands shook as she turned the brittle pages, her mind racing to connect the dots between this account and the historical events she knew so well.

"Clovis I," she muttered, scribbling furiously in her notebook. "The Battle of Soissons, the eclipse... it all fits." Her pen flew across the page, mapping out connections and theories.

As she delved deeper into Merona's story, Dr. Thompson felt a growing obsession take hold. The witch's unwavering courage in the face of supernatural forces and her determination to change history resonated deeply with the historian.

"How have we missed this for so long?" she asked herself, running a hand through her disheveled hair. "A witch shaping the very foundations of Frankish power, of Christianity's spread across Europe..."

Her eyes burned from the strain of reading the faded script, but she couldn't bring herself to look away. "The implications are staggering," she breathed, her mind reeling with the potential impact of her discovery.

As dawn began to creep through the study windows, Dr. Thompson realized she had been reading through the night. But sleep was the furthest thing from her mind. She was on the cusp of rewriting history, and nothing would stand in her way.

Dr. Thompson's gaze darted to a weathered chest tucked away in the corner of her study. Her heart raced as she approached, fingers trembling as she lifted the heavy lid. A cloud of dust billowed forth, revealing a collection of ancient scrolls nestled within.

"My God," she whispered, carefully lifting one from its resting place.

The parchment crackled beneath her touch, its surface adorned with intricate symbols and illustrations. Faded ink depicted a woman with raven-black hair and piercing blue eyes, surrounded by elemental forces.

"Merona," Dr. Thompson breathed, recognizing the witch from her earlier readings.

With painstaking care, she unrolled the first scroll. Her eyes widened as she deciphered the cryptic text.

"The eclipse of Tolbiac," she murmured, excitement building. "It wasn't just a natural phenomenon. Merona... she channeled the elements to influence the battle's outcome."

Dr. Thompson's mind raced, connecting dots between the scroll's account, and known historical events. "This changes everything we thought we knew about Clovis I's conversion."

She grabbed her notebook, scribbling frantically. "The witch's influence extends far beyond what I initially imagined. But why? What was her ultimate goal?"

As she continued reading, a chill ran down her spine. The scroll hinted at a cosmic struggle, with Merona at its center.

"A destiny intertwined with the very fabric of time," Dr. Thompson muttered, her voice a mix of awe and trepidation. "What have I stumbled upon?"

Dr. Thompson leaned back in her chair, her mind reeling from the implications of her discovery. The weight of history pressed upon her, heavy and palpable in the dim light of her study.

"If Merona truly shaped these pivotal moments," she mused aloud, her voice barely above a whisper, "what does that mean for our understanding of the past? Of the present?"

She stood abruptly, pacing the cluttered room. Her fingers traced the spines of ancient tomes as she passed, each one a silent witness to her internal struggle.

"The witch hunts, the rise of Christianity in Europe... were they all part of some greater design?" Dr. Thompson's brow furrowed. "And if so, what echoes of Merona's actions still resonate today?"

She paused at the window, gazing out at the modern world beyond. "Could understanding her story inspire change even now?"

With renewed determination, Dr. Thompson turned back to her desk. "I need more," she declared, grabbing her coat. "This is just the beginning."

Hours later, she found herself in the depths of the university library, surrounded by stacks of obscure historical texts. The librarian, a wizened old man, peered at her over his spectacles.

"Dr. Thompson, you've been here since opening. What exactly are you looking for?"

She looked up, eyes bright with fervor. "I'm tracing the footsteps of a witch through history, Mr. Harding. One who may have changed the course of empires."

The librarian raised an eyebrow. "Sounds rather fanciful for a respected historian."

"Sometimes truth is stranger than fiction," she replied, returning to her research. "And sometimes, the most important stories are the ones hidden between the lines of accepted history."

As night fell, Dr. Thompson emerged from the library, her bag heavy with notes and photocopies. "Next stop, Soissons," she muttered, hailing a taxi. "If Merona's influence reached Clovis, there must be traces left behind."

Dr. Thompson's fingers trembled with excitement as she carefully unfolded the yellowed parchment. The air in the Soissons archives was thick with the scent of aged paper and leather, but she barely noticed, her eyes locked on the faded script before her.

"Incredible," she whispered, heart racing. "This decree... it mentions a 'woman of great power' present at Clovis' court." She glanced up at the archivist hovering nearby. "Do you realize what this could mean?"

The archivist, a middle-aged woman named Marie, leaned in with curiosity. "It's certainly an unusual reference. But how does it connect to your witch?"

Dr. Thompson's eyes gleamed. "It's not just this. Look at the symbolism in these illuminations." She pointed to intricate designs bordering the text. "These aren't standard Christian motifs. They're pagan -- no, pre-Christian Frankish symbols associated with magic."

Marie's brow furrowed. "But Clovis converted to Christianity. Why would he allow such imagery?"

"Exactly!" Dr. Thompson exclaimed, her voice echoing in the quiet room. She lowered it, continuing intensely, "What if his conversion wasn't as absolute as history records? What if this witch -- Merona -- influenced him more than we ever knew?"

As she spoke, Dr. Thompson's mind raced. Could Merona have been a voice of moderation, tempering Clovis' newfound Christian zeal with older wisdom? The implications were staggering.

Her reverie was interrupted by Marie's cautious voice. "Dr. Thompson, there's something else you should see." The archivist retrieved another document, this one bearing a royal seal. "This is a copy of the Salic Law, enacted by Clovis."

Dr. Thompson's breath caught as she read the passage Marie indicated. "It forbids witchcraft... but only if it causes harm to others." She looked up, eyes wide. "This is unprecedented for the time. It's almost... protective."

"A compromise, perhaps?" Marie suggested.

"Yes," Dr. Thompson murmured, her mind whirling with possibilities. "A compromise between old ways and new. Between a king and a witch who shaped history from the shadows."

She stood abruptly, gathering her notes. "I need to cross-reference this with other sources. Thank you, Marie. This could change everything we thought we knew about the Frankish conversion."

As she rushed out, Dr. Thompson's heart pounded with a mixture of academic excitement and something deeper -- a sense that she was on the verge of uncovering a truth long buried, one that could reshape our understanding of power, faith, and the hidden influences that guide the course of history.

Dr. Thompson's fingers trembled as she leafed through the ancient text, her eyes widening with each revelation. The significance of Clovis' baptism in 508 AD unfurled before her like a tapestry of intricate threads, each one connecting to form a larger, more complex picture than she had ever imagined.

"My God," she whispered, her voice barely audible in the hushed confines of her study. "It wasn't just a personal conversion. It was a pivot point for an entire continent."

She closed her eyes, envisioning the scene: Clovis, the powerful Frankish king, submerging himself in the baptismal waters, his long hair trailing in the ripples. Behind him, perhaps hidden in the shadows, stood Merona, the witch whose influence Dr. Thompson had been tracing through the annals of history.

"But why?" Dr. Thompson murmured, her brow furrowing. "Why would a witch encourage a conversion that would eventually lead to her kind being persecuted?"

She reached for her notebook, scribbling frantically. "The adoption of Nicene Christianity... widespread conversion among the Franks... religious unification across modern-day France, Low Countries, Germany..."

Her pen paused, hovering above the paper. "The alliance between the Franks and Catholicism... Charlemagne's coronation... the birth of the Holy Roman Empire."

Dr. Thompson leaned back in her chair, her mind reeling. "It's not just about Clovis or Merona anymore. This is about the shaping of Western civilization itself."

She stood abruptly, pacing the length of her cramped office. "But where does Merona fit into all this? What was her endgame?"

As if in answer, her eyes fell upon a small, ornate box she had discovered among the artifacts. With trembling hands, she opened it, revealing a delicate silver pendant bearing an intricate pentacle design.

"Of course," she breathed, tracing the symbol with her finger. "Balance. It was always about balance."

Dr. Thompson grabbed her phone dialing her research assistant. "Alex? I need you to pull every record we have on pagan symbols incorporated into early Christian artifacts. Focus on the Merovingian period."

She paused, her gaze drawn back to the pendant. "I think we've been looking at this all wrong. Merona wasn't fighting against the tide of history. She was guiding it, ensuring that the old ways weren't lost entirely as the new faith took hold."

As she hung up, Dr. Thompson felt a surge of determination, unlike anything she'd experienced in her academic career. This wasn't just about uncovering hidden history anymore. It was about understanding the delicate interplay of forces that had shaped the world as she knew it.

"You clever witch," she murmured, a smile tugging at her lips. "You played the long game, didn't you? And we're only just beginning to understand your moves."

Dr. Thompson's fingers flew across her keyboard, her eyes alight with a fervent energy. She paused only to glance at the silver pentacle pendant, now resting beside her monitor like a talisman.

"This changes everything," she muttered, her voice thick with excitement. "The world needs to know about Merona."

She reached for her phone, punching in a number she knew by heart. "Professor Blackwood? It's Emily. I've made a breakthrough that's going to rewrite medieval history as we know it."

As she spoke, her free hand absently traced the outline of the pentacle. "I need your help to get this published. It's big, James. Bigger than anything we've ever tackled before."

She listened intently, nodding. "Yes, I know the risks. But think about the impact! This could change how we view the entire Christianization of Europe."

Dr. Thompson's gaze drifted to the window, where the first hints of dawn were breaking through the night sky. A metaphor, she thought, for the light she was about to shine on centuries of hidden history.

"I'm not just doing this for academic recognition," she said softly, more to herself than to the professor on the other end of the line. "This is about giving voice to those who were silenced. It's about understanding our past to shape our future."

As she hung up, Dr. Thompson leaned back in her chair, her mind racing with possibilities. The story of Merona, the witch who had shaped history from the shadows, deserved to be told. And she, Emily Thompson, would be the one to tell it.

"The true magic," she whispered, her eyes fixed on the brightening horizon, "isn't in spells or rituals. It's in understanding. In acceptance. In seeing the threads that connect us all across time."

She stood, stretching, feeling the weight of her discovery settle around her like a cloak. "Your story will inspire, Merona," she promised the empty room. "The echoes of your past will help us build a brighter future. I'll make sure of it."

About the Author

Michaela Riley resides in the picturesque landscapes of Virginia, where she shares her life with her husband and two beloved dogs: a striking red German Shepherd named Morrigan, who carries an air of grace and strength, and Carlos, her energetic Chihuahua-terrier mix, who never fails to bring a smile with his playful antics. Michaela's deep-rooted passion for exploring her family heritage drives her to delve into her ancestry, allowing her to uncover stories and traditions that connect her to the past.

In her free time, she finds joy in hiking, often embarking on long treks through the serene trails that the local mountains and forests offer. It is during these tranquil moments in nature that she feels a strong connection to her ancestors, particularly Clovis I, a figure of historical significance in her lineage. The winding labyrinth trails she navigates with her faithful canine companions not only provide physical challenges but also serve as a metaphorical journey into the complexities of her heritage.

This book was born from the inspiration drawn from these experiences; each hike a path leading her closer to understanding her roots, and each trail a reflection of the intricate journey that shapes her identity. Through her writing, Michaela hopes to share the beauty of these explorations and the profound connection she feels with her past, inviting readers to join her on this remarkable journey of discovery.

www.michaelariley.com

www.meronarebirth.com

495

Acknowledgments

Thank you to my husband for your patience while I take valuable time away from us to pursue my passion of writing…you give me faith in humanity. Your love is my sanctuary, enveloping me in warmth and comfort, wrapping me in an everlasting embrace. It stands resilient against life's tempests, creating an unbreakable bond that intertwines our souls. I love you!